Praise for
If You're Reading This, I'm Already Dead

'A marvellous novel, breathless in its pace, assured in its structure, and by turns witty and intelligent. There is a certainty about Nicoll that exults in extravagant plots, outlandish characters and exotic settings. This is the real deal' *The Herald*

'It's not often that a book actually merits the breathless "I couldn't put it down" of back-cover blurbs, but this one does. [A] spellbinding and thoroughly entertaining account' *The Scots Magazine*

'One of the many pleasures of this novel is to be found in Andrew Nicoll's assured mastery of tone. His style is admirably fluent, capable of moving seamlessly from reflection and comment to rapid story-telling' *The Scotsman*

'Nicoll writes with fluency and flair [and] offers his readers a jeu d'esprit of character and plot, which celebrates the art of storytelling, almost for its own sake' *bookoxygen.com*

'Nicoll uses dark humour to great effect . . . The ironies are immaculate: the delusional fantasies, historic terrors and moving sincerity flow together seamlessly, and the counterpoints are deeply gratifying, and sometimes horrifying' *Edinburgh Journal*

'Roll up, roll up and prepare yourself for an encounter that is as wacky and entertaining as a night in the company of the Barnum and Bailey circus' *thebookbag.co.uk*

'[Just as] Renton in Irvine Welsh's *Trainspotting* or John Self in Martin Amis's *Money* stayed in the head after I closed the book, Otto is in there too now, laughing his head off and sitting on a camel. That's the trick. Great if you can pull it off' *Big Issue*

Also by Andrew Nicoll

The Good Mayor
The Love and Death of Caterina

IF
YOU'RE
READING
THIS
I'M
ALREADY
DEAD

ANDREW
NICOLL

Quercus

First published in Great Britain in 2012
This paperback edition published in Great Britain in 2013 by

Quercus
55 Baker Street
7th Floor, South Block
London
W1U 8EW

A CIP catalogue record for this book is available
from the British Library

ISBN 978 0 85738 494 2 (PB)
ISBN 978 1 78087 358 9 (EBOOK)

10 9 8 7 6 5 4 3 2 1

Typeset by Ellipsis Digital Limited, Glasgow
Printed and bound in Great Britain by Clays Ltd, St Ives plc

For Libby, who taught me to tell stories

We were in Pest when this story began. Christ, was it Pest? It might have been Buda. One of them is up the hill and the other one is across the river. It doesn't matter. We were in Budapest when this story began and I was a young man and as strong as an ox with the looks of a young Hercules, whiskers like the horns on a prize bull and a whang you could hang wet towels off.

Now I'm an old man and I'm shit-scared and I've left it too late and, if you're reading this, I'm already dead. I've always wanted to write that: 'By the time you read this I shall be dead.' That and 'It was a dark and stormy night.' Stories come after words like that.

Well, this is a dark and stormy night all right, pitch black except for where the fires are burning all along the docks, black as hell, except for the flashes of bombs going off, thunder and lightning, the fires screaming like a gale, lumps of metal the size of pianos falling out of the sky and screaming all the way down and bits of shrapnel, fizzing and spitting off the roof like a rain of red-hot needles.

Two hours ago I was in Wilhelmstrasse. There was this

kid – I don't know how old he was, maybe fourteen, maybe fifteen, I don't know, they're throwing anybody they can get into the mincer now. So there he was, in his crappy uniform, proud as a dog with two pricks, marching a column of Italians back to spend the night in the docks. That's the punishment for our gallant allies. That's what they get for throwing in the towel. Screw the Axis. Stuff the international brotherhood of Fascism and National Socialism. To hell with all of that. We work the poor bastards half to death all day and then we tuck them in at the docks to see if another night of bombing might cheer them up a bit.

They shuffled along in their cardboard shoes with the kid pretending to march, acting like he was driving them on when the only thing keeping them going was the thought of black bread and cabbage soup. And, all of a sudden, he shouts, 'Halt!' and he looks at me like I'm Winston Churchill, sticks me with his rifle and demands to see my papers. Little shit. I'm seventy-three years old, for God's sake. How many seventy-three-year-old spies have you ever heard of?

I reached into my jacket while he stood there, keeping me covered, half hunched, two hands on the rifle, ready to spring into action if I should suddenly decide to overpower him and steal his Italians. So of course, when I produced my papers like a good citizen of the Reich, he couldn't take them because his hands were busy.

'Open them,' he said.

I did.

'Hold them up a bit higher.'

I did.

'That can't be right.' He was looking at me really hard, his eyes darting to the picture on my pass and then back at me again.

'Bring it closer,' he said.

So I did. I was right up against him with my hand in his face when I felt the rush of wind and the kid wasn't there any more. No warning. Not even a siren. Just a bomb that dropped so close we didn't even hear it until it landed, straight through the roof of the house on the corner and right down to the ground floor. That whole wall disappeared just as if somebody had cut it out like a slice of cake, and it took the kid and it left me. Nothing touched me. Not a brick, not a stick or a bit of broken glass. Nothing. I felt the fire of it pass me and I thought I was going to die. I felt it roar and growl and rumble so it shook my heart inside my chest and now every bone aches like I've been three rounds with a Turkish wrestler or three days in a Turkish brothel, and my suit's scorched and there's plaster between my teeth but I didn't die. The kid died but I didn't die. I ran – and I can still run, believe me. I ran until I got back here to my little caravan and I climbed inside and I locked the door as if a few slats of wood and a couple of sheets of tin could keep the bombs out. I got away with it, but I expect to be dead by morning. It's been five months since the Allies landed in Normandy and the radio says our unstoppable forces are about to throw them back into the sea any day now. In the meantime they come as they please and the bombs fall in long lines, crump, crump, crump, like an angry child trampling on sandcastles, flames bloom in the night like jungle flowers, kids vanish in the gale of a bomb. That's what we get. That's all we deserve for following that stupid, Jew-hating bastard into hell.

But I can't sit here all night just pissing my pants and waiting for the bombs to drop, and that's why I'm writing this.

I want one final round of applause before the curtain. I want somebody to come picking through what's left of my caravan to find this and say, 'That can't be right,' the way that kid said, 'That can't be right,' when he saw my pass. I want people to know how Otto Witte, acrobat of Hamburg, became the crowned King of Albania.

A story like that needs a drum roll and trumpets. It needs girls with feathers in their hair and spangled tights. It needs coloured lights and velvet curtains. You can't start that story with an old man pissing his pants in an air raid. I'm going to tear this up and start again.

We were in Pest when this story began. Christ, was it Pest? It might have been Buda. One of them is up the hill and the other one is across the river. We were in Budapest, that's where we were. There was me, Otto Witte, acrobat of Hamburg; my old mate Max Schlepsig the sword swallower and professional strongman; Professor Alberto von Mesmer, the Human Encyclopaedia, who did a mind-reading act with his gorgeous daughter, Sarah; and Tifty Gourdas. Tifty said she was a Magyar countess, kicked out of the family palace because she fell in love with a humble dancing master. We all thought that was probably a lie, but she could dance to set the sawdust on fire and she knew how to strip. And when she said 'fell in love with a humble dancing master' that probably meant something else altogether. Tifty and me, we used to do something else altogether from time to time, just for a little bit of comfort on the cold winter nights. It gets cold when you're sleeping out under canvas. You couldn't blame her. I was gorgeous.

Tifty used to do private performances for select groups of gentlemen after the last show. Just for the quality. None of your riff-raff. We'd all hurry and get the bears and the ponies bedded down for the night, sweep up the horse-apples from the big top and spread a velvet cloth over a couple of benches in the ringside seats. Then I'd go and untie the tent flaps and they'd be waiting there in the shadows, one or two of them, gentlemen of quality, with their canes and their opera capes and their fancy bow ties. I've no idea how they found out about it. We never advertised as far as I knew, but I suppose word got round. There's not much to do in Kosice on a Monday night, and by God she could strip.

Me and Max used to stand around at the back. Tifty liked to have us there, just to make sure that these intimate little performances didn't get too intimate. We took the cash and never kept a penny for ourselves. That was fair enough. Nobody was paying to watch us take our pants off. No, we gave every farthing to Tifty, but she always saw us right one way or another – in cash or kind. I was never stuck for a beer or a cuddle when Tifty was around, and I'm guessing neither was Max. Well, that's fair enough too. We shared everything else.

So there we were in Budapest, me and Max and Professor Alberto von Mesmer and the girls.

We had the afternoon off between shows and I fancied a few beers, but Max wanted to go to the pictures so we all went. Going to the pictures was a different thing entirely in those days. For starters, there was no such thing as a picture house. These days a picture house is a magnificent palace with seats for hundreds and mirrors and chandeliers and fancy curtains and girls with trays of ice cream. Of course, that was when we still had ice cream and before the picture houses all got bombed flat.

Back then they used to put on a picture show in any old beer hall. You could get a bit of singing and a beer and maybe a comic or dancers, unless it was a Sunday, or performing dogs – I always liked that – and then they'd turn the lights out and put the pictures on. A film show was just one more item on the programme. Nobody ever thought they were going to last.

So there we were, all together, sitting on this long bench. I can see us now, my old mate Max at one end and then the Professor and then Sarah – did I mention the Professor was blind? Sarah was sitting next to him so she could whisper in his ear to tell him what was happening on the screen.

It was really good in those days. They could make a picture in England or America or Germany and it didn't make any difference because there weren't any words. Anybody could understand it. That was proper acting. Now it's all in the words. It's no use showing an American picture in Germany even if we could get them. Talkies ruined the films, I'm telling you. Nobody acts any more.

So there was my old mate Max, and the Professor, and Sarah whispering in his ear. People get so excited about that kind of thing now. They don't like chatting in the middle of the show. There's a lot of 'shushing' and I just call that rude. Back then people used to join in a lot more, shout out at the people in the picture and tell them to 'look out' or 'hurry up'. Now it's all so polite. Anyway, I suppose people made allowances since the Professor was blind and he wasn't going to get his money's worth unless somebody told him what was going on. And Sarah was sitting on my left and I got my hand down her skirt in the dark and gave her bum a bit of a tickle and Tifty was sitting on my right and I got my other hand down her skirt and gave her bum a bit of a tickle too, and I'm not going to tell you what Tifty was doing with her hand while I was doing that. Luckily Sarah wasn't that kind of girl. There would have been hell to pay if their hands had touched but Sarah was a good girl. Sarah was the kind of girl you marry.

It's a great thing, sitting in the dark with a pretty girl, but sitting in the dark with two pretty girls is even nicer.

Now, if you're like me I don't suppose you remember too many films. If you went to the pictures one day and something came on in the second feature and you'd seen it before, it might come back to you, but how many films could you actually remember, frame by frame, scene by scene, and play them over again on the inside of your eyelids if you sat down in the dark and closed your eyes?

Well, I can remember that one. Every last cough, spit and fart of it. By God, that was a picture. I'd never seen anything like it. It was a sensation. As far as I recall the people who made it stole the idea from somebody else's book, which sounds like a very fine plan to me. Somebody else has all the trouble of making up a story and all the labour of writing down a mountain of words (which is no small thing, as I am discovering) and then you just come along and make a picture out of it. When you think about it, that really is the easy bit. A picture paints a thousand words right enough. You don't have to waste a gallon of ink describing the hero's jutting jaw or his prancing stallion. You don't have all the bother of coming up with fancy metaphors; like saying that the princess has skin as soft and white as goose feathers or anything like that. You just take their pictures and anybody can see for themselves that the princess is a knockout and the hero has a jaw like the prow of the *Tirpitz* and a horse the size of a train.

But, like I said, I don't blame them for stealing this story. It was such a good story it almost made me want to read the book. It was called *The Prisoner of Zenda* and it was about this bloke who went to a faraway country and found out that he was the living image of the new king, only the king was locked up in a dungeon, hidden away by his villainous cousin and, if the king didn't turn up for his coronation, the cousin would take the throne. So the king's friends found the bloke who looked exactly like the king and passed him off and got him crowned and rescued the real king and then, by way of thanks, they kicked the doppelgänger out of the country.

It was a fantastic picture. It had everything: romance and suspense and sword fights – lots of sword fights – and I remember the pianist was very good, really caught the mood, knew what to play for the kissy bits when the bloke was making up to the princess and what to play when the villains came on and what to do when they were having their sword fights. And this was proper sword fights, none of this nancyboy stuff like they do in those fancy student houses, where they stand on milking stools and whack each other about the head until somebody ends up with a lump sliced out of their face to prove what an aristocrat they are while they're killing little Jewish girls. No, this was the real thing, with running about and climbing up and down stairs and throwing the furniture around. By God, it was good.

None of us had ever seen anything like it. Sarah was gabbling away in her father's ear, telling him what was happening and what it said on those signs they used to put up on the screen when there was something important to explain and – I've got to say – people were pretty good about it. I like to think that's because people in general are pretty nice and they wanted to be a bit kind to an old blind man and help him out a bit. Or it might have been because they saw me and Max and they decided not to make a fuss.

Sarah was pretty good at that storytelling business. The Professor was sitting there stone blind, but I don't think he missed a single thing that I saw with my own two eyes. Sarah was even putting in the colours and the smells and the Professor was getting ahead of her, guessing what was coming next or telling her to hurry up, 'What's happening now? Watch out for that step!' and when it came to the sword fights or the chases on horseback our whole bench was bouncing along and Sarah was getting more and more excited – you could hear it in her voice – and bouncing along all the faster and so was Tifty. By God, that was a good picture.

But all good things must come to an end and, before too long, the lights went up again and I got my hands out of the girls' knickers and back in my own pockets just in time for the performing dogs coming back on.

My mate Max said, 'I've had enough of this. You coming?'

I wanted to see the dogs. I like dogs. I've always liked dogs, and dogs like me. Nobody else could be bothered. After a picture like that, things were bound to go a bit flat, I suppose, so they all decided to move on; it was almost time for us to get ready for that night's show anyway.

'I'm staying for the dogs,' I said. Also there was a barmaid who was making sheep's eyes at me before the picture show and she was still making sheep's eyes at me after the picture show and I thought I might let her feel my muscles.

So Max said, 'Fair enough.' Never a cross word, me and Max. If it suited me, it suited Max, and if it suited Max, it suited me, and he gave me the money for another glass of beer before he left.

I didn't stay long after that. God, this is long-winded and those bombs aren't getting any further away. I'm going to have to write a bit faster if this story is going to get told before I get blown up. This isn't how a king should tell the story of how he got to be the king. I'm going to tear this up and start again.

But now I need to pee. It's no fun being old. Even for kings.

We were in Buda when this story began. Definitely Buda and not Pest. I remember it all so clearly now. It's all coming back to me. Buda is up the hill and Pest is across the river and after me and the barmaid from the beer hall got finished I went across the river and up the hill so I was definitely in Pest and going back to Buda, so that's that sorted out.

Anyway, it's a lovely town – or two lovely towns. Or it was, at any rate. God knows what it must be like now. Joining up with us might have been better than getting bent over the table to take it roughly up the chute from our heroic Aryan storm troopers but it comes to the same thing in the end. We signed up for a one-way ticket to hell, and they decided to come along for the ride, so some place in Budapest tonight there's probably an old man like me, sitting in the dark and trying not to piss his pants as the bombs fall all around him. We should drink a toast, him and me. I've still got a little bit of sloe gin left in the bottom of the bottle. I was saving it up for my chest in the winter but, since I might not have a chest by the morning, there's not much point.

So here's to you, old man in Budapest (I should say here that I have been under the sink and got the bottle. It's pretty sludgy, full of dusty bits of broken sloe berries and even a couple of leaves. I will strain it through my moustache). Here's to you, old man in Budapest. You're as shit-scared as I am and you didn't want this war any more than I did so God bless you and see you safe through the night, old man in Budapest. Or old woman. There must be an old woman there too, under those bombs, and young women and little kids. God bless you all, you poor bastards.

Maybe she's there. The barmaid. She would be getting on a bit now. Sixty or so, I suppose. Fifty anyway, which is old for a woman – especially in wartime.

I can't remember her name and I'm not going to try. I don't know if I even knew it. I bet I said, 'What's your name?' and she would've told me and I'd've said, 'That's a pretty name,' without even hearing it. If she'd asked me right there and then, that very second, what her name was, I couldn't've told her.

I didn't give that girl anything like the time and attention she deserved, but she wasn't alone in that, poor kid. No, she was not alone in that. I suppose, given the circumstances and how it's very likely that a ton weight of exploding iron is going to come through my roof any second, I suppose that is something I should repent. Well, I do repent it. I could've shown a great deal more care and

13

respect in a lot of cases and, I have to acknowledge, if I'd've had a sister and somebody like me had come along then, in fairness, I would not have been pleased.

I was never cruel to anybody. I never made anybody any promises and, consequently, I never let anybody down. I was careful about that and, if anybody started building castles in the air and putting Otto Witte inside them, with his magnificent whiskers and his magnificent muscles and one magnificent muscle in particular, that was not my fault. This is not to excuse myself.

But that girl in the beer hall, that girl who might be sitting now, under a storm of bombs, right now, maybe with a pack of grandchildren round her knees (and, God forgive me, I'm not even going to think about the end of that sentence), that girl I did not give the attention she deserved. No, it was just down to the cellar, a quick kiss and a cuddle, 'Oh, Otto, ain't you strong!', knickers down, up on a barrel and away we go!

Now, I was always careful. Nobody left the party until everybody got a dance, if you know what I mean, but I could've taken a bit more time and had a bit of a cuddle afterwards. Girls do like a cuddle afterwards. The fact is, there just wasn't time. I had to get back up the hill for the next show and, anyway, her dad was coming down the stairs, yelling and screaming. I don't know what he was saying. I could never make out a word of Hungarian – even written down it looks like an explosion in a sign-writers' shop – but he did not sound happy so I buttoned my trousers quick smart, hauled myself up to the roof by my fingertips, swung my feet up to the cellar trapdoor, where the barrels came in, kicked it open and flew out on to the street. By God, I was fit then. Still am. I bet I could still do it now.

As it turns out, and for the record, I couldn't do it now. I had a go and it didn't work out entirely to plan. It was all right when I reached up to the rafter – which is really remarkably sturdy considering how this caravan rattles about in every breeze – but I didn't quite get my feet up to the roof before I fell off. And I hit a shelf on my way down and the coffee can hit the floor and the few little bits of brown dust I was saving for Christmas fell out. I salvaged something – most of it, I think – but there's probably even less coffee in there than there was before and a good deal more floor sweepings.

I've got to stop doing this, this babbling about coffee cans and falling off the roof and the fun I had with this girl here and that girl there. It's got to stop. The words come easier if I imagine that the person who finds this is a friend and we are sitting round yarning about the old days and death seems more distant with a kind friend in the room, but I don't have time for all this wandering about in the story. And it is inappropriate. This is a story about a king, and kings don't fall off the roof and kick their coffee can on the way down. Kings don't have to button their trousers up in a hurry when an angry daddy shows up in a pub cellar. No, we need a bit of dignity. I am definitely going to tear all these pages out and start again.

To begin.

We were in Budapest when this story began, twin capital of the Austro-Hungarian Empire that lay, like a sleeping dragon, sprawled across Europe from the Adriatic to Russia, from the Alps to the Carpathians.

How can we tell of the grandeur and the beauty of this place, crowded with the plunder of centuries, groaning with the weight of its own Imperial power, awash with treasures and art, its magnificent buildings and wide avenues expressing more eloquently than mere words its glorious history and kissed by the sparkling Danube at its very heart? How—

Jesus Christ! That one was close. Not so close as the one that got the kid this afternoon but pretty damned close. It whistled all the way down and then the ground shook and then there was this thunderclap that rattled my teeth and shook my heart around inside my ribs and that damned coffee can fell off the shelf again. My little caravan was pelted with stones and bits of earth, as if somebody was firing bags of nails out of a cannon, but I don't think any of them came through. It probably sounded a lot worse than it was — like being inside a drum. It's a good thing I closed the shutters or I wouldn't have a window left, and whatever else that bomb has done, it's completely knackered my literary good intentions.

Screw high-flown prose style, I'm going to go back to talking to myself. Or you. I wonder who you are. A little boy come out of the shelter after a night of explosions and looking for a really good bit of shrapnel, maybe? They do that, the kids, the ones who haven't been dragged away from their mothers and sent off to defend the Reich. I've seen them stopping to pick up lumps of jagged metal from the street and swapping them with their mates. Hideous. What a world we have made for them that they think broken bombs are playthings. No, I wouldn't want it to be you. I wouldn't want a kid to find my little caravan all blown to bits and me plastered all over it. And I wouldn't want you here with me now.

I wish my old mate Max was here. That would be really nice. But Max would probably have his own version of this story. He'd be bound to remember it different and he'd want to tell it different. But I reckon Max would stay and hold my hand. Fair's fair. I did it for him, and it was always turn and turn about with me and Max, but he's already done his fair share of dying, and I reckon I'll get to shake him by the hand before too long anyway.

It might be nice if you were a pretty girl, young and easily impressed, but supposing you were, then what? I am not the man I was. Best not.

A dog would be nice. Dogs are good at listening but not

too good at reading books. So it's you. You're just a bloke. A decent bloke. Not heroic, not interested in politics, just doing your best. A plumber, or a schoolteacher and an air-raid volunteer, and you're going to come along and help to clear up the mess, and you'll find my book and you'll put it in your pocket and you'll get your shovel and put me in a sandbag and you'll tuck me up all cosy and wipe your hands and say, 'Poor old bugger.' But before that happens we'll sit here and have a couple of beers and yarn about the old days.

Sit down, friend, pull up a chair, pour yourself a glass of something and don't pay any attention to the bombs. It's only thunder. It can't hurt you. Now, I've got a story to tell you.

I was in Pest when this story began. No doubt about that. I was in Pest and I'd had a couple of beers and I'd had a bit of fun with a pretty girl and I'd come bouncing out on to the pavement like a bat out of hell. It was a bright sunny day in May. Or June. Or August. Well, in the summer, definitely, and I took off down the road like a rabbit running from a fox.

It didn't take long before I got to the river, all green and sparkling, with queues of barges moving up and down it and the sides all built up with big stone blocks. The place was heaving – people rushing back and forth, carts loaded with stuff and horses tramping like marching soldiers, and fancy coaches, all shiny and painted, with their spindly little wheels and matched pairs trotting along on dancers' legs, footmen on the back making solemn faces and grand ladies inside with their big hats and pretty dresses, peeking out from behind their gloves at me and wondering. Believe me, the toffs are the worst of the lot. Don't you go thinking that they're any better than that landlord's daughter. Look at Tifty – not that I'm judging. Anyway, everybody in Pest was heading for the same place, all of them crowding along the riverbank to the big bridge – I forget what they call it, but it's all hung with these huge, great, square-linked chains, enormous things with enormous stone lions at either end. It's a very handsome thing. Or it was.

So everybody in Pest was crowding on to this bridge to get to Buda and everybody in Buda was trying to get to Pest. It was a very handy thing, that bridge, and when I got to the other side I climbed the stone stairs that wind up the side of the hill, right the way to the top. It's lovely up there, all those little streets and the arches and the palaces and the music hall where Beethoven played and the spun candy towers and the views all around. I remember one little place with a tavern where we used to go sometimes and, marching all along the walls, a whole parade of stone lions, right up to the corner where two poor lions had to share one head. But I didn't have time to stop for a drink. I ran along the little streets, across the square beside that big church and through the gate in the town wall at the other side. That's all I remember – not that it's the end of the story, but I couldn't tell you exactly where I went after that. I couldn't draw you a map. All I know is it was quicker to run up one side of Buda hill and down the other than it was to run round to the flat field where we had our tent.

Oh, my friend, that tent. I miss that tent. Sometimes, you know, I go there still in dreams. The smell of it, the lamps hung all around the ring, the straw, the sawdust, the animals, the noises they made, the way they smelled, the warmth of them, the heat of their bodies — you have no idea how damned hot a tiger is — the drums and the music, the girls all dressed up, and my friends. I see them now. I see them just as they were. Night after night they stand there smiling. My old mate Max throws back the tent flap and suddenly the shadows are bright with his lantern and he beckons me inside and they are all standing there waiting, Max and the Professor and Tifty and Sarah. My Sarah. Sometimes I wonder if that's what it might be like. On a night like tonight, when a big black exploding piano comes crashing through the roof, or some other night when my heart just seizes up and the blood stops moving in my veins, I wonder if it might be like that, if I might find myself walking across a shadowed field towards the light of a lantern that's shining out from a warm tent, with my good friends waiting inside. Sometimes I wonder that and then I wake up in my little narrow bed, in my little tin house, and it's dark and all the blankets have fallen off and, in the space of a night, I have grown old.

But not then. Then I was young.

I must have run for miles by the time I got to the tent and I don't think I'd even broken a sweat and, when I arrived, Tifty was standing there in her pink tights, looking like a Roman statue.

She had that smile on her face, that naughty smile she used to get when the nights were cold and she needed a cuddle.

I smiled back.

Tifty smiled some more. She had a lovely smile. She was

a lovely girl, but it wasn't all that long since the cellar of the beer hall and I suppose I could have managed something, a little something, but time was really getting short and we had a show to put on.

Tifty was still smiling.

'What?' I said.

'Oh, nothing,' she said. And she went away across the sawdust ring, carrying a bucket of horse-apples and swaying like a palm tree on a desert island.

Well, I kept on walking through the tent after her. I had things to do, stuff to get ready, fancy painted barrels for balancing on, seesaws for bouncing, that kind of thing, and then there was Max grinning at me like a bear having a seizure.

Now I'm not stupid. I could tell something was going on, so I said, 'What?' again. 'What?'

'Nothing.'

'Come on, Max. What's up?'

'Nothing.' But it was all he could do to stop from bursting out laughing.

'What?'

'Nothing.'

'Look, I had a bit of a tumble with that barmaid, all right. Is that it? You'd've done the same. Is that what this is about?'

Max looked astonished. 'You never did!'

'Yes, I did.'

'You lucky bugger. You lucky, dirty bugger.' But he wasn't angry or jealous. We were friends. He was just congratulating me. It's no loss what a friend gets, that's what we used to say.

'So it's not that?' I said.

'No.'

'What then?'

Max made his big bear grin again and he said, 'You're in the paper, mate,' and then he reached backwards, took the rolled-up newspaper out of his back pocket and handed it to me.

But it was no damned good. I can read well enough. I am neither stupid nor ignorant but, unless it was coming from an angry daddy stamping down the stairs, that Hungarish stuff made no sense to me and I knew it made no more sense to Max.

Max said, 'Page three.'

I opened the paper but there was nothing to see. Just a jangle of letters that would make your eyes hurt. I said, 'Stop messing about,' and I gave him his paper back.

But by then Tifty had come back from emptying the horse-apples and she said, 'Darling, it's quite true.' With an elegant finger she pointed to a picture in the middle of the page. 'That's you, darling, isn't it? Now what have you been up to? Have you been naughty, darling? Tell Tifty.'

'No, I have not been "naughty". Well, a little bit naughty –' they laughed then, Tifty and Max – 'but nothing that would get me in the papers.'

'Silly Otto,' she said. 'Tifty's just teasing.' She was trailing her fingertip over my ear. 'Darling, you know how Tifty likes to tease.' I did know. There was this thing she did with that finger. I'll tell you about that later. Maybe. 'Darling,' she said, 'did you forget that this is my native land and this is my native –' tapping that lovely finger on Max's paper again – 'tongue?'

'That's still not my picture,' I said.

'Are you sure? Really sure?'

'What's it say, Tifty?'

'Oh, darling, it's a very boring article. Very boring. Nobody would ever have read it if your picture hadn't been at the top of it.'

'Tifty, what's it say?'

'My dear, if you must know it says, "*Albánok keres új király.*"' Tifty had a voice like fairy bells dipped in rum and smoked out of a meerschaum pipe. If anybody else said something like that it would sound like a bag of marbles falling in a tin bath. She could say it and make it sound like angels kissing your ears.

Still, I was getting impatient and it must have shown in my eyes.

Tifty said, 'It means, "Albanians seeking a new king."' And then she read out the whole thing, all about this silly little country that nobody ever heard of before, the haunt of pirates and bandits and how it used to be under the heel of the barbarous Turk but now it was breaking free and it was looking for a king.

'And it seems they have chosen you, darling. It is you,' she said.

Max said, 'Looks like you.'

'It does, you know,' said Tifty.

'It's nothing like me.'

'We can settle it,' Max said.

'We can settle it,' Tifty said.

Now, we never argued, my friends and me, but if there was ever a disagreement, we knew how to settle it; we'd ask Professor von Mesmer. So that's what we did. We all of us trooped out of the tent and round the back to the caravans. Sarah was just going up the steps when we arrived, carrying a tray with her father's coffee on it, and Tifty asked if we could see him. That's how it was. You couldn't just walk in on Professor von Mesmer.

'Just a moment,' Sarah said. She went inside with the coffee tray and, a little bit later, he came out on her arm.

They say the doctors have this trick where they make you look at ink blots and decide how mad you are by what you can see there. The Professor wore eyeglasses like great round pools of ink. I won't tell you what I saw there in case those doctors decide to lock me up. Nothing good. Like an evil butterfly clamped across his face where his eyes should be.

He got to the bottom of his caravan steps and he leaned on his cane and he said, 'How can I help you?'

Bold as brass, Max steps up and holds out the paper. 'Settle an argument,' he said. 'Is this Otto or is this not Otto?'

The Professor knew there was something there. He felt the weight of it in the air against his skin or he heard it where the smell of Tifty's perfume should be or something, but he knew and he put his hand out in front of him, but

Max was too slow. Max was always slow, and he just waited that little bit too long so the Professor was left waving his arm about, snatching at nothing, looking like a cripple.

'Sorry,' Max said, and gave him the paper and that was even worse somehow.

'What am I looking at?'

Max said, 'It's a picture of Otto.'

But the Professor ignored him. 'What am I looking at?' he said.

It was Sarah he was talking to. She stood behind him, her lips close to his ear. She said, 'It's a newspaper picture of a man. He is not yet forty. He has sharp eyes, quite a nice nose, not too big, not too small, a thick neck – he looks strong – he has a fantastic moustache that curls like a great sea wave and he's wearing a fez.'

The Professor said, 'It bears an astonishing resemblance to our own dear Otto,' and he said it like Moses coming down the mountain with the Law of God tucked under his arm.

'I'm sorry,' I said. 'I don't even own a fez.'

Tifty said, 'Darling, according to the paper he's wearing the fez because he's another of those barbarous Turks. His name is Halim Eddine, the son of the Sultan, and they have offered him the throne of Albania.'

'They must like him a lot.'

'According to the paper they like him enough to give him the Imperial treasury too. And a harem.'

'They must like him an awful lot.'

'Darling, they've never met him. They've never even seen him – except in newspaper pictures.'

'He looks just like you,' Max said.

And the Professor said, 'You could certainly fool me.'

And Sarah said, 'It's just like the story in the picture show.'

So I said, 'Is it far?'

I know what you're thinking. You're thinking that you never heard of anything so stupid in all your life as the idea of setting off to invade a foreign country on the say-so of a blind man. But it was obvious. It made perfect sense.

I looked so much like that Turkish prince that even a blind man could see it, and if Professor Alberto von Mesmer could see it through his black eyeglasses then it was a racing certainty that those king-hungry Albanoks would see it too.

'I don't speak Albanian,' I said.

Tifty said, 'Darling, nobody speaks Albanian. Anyway, he's a Turk.'

'I don't speak Turkish either.'

Then the Professor said, 'I don't think they want you for your conversational skills. They want a king. In my experience, kings are far too grand to speak to anybody who is not a king. I should say that they have ministers for that sort of thing. And viziers. If you can look stern and unapproachable and if you have a vizier who can speak Turkish, I don't see any problem. Luckily, my boy, I can speak

Turkish. In fact, Turkish is one of thirteen languages I can speak.'

So, as it turns out, I was right the first time. We were in Buda when this story began, not in Pest at all. It all started right there, at the back of the tent with Tifty, my mate Max, a blind man and his beautiful daughter.

It occurs to me that I should say something about Sarah. I should paint you a picture. I should describe her to you. I should find some way to set her down in this book and press her between the pages like a precious flower so she will last forever. That's what this is all about, after all. That's what all this scribbling is for – so there will be something of me left poking out of the wreckage, and the best part of me is Sarah so there should be something of her too. I can't do it. I am more and more filled with admiration for people who write books, the way they pack those descriptions in so you can see everything laid out there in front of you like a picture show, but it's beyond me. And there's more than that.

God gave us memory so we can have roses in December, that's what they say, but then, one day in late November, you discover that the smell of the roses has faded and it won't come back. Sometimes I fear that I have forgotten her, the way I have forgotten my father's voice, the way my mother's face has gone. I see her in dreams but I cannot grasp her. How can I tell you? Should I say how tall she was, what her hair was like, her eyes, the shape of her mouth? It wouldn't tell you a thing, friend. You'd be no wiser, so let me tell you this: she was like morning. Think of a girl who looks like morning, smells like morning, talks like morning, and that's Sarah for you. Beautiful, and as smart as paint.

You'll just have to imagine her standing there with me and her dad and Tifty and Max, and me saying, 'Is it far?'

It was time for the show and, as far as I remember, everything went to plan. Tifty went round and round the ring on her big grey pony, doing all the tricks she usually did, standing up on his back, balancing on her head with her legs in the air, bouncing from one side of him to the other as he cantered along and then the big finish when she jumped him through a ring of fire, and of course she was always careful to make sure that all the men in the audience got a good look at her legs and her gorgeous bum.

We had a talking-dog act – Doctor Schmidt's Incredible Canine Choristers, they were called – and all the usual stuff you'd expect from a show like ours: clowns throwing buckets of confetti into the audience, dancing girls, the tiger leaping from one upturned barrel to another and snarling at the whip, elephants, camels, me with my acrobatic act, jumping, tumbling, balancing, swinging, climbing up and down ropes – all the stuff that looks easy until you try it. Max was good. Max was great. He had a real act. He could swallow a sword a foot long, haul it out again and then bend it round his neck while he lifted a dumbbell with his free hand; he could take on Tifty's pony in a tug of war – and win. I wasn't in bad shape, but my mate Max was a giant.

And then there was Professor von Mesmer and Sarah. They always had a couple of spots. He did his Human

Encyclopaedia act, where people would yell out questions from the audience: 'Who won the Battle of Austerlitz?' or 'What's the biggest warship in the world?' or 'What's the capital of Burma?'

We didn't have too many university professors at our shows and old Alberto was fast enough on his feet to cope with most of the customers. If he got something wrong, then nine times out of ten they wouldn't know any better or dare to challenge him in front of a tent full of people, and if they did he would always have an answer like, 'Yes, sir, it is a commonly held belief that the Great Ongo-Bongo was the fifteenth Mexican Emperor, but in fact he was never crowned. Next question, please!'

By God, he had a convincing manner – exactly what I needed for my grand vizier. And he had Sarah.

I can see them now, Sarah standing on the edge of the ring in her pretty dress, walking amongst the audience as dainty as a blackbird going from branch to branch in a garden, and the Professor in his black suit, his hair slicked down with oil and those black glasses glittering over his eyes like pools of tar. He commanded respect. In fact, the truth is, I was more than a little afraid of him. He could see things with those blank eyes, see inside things, see *into* them, and when Sarah went through the crowd, holding up watches and pens and scarves and saying, 'What's this?' or 'What colour is this?' he knew every time. Now, I've seen mind-reading acts before that and I've seen them since, but never like that. If they had some sort of code, I never spotted it. Nobody spotted it. If Sarah called out to him or if she picked on some little kid from the crowd and let them ask the question, it made no difference, Professor von Mesmer would guess it anyway, whatever they were holding up, whatever colour it was, however many there were. If it wasn't a miracle, it was something very close to one, and it was the same as every other night. Ordinary. I can't recall a single thing about it.

But I remember how we all gathered at the Professor's caravan after the show. We had to talk. We had to think. We were conspirators. We had to decide if we were going to do this thing. It was outrageous and daring and dangerous. I had the most to gain by it if it worked and my head would be loosest on my shoulders if it failed. I didn't fancy doing it without them, but they couldn't even begin it without me, and a chance like that never comes twice in a man's life.

We were all sat around in the last of the evening, lights springing up in the houses on Buda hill behind us, like stars coming to life at heaven's back door. The Professor sat there on the steps of his caravan, Tifty over there, her coat wrapped round her shoulders and Max beside her, thinking that she might be feeling the cold, with Sarah going round amongst us all with the coffee pot until she sat down next to me and gave my hand a little squeeze in the shadows.

The Professor took a sip of his coffee and he said, 'You asked how far it is to Albania, I think.'

I nodded to him to signal my agreement – not that he would have seen me since it was getting along for dark and he was stone blind anyway.

'Very often, if a man asks a question like that he means something else altogether. Not "How far is it?" but "How long will it take to get there?"'

'That's what I meant. So how long will it take to get there?'

'But the question is, my boy, not how long it will take to get there, but *how* to get there.'

'So, can we get there?'

'Oh, we can get there, but again you are asking the wrong question. What you should be asking is whether we can get there before the dreadful Turk.'

I was getting fed up with all this babble and him showing off how clever he was and how stupid I was, and I suppose it must have shown because Sarah gave my hand another little squeeze and she said, 'Tell him the rest, Daddy.'

'Yes,' he said. 'Before you decide to embark on this great adventure, you should know something more about the Albanians.'

And then he said nothing more. He just sat sipping on his coffee, and I was damned if I was going to play his stupid games any longer so I sat sipping my coffee too until Tifty said, 'Professor, darling, tell us what we should know.'

That was all it took. He said, 'My boy, the Turks have been in Albania since the fall of Constantinople. They have ruled there these four hundred years, but the empire of the sultan is very nearly as old and decrepit as I am. It's ripping apart at the seams and Albania is simply the latest bit to fall off. For centuries the Mussulmans have gone about the business of converting the natives at the point of a sword,

35

forcing them to deny Christ, ruling by rapine, but they are the only people in that country with a shred of civilisation about them. All the rest are bandits and brigands and warlords and smugglers and condottieri, and the Mussulmans are manning the barricades against them. There's one little white-haired gentleman called Ismail Kemali who is trying to keep the lid on the pot. He's made himself the Prime Minister.

'But the thing you should know about the Albanians is that they hate the Turks. In fact, the only thing they like better than a Turk is a dead Turk, and the only they like better than a dead Turk is a Turk they can torture to death.'

This was disappointing news. So I said, 'We'd better get a move on!'

It's been quiet for a bit. No explosions. No whistling and screaming as the bombs fall. It's not the end. I've seen this often enough to know how it goes. We get the thunder and lightning, then it goes quiet and then the next wave comes in. This is just the eye of the storm and it'll go on until dawn — not that daylight matters very much these days. They come and go as they please.

I found the courage to look out the window. Just pushed the shutters back a bit and then I went right outside. I opened the door and I went out and damn the blackout — as if my little lamp is going to make any difference to the bombers when the whole town is a bonfire. You should see it, friend. I could hardly believe it. It's like a blizzard out there and I thought, It's only November. It's early for snow. And then I looked again and it wasn't snowflakes, it was little wisps and curls of ash and bits of burnt grey paper, some of them glowing orange round the edges, all blowing past like goose-down in a pillow fight. I went out in it, in the burning, scorchy smell of it, and I laughed and danced like a child in a snowstorm. I laughed and I howled

37

and I snatched at the little bits of paper until I managed to catch one and I read it and it had the crooked cross in one corner and 'Judentransport' written underneath. I let it go then. Something's burning. Half the town is burning. It's our own fault. We set the world on fire and we stood too close to the flames.

I boiled the kettle and made myself a cup of hot water. It's tiring, this writing business, and waiting to get blown to bits is exhausting. Even though I know I'm going to die, I'm still drinking hot water, still saving my silly spoonful of coffee-scented dust, still hoping for better days. We get a little bit of something and we hang on to it, hoard it, save it up for our old age and then, suddenly, we are old and we can't enjoy it, and then we're dead and some other bugger gets the lot. Every year there are thousands and thousands of bottles filled with champagne, millions of them maybe, but eventually every vintage runs out. Eventually there are just a few hundred left, then a few dozen, then a handful and, finally, just one. Everything gets to be too precious to use up, the last days, the last little bit of coffee, the last of life, the last of love, so we scrape them all together and keep them in a tin, thinking we can preserve them, and so they are wasted. A bottle of champagne on the cellar shelf is a dead thing. It's not preserved. It's wasted unless it's in the glass and getting itself drunk by a pretty woman. That's what it's for. That what life is for. We forget that or we learn it too late.

But back then, back in Buda, I was ready for anything. I was ready to pop the cork on life and glug down every last drop. I was a guzzler in those days and I knew what had to be done.

'I am very grateful for the advice,' I said, and when I stood up I found I was still holding Sarah's hand. The Professor didn't seem to notice that, but he noticed when she stood up beside me. There was a tiny movement of his head that made his glasses glitter in the firelight. I saw it. 'Here's what I think. I think we have to get to Albania as fast as we can. We have to get there before any other new kings get there to claim what is un-rightfully theirs much as it is un-rightfully mine. I think we have to tell those Albanoks that I'm coming, get them to put the kettle on and, above all else, warn them to look out for impostors. We need flimflam. We need something to dazzle the eye. We need to make a splash. A tiger would be good, but he's probably too dangerous. An elephant would be ideal, but it's big. The camel will have to do. We need money, so I propose we break into the strongbox, nab the cash and throw it on the camel with a lot of fancy dressing-up clothes and get out of here tonight. So are you in or are you out?'

I might have said some other stuff too, about friendship, sticking together, the undeniable tidal pull of Dame Destiny and something about a yacht at Monte Carlo, but it pretty much added up to 'Let's grab what we can and run.'

Sarah was standing beside me holding my hand, so I was pretty sure she was up for it, and if Sarah was coming, her dad wasn't going to stay behind. Anyway, he'd been practising for the role of grand vizier all his life and he wasn't going to miss his chance, but there was still Tifty, and I didn't want to land my mate Max in anything that he wasn't up for. So, when I got finished, I was a bit upset to see that Max had gone. I couldn't blame him. Max was a good, honest bloke. He'd never taken a penny in his life that didn't belong to him, so the thought of stealing a camel and a cash box was too much to ask.

But I was delighted to see Tifty stand up at the other side of the fire and button her red velvet coat. My friend, with the firelight licking up all around every curve of her she looked like she was getting ready to take coffee and cakes in hell, and then she put her big hat on and said, 'Darling, I'm already packed.'

So that was it. Me, a Hungarian countess with an odd line in exotic dance, a pretty girl and her blind father the mind-reader. 'I'll get the cash box,' I said.

But then my mate Max turned up again. He said. 'Done that. I left an IOU. I can write enough for that.' He had a big iron chest on one shoulder and he was tugging on a rope with a camel on the other end of it and he said, 'We're never going to get this on the train.' What a bloke he was. I bet Max could have punched that camel's lights out and carried it all the way to Albania if he'd wanted to, but he did something better than that. He gave up his good name on my say-so. What a sacrifice. That's love, that is. That's real friendship. And there he was, walking off across the field into the darkness, singing lullabies to a fractious camel and carrying a box full of stolen money, so we followed on behind with our coats and our hats and our little bags of stuff, into the dark, as dark as the Professor's eyeglasses, twisting through the narrow streets, up the hill and down the hill, with the camel walking ahead of us, polishing the cobbles with his carpet-slipper feet, with no sound but the tap-tap-tap of the Professor's cane, all the way to the railway station.

Imagine an opera house, the biggest, swankiest opera house you've ever seen, covered in curlicues and folderols and statues and columns and fancy carvings, with flowers and foliage chiselled over it. Imagine twisting iron pillars painted white and gold and varnished woodwork and mosaic pictures up the walls and arches and a domed roof and coloured glass twinkling and cut crystal globes shining on blazing gas lamps. Now imagine that same opera house went out one night and met the fanciest wedding cake anybody ever saw, four storeys high, with row after row of little Greek columns and covered in artificial roses and sugar Cupids. And the opera house and the wedding cake danced all night, they talked and they laughed and they had a great time, the way that wedding cakes and opera houses will, and then, nine months later, Budapest Railway Station was born. What a place. We stood together in the square in front, glad that people were too polite to mention a camel draped in dressing-up clothes, and admired it.

Even in the middle of the night it was packed with people: people pouring off the trains that came from every corner of the empire, people shoving through the doors to travel, well, any place in the world, I suppose. But not, as it turned out, to Albania.

'It is a well-known fact that there are no railways in Albania,' the Professor said – and he said it almost triumphantly.

'Oh, everybody knows that,' Sarah said. 'In fact, Otto was just remarking on that to me on our way to the station.' And she gave my hand a little squeeze.

'I didn't notice that – and my hearing is remarkably acute, perhaps by way of a natural compensation for my lack of sight.'

'I was whispering,' I said, 'so as not to alarm the camel.'

'This is a more than usually jumpy camel,' Max said.

Now I could see that the Professor was not pleased. I suppose that might have been because Sarah had chosen to stand by me and, maybe, put him in his place a little when he wanted to get one over on me, but it seemed as if he felt snubbed or slighted somehow, as if this whole adventure had been his idea all along, his ball to play with, and I was stealing it from him. I didn't want to fall out with the Professor. He was the only one of us who could speak Turkish after all, and by God we needed somebody who could do that, but aside from that he knew stuff: which spoon to use for chilled monkey brains, how to bow – who to bow at – stuff like that. And he was a thinker. You could see him thinking. It gave me the creeps. So I wanted the Professor onside – for Sarah's sake if nothing else – but there's only ever room for one king at a time.

43

The Professor turned his spectacles up to the sky and he asked, 'Since we are all agreed there is no train service to Albania, why are we here?'

'We're here because of the telegraph office. We need to send a telegram to the Albanoks, that Prime Minister bloke – what was his name?'

'Ismail Kemali,' said the Professor.

'Him. And it needs to be in Turkish. Tell him that His Excellency, the Heaven-born, beloved of Allah, has generously consented to take the throne, that he is hastening to his country with all speed. That, for reasons of urgency, His Supremacy will travel with only a tiny retinue, that a full accounting of the Treasury will be demanded of old . . .'

'Ismail Kemali.'

'Him. And his life depends on it and, above all else, to watch out for impostors and pretenders. Tell him that all future correspondence from His Magnificence the Heaven-born et cetera, will be sent using Code 17c of the code-book and, if it's not in Code 17c, then it's a fake and a phoney and must be utterly disregarded.'

'I don't know Code 17c,' said the Professor.

'There is no such thing. I just invented it, so it will be hard for anybody to send it and just as hard for them to decode. So tell him that you are sending the exact time and place of our arrival but in code. Give them a few spurts of random letters, enough to keep them guessing.'

'You seem to have thought of everything,' said the Professor.

Sarah said, 'It is a very clever plan,' which probably wasn't helpful.

The Professor was very sniffy. He said, 'They charge by the word in the telegraph office, you know. How is this to be paid for?'

'There's plenty of cash in the strongbox,' Sarah said.

'And it's locked,' he said triumphantly.

But then there was a terrible crunch from behind the camel, and Max said, 'It's open now.' My mate Max.

We went to look. The box was stuffed with sacks of money, kronen and kronen of the stuff, and, I must admit, in a strange way it salved my conscience to see how much was in there. I didn't feel nearly as bad about taking the boss's cash when I saw how much he'd stashed away when he was always telling us how hard up he was.

Tifty said, 'I'm thinking hats. Something with feathers.'

'After we get back,' I said. I took out one of the bags, closed the lid again and pushed the broken padlock back into place as best I could. It was no security. My mate Max was all the security I needed. I asked Tifty to hold out her bag and I emptied half the coins into it. 'Would you please take the Professor to the telegraph office and help him send the message?'

'Darling, we'll be delighted – won't we, Professor?' And she held out her arm and waited for him to find it, 'But what will you be doing?'

'We have to get a ticket for the camel.'

In my humble opinion, everybody ought to run away from home and join the circus at least once in their lives. It is an education. It broadens the mind. It equips a person for taking his place in the world. Of course, me taking my place in the world meant running away from the circus to become a king but, on solemn reflection and after some years of careful thought, I can tell you, if you're running off to become a king, then a circus is a great place to start. They've got everything in a circus: talented people, tools, rope, chain, clothes for every occasion and, if you wrap them all up in a big bundle, then a camel is ideal for carrying the whole lot around with you.

We had a look in the luggage, me and Max and Sarah, and we dug out the ringmaster's uniform – a shiny black claw-hammer coat and one of those silk hats that packs away flat in case you have to carry it from place to place on a camel at any time, but pops back up to full size again if you bang it on your knee.

Max gave me a rub-down to get the worst of the dust and the camel hair off my coat and Sarah tied my tie and gave my moustaches a bit of a twirl. 'You look lovely,' she said. 'Like a bridegroom.' And that made me look down at her a bit quickly, even though she still had a good grip of my whiskers.

Her eyes were damp and shining in the lamplight and I could see she was scared, poor kid, as if all that we were daring had suddenly come home to her. 'Otto. My Otto,' she said, 'you've always been a king to me.' And then, with a final brush of my lapels, she sent me off.

'Wait here,' I said. 'Look after the camel.'

Now, I'm a performer. I know how to put on a show. But, until then I had never been an actor. I was Otto Witte the circus acrobat, but by the time I got to the top of the railway-station steps, I was somebody else. When I pushed those big doors open, when I walked into that glorious, glittering hall, swinging my cane, clattering it down on those polished tiles, I had forgotten who Otto Witte was. I forgot I ever knew him. Otto Witte was a decent bloke who didn't let people push him around and didn't push anybody else around either. But the bloke in the railway station had never heard of Otto Witte. The bloke in the railway station walked right through the middle of the hall, right to the first ticket window, right up to the front of the queue and banged his cane on the counter.

'A thousand apologies, madam,' I said to the lady at the front of the queue. 'A thousand apologies. Imperial business.'

The man behind the counter was gaping at me and he did not look pleased. He had a fancy uniform with a lot

47

of brass buttons and a good set of whiskers – but mine were better. He was all set to jump down my throat, but if there's one thing an acrobat knows about it's timing, so I waited, just a tiny moment, and the very instant he opened his mouth to speak, I said, 'Where the hell is my camel car?'

He just looked at me.

I said, 'Are you deaf, man? Where the hell is my camel car?'

When we move camp we undo all the guys around the big top and then we take down the mast in the middle, and when that happens all the canvas folds and sags and collapses. That's what happened to the little chocolate soldier in the ticket booth.

'Your camel car?' and then he said, 'Sir,' which I liked a lot.

'My camel car!' and we said that to each other, back and forth another couple of times.

'Your camel car, sir?'

'My camel car!'

Until I said, 'You've got no idea what I'm talking about; have you?'

'I'm very sorry, sir. I don't.'

'Get me the stationmaster,' I said. 'Get him now. In fact, get him yesterday!'

'Yes, sir,' he said. 'Who shall I say is calling? Sir?'

I rolled my eyes and tutted. I was doing my best to look like somebody who expected to be recognised by railway clerks across the empire. 'Tell him it's the Graf von

Mucklenberg, Keeper of His Imperial Majesty's Camels.'

The little man got up from his stool and dashed away from behind his window. Then he came back and pulled down the linen blind.

The people in the queue behind me gave an angry groan. I turned round and scowled at them. 'A thousand apologies,' I said again. 'Imperial business. For your King and Emperor.' They just took it. I was amazed, but they took it. It was a horrible moment. The dreadful realisation that if you say, 'Because I say so!' loud enough, people will do as they're told. They will stand in line or stop standing in line. They'll let somebody else jump to the front of the queue and take what should be theirs and, if you yell at them loud enough and long enough, they will shoot some bloke they've never seen before, spike his kids on bayonets and swear it's all the work of God. It starts with jumping the queue and it ends up with bombers circling overhead and cities on fire.

Now there was nobody in the whole empire quite as grand as the stationmaster of Budapest. Of course, these days, he'd look downright ordinary alongside real heroes like Goering or Himmler but back then he only had to compete with the likes of the Emperor and a couple of archdukes and he had the uniform to do it.

The stationmaster was like the captain of an ocean liner – king in his own country and the only appeal over his head was direct to God Almighty. And, like the captain of an ocean liner, he sat up on his own bridge, looking out over the whole railway station from a glorious office, lined with polished oak and mahogany and studded with polished brass, brass rails around the tops of the desks to stop his pens falling off, brass lamps, brass door knobs and big brass buttons studding the banister of the stairs that led to his door, just in case there were any naughty schoolboys who might take it into their heads to slide down it.

In the ordinary course of things I would never have given a great man like the stationmaster of Budapest a moment's thought. If I had troubled to think about him at all, it would have been the same way that I thought about the Archbishop. I knew he existed. I knew there must be somebody called 'the Archbishop of Budapest'. The town was full of churches and every church had a priest and somebody had to be in charge of them all, so it made sense to imagine that there must be an archbishop in a fancy palace some place, but I gave him no thought since the Archbishop was not likely to send his card round and ask for an acrobatic performance. I suppose he might have sent his card round demanding a private show from Tifty, but that would have been none of my business. And, in just the same way as there was somebody called 'the Archbishop of Budapest', there must be somebody called 'the Stationmaster'. They had a railway station and plenty of trains and somebody had to be in charge of them, but I didn't expect him to ask me in for a drink.

And yet, there I was at the bottom of those stairs, about to be shown into the holy of holies.

The man from the ticket office left me on the landing. 'Wait here, sir,' he said, 'and I'll announce you.' But I had no intention of doing that. The Graf von Mucklenberg, Keeper of the Imperial Camels, was not the sort of man to wait about on the back step.

I watched the ticket clerk while he knocked on the door, waited politely and went in. Then I counted to seven and I ran up the stairs after him. The door bounced on its hinges and the glass rattled and I said, 'Mr Stationmaster, where is my camel car?' like a bomb going off in the office.

The ticket man was standing on the gorgeous Turkey rug in front of the stationmaster's desk and he flinched at the sound of my voice as if it had been a pistol shot in his ear. I could read the horror in the shaved hairs on the back of his neck and he looked at me and he looked at the stationmaster and, when I put my cane on his shoulder, he stepped aside, as meek as a lamb and I was confronted with the Magnificence.

The buttons on his uniform were gleaming like the portholes on an ocean liner, he had a set of whiskers like a frozen hedge and I knew then that there was nothing in the world standing between me and the throne of Albania that was half as big, half as terrifying, as the stationmaster of Budapest.

'That'll be all, Barna,' he said. 'Hurry along, you have passengers waiting. I'll deal with the gentleman.'

I heard the door closing quietly behind me and I tried very hard to remember that I was not Otto Witte.

The stationmaster said, 'How can I help you, Mr . . .'

'Graf!' I said. 'Graf von Mucklenberg, Keeper of the Imperial Camels.'

The stationmaster stood up from behind his desk and made a sharp bow. There was a fancy gilded inkstand on his desk and he almost had an eye out on the big black pen that was sticking out of it. He said, 'You do my humble railway station too much honour, Erlaucht,' and then, smooth as silk and soft as butter, he said, 'May I see your credentials?'

Such a simple thing. So obvious. So straightforward. What could be more natural or less offensive? What could be more ordinary? Why hadn't I thought of that?

I did the only thing I could do. I gaped like a codfish and I flapped my jowls at him. 'Credentials? Credentials? Are you asking to see my papers? Some form of bona fides, is that it?' I'd been paying attention to the Professor and now I was off and running. 'I'll show you my credentials, sir. My "credentials" are standing outside your railway station right now. Or do many of your passengers turn up looking for a third-class return for one of His Imperial Majesty's camels?'

The stationmaster spread his hands in a gesture of help-less resignation. 'Forgive me, Erlaucht, but until this moment I had no idea that His Majesty possessed even a single camel.'

I gave him a look that was intended to convey contempt and disbelief of his astounding ignorance but he went on, apparently without even noticing.

'Unless I have some form of identification, then for all I know, Erlaucht, you could be on the run from a travelling circus with a stolen camel.'

Well, you can imagine how I felt. Here I was, on the way to a foreign country I'd barely heard of until that afternoon, gambling my life – and the lives of my friends – on persuading everybody that I was the rightful King of the Albanoks, and the stationmaster of Budapest had seen through me right away and spotted me for a simple camel thief. I felt the colour drain right out of my face and, I can tell you now, most of it was heading straight for my trousers. I very nearly fell flat right there – but I didn't. I gripped on to the edge of his fancy desk and I leaned right forward, right in his whiskery face, so what was nothing more than panic he read as blind fury. I was gritting my teeth together so as not to be sick and I said, 'I know your game. You're playing for time. You had no more idea that I was coming than that little ticket clerk of yours did. You've fouled up. You were well warned. The Palace doesn't make mistakes with stuff like this. I've known them long enough to know that. The Palace. Does Not. Make. Mistakes. So you've made a mistake. You're responsible. You're to blame. They sent you the telegram. They told you what to do, but you made an arse of it. Somebody dropped it down the back of a sofa. Somebody lit their pipe with it. Well, I was ready to help you out. I was ready to meet you halfway, but not now. Now you're going to send a telegram to Vienna. You can do that, can't you? If I stand over you to make sure you get it right? Surely there must be somebody in this shitty little railway station who can get something right! You're going to send a telegram back to Vienna in it and you're going to tell the Emperor that you're really very

53

sorry but you seem to have mislaid his instructions and does he really want you to put the Graf von Mucklenberg on a train with His Majesty's camel? And then you're going to write, "PS I resign."'

By the time I'd finished with that lot there was hardly a breath in my body and there was quite a lot of spit on the stationmaster's nose. He didn't wipe it off.

But he still wasn't sure. He still couldn't decide if I was Franz Josef's right-hand man or just a common-or-garden camel thief, so I gave him one last shove. I reached across his desk, opened his cigar box and took one out.

The stationmaster picked up his pen, 'How many in your lordship's party – not counting the camel?'

That was how we came to be on the night train out of Budapest: me, Otto Witte, acrobat of Hamburg; my mate Max; Professor Alberto von Mesmer; Sarah and Tifty. And the camel.

I had pulled it off. I could hardly believe it myself and – I have to admit – I was pretty well bursting with pride. I had defeated the stationmaster of Budapest, and if I could do that, the rest would be simple. How wrong can you be?

There was one more tiny hitch before we got on the train. There I was in the stationmaster's office, sitting in an easy chair, smoking a fat cigar, his fat cigar – a fat cigar he lit for me with his match – legs flung out in front of me, as happy and exhausted as I was in the cellar of the beer hall. And then the stationmaster looked up from his desk and said, 'I am preparing tickets for sleeping cars for you, your four companions and all necessary accommodations for His Majesty's camel.'

'Very good,' I said, and I took another tug on his cigar.

'Where would you like to go, Erlaucht?'

And I was baffled again. Another damned stupid, obvious

question. 'Please may I see your papers?' and 'Where would you like to go?' and I had no answer. The stationmaster was teaching me some valuable lessons on my road to becoming the king.

'Hasn't this been explained to you?'

'As you pointed out, Erlaucht, there appears to have been some kind of clerical mix-up. If you could just refresh my memory . . .'

It seemed I had only two weapons in my armoury. I could either rage like a lunatic at this man, or I could wait. I breathed his delicious cigar smoke deep into my lungs, held it in my mouth and puffed a smoke ring towards his moulded ceiling. 'His Majesty's camel is intended as a gift for the newly installed King of Albania.'

'Yes, Erlaucht.'

'There are no railways in Albania.'

'No, Erlaucht.'

'Therefore, I shall complete the journey by sea.' I was kicking myself as soon as I said that. For all I knew, Albania might be landlocked. The stationmaster said nothing. He sat with his pen poised.

'Go on then, man. Make the necessary arrangements.'

'But which sea, Erlaucht?'

I sat up. 'Are you playing with me, Mister Stationmaster? Which sea, indeed? The Atlantic, of course!'

You know, I think he was teasing me. I think that might have been one last test. I think he might have been unsure about me even then and I failed his test. But, whether it was because I put enough aristocratic sarcasm into my voice or whether it was because he was just glad to see the back of me, the stationmaster never turned a hair of his magnificent silver moustache.

'Forgive me, Erlaucht. A ridiculous question. Of course, our only sea coast is on the Adriatic. I imagine you will be joining the fleet there.'

I simply rolled my eyes to the ceiling again.

'I will make out the appropriate documents for Fiume.'

'Yes,' I said. 'Fumey. You do that!'

The stationmaster picked up the gilded telephone from his desk and turned the crank. He yelled into the mouthpiece, 'Stationmaster here,' he said. 'The Graf von Mucklenberg, Keeper of His Imperial Majesty's Camels, will be leaving on the night train for the Adriatic with a party of four and a camel. Make all necessary arrangements. I will supply the papers.'

And then he said, 'Outside.'

And then he said, 'If you go outside the station and find a camel, I imagine that will be the appropriate camel.'

He put the telephone down and he picked up that big black pen from his fancy inkstand. The stationmaster wrote carefully. He took his time, writing in a book of printed forms. He tore six of them out, one at a time, and folded each into an envelope.

I waited. It took nearly half a cigar. The stationmaster struck another match and lit the wick on a long block of sealing wax. He took the envelopes, sealed every one of them with a big red blob of wax and stacked them up and then he turned to me again.

'Honoured my lord . . .' He stood up and came round the desk. 'Honoured my lord, your tickets.'

He was making a bit of a fuss. I suppose I should have made a fuss too, stood up to receive them or something, that would have been nice, and Otto Witte would have done that, but not the Graf. Oh no. The Graf just held out his hand, shifted his cigar into his cheek and said, 'Thanks a lot, old man.'

The stationmaster was disappointed but he tried not to show it. 'If you will follow me, Erlaucht –' he took his hat from the stand by the door and stood aside to let me out – 'the train is waiting.'

I stood up and brushed some of the stationmaster's scented cigar ash from my trousers. That fine grey ash. Fine grey ash like those little burning bits of paper blowing past my windows. It's hard to remember which one was first. It's hard to think which one was thirty years ago.

I followed. He waited for me at the bottom of the stairs, straight as a poker, face like a carved mask. 'This way, Erlaucht.' And then he never said another word. Too proud, I suppose, too humiliated, too angry, too ashamed. He made his way through his station and I walked alongside until we reached the gates at the end of Platform One and then, at some secret signal, the band started up. The Radetzky March. Lots of lovely Imperial oompah, and there was Max on the platform grinning like an idiot, and Tifty looking good enough to eat, with the Professor on her arm and Sarah smiling at me and, down at the other end of the platform, the camel was being loaded into a nice comfy wagon.

The stationmaster made a smart bow. 'I leave you here, Erlaucht.'

'Very grateful,' I told him and then, because I was feeling generous, I offered my hand. 'The Emperor will hear of your excellent work.'

He held my hand and leaned in close. 'Those tickets in your pocket – strictly one way. I have no idea who you are, but you are somebody else's problem now. I will report to the capital on your safe departure, inform the Palace that the Keeper of the Imperial Camels is safely on his way to the sea. I don't expect that they will ever have heard of you and I doubt that we will ever meet again.' And then he said, 'Erlaucht.' But he said it like he didn't really mean it.

He was a wise old bird. I liked him a lot.

And, like I said, that was how we came to be on the night train out of Budapest: me, Otto Witte, acrobat of Hamburg; my mate Max; Professor Alberto von Mesmer; Sarah and Tifty. And the camel.

I like a train, don't you? It's ages since I've been on a train. I don't even know if they are still running. There are no railway lines near me so I wouldn't hear them on the tracks, and the Allies bombed the station and, I suppose, most of the trains are needed for moving troops and guns and stuff like that. Still, there must be trains, surely.

I was often on a train in the old days and I liked it a lot. I remember one time, it must have been when we moved the whole damned circus from Heidelberg, way down to Ulm for the spring fair. By God, it was hot that day. A real warm spell. So we got everything loaded up in the wagons, and I don't know how she did it but, somehow or another, Tifty managed to keep a whole compartment for herself. Everybody else was jammed in tight, hanging off the luggage racks and sitting on one another's knees, and I was just about to squeeze my way into the third-class smoking car

– I was actually holding on to a leather strap in the roof to haul myself inside – when Tifty grabbed me by the shirt tails and dragged me back out.

'I know a better place,' she said, and she slammed the door on the carriage, took me by the hand and trotted off down the platform to her own little compartment.

Trains were different in those days. No corridors. Just a room on wheels with a door at either side. We had that one to ourselves, and once it started moving it was a little world of its own. No way in or out. Completely private.

I was standing at the window, looking discouraging, just in case any latecomer might want to spoil the party and, I swear, by the time that train was out of the station, Tifty had her clothes off.

When I turned round from the window there she was, as naked as God made her and smiling up at me with her dress all folded up like a pillow beside her.

'May I examine your ticket, madam?' I said.

'Otto, darling, you can examine anything you want.'

I think that was the second-nicest train ride I ever went on. Everything was so sunny and green and the cows looked so happy in the fields and there were flowers waving and twinkling all along the sides of the railway and flashes of emerald-coloured light splashing off the young leaves of the trees. Maybe I have just imagined that. Maybe that's just one more lovely thing that memory has added in to make that trip even more perfect because, to tell the truth, I don't think I spent too much time looking out the window. A couple of coaches along, my mates were jammed in together, clinging to the luggage rack, hanging off the straps and having a great time – just like Tifty and me!

But everybody was respectable when we drew into the next station. I jumped out and ran back to the third-class smoking car and banged on the door. 'All change,' I said. 'There's plenty of room further up.'

I don't know how many of them fell out on the platform when I opened the door but there must have been at least a dozen, and they all ran off along the platform, laughing and yelling, and they jumped in beside Tifty.

We were always having fun in those days, always happy. Well, mostly. When I got back into third class and sat down, Sarah was there on the bench opposite. I smiled at her and she smiled back but she looked a little sad, as if she knew what I'd been up to and it hurt her. Sarah and I didn't. Not at that stage, you understand. She had no right but, still, it made me sad that she was sad and I think I felt a little ashamed. It took the gilt off the gingerbread a bit and that's why the trip to Ulm is officially only my second-nicest train journey ever.

Now, my very favourite train journey ever was the one on the night train from Budapest.

I've had some great times in third-class smoking cars, but this was nothing like that. No slatted wooden benches for us, but a saloon car with big, button-back velvet armchairs as plump and curvesome as Tifty herself. They have dirty tin oil lamps in third class, oil lamps with bare wicks, but we had proper lamps with glass globes and polished brass reservoirs and we had carpets where they had bare boards.

We even had a steward – not that he had much to do once he'd filled the champagne glasses.

And Tifty had a bag full of gold, enough to pay for anything we wanted. The steward brought us cold chicken and, after Tifty had crossed his palm with silver and he withdrew again, she asked me for the tickets.

'You can have this one, Otto. I'll put the Professor next door to you, then Sarah, then me and dear Max right at the end.'

My mate Max took his ticket and gave me one of his big bear grins. 'Right at the end,' he said. 'In case the camel needs a glass of water in the night.' But Max wasn't only next door to the camel. He was next door to Tifty, and camels can go a long time without a drink.

And, as well as making sure that Max was right next door to her, Tifty had also made certain that the Professor was between me and Sarah so, no matter how often that camel got watered, I was going to be pretty far from the oasis.

'I'm sure we'll all be very comfy,' Tifty said.

'I'm sure we will.' I was trying not to sound huffy. 'And now we are safely on our way and heading south to the Adriatic and Albania.'

'West,' said the Professor. 'We're heading west towards the Atlantic and America.'

'West!' Everybody jumped up and started looking out the windows and I must have snorted half a glass of champagne out of my nose.

'West,' I said, as if I'd known that all along. 'You're sure?'

A train could be a comfy little love nest on wheels, but it would make just as good a jail cell, and I was beginning to wonder if the stationmaster had decided to have the last laugh by sending me and the Imperial Camel straight back to Vienna.

'West,' said the Professor.

Max shrugged from the window. 'It might be west. It's hard to say. Too dark.'

Sarah looked at me and nodded.

'Sarah says I'm right and you may take it that I am right.'

'Professor, darling, you are uncanny.' Poor Tifty flopped down in a velvet armchair and poured herself some more champagne with the look of a woman who expected not to see any more for a very long time.

The Professor held out his glass. 'There's no trick to it, even for a blind man. There are signs anybody can read: the wind, the prevailing weather in Central Europe at this time of the year. Also the railway timetables. It is a well-known fact that all the trains from Budapest to the Adriatic first go west, not south, avoiding the mountains. Tonight we will travel along the shores of Lake Balaton – I'm sorry to miss it. I hear it is quite lovely – and we'll be at the Adriatic in the morning.'

The old bugger was showing off again, but I knew I couldn't afford to deal with him as I had the stationmaster. Even looking me full in the face, the stationmaster wasn't quite sure that he could see me, but the Professor's inky glasses might as well have been fitted with X-rays.

'Why don't we have a brandy before we turn in?' I said.

Max obviously thought that was a great idea, but I said, 'Just you and me, Professor?'

'I am quite tired. I think I should go to bed.'

I put my hand on his arm, just to show that I meant it, and I said, 'Please. Important state business for the King of the Albanoks and his grand vizier,' and, although he was halfway out of his chair, the weight of my hand on his elbow was enough to make him sit down again. Some things, I have discovered, weigh a lot heavier than you might think. A kiss, for example, can be a weighty thing, or those little bits of ash drifting by on the wind. They float along on a breath of air but they crush everything they land upon.

'Very good,' he said. 'I am at Your Majesty's command.'

I signalled to the steward and ordered a couple of stiff ones and my mate Max suddenly noticed that he was awful tired and, funnily enough, so did Tifty. Sarah patted her dad on the back of the hand and said, 'Don't sit up too late,' but, as she passed my chair she let her fingers trail on my shoulders. 'Goodnight, Otto.' That was all she said.

After a bit, after the saloon door had clicked shut, after I had swilled my brandy round in its glass for a bit, after I had let the train go clickety-clack through the night for a bit, I said, 'How did you get on with that telegram, Mr Grand Vizier?'

'Very well, I think. I sent it, with the help of the Countess Gourdas of course, and we paid an extortionate sum, but such things are always so much less painful with someone else's money and, almost before we left the counter, a reply was coming through.'

'What did it say?'

'I have it here.' The Professor took a regulation slip of blue telegraph paper from his inside pocket, unfolded it and held it out to not quite where my hand was. 'According to the Countess Gourdas they are thrilled to hear of your approach, they are wondering why you are currently in Budapest and they demand further details of your arrival.'

'And what did you tell them?'

'I gave them a full and detailed account of the celebrated rogue and camel thief Otto Witte – and every word of it in code 17c, of course. A few drunken streams of letters, that's all. Then I broke off the line.'

'You did well, Mr Grand Vizier. No king ever had a more able minister.'

He took a sip of his brandy and said, 'Your Majesty is most generous.'

Then it was my turn to do some brandy-sipping. It's a useful thing, a glass of brandy. It can help the time pass without anybody noticing that nothing is happening and nothing is being said. Looking out the window is just as good, but it was night and there was nothing to see, just inky panes of glass shining back as flat and black as the Professor's spectacles. I said, 'A king and his chief minister should be able to speak frankly with one another, don't you think?'

'I think it's essential.'

'Then tell me frankly, what do you think of our chances?'

'Slim.'

'Slim? Didn't I get us on this train – and the camel?'

66

'I expect to suffer death by impalement within the week.'

'And yet you've come along.'

'Yes.'

'And you don't trust me.'

'No. You are a libertine and a camel thief. You are not to be trusted.'

I had no idea what a libertine was, but I knew it was not good, just as I had known the landlord coming down the stairs in Budapest was not happy. The words made no sense, but their meaning was clear enough.

I said, 'It's no job for a choirboy, you know, this snatching countries business. Julius Caesar, Alexander the Great, Attila the Hun – they probably knocked off a couple of camels in their day. Nobody minds a camel thief as long as he's a successful camel thief. The trick is to steal thousands of camels. Grab everybody's camels and call them your own and you're not a camel thief any longer – you're a king.'

'An interesting political theory,' said the Professor. 'But it doesn't really amount to a plan. Have you worked out how you're going to grab all the camels?'

I had to admit that I had not. 'I got us on the train, didn't I?'

It was pathetic, and if he had owned a pair of eyes, the Professor would have given me a hard look.

'I'll think of something,' I said. 'I'll improvise. How can I plan for something when I don't know what it is I'm supposed to be planning for?'

'Tomorrow, when we reach the sea, what then?'

'Then, Mr Grand Vizier, I'll put you on a boat.'

'A boat? Just any old boat? Do you expect the Albanians to strew petals in your path as you step off some peeling trawler, stinking of fish guts? Time is of the essence. We have to get there before the other king; don't you see that?'

'I promised you a boat and you'll get a boat. That's a damned sight more than the Children of Israel got. They had to walk.'

The Professor turned his blank eyes to the roof and sighed. 'We're doomed,' he said.

'And yet you're coming along. You don't believe I can do this, but you're coming along anyway!'

He buried his nose in his brandy glass and he said, 'I don't have to believe. Sarah believes.'

'What?'

'You heard me. Sarah believes you can become the King of Albania. She even believes you will make her your queen.'

And then everything made sense. They had talked about that newspaper story long before I ever got home to the circus. It was Sarah's idea all along. It was Sarah who described that picture in the paper – after she went into the Professor's caravan with his coffee, after she had said God knows what to him – it was Sarah who stuck up for me when her father was sneering over how little I knew about the railways of Albania, Sarah who got me dressed up in the ringmaster's tailcoat. 'You've always been a king to me.' That's what she said. 'Like a bridegroom.' She'd said that too.

'Now you know!' said the Professor, and he drained his brandy glass at a gulp.

'Now I know.' I finished my brandy too. 'So what will you do?

'I will come with you and die too. What else can a father do?'

'No dying,' I said. 'Nobody's dying. This is about having a bit of fun and getting stinking rich. I won't let anything happen to her. I promise you.'

He said nothing.

'The word of a king,' I said, and I clinked my empty glass off his, 'and, in exchange, you have to promise me something, all right? No more showing off. No more trying to make me look silly. Save your brains for the Albanoks. Let's make fools out of them.'

'To hear is to obey. It shall be as Your Majesty wishes,' and we clinked our empty glasses again.

After that it was time for bed. I heaved the Professor out of his chair and gave him my arm as we went into the bouncing, rolling corridor.

Max's bunk was silent, Tifty's was alive with the sounds of two people making a great effort to be very quiet, Sarah's cabin was all in darkness, and then we were at the Professor's door.

'This is yours,' I said. 'Need any help?'

The lamps were lit in the Professor's cabin – which seemed like a waste of paraffin to me, but it let me see the carpets and the velvet curtains with their thick gold tassels, a neat porcelain sink in the corner, the mirrors, the polished wood and a little bed, as white as a goose and as plump as a widow.

'I'll be fine. Goodnight.' And he shut the door in my face.

My room was in darkness but, when I opened the door, the light from the corridor was enough to show me Sarah standing there, waiting. That's why the night train to the Adriatic was my very favourite journey ever. I don't want to say any more. I can't say more.

She put her fingertips across my lips and said, 'Promise me, after this, no more Tifty.'

There never was. Never again. I can't say more. I can tell you about Tifty or that girl in the beer hall, that's all right. I can talk about that. That's just a bit of fun. But Sarah was my wife.

Fish swim together in the seas by their thousands, great shoals of them, moving and heaving and circling together, never stopping, never making a home in one place. When the day comes and something tells them that it is time to continue their race, something in the water or some strange pull of the moon, then they mingle and have their joy of each other and cast their babies adrift in the sea, clouds of them, baby fish by the millions scattered across the whole ocean with never a mother to bring them up. Hundreds of thousands are gobbled up, hundreds of thousands more sink to the bottom, hundreds of thousands of others grow up and starve to death but thousands live, swimming alone through the endless ocean. They never see themselves, they have no one to tell them who or what they are and yet, somehow, they come together again. They find their way across all the unmeasured sea. They find one another again, their own kind. They recognise one another and they never part again.

That was Sarah and me. We found one another.

I remember every moment of that train journey, even

the ones I spent asleep, and we did sleep, eventually, the comfortable, exhausted sleep of two happy people jammed into a single bed. Some people say they can't sleep on a train. All the rattling and bumping, the endless clickety-clacking keeps them awake, but for me it was like a lullaby, it was like being rocked in a warm cradle and I fell asleep, holding Sarah.

That lovely old train went trundling through the night, taking our hot little bed with it. From time to time we stopped, wheels squealed, signals clanked, coal rattled into the bunkers, water gushed on board in torrents and disappeared again in hisses of steam, and then we would wake up and, all amazed, discover one another again. I hope you know what that means. I hope you know what it's like to wake from a dream and discover that, after all, it's true. You do. I know you do. But not everybody knows that sometimes it can be a happy thing. I hope you know the surprising joy of that.

The train gave another jolt and, when it woke us, there was a soft grey light coming through the crack in the curtains.

'I have to go,' she said, and she crept away.

Not long after that the steward was working along the carriage, waking everybody up with jugs of hot water. I had a shave in the tiny little sink, brushed my teeth, combed my face and, when I was looking respectable again, as the Imperial Camel Keeper deserved to look, then I went along to the saloon for my ham and eggs.

My mate Max was already there, sharing a table with

the Professor. I watched them from the door for a moment, Max with his great bear paws, holding the Professor by the elbow, helping him into his seat, pouring out his coffee. Tifty had the decency to arrive a bit late for breakfast. She came up behind me in the narrow doorway and gave me a little goose to hurry me on, 'Come on, darling, we can't have you blocking my passage!' and she laughed that beautiful, filthy laugh of hers and squeezed past me.

Tifty was every bit as gorgeous as she had been the night before – perhaps the more so, since she had that replete glow about her which sometimes hangs on a woman after a night of love, or something very like love. She was a hell of a girl, Tifty, and I had gone to bed the night before envying Max, but that morning I knew better.

I sat down at the table with the others – the Professor staring straight ahead, looking at nothing, Tifty and Max playing footsie under the table and trying not to giggle, and me, sitting with a cup of coffee and looking at the door that led back to the sleeping car. Sure enough, Sarah came through it. She was like summer; I told you that, didn't I? Well, imagine what it would be like if it had been winter all your life and it was, all of a sudden, summer. That's what it was like when Sarah came in. All along the sides of the track flowers burst into bloom and the windows filled with sunshine and nobody seemed to notice but me.

This is where I trip up and fall flat on my face, writing nonsense like that. I've read a book before. I know how it is. I'm supposed to tell you how I felt. Well, I felt like that. And I'm supposed to write about what it was like to be inside Sarah's head and in her heart and tell you how she felt, seeing me, but I can't do that. I can't write about how 'her heart leapt like a startled deer in the forest'. I can't do that. All I can tell you is that I saw her and I loved her and I knew she loved me.

Sarah said, 'Good morning, everybody,' sat down beside her dad and gave him a kiss. 'So what's the plan, Otto?' She said that – Sarah, who had been running the whole show from the start without my noticing.

I took out my watch and wound it. 'The steward says we should be in Fumey in about an hour. Professor, over to you.'

'Fiume' – he was careful about the pronunciation – 'is the principal harbour of the Kaiserliche und Königliche Kriegsmarine, the naval force of the Austro-Hungarian Empire and home of the Naval Academy. Fortified since Roman times, its natural harbour on the mouth of the Rječina and at the head of Kvarner Bay, an inlet of the Adriatic Sea, overlooks the islands of Cres and Krk to the south. The city is ringed by mountains on the other three sides, creating a humid, subtropical climate with frequent rainfall and cold "bura" winds in the winter.'

When he was finished, it was as if somebody had flipped a switch on one of those musical clockwork monkeys. Snap! And it all stopped and he went back to looking at nothing and lifting bread to his mouth.

'So there we have it,' I said. 'This is the end of the line

and as close as we can get to the poor, lonely Albanoks, crying out to meet me. I reckon we have to get the camel unloaded – can you take care of that, Max? He seems to like you.'

Max nodded. Nothing was ever too much trouble for my mate Max.

'Then we have to get down to the docks and find a boat.'

Max said, 'I would think that the Keeper of the Imperial Camels ought to be entitled to a berth on board any ship of the Kaiserliche und . . . what he said.'

The Professor said, 'We can't just commandeer an Imperial warship.'

'Oh, but it's all right to steal an entire country, is it? Anyway, I wasn't talking about anything fancy, just a cruiser or something.'

'A cruiser!' And the Professor turned those black goggles to the roof again.

It was up to Sarah to calm things down. 'Let's just play it by ear,' she said. 'We'll get the camel off the train first, like Otto says, and then we can see about boats and things – don't you think, Otto?'

So that was the start of it. That was the very first time I ever had to make a choice between siding with Max and siding with a woman – any woman – and it turned out to be Sarah.

'Yes,' I said, 'that's what to do. One step at a time and, you know, Max, even an Imperial cruiser might be a little bit ambitious.'

Tifty put her spoon down in her saucer with a noise like

a tiny silver bell. She said, 'I don't know about that, darling. I seem to recall a young man I used to know. I'm sure he's something in the navy.'

I'm cold and my fingers are getting stiff. I've boiled the kettle again and made myself another cup of hot water, but there's nothing to put in it: no sugar, no tea, no coffee, well, none to speak of. I have been sitting here, holding my cup, warming my hands on it. Do you do that? There's no fuel. I sit here in my coat and my hat with my scarf wrapped round my chin but I'm still freezing. It's as if the cold has been injected under my skin. There's never enough fuel. There's hardly been anything for months. If we were wise we would pool our resources — like the Bolshevik hordes who are definitely not about to come charging into town any minute now because our gallant forces are on the brink of wiping them off the face of the earth. They might be half-human Slavic apes, but they share what they've got.

I don't have enough to heat a quarter of my little caravan but, if there were four old men all jammed in here together, we could pool our rations. We'd be warm and we'd have somebody to talk to in the middle of the night. But we don't do that. That's not the German way. We respect the dignity of private property, so long as it's not the dentist's property, or the lawyer's property or a jeweller's or a furrier's, of course. No, we sit alone in our own cellar or our own attic or our own shitty little tin house on wheels, all dignified and respectable, wondering if we'll freeze to death before the bombs get us.

Well, friend, it seems to me that the Bolshevik way is a damned sight closer to everything I was taught in Sunday school. I can say that of course, because I will be dead soon. These days, dead men are the only ones entitled to free expression of their opinions. It's only because I am dead that I can speak my mind. I am beyond hurt. But you are still alive. Feel free to rip this page out if you like. I won't think less of you.

Anyway, I got my hands warmed up on that cup of hot water and then I had a brainwave. I boiled the kettle again, cooled it down a bit with a splash from the tap and then I filled up the old bottle that used to hold my sloe gin. I seem to have a lot of socks, and I can't get any more of them on my feet, so now I have something like a hot-water bottle, wrapped in a nice warm sock. I should have thought of this a long time ago. We haven't had hot-water bottles for years. They need the rubber, I suppose.

And now I see I have wasted page after page, rattling on about Bolsheviks and hot-water bottles and already there is quite a little pile of pages but my friends and I haven't even got the camel off the train yet. Let's remedy that.

Forget about all the handshaking and the formal thanks and the generous tips paid from circus funds and the noting of names and the firm assurances that a detailed account of loyal and excellent services rendered would be conveyed directly to the Imperial ear. That was all a lot of rubbish. That was about as sincere as saying, 'But we will always be friends,' to the girl you've just dumped, or, 'Promise you'll come and visit,' to someone you meet on holiday – and then you write a false address on the back of a cigarette packet, just in case they ever try. Forget all that and come directly into the high street of Fiume (yes, I learned how to say it).

Now, it seems to be an unwritten rule in life that the further away you get from the capital, the less you get of everything: paved roads, flush toilets, pianos, good coffee, music halls, all the things that make life nice – or used to. Well, Fiume was about as far away from the capital as you could get without falling off the edge, but it had the lot. Fiume was the empire's toe in the water, the one place on earth where old Franz Josef could take his boats out of the bath and put them in the sea. That was why the railway went there, twisting and turning, puffing and panting all the way back to Vienna. There was a railway station, a port full of sailors and, in between, a town ready to supply anything and everything that a sailor might want, all done in the best possible taste, you know. The big bow-fronted shops got their windows polished every day, the pavements were nicely swept, boys would brush the horse-apples off the road for ladies who wanted to cross the street, take a penny and brush them back again. There were big government buildings, all carved with fruit and flowers and eagles and naked ladies and some nice, quiet houses with gardens and heavy lace curtains where the naked ladies stayed on the inside.

My worst enemy could not accuse me of being stupid – well, there was that one time outside Stuttgart, but it's got nothing to do with this story – and I knew we had to hurry. If it was morning in Fiume, it was morning in Buda. If we were getting up and having breakfast then, eventually, the boss would be getting up too, and even he would spot that he was missing a cash box and a large camel.

A camel is not an easy thing to put in your pocket. A camel gets you noticed, and I knew that, before too long, stories of the Graf von Mucklenberg and his friends would be clacking up and down the telegraph wires.

'We need to get out of town,' I said, which was a statement of the blindingly obvious if ever there was one. But the camel would not budge. He had stopped on the corner of the street to get rid of last night's hay and, until he'd finished, not even Max could shift him.

A surprisingly large number of people seemed interested in what our camel was doing and, even when he stopped doing it, they were still interested. There was next to no chance of making a quick getaway without drawing a lot of attention and, I have to admit, I was beginning to panic a little.

And then, while I was standing there wondering what to do, I noticed the Professor. He had stopped looking at nothing. He cocked his head a little and then he turned and looked back up the street, listening to nothing instead. He could hear something, I knew it, and the very next second a man in uniform came around the corner at the other end of the street and, right behind him, came a band.

'Shape up,' I said. 'Everybody get in line right across the street. Camel in the middle, and walk away smartly.'

The music was getting louder. The band was getting closer, and I knew it was only a matter of moments before they caught up. So there we were, me and Tifty on one side, my mate Max with the camel, and Sarah, arm in arm with her dad, on the other.

'Wave,' I said. 'Smile and wave. Acknowledge the loyal adulation of a grateful people — and walk slow!'

That's what we did. We walked nice and slow down the street, waving at the people who came to watch. There was no way to get out of town without being spotted so we let them look, we hid in plain sight. And there was no way to keep up with a marching band leading the way — not with a blind man in the company — so we walked ahead of them, slowly. When we started walking, the band was at the other end of the street. By the time we got to the corner they were right behind us and the bandmaster was snarling to 'Get out of the way', only less politely than that. We ignored him so he said it again, louder, and we ignored him some more.

I grinned like a lunatic and said, 'Keep waving.'

All along the pavement, people were waving back, kids were running along, looking at the camel and waving and letting the band go by and then running again to get another look.

The bandmaster was beside himself with fury. He was

nearly spitting, but he couldn't just push us off the street because a camel is a difficult thing to move and he didn't want to be seen roughing up women and an old blind man. How times have changed. So he said again, in a very angry whisper, 'This is the marching band of the Kaiserliche und Königliche Kriegsmarine, and I'm telling you to get off the damned road.' And then he took his big fancy stick and he poked the camel.

That wasn't a nice thing to do and the poor camel didn't like it at all. He made an unhappy noise but he didn't walk any faster, and then the bandmaster poked him again.

That did it. My mate Max wouldn't put up with that kind of needless cruelty so he grabbed the bandmaster's stick by its pointed end and jammed it under his own arm. The bandmaster was not pleased. I turned round and there he was, cursing like a sailor, face like a beetroot, tugging on his stick with two hands and not budging it by an inch and then, without even letting go of the camel's reins, Max broke the end off the stick with his free hand and passed it back to him.

'Do that again,' he said, 'and I'll jam it up your arse – splintered end first.'

All credit to the bandmaster – he looked like he might burst into tears when he saw his stick in bits, but he never even broke his stride and the band never missed a single oompah. We seemed to reach an accommodation so that, before we got to the end of 'Unter dem Doppeladler', we were marching through the dock gates in good order.

Sailor sentries standing inside little wooden houses

snapped to attention as we walked past but, once we were through the gates, with no more crowds of happy Fiumers to cheer us on, things were getting a little chilly.

The bandmaster stood marching on the spot, holding his broken stick up over his head and yelling orders to his men until the final clash of the cymbals . . . 'and HALT!'

None of his men fell out. They just stood there, wrapped in their euphoniums and balancing their glockenspiels and looking angry. The bandmaster put his hand on my shoulder – not Max's shoulder, you'll notice – and he said, 'Now then. A word.'

Max looked at me and I looked at Max. I knew the fun was about to start and we were going to have to talk fast or punch hard. Max had already decided which one he was going for. He dropped the camel's rope, made a fist the size of a ham, picked his spot and landed one of his famous haymakers right on the bandmaster's chin.

The poor bloke went about four inches up in the air and came down again like a sack of potatoes and then the whole thing kicked off. The sailors in the band were loyal, I'll say that for them, and they took a dim view of Max clocking their boss. Drums went flying, trumpets went flying, Sarah grabbed her dad by the hand and ran round the other side of the camel with him, I got a two-handed grip on my silver-topped cane and Tifty, God bless her, Tifty came to stand beside me, holding a glittering steel hatpin about a foot long.

It looked as if things were about to get very boring indeed, but for some reason not one single bandsman broke rank.

Instead they all came to attention – except for the bandmaster, who was sitting on the ground shaking his head with his legs spread out like a starfish. Just for a minute I thought my natural air of authority must have won through – that or the terror of a poke in the pants with Tifty's hatpin – and I was just about to congratulate myself on another job well done when a voice behind me said, 'What's going on here, then?'

I am sorry that we seem to have fallen out of love with whiskers. All over the Austro-Hungarian Empire, back then when there was an Austro-Hungarian Empire, people set great store by whiskers. You could tell a man of standing by his whiskers, and nobody who wanted to get on in the world would ever leave his top lip exposed to the elements. Every officer of the empire from the humblest to the highest, every village postman, every sergeant major, every arch-duke and general all the way up to old Franz Josef himself, knew exactly where he stood by the size of his whiskers. And, even at home in Germany, we knew a thing or two about facial hair in those days. Bismarck unified the nation under the shadow of his magnificent moustachios, and the Kaiser sat in Berlin wearing a big brass helmet with a thing like a shellacked sparrow on his upper lip. Everybody had a moustache. Moustaches were everywhere.

Now there is only one moustache that counts and it's a pathetic, pitiful, weedy, silly little thing, one stupid thumb-broad stripe on one single top lip, a woeful nosebleed of a thing, the sort of moustache that's worn by a bandy-legged, pigeon-toed clown in the picture shows and by our great leader. Our schoolboys have let us down badly. They could have prevented all this. A little mockery, a few gentle catcalls: 'Call that a moustache? My grandma could grow better!' A little bit of tittering and that moustache would have shrivelled up and fallen out by the roots. But, no, we all had to pretend that we took it seriously. We treated that moustache with a great deal more respect than it deserved. And look where that got us.

But when I turned round, well, there was a set of whiskers worthy of a proper regard, enormous whiskers which started out as sideburns and grew into a vast handlebar moustache, hanging down and out, rigidly, like a pair of scallop shells attached to a face, a dress-circle balcony of a moustache and, to crown it all, it was flaming red, past ginger, past carrot and damned near vermilion. I don't know if you have ever seen hair of that colour but, in my experience, it almost always goes with a complexion like a day-old corpse and this man had that too. He was only a short little fellow, barely up to my shoulder, and slightly built, but he stood there, with his soft cap sitting on the back of his head, his hands jammed in his trouser pockets and his legs apart as if he was braced against the rocking of the storm. He looked so fine in his uniform, his jacket as blue as the deep-sea waves, a shirt as white as a gull's wing, his neat little bowtie hanging down limp as a flag in the tropics and gold on his cap, gold on his shoulders, gold on his wrists. Gold everywhere. Every little bit of him that could be covered in gold was covered in gold.

'What's going on here, then?' he said.

You know, I really think I learned more about being a king in those half-dozen words than you ever could from a library of books – not what he said but the way it was said, no yelling and shouting, no pushing anybody around; he just said what needed saying, knowing that the right to say it was his.

'What's going on here, then?'

The bandmaster spat a bloodied lump of tooth out on to the ground and said, 'He broke my stick!'

'You poked my camel!'

'And he punched me in the mouth.'

'You poked my camel.'

'And he obstructed the band. Walked in front of it and wouldn't get out of the way.'

'I see,' said the little red-haired man. 'You obstructed his band, he poked your camel and you broke his stick and knocked his tooth out.'

'Two teeth,' the bandmaster said.

'Really? Two?'

'Well, he poked my camel twice.'

'So it's a case of an eye for an eye and a tooth for a camel-poke, is it? Anyway, it's all most unfortunate. I hope it's done nothing to spoil your rugged good looks, Herr Oberstabs-bootsman. Now get up off the ground, there's a good fellow. You're making the place untidy. Get up and place these people under arrest – and take their camel away. I can't have it cluttering up my dockyard.'

This was a setback, but the red-haired man had taught

me a valuable lesson. I decided to take a leaf out of his book and speak as if I meant to be obeyed. 'That won't be necessary,' I said, and I stuck out my hand. 'Graf von Mucklenberg. I imagine you're expecting me. Forgive me, I was in the cavalry. Never really got up to speed with navy ranks. Whom do I have the honour of addressing?' I was very proud of that little pronoun.

And he took one hand out of his trouser pocket, and he shook me by mine and he gave me his name – I remember it to this day. He said, 'Fregattenkapitän Imre Varga, at your service. Be so good as to place yourselves under arrest.'

'Delighted,' I said. 'For my own part nothing could please me more, and of course my associates will obey without question, but as a brother officer and, speaking as a friend, thinking of your future prospects, I would strongly advise you against arresting the Emperor's camel.'

I think his pale face might have turned half a shade paler, but his moustaches were set solid and his top lip gave never a tremble. 'Nobody mentioned that this was the Emperor's camel.'

'Nobody told you?' I said. 'Nobody told you we were coming? Oh, I beg your pardon, Varga, I thought you were in charge here.'

'I *am* in charge.' There was just the tiniest falsetto squeak in his voice. He cleared his throat. 'I'm in charge. Me. I'm the one in charge. Nobody mentioned the Emperor's camel was coming.'

I took him by the arm and walked a little way off, for a

confidential chat. 'Look, there seems to have been some dreadful misunderstanding. I, and, of course, my associates, we are transporting His Majesty's camel as a gift to the new King of Albania. I take it you know about the new King of Albania.'

Varga snorted under his whiskers. 'Pwah! I may be a humble sailor, but I keep up with events. We're not completely cut off from affairs of state in Fiume, you know. Everybody knows about the new King of Albania.'

'Obviously. So I needn't explain that the Queen of Albania is simply camel crazy.'

'Everybody knows that too. Do you take me for a complete idiot?'

'Oh come now, how could an idiot become Fregatten-kapitän in His Majesty's navy?'

'You'd be astonished,' Varga said.

'Then I needn't explain another thing. Naturally I assumed you were expecting us and, when I saw the band – very fine band, by the way, Varga – when I saw the band coming down the street I stupidly jumped to the conclusion that it was intended for us. Then there was that little misunderstanding between your bandmaster and my camel handler. One feels very foolish.'

'Think nothing of it.' With his arm linked in mine, Varga spun me round and we turned back the way we had come, strolling along together side by side and chatting like old friends. I noticed that the camel was now under armed guard.

'Forgive me,' he said, 'but your remarkable and unbelievable story does nothing to alter the fact that you and your party are guilty of a dreadful assault on one of my men – to say nothing of the damage inflicted on the band-master's baton, which is Imperial property every bit as much the camel. In fact, probably more so.'

'So you do intend to arrest the Emperor's camel, after all? That is a courageous and potentially career-limiting decision.'

'Yes. I'm afraid I must insist that you remain here, as my guest, while I investigate further.'

There was no point in making a fuss. We couldn't fight our way out, not after the guns had come out. In my heart of hearts I knew that our little adventure had hit the buffers, but I wasn't ready to give up. I said, 'Varga, this is a matter of national policy. We are mere pawns in a vast European intrigue, and the fate of the Balkans may hinge upon it. I would urge your discretion. Even if public failure means nothing to you, consider how you might endanger my mission.'

But the little sailor seemed not to hear me. As we approached, Tifty stepped out from behind the camel, her delicious hat re-pinned on her lustrous hair, dark eyes gleaming, sinuous as a treble clef, holding her gloved hand out to be kissed, letting it droop from the wrist like a broken flower.

Varga said, 'Won't you introduce me to this beautiful creature?'

'Forgive me. Countess Tifty Gourdas, permit me to present Fregattenkapitän Imre Varga.'

Tifty smiled. She wiggled her fingers. She wiggled them some more. But her hand went unkissed.

Varga looked at Tifty and he looked at me and he said, 'Not her. The camel handler. Introduce me to the camel handler. My God, those muscles!'

Now, I'm a man of the world – I hope that much is clear – and I hope I'm pretty much a live-and-let-live kind of bloke. I don't really care what people get up to so long as they don't do it in the street and frighten the horses and, although it does me no credit, I have to admit I would have been quite willing to let little Varga try his luck with Tifty.

Tifty was up for it too. For God's sake, that was Tifty's hobby! She was a real sportsman and, as the old saying goes, 'You never miss a slice off a cut loaf.' Anyway, it was all for the greater good. Invading Albania was a team effort, after all. The Professor brought his encyclopaedic knowledge, Max brought his muscles, I brought my kingly bearing and a little rat-like cunning, I wasn't altogether sure what Sarah was adding to the cake, but Tifty was definitely the glamour. Tifty was the pretty girl who wiggles her bum just as the magician makes the rabbit appear. So, no, I admit, I would have had not one moment's concern about throwing her right into the slavering jaws and quivering red whiskers of the little Fregattenkapitän – no more than that bloke in the Bible who turned his daughters over to the mob to stop them doing the dirty with those angels who had unexpectedly dropped in for coffee and cakes. But, somehow, I was not willing to hand my mate Max over to a fate worse than death. Greater love hath no man than that he lay down his friends for his life and all that, but, no, offering up Max's peachy arse to that little ginger shirtlifter was asking too much.

And Tifty wasn't impressed either. She stood there, her tiny hand unkissed, with a face like thunder. 'Gentlemen who are short and ginger should make more of an effort to be likeable,' she said. 'I think you are very rude.'

'Oh I am! I am! Now who's your big friend?' The little sailor went skipping over to Max and said, 'Nice camel!'

Max said, 'Thanks. I'm fond of him,' and looked at his shoes.

'Lovely camel.'

'He's not mine.'

'No. I hear he belongs to the Emperor!' He stuck out his hand and said, 'I'm Fregattenkapitän Varga but you can call me Imre.'

They shook hands. 'Schlepsig. Max Schlepsig.'

'You know –' Varga wagged his little white finger – 'I shouldn't like you, Max. You hit my bandmaster and that was very naughty, but I have the feeling we're going to be firm friends. And, since you're under arrest anyway, why don't we go for a walk before lunch?'

Max said, 'All right.' What else could he say?

'Excellent.' And little Varga reached out, took the camel's rope out of Max's hand and gave it to Tifty, who was every bit as horrified as he hoped she would be. 'Why don't you bring it along?' he said. 'For the exercise, you know.'

Tifty couldn't think of a single thing to say and she fell in, as meek as a lamb, but dragging that damned camel around was too much for her so I took it and suggested she might like to take care of the Professor instead. 'Be his eyes,' I said. 'Tell him everything you see. We might need it later.'

Of course that left me free to walk side by side with Sarah and we started along, Sarah, the camel and me, behind Tifty and the Professor with Max and Varga leading the way and a couple of sailors bringing up the rear, their rifles slung over their shoulders.

Tifty swayed along the gravel path, one arm linked in with the Professor, her free hand wandering idly to caress that vicious hatpin as she glared at Varga's pale neck. 'We're just coming up to some sort of processional arch. There's a long garden. I can see the Naval Academy up ahead.'

'How many columns on the arch?'

'None. It's all one big block with a hole through the middle.'

'Roman, like the Arc de Triomphe.'

When I was sure the Professor was listening to Tifty and not to me, I gave Sarah's arm a squeeze and I said, 'Thank you so much for last night.'

She put a finger over my lips. 'Shh. You say that, you make it sound like a transaction. It's not. You didn't pay me for it and you can't thank me for it.'

'I can say thank you if somebody does a nice thing for

94

me. I say thank you if Max buys me a drink or gives me a fill of my pipe – but I'm not allowed to say thank you to you?'

Sarah gave an exasperated little sigh. 'Why don't you understand this? Some things are too big. Some things make "thank you" too small. You can't say thank you for the stars. You can't say thank you for the Grace of God. Some things are so big you just have to accept them. That's what I'm like.'

'As big as the stars or the Grace of God?'

'Exactly.'

'Good God.'

Sarah laughed at me then. 'If Max buys you a beer or gives you a fill of tobacco, you have to say thank you; because you owe him until it's your turn to buy. But you don't owe me. You repaid me magnificently.'

I twirled my moustaches and puffed my chest like a pigeon then. I always took a foolish pride in those accomplishments. Very silly.

'Anyway –' she cocked an eyebrow up ahead – 'do you think Max knows what's expected of him?'

'Oh, Max isn't stupid. He'll catch on quick enough, if he hasn't worked it out already.'

'And what do you think he'll say if the little sailor offers to fill his pipe for him?'

'A man who's prepared to take on the navy to defend the honour of his camel? I don't think it will go well.'

At the front of our little procession, Varga flung his head back and tittered. He turned to look back at us confidentially. 'Your friend! So funny!' and then he laughed some more and squeezed Max by the arm.

Tifty looked back at us and made a great pantomime of throwing up. 'What are we going to do?' she hissed.

Varga put his hand up and waved, 'Everybody, everybody! You must stay for lunch.'

'But we just had breakfast,'said Sarah.

'Varga, it's very kind,' I said, 'but we really must get on our way. I've got a camel to deliver.'

'Nonsense. A few hours won't make any difference Anyway, we're having such fun and, as I mentioned, you're all under arrest while I carry out my investigations – even you, Maxxie,' and he reached up and gave my mate Max a little tug on the nose. Max was beginning to catch on to something and I thought he might have been working up to another one of his famous haymakers, but he looked at me first and I shook my head.

Varga said, 'I can't have you shot before you've had something to eat. That wouldn't be nice.'

'Varga, be serious! You can't have anybody shot.'

'Oh, I can. I do it all the time. I am the Lord of Life and Death. Have 'em flogged, have 'em shot – it's all the same to me. I have absolute Pharaonic power. I can have you all shot – oh, not you, Maxxie!' He gripped Max by the elbow and his thin, sing-songy voice went all husky and reassuring. 'Not you. We're friends forever, but those others, starting with Little Miss Hatpin there . . .'

Max said, 'You are not allowed to shoot my friends.' He was a man of few words, my mate Max.

'No, Maxxie. No.' Back to the lullaby voice again. 'Naughty Imre won't shoot anybody if Maxxie doesn't want it, but if, just supposing, I did decide to have that one –' his finger poked out, white as a root, and pointed straight at Tifty – 'if I decided to have her shot, she *would* have to face the firing squad in her corsets. That's such a pretty dress – far too nice to make holes in – and it's just my size too. Now hurry along, everybody, keep up. There's something you must see.'

He marched us off around two sides of the Naval Academy and down a path between two low hedges. When he turned the corner and while he was out of sight, one of the sailors walking behind said, 'He's not joking, you know. He means it. He's done it before. Mad as a box of frogs. You watch yourselves.'

And then Varga was in sight again, hopping about and clapping his hands and tittering, 'Look everybody, a croquet lawn! It's so fashionable. They play it all the time in England, you know. Now get into your teams – Maxxie's on my side.'

'I am blind,' said the Professor.

'We'll make allowances,' said Varga.

And so we all had to play his damned stupid game, except for the camel, who stood cropping the ornamental bushes with his big purple tongue while we fooled around with croquet mallets. None of us understood what was going on, of course, and I doubt that Varga did either. He seemed to make up the rules as he went along and he wasn't afraid to add in a new one any time it suited him. He could whack our balls out of the way if he felt like it, but we couldn't hit his because it was red or he got two free kicks at somebody else's ball if it went through one of those little loops stuck in the grass, but we never did. It was all madness, and he went through the whole thing like a spoiled child with a new toy, never letting anybody else have a turn and always threatening to throw a tantrum, which is bad enough with any child but a million times worse if he's armed.

It was a terrifying time, but at last, thank God, the game was over. I don't know why it was over or how it ended, Varga simply announced, 'That's it! We've won – me and Maxxie! The winners! Well done, Maxxie, you were wonderful. Are you sure you've never played this before?' And the two sentries, who had been standing at the side of the lawn looking bored to death, put their rifles over their shoulders and clapped like lunatics.

'Lunch now. Lunch everybody. Come along.'

At the other side of the lawn, French windows opened in the side of a building of golden stone and a steward in a white drill uniform came out, it seemed without moving his legs, like the little wooden farmer who looks out from one of those damned stupid chalets they make to let you tell the weather.

Max said, 'It's not even ten o'clock yet.'

'Lunch starts with drinks, Maxxie. Lots of drinks. Don't you know anything, you silly boy?'

It was the first time I'd felt hopeful for a long time. I reckoned that I could come a good third place behind Max and Tifty in any drinking contest and Varga would be unconscious before the soup arrived but, even if that failed and he went ahead with his plan to have us shot, at least I'd be drunk when he did it.

We made our way across the lawn to the French windows, and the steward stood there and fawned with an undertaker's smile, pointing the way to the dining room as if it were the way to the grave.

I wonder if I am making this up. Am I making this up? I swear I'm not, but I feel like a fraud, like a kid who remembers clearly every little detail of a photo from his granny's album and all the stories that go with it: who stood where, who said what just at that very moment when the picture was taken, although it was taken a year before he was born. Or like an old uncle reciting the same anecdote over and over again for years so the whole family knows every word of it and remembers where to laugh.

But even the kid with his granny's photo album can be telling the truth. Even if he didn't see it, the story can still be true.

And when the old uncle tells his stories, there's something at the bottom of them. He knows it all off by heart because that's how it was when it happened and he got it all sorted out in his mind and told the story and told the story and told the story until it stuck like that. But it's still true. Those boys up there tonight in the bombers, if they come through this, if they don't get themselves killed trying to kill me, they'll have stories to tell their grandchildren, and the grandchildren will be bored to tears, but the stories will be true anyway. Am I boring you? I never thought of that. That would be embarrassing. I'm sorry. But I can't stop. I have to get this written. You can stop reading, of course. Stop for a bit and come back to it, snap the book shut and shut me up with it. I hope you'll come back. Carry me round in your pocket until you're ready to sit down and listen to the story again. I hope you'd like to do that. Just don't, for God's sake, throw this book away, please. Read it or don't read it. Give it away to somebody else who might want to read it. Or keep it under your bed in an old shoebox so it ends up in a junk shop after you're dead too and maybe forty years from now, or fifty, or into the next century even, somebody will find it and buy it for almost nothing and start to read it and say, 'That can't be right!' just like that poor little bastard this afternoon. Just don't throw this away. Out there, outside this little tin caravan, people are dying, lives are ending, disappearing as if they had never even been here. Nothing left but blizzards of ashes floating by on the wind. I don't want that to happen to me. I want to leave a tiny little scratch in the dust of history. Don't let that happen to me. I'm relying on you. I'm gambling on you. But it doesn't matter what you do – I have to get it written down anyway.

I was wondering if I might just be making this stuff up because of all the food. Maybe it's because there's so little of it these days. Get your hands on a month-old turnip and it's like Christmas Eve, but it seems to me I can remember everything about that meal with Varga. Can there really have been so much? Those piles of fruit? My God, he had oranges, just sitting there in dishes on the sideboard, heaps of them. Oranges! I can't have made that up, surely.

And I know I haven't invented the drink. It started the minute we walked through those fancy French windows. No sooner had the little ginger lunatic put down his damned stupid croquet bat than he unsheathed his cutlass and I have to admit I might have gone just a tiny bit squirty when I saw that bloody great knife in the hands of that tiny little madman, but it was just more show-offery. He led the way, running in from the garden like he was storming the decks of an enemy vessel, although I doubt he would have been at the front of the charge if there had been anything more terrifying than champagne bottles waiting to meet him. But there were battalions of champagne bottles waiting in that dining room and little Varga snatched up the first one he came to and set about it with his cutlass, one long swipe up the neck that took the top right off it so it spluttered a jet of foam and soaked the carpet, a lovely, celebratory way to die.

'Have a drink!' he said, and it sounded like an order, not an invitation. So we had a drink and another one and another one and the steward with his white drill jacket and his piped trousers and his gold buttons went twittering about between us, smirking and pouring, smirking and pouring and, thank God, he opened all the other bottles in the traditional way, with his fingers.

Sarah came up to me, giggling. 'I've never had champagne before,' she said. 'The bubbles go up your nose.'

Every girl I ever knew who ever had champagne always said that 'the bubbles go up your nose' as if it was some deep and original insight. It's not, of course. You know what it is? It's old age and death knocking on the door. When a girl says, 'The bubbles go up your nose,' and you think it's boring and silly, when she laughs with the undiscovered joy of it and you don't, when you can't share in the fun of something that's wonderful and new, then that's a nail in your coffin, my friend. When a little kid laughs at a balloon or cries when it bursts and you don't, that's another one and, I'll tell you this, there are only thirteen nails in a coffin. Don't use them up too quick.

I laughed and gave her a quick little peck. 'See if your dad can prise Max away from Varga. Engage him in conversation about naval badges of rank or something. I need to have a private word with Max.'

She managed it, the minx. I think the Professor must have used his mind-control powers or something, but before too long he had Varga jammed in between the wall and the sideboard and he wouldn't let him escape until he'd wrung every drop of information out of him.

Max took his chance and wandered over. 'My old boots! For God's sake, Otto, you've got to rescue me. He fancies me rotten.'

'Aww, shut up and take it like a man!' I poured him some more champagne. 'Look, you know I'm not going to let anything happen to you. Just play along with him for a bit. Sit beside him at lunch. Play footsie with him under the table. Christ, hold his hand if he wants. Please. I've got this under control.'

'You'd just better.' But he wasn't convinced.

And then there was more champagne until Tifty and Sarah hugged each other round the neck and hooted with laughter and, at last, the steward came fawning up to Varga, who clapped his hands and announced, 'Time to eat,' and led us to the table.

Lunch. There was soup to start with, I know that, and mountains of food – mountains of it – and more drink, a different wine with every course, and meringues to finish and liqueurs and coffee, but the thing that sticks in my memory the most is the camel, standing tethered at the window and flicking at the rose bushes with his long purple tongue.

Varga was at the head of the table, of course, with Max beside him, and from time to time, between drinks, he reached out to give Max's hand a little squeeze. I was at the far end of the table – which was a bit of a comedown for an actual Graf and the Keeper of the Imperial Camels – but it gave me the chance to slop some drink into the soup tureen when Varga wasn't looking.

He was never the sort of bloke you could call quiet, but by the time that creepy little steward came round with the nuts Varga was making my ears bleed. I've always said that drink is a magnifying glass. Drink makes you the person that you already are but just a bit more. If you're a happy person, drink makes you happier. If you're a miserable person, it just makes you more miserable, and I understand that our great leader is a staunch teetotaller, which is probably just as well, since his magnificence magnified would be more than we mere mortals could bear. For my own part I tend to find that the more I drink, the more attractive I become to women, but Varga, well, Varga was a vicious little turd stone-cold sober, and drink did nothing to add to his lustre. Down at the other end of the table, I could see things were getting out of hand. Max was doing his best to stick to the plan – even though he had no idea what the plan was and, to tell the truth, neither did I – but once or twice he looked down the table at me with a glance that said, 'This guy's really asking for it!'

I made soothing gestures and Max could see that I was watching, keeping an eye on things while I played with my brandy glass, but then Varga's hand disappeared under the table, and the very next second Max shot to his feet, his left fist winding backwards for a punch.

'Herr Schlepsig!' I said, not yelling, but with that kingly authority I was learning to cultivate. 'Herr Schlepsig, that will do!'

I wasn't loud, but silence fell across the drunken table after I spoke the way it comes rolling back after a thunderclap. Nobody knew where to look. Max sat down and I stood up, my cigar in one hand, my brandy glass in the other, and I walked slowly up the length of the table to Varga. 'You are not a gentleman,' I told him. 'You are a disgrace to the uniform of the Emperor. You have taken unspeakable liberties with my servant, a man so far below you in society as to be unable to defend himself, a man who looks to me as his master for protection.'

'You don't object, do you, Maxxie?'

'I object,' I said, and I emptied my brandy glass over his head. 'I'm calling you out, Varga. I demand satisfaction.'

He sat there, wiping brandy out of his hair with one of his big swanky napkins and tittering like the madman I knew he was. 'Bloody fool. Why should I shoot you when I can simply have you shot? A man doesn't keep a dog and bark himself, you know.' He gave his face one more wipe and smacked his lips to catch the last drops of brandy. 'Anyway, duelling is illegal.'

'Technically,' said the Professor, who seemed to be taking extra care over his words. 'Technically only officers may duel and technically of course, in law and following the letter of the Bishops of the Austro-Hungarian Empire, it is entirely illegal and improper for any officer to take part in a duel in any way.'

'See? What did I tell you? Now be a good fellow and go out outside and stand against the wall. I'll have somebody come out and shoot you shortly.'

'On the other hand, as recently as 1884, Josef Hintner, Lieutenant of Reserves of the Tyrolese Jaeger Regiment, was cashiered for "absolute refusal of a duel". Stripped of his rank and kicked out in disgrace.'

'Step outside,' I said. I heard Tifty gasp, and behind me Sarah was whispering my name over and over, like a charm. 'Otto, Otto. Oh, Otto.' Exactly what she had said the night before. Exactly the same frantic whisper, but this time it meant something different.

'It was thirty years ago,' said Varga.

'For ex-Lieutenant Hintner, it must seem like yesterday. Fight me, you bloody coward. You might win.'

I knew then, with that hesitation, that if I could make him fight me, he would lose. I've been in a few fights in my time and I can tell you this – maybe the most useful bit of information I have to pass on to you – nine times out of ten, it's not about who's the biggest or the strongest, nor who's fastest on the draw; it's about resolve. Resolution, that's what it is. Determination The man who is determined to do this thing and no half-measures, just get it done, whatever it takes, that's the man who's going to win, and the other man, it's the other man who's going to lose and I was ready to kill Varga then. I was resolved to do it, and he wasn't. He was happy enough to kill me if he could get somebody else to do it. He'd have stood around laughing his stupid ginger head off if we'd been obliging enough to line up for his firing squad, but he wasn't ready to do it himself, not if he might get his hands dirty and certainly not if there was any chance anybody might try to hit him back.

I leaned in close to where Varga was clawing at the table-cloth as if he was trying to keep from falling off his chair. 'I am challenging you to a duel, Herr Fregattenkapitän. Come outside and try to kill me if you dare.'

He didn't say anything.

Max said, 'You don't have to do this on my account. It's not that important.'

'Oh, but it is,' I said. 'And you know it is, don't you, Varga? I've called you out. And your little friend the waiter over there knows I've called you out. Those sailors standing outside with their rifles at the ready – he's going to tell them that I called you out and it'll be all over the naval college this afternoon, it'll be all over town tonight, all over the dockyards, all over every ship in the navy, sailing out all over the world.' I kept my eyes drilled into him and I said, 'You see, Herr Schlepsig, if he doesn't come outside and fight me right now, his name is mud. He either kills me, or he might as well kill himself.'

Varga let go of the tablecloth. 'I take it, as the party facing the challenge, I may choose the weapons.'

'If you like.'

He stood up. 'I assume you have no sword.'

'It's in my other trousers.'

He drew that cutlass again, the same one he used to open our first bottle of champagne, and it came out of the scabbard with a hiss of warning. 'Have mine,' he said, and then, with a smart bow, he indicated the way out through the French windows. 'After you, Erlaucht.'

I went outside, out into the middle of Varga's damned stupid croquet lawn. I took my coat off, rolled my sleeves up, swung that big knife around a bit, limbered up a little. When I looked back to the house, there was the steward, hunched over, whispering to the two sailors who stood, gripping their rifles, looking from him to me and back to him. My friends stood crowded round the doorway, Max and Tifty looking worried, Sarah clinging to her father and babbling to him, telling him the story he could not see. Her face was the colour of the wall and I suppose mine must have been too. I may tell you, friend, I was damned near shitting myself.

Varga came out, pushing his way past Sarah and the others and down the steps on to the grass. 'Ready?' he said. He was walking towards me pretty quick but he was still a good way off. 'Shall we begin?' and, before I had time to answer, he said, 'Good!'

And then that little turd reached into his jacket and came striding across the lawn towards me with a gun in his hand aiming right at me. That first bullet damned near brushed my whiskers. If he'd had enough brains to stand still and take a proper aim, I reckon he could've put one between my eyes, but I wasn't about to make myself a target. I ran. Not away. I didn't run away. I've never run away and, like I told you, it's resolution that counts. Resolution is the only thing that counts. The willingness to fight, that's what matters. No, I ran right at that little bastard and he was squaring up to fire on me again when I threw myself into a flick-flack, hands down, feet up, spring, roll, feet down, hands up, bouncing across the soft, flat green grass with the bullets whizzing and spitting and chewing up the turf, until I hit him, skittled him right over and his gun went flying and the air went out of his lungs with a wheeze. I put the point of that sword on his throat and I looked at him for a bit.

I said, 'I want a boat, Varga. Just whatever you've got lying round. Something big enough for a camel. Nothing too fancy. A cruiser should do nicely.'

He gritted his teeth and chewed on his moustaches for

a time and he said, 'I can't do that! I'm not giving you a warship.'

'Too bad,' I said, and I leaned on the blade a tiny bit, just so he could feel the point of it through his white collar.

'Wait, wait!' He was flapping and wriggling on the grass like a newly landed fish. 'I'll give you my yacht!'

My mate Max was the first to reach us. He bent down to the grass and palmed Varga's pistol, 'Just in case,' he said. 'There are two bullets left, so don't get any funny ideas. I told you, you are not allowed to shoot my friends. I take a dim view of that.'

I reached down and offered Varga a hand up, but he ignored me, rolled on to his knees and stood up. 'Where did you learn to bounce around like that?' he said.

'Never mind me, where did you learn to shoot? Four bullets and every one of them wasted. You couldn't hit a cow's arse with a banjo if you were standing behind the cow. Now, Max here, Max is a crack shot. He could blow off a gnat's goolies at ten paces.'

'I quite believe it,' said Varga. 'A crack-shot camel wrangler and the bouncing Graf. You might be a travelling circus act for all I know, but I know this much – you are not quite a gentleman.'

'Well, that makes two of us.' It gave me great pleasure to stab Varga's sword through the fine turf of his croquet lawn and leave it standing there while I put my jacket back on. I think Varga might have cast a troublesome eye on it for just a moment, but I heard Max say, 'Steady,' in the way he spoke to the camel, and nothing came of it.

And then Sarah arrived with my hat, fussing and clucking and fretful and full of solicitous kisses and a few tears as well.

'He might have killed you!'

'Well, I didn't let him.'

'Otto, I was scared.'

'No need. I had it all under control.'

'But are you all right?'

'Not a scratch.'

'Oh you stupid man!' And then she hit me, punched me in the chest and called me, 'Stupid! Stupid! Stupid!' again and rubbed her snotty nose on my clean shirt front for a bit and had a little snivel while I held her, which was nice but it didn't last long. Girls are funny. She went from being worried about me to being angry, then all weepy and, from there, it was but a short step back to blind fury again, only this time it was Varga she was after.

She called him a lot of words which I was surprised she knew, and I think she was working up to hitting him when Tifty arrived, hauling the Professor in tow. 'Darling, you mustn't be silly. Don't soil your hands with him. Dignity, darling, always dignity. Remember that you are a lady. But I, on the other hand, am a fallen woman,' and she whirled round and slammed her hand into the front of Varga's trousers, muttering fiercely at him in that awful Hungarish and squeezing so hard it made *my* eyes water.

The poor blighter was helpless, skewered like a moth in a glass case, up on his tiptoes and dancing about weakly as if he wanted to escape from Tifty's grip by climbing up an invisible ladder.

And, just like I couldn't understand a word of what the daddy in the beer hall said although I picked up the meaning, it was pretty clear that Tifty was making a point with Varga along the lines of, 'Do we understand each other?'

He barely had a breath left in his body, but somehow, he managed to squeak out '*Igen, igen, igen,*' which is how I learned Hungarish for 'yes'. Funnily enough, that girl in the cellar had said exactly the same thing in a slightly different way.

I said, 'Put him down now, Tifty. Be nice. After all, Varga's taking us boating.'

'That's kind,' she said, and she let him go and he fell over on the grass again.

'Oh, pick him up. We have to catch the tide.'

Varga managed to say, 'It's not a boat, it's a yacht,' in a more than usually annoying way, and Tifty made a face and said another rude word which I did not recognise as I had not heard a pretty girl saying it any time recently, but I was having none of it. I told her to shut up in no uncertain terms and offered Varga his sword back.

'I reckon it's safe enough, if you're as good with a blade as you are with a pistol, and anyway, Max has his eye on you.'

Max made a bulge in his pocket and said, 'Pop,' just to make the point.

Varga feigned outraged concern. 'It's very silly to carry firearms down your trousers, Maxxie. That's how accidents happen, and that would be such a terrible waste.'

'Are you offering to kiss it better?'

'Any time, Maxxie, any time.'

Max looked to be pulling back for another one of his haymakers so I had to step in again. 'Varga, just get us on the damned boat.'

'It's a yacht.'

'Just get us on it.'

So we gathered up the camel, who was picking his way round Varga's garden like a burgermeister at a civic buffet, and we made our way back to the docks.

If Varga had been a better officer, if he'd been better loved by his men, or perhaps just not a raving nutter, he could still have had us in irons in a minute and up against the wall the minute after that, but he was the man he was. Varga could not bring himself to cry out, 'Help, I'm being kidnapped,' because he knew very well that every sailor in the academy would gather round in a body and help to shove him on the boat, so he simply smiled and nodded and returned the necessary salutes and he told the harbour-master, 'My friends and I are going on a bit of a cruise. Back tomorrow.'

That was all there was to it. Varga led us quickly down the quayside to where his yacht was waiting, a magnificent thing, sleek as a greyhound, elegant as a duchess and fast. I know nothing about boats, but you could see she was fast. Even tied up at the dock she looked like she was racing along, every line of her stretched and straining, every plank and beam polished like a nut, every inch of rigging taut.

Varga couldn't hide his pride. 'Isn't she something? Took her off a Turkish smuggler. It was quite a chase, I can tell you. She goes like shit off a shovel.'

I gave him a little poke in the chest. 'Please remember that there are ladies present,' which made Sarah very happy, and he was all set to say something smart but he saw from my face that I meant it. 'Time's a-wasting. Get the camel on board and let's get going.'

'You're not taking that camel on my lovely yacht.'

'Well, we're not leaving him here,' said Max.

'Have you forgotten that I am Keeper of His Imperial Majesty's Camels? I have to deliver this magnificent animal to the King of Albania. That camel is the point and purpose of our journey.'

'You're not serious?'

'Never more so.'

'But my beautiful polished deck.'

'Oh, his feet are as soft as thistledown,' said Max. 'He'll polish your deck up something lovely.'

'It's out of the question. I can't allow it. I simply won't permit it. I absolutely and utterly . . .'

He was going to say 'refuse', but, about the time he got to 'absolutely', I gave a nod to my mate Max, who landed a little tap right in Varga's guts. It wasn't much of a punch. Like I said, just a little tap, nothing at all compared to what he could've done. Max was a man who bent steel bars for a living, after all, but Varga turned green and all the breath went out of him in a wheeze.

Max put a friendly arm around him and held him up. 'Sorry about that. It'll pass off in a minute. Just breathe. Breathe.'

It must've hurt like hell, particularly after what Tifty had done to him, but I was less than sympathetic. Once Varga managed to get his eyes uncrossed again, I told him, 'You're not giving the orders any more.'

Tifty was gleeful, glinting with a sharp spite. 'No,' she said. 'We're giving the orders now.'

You couldn't blame her. A couple of hours before Varga had been all set to have her shot in her shift so he could steal her dress, and all that champagne was beginning to wear off, and champagne always left her with an angry headache. Tifty suffered from no more than the usual dose of ordinary human viciousness, the natural urge to do unto others what they would have done unto you if only they got the chance, but I couldn't let her off with that. I said, 'Actually, Countess, I think you'll find that *I* give the orders now.'

Any sentence that contains the phrase 'I think you'll find' or the words 'Don't you know who I am?' is doomed before it's even out of your mouth. It was a very grand thing to say and, looking back on it, it might have been a mistake. Tifty wasn't stupid. I think she had already seen how things were with Sarah and me and, when I spoke shortly to her like that, well, I think she took it harder than I intended, especially when Sarah took my arm and cuddled in proudly, as if to make that 'I' into a 'We'.

No, if I had been wise, I would have apologised right there and then, said sorry and explained that it didn't come out right. But I was stupid, acting like the king I was not, and Tifty complained in the only way she could, crossing her legs and dipping a deep curtsy that would not have been out of place in the Hofburg. It almost convinced me that she was telling the truth and she really was a countess after all. By God, that girl had a magnificent cleavage. She stayed down there long enough to let me admire it and then rose again, smiling at Sarah, once she was sure that I had.

'Get the camel on board,' I said. 'There's no time to lose.'

There wasn't much Varga could say to that. He rolled his eyes and said, 'Make it stand in the prow.' And when Max didn't move, he rolled his eyes again and said, 'Oh for God's sake! The pointy bit at the front.'

That camel was surprisingly cooperative. He seemed to trust Max completely and he paid no heed to the gang-plank and took his place at the front of the boat, as calm as a carved figurehead, while we busied ourselves helping Varga get the boat ready for sea. None of us knew the first thing about boats or which rope to pull or which to let go, of course, and the Professor just stood there, turning his face up to the sky, catching the warmth of the sun on his skin and fiddling with his cane while we ran all about him. To tell the truth, he was probably the most useful of us all – unless you count the camel – since at least he did no harm but, somehow, eventually, Varga got the thing moving and we pulled out on the dropping tide. It's a strange moment, that. It's almost like falling in love. Or maybe like watching somebody dying. You can think of the time before it happened, and you can think of the time after it happened, but it's hard to put your finger on just the very moment when it actually happens. It's like that on a boat. One minute it's a lump of wood, a dead thing, a stripped, shaved, nailed tree, fixed to the land, as lifeless as a staircase, and then something happens and you're not very sure if you imagined it, but it seems as if there's a gap that's opened up just a little between the boat and the harbour wall. One end is just a little bit further out than it was before, so that must mean that the other end is closer, but, when you turn to look, it's not, there's a gap opening up there too, like a wound, and then, the next second, there's no tiny bit of the boat left touching the land and you know that now, for sure, she's afloat and moving, moving under your feet and through the water and through the air, moving away from everything that ever held her, and she's alive, changed into something new and different and better. That's what happens to people when they love. That's what happens when a soul sets out on its journey. I know. I've seen them both.

In no time at all Varga had us heading out through the harbour of Fiume, past the great warships that lay at anchor there and towered over us like huge steel castles. It was hard to believe they could ever have uprooted themselves and sailed out into the ocean like trees walking out of the forest. They seemed so fixed and solid, but Varga's yacht went running around between them the way those little farm dogs do when they are herding cattle, jinking in and out between their hoofs or dropping down, belly flat, to avoid the kicks. And then we were out in the bay and the warships were further and further apart and the town was dropping away behind us, getting smaller and smaller, and the shore was just a jumble of rocks.

I looked back. Varga was at the wheel and he was actually smiling and I smiled too, because with every wave I was getting closer to my kingdom.

Suddenly everybody was happy. Everybody was smiling, except for the Professor, who stood in the stern, holding on to the rail and looking about him with blind eyes.

I went to him, leaning over on the tipping deck, swinging along, hand to hand from one rope to another.

'Everything all right, Professor?'

'He's put out flags, hasn't he? Near here? I hear them flapping.'

'Yes. On a little pole at the back.'

'Tell me.'

'A lot of blue flags. One all blue and white, checked like a tablecloth, and one with a white stripe along the middle.'

The Professor heaved a sigh. 'N and J. The international signal for "I am under attack". Make him take it down.'

The smart thing would have been to shoot him right there and dump his body over the side. That would have been the smart thing, except that none of us had the first idea how to work the boat and he knew it. He took the flags down – or at any rate I took them down for him. He was damned lucky I didn't jam them down his throat, but he treated it all as a great joke. 'You can't blame me for trying.' That's what he said.

Max said, 'Would you like me to hit him again?'

'Oh don't be so stupid. You want to get to Albania, and I'm the only ticket you've got.'

Of course he was right, and of course I couldn't let Max hit him again. So I hit him. Back-handed. Right across the chops. Varga must have been pretty sick of getting beaten up and he looked as if he was about to burst into tears, so I waited until he'd got a grip of himself again and then I said, 'Understand this. You belong to me. We all know how much you value your own skin and you bought it for the price of this boat. I would've been within my rights to stick you with your own sword back at the academy, you little coward, so don't start getting any courageous ideas now. And here's the truth of it: we are going to Albania or we'll die trying. We'd rather stay alive, but we will die trying, and if you want to live you'd better get us there.'

'It's the other end of the Adriatic.'

'Varga, can you get us there?'

'I am a Fregatenkapitän of the Kaiserliche und Königliche Kriegsmarine. Of course I can get you there.'

'How long?'

'It's two hundred sea miles to Split, another hundred to Dubrovnik, and a bit less than that to Durres.'

Sarah said, 'Is he telling the truth, Daddy?'

'Yes, more or less.'

'How long?'

'If we pile on the sail, if the wind holds from the starboard, we might make better than ten knots. But that'll be hard sailing for a week or so.'

Professor von Mesmer gave a polite cough. 'Forgive me, but ten knots for twenty-four hours is two hundred and seventy-six miles. We can do it in two days.'

'Impossible. We can't sail at night.'

'Yes, we can,' I said. 'It seems to me that ships come from Australia, from America, from all over the world, and they don't stop in the middle of the night, bobbing about in the middle of the ocean until it's time to wake up again.'

'They have a crew.'

'We are your crew.'

'I have to sleep.'

'Of course you do, and while you are sleeping, one of

us will steer. If there's any bother, we'll come and get you. None of us wants to drown any more than you do, Varga.'

'There are islands.'

'I know. I saw them on the map. Get us through the islands and then you can sleep. We sail –' I pointed out the direction – 'that way.'

'South-east by south,' said the Professor.

'See how easy it is? A blind man could do it.'

You would think, wouldn't you, that I would have more to say about sailing night and day, canvas cracking, ropes creaking, with a lunatic in command and a blind man at the tiller. You would think, since I have filled pages with the business of getting on a train and pages more with the business of getting on a boat, I might have had something to say about the actual voyage. The truth is, I don't.

I remember the oranges piled on Varga's sideboard at the Naval Academy and the sound of the camel's feet on the cobbles in the streets of Budapest, but that sea voyage seems to have passed without leaving too much of a mark on my memory. I know we got on the boat and I know we got off the boat and, it stands to reason, something must have happened in between, but to tell the truth, there's not much to say.

If you or I were up in the sky tonight, in one of those planes, up in the blazing, burning clouds, following the fires and dodging the flak, circling, waiting, watching for the fighters to come at any moment, I know we'd remember every second of it, from the time we took off to the time we landed again. But I bet they don't, those boys up there.

For them it's just hours and hours of hard work and routine with a few moments of blind terror now and again. If they did it twenty times, or thirty, hour after hour, flying through the night with death sitting on their shoulders there and back again, how many of them do you think would come home with even one good story to tell their grandchildren? Damned few, and if they did, it would probably be the tale of the time the dog ate the general's trousers, not some nonsense about flying home with their tail on fire and the wings full of bullet holes.

And isn't it amazing how much of our lives passes that way? All the million, million moments from the moment we first crawl, screaming into the world until we crawl, screaming out of it again and all the moments in between those two screams of fear and regret, how many of them do we actually remember? In each of them the sun is just as warm, just as yellow, the sky is just as blue, the clouds are just as white, roses just as red, birds sing, snowballs fly, women laugh, every plate of soup is just as hot and tasty as the next, cowsheds smell the same, grass feels the same under bare feet, and everything in the world that is there to be enjoyed is enjoyable time after time so we forget to notice and, before we even realise, all that vast store of moments is gone, worn out and eaten up with no record kept. Or that's how it was with me. One minute I was a boy, running away from school, the next I'm an old man waiting to die in a little tin shack. Be warned. I'm wasting my breath. You will not be warned. I was warned, and I took no heed. I doubt if it is even possible for mere men

123

to live, savouring every minute. It's not in our nature. Life itself is as much as we can cope with, never mind storing it all up as we go like an endless newsreel. Nobody's head is big enough to hold all that nonsense.

It's as if we spend our whole lives in a railway-station waiting room, sipping endless cups of coffee with the same people, handing round the newspaper, doing anything to make the time pass while, outside, people go by in droves, pretty girls and clever men, heroes and scientists and geniuses and simple, loving people by their thousands. We never meet them, we never speak to them, we never hear their stories. We stay in the waiting room, with the same people and the same newspaper, waiting for the bell to ring so that, perhaps a dozen times in a lifetime, we can rush out on to the platform and see a train arrive, actually experience something that makes a mark on our memory before we go back inside.

And what things we choose to remember. Brahms is dead. I know he's dead, but I don't remember when it happened. A mountain like that shifts away and I can't say what I was doing when I heard the news, not the day of the week nor the month of the year, but ask me about the time my mother came home from the fair with the giant blutwurst and I can remember everything.

I heard tell once about this bloke, I'm almost sure he was French, who spilled out his whole life story, from the time he was a boy, filled book after book with it and it all came back to him because he ate a cake. That's a lot of tripe, I can tell you. Writing even one story is damned hard work, and I'm sitting here, racking my brains, trying to think of a single thing that happened on that voyage. Of course, the French bloke wasn't sitting down to write in the middle of an air raid, and I haven't got any cakes, so we're not exactly starting on an even footing, but let's see what I can do . . .

I can see myself sitting at the tiller with Varga, and Sarah is coming up the little wooden stairs from the kitchen with coffee on a tray for us. Varga wouldn't have taken it from Tifty. He didn't like Tifty, and he knew she didn't like him, but he was nice as pie around Sarah, and he took the coffee and thanked her like a gentleman. Of course Varga didn't like me either, but he knew I wasn't going to spit in his coffee and he knew that I was serious. I was going to get to Albania or die trying, and we had to get along.

I suppose, considering that he tried to murder me and considering how often he'd been slapped and punched and cruelly squeezed, we got along pretty well.

He got a bit upset when the camel discharged some ballast all over his nice deck and he started shouting and screaming about his lovely varnish, but Max shovelled the whole lot over the side and sloshed a bucket of sea water over the spot and that calmed him down again so, on the whole, we got on pretty well.

Varga stayed at the helm all through the afternoon and long into the evening, leaning on the tiller as he guided us down the passage between the islands, and in that time he taught me just about everything I needed to know about sailing a boat. There's really only two difficult things about a boat: making it start and making it stop. I couldn't get one started and I couldn't get one stopped – well, not without ramming into something, which isn't a good way of stopping, or just hauling in all the sails and dropping anchor, which will also work. The trick is to stop neatly at a quayside so you can get off without getting your feet wet, and I couldn't do that. But keeping it going wasn't too hard. The wind was steady and Varga showed me two little cranks to turn to let the sails out a bit if it started to blow too strong or pull them in a bit tighter if the wind dropped. I think that was it. It might have been the other way around. There's another bit of useful knowledge that I've misplaced.

Anyway, the important thing was not to let the wind blow us too far over to one side, just keep things steady, not to try and race ahead too much and, I must say, that made sense, because if the boat tipped over, the camel might fall off. Apart from that, all we had to do was keep heading in the same direction. Varga showed me the point on the compass – not that I took his word for it, I checked with the Professor first – and then I got a turn at steering.

It was harder than it looked – the waves tried to knock us off course and the boat wanted to turn out of the wind like a weather-cock – but with a bit of effort I could get it done.

And then, after a bit, it wasn't hard at all. Have you ever worked with a horse when it's working, but not too hard, when it's hauling a load or pulling a cart and that horse is almost laughing out loud because the work is easy? It's like he's saying, 'I could do this all day and, if I wanted to, I could knock you down and kick you over the rooftops and still haul this load, but I won't because I like you, and anyway this is fun.' That's what it was like sailing that boat. Out at sea she was a living, breathing thing with a heart beating under her masts and muscles pulsing through the water. You could feel the strength in her, feel the waves passing under her and vibrating through the tiller, feel the wind thrumming through the ropes and buffeting the canvas. I swear, sitting there, I could see the air swelling the sails, filling them up and pouring out over the edges in torrents, like water from a bowl as the boat panted through the waves.

We smiled and we laughed, sitting there together drinking coffee, me and Sarah and Varga, or sometimes all of us in a row, Max and Tifty and the Professor too, because Max had to learn how to steer as well. Max was better at the hard work of steering but, with Tifty there to remind him about looking at the compass and letting the sails out and in, he did all right. You could rely on my mate Max.

So there we were, all of us sitting in a row and bouncing along, just like we did on that bench at the picture show except without the tickles this time. Strange to think that only a day had passed and yet everything had changed.

Only the day before we were all together in the dusk of Budapest and now, a day later, we were on a boat in the Adriatic watching the stars come out, still together, but changed. In Budapest I had a girl on each arm. On the boat I sat with Sarah, but Tifty sat with Max. Something had changed. I had changed. I had spoken harshly to Tifty, not once but twice, and I'd put my foot down with the Professor.

We were still friends. We still loved each other, but something had changed. Everything was the same, but everything was different, as if we had gone to bed at night and woken up to find all the furniture moved round – the same old comfortable furniture, but in a different place entirely.

It grew dark. From up in the prow the camel gave a contented belch and sank to its knees, ready for sleep, jawing away like an old man with a plug of tobacco and looking up to count the stars.

Varga rubbed his hands together and turned his collar up against the wind. 'Now,' he said, 'I wouldn't want you to use this as an excuse to throw me over the side and seize the ship and, bearing in mind possible emergencies and the finer points of pilotage, reading of charts, lamps and signals and so forth, that would probably be a very bad idea anyway, but I'd say you've turned into a very able crew.'

'So you reckon we could sail her,' said the Professor.

'Well, I wouldn't want to throw you out in mid-Atlantic in the teeth of a nor'easter with the waves as high as steeples but, for a cruise like this, you'll do.'

'But we could keep her running on this course, saving emergencies,' I said.

He looked a little nervous. 'But that doesn't mean you can make me walk the plank. Emergencies. You have to bear in mind emergencies.'

'Exactly, and for that reason I want you close at hand and fresh and alert. I suggest you turn in, Herr Fregattenkapitän. Get some sleep. I am relieving you of command.'

He stood up and saluted and hurried down the stairs into the boat, pleased that he was going to bed and not going overboard. 'Keep her on her current heading,' he said. 'There is nothing between us and Dubrovnik. Watch out for the lights of other vessels. The *slightest* difficulty – the slightest difficulty – call me at once.'

As soon as he was gone, I gathered the others around. 'Do you remember that puzzle from when we were kids, the one about the farmer with a fox and a goose and a bag of grain and he has to get them all over the river but he can only take one at a time? Well, that's us now, and Varga is the fox. He's bent over backwards since we left port, but I don't trust him. I want him watched at all times, whether he's down below or up on deck. Professor, why don't you bunk up with him? For all we know he's down there right now pulling the plug out. Your eyes are as good as his below decks at night. Make sure he puts all the lamps out, and watch him like a hawk.'

The old man seemed happy to be useful. He found the stairs easily with his cane and wished us all a good night.

The nights are not long at that time of year. I fixed it with Tifty and Max that they would get some rest while I stayed at the tiller with Sarah.

'I'll wake Varga in a few hours and he can share a spell with me and then, a few hours after that, you can take over and watch him. If he gives any cause for concern, just shoot the little bastard.'

But Max said, 'Otto, mate, I don't think I'm much of a killer,' which was good because I wouldn't have liked him nearly as well if he had been. Still, it made me think about this king business. The day before I was running away from an angry daddy as fast as my legs would carry me, and now I was blithely issuing orders to have a man killed. Max was my conscience. Every king should have a conscience, and Max was mine.

'Don't worry,' said Tifty, 'I'll do it. It would be a treat.' She had a rare gift for bearing a grudge, that girl, and she gave me a wink and took Max by the hand to lead him downstairs into the dark ship.

'Go to sleep, you pair. I mean it. Get some rest.'

'Yes, Your Majesty. Soon, Your Majesty,' and she laughed that laugh, that gorgeous, filthy caramel laugh that came echoing up from below deck.

And then we were alone, just me and Sarah, with no noise but the noise of the wind rolling in the sails, the camel's gentle belches and the strange musical ripple of the water disappearing behind the boat, sparkling and bright, like an endless, unbroken apple peel, unfolding itself from the prow.

Sarah took my arm and leaned in close, with her cheek in my coat collar. I could smell her hair and it was wonderful, sweet as a night garden. 'Tifty doesn't mean it,' she said. 'She's not a killer.'

'I'm not so sure.'

'Then the job's done. If you can't be sure, then Varga can't be sure, and so long as he thinks she might do it, he'll be good. It's not what's there that counts, it's what people think is there. You know that. You work in a circus.'

'I used to. Now I'm a king.'

I had to lean into the tiller for a moment to keep the needle in the compass lined up just so and, as I leaned, Sarah leaned with me, her weight against me, holding on to my arm, pressed against me down the length of my body, smiling up at me as the candle in the compass-house made pretty shadows on her face. 'That's quite a promotion,' she said. 'How are the wages?'

'Pretty good.'

'Do you get your own caravan?'

'I hear there's a house comes with the job.'

'And who will live with you in your new house, King Otto?'

'Oh, palace guards, advisers and ministers, my grand vizier of course, Max and Tifty and the camel and dancing girls, lots and lots of beautiful, fat dancing girls with their hair in ringlets.'

She punched me. 'Anyone else? '

'No. Nobody in particular.'

She punched me again. 'Nobody?' Punch. 'Can't you think of anybody a king should have with him?'

'Apart from fat dancing girls with their hair in ringlets?'

'Yes,' punch, 'apart from fat dancing girls with their hair in ringlets. Cat goes with mouse, cheese goes with crackers and king goes with . . .?'

'Dancing girls?'

'Otto, do you want another punch?'

'Queen! Queen! I meant "queen".'

'Of course you did, Otto. I will be your queen.'

'Thank you. I was afraid to ask.'

'I know. It's the only reason I was forward enough to apply for the post.'

'Consider yourself hired.'

'Thank you, Otto.'

That girl. My God, but she was pretty. She lay there with her head on my chest, letting her hand trail the length of the tiller to play with my fingers and back again to brush my face in the dark. And somehow she had decided to marry me, and somehow I had agreed.

'What are the duties, Otto?'

'Of the queen? Oh very light. Almost negligible. Mostly they include keeping the king happy, seeing to his wants.'

'Blimey, I thought you got your wants seen to last night. I don't call that "light duties".'

'Oh, very light. And don't say "blimey". Queens don't say "blimey". Say "my word" or something like that.'

'My word, Otto, I don't call that light duties.'

'Very good.'

'Thank you, Otto. What else, Otto?'

'Well, obviously, there's number one on the list: the supply of an heir.'

'I think that's probably a natural consequence of "light duties".'

'Probably, yes. And there will be the business of curtains to make up for the royal palace. Miles and miles of curtains and bedrooms to decorate, and there's forks and knives to choose and plates.'

'Otto, they must have plates!'

'Maybe, but this is the good stuff for when the King of England comes to visit – and the President of America.'

'Will they come?'

'Sure to, love. And the Sultan. Maybe even the Czar. Everybody loves Albania now. They will all want to woo us to one side or another.'

'And will you be wooed, my king?'

'I will act always and only with the interests of the loyal and loving Albanoks at heart. I will be immune to the blandishments of the Great Powers, except in so far as they extend to harbour improvements, railways and model farms, caring only to secure for the people of Albania their rightful place on the stage of world affairs. And, since we start with "A", that's pretty close to the front.'

'And while all this wooing is going on, and all the blandishments and stuff, what will I be doing – aside from providing heirs?'

'You'll be in the garden, dear, talking to the queens who come calling. You must discuss pug dogs and the difficulties of successful rose growing and dull books and boring music and how difficult it is to bring up little kings and the charitable home you have established for the rescue of fallen women.'

'I have?'

'We'll make Tifty the matron.'

Sarah laughed then. She held on to me and she laughed until she cried and then she kissed me and cried some more, still in a happy way but a different kind of happy.

I made a lot of crazy promises in between those kisses, stuff about palaces and plenty and peace and bread on tables and children in schools when, all the time, we were sailing to murder and greed and ice-cold lust.

We met the last of those three devils in Dubrovnik. It's a beautiful spot, all honey-coloured stone and pantiled roofs and great, round towers standing guard over the harbour and, behind them, a million crazy little lanes that run through the town like mould through cheese, and each little lane has a thousand blank doors opening on it, some of them painted green, some of them where the paint fell off a hundred years ago, some of them never painted at all but oiled and polished so the wood glows and the edges have all been rubbed off the carvings.

They call it 'the Pearl of the Adriatic', but the thing with pearls is, every single one of them starts out with a nasty little bit of dirt at the middle of it and years and years of pain.

I'll say this for Varga – he was a sailor. He took us into the harbour with barely a ripple. I remember standing on the side of the boat, hanging out a necklace of woven rope bumpers, but there was no need. Varga brought us to a stop a hair's breadth from the harbour wall without so much as a scuff in his pretty varnish, and I jumped and Max jumped and we got her tied up fore and aft.

The place looked dead, as if a plague had struck it and all the people had buried themselves alive and each door was a shut coffin lid. But there was one little boy, I don't know, maybe ten years old, a beautiful child, clean as a fish, with hair that gleamed like cut coal, an angel of a boy who looked as if he had folded his wings and fallen from the sky and landed, right there in a pile of nets to sleep. He lay there, so beautiful and nearly naked. No shirt. Trousers he must have put on two winters before, halfway up his leg and worn through in the seat and, on his hip, a long, gleaming knife, like a claw. That's why I remember him, because he looked like a killer.

My mate Max was busy getting the camel off the boat. The creature looked pretty keen to get back on dry land, but he didn't want to make that little step across the gap at the quayside where the water gleamed down below so, instead, like the rest of us, he stood and grumbled about all the things he wanted but hadn't the courage to do.

All the grunts and bellows woke the kid. He sat up from his nest, took one look at the camel and ran off, his little feet slapping on the dusty cobbles as he went.

'So it's that way to town,' said Varga. 'We need some supplies. Bacon, bread, coffee, the usual stuff.'

'And forage for the camel,' said Max. 'I'd like to find a little bit of growing grass he could crop.'

'Oh, fish! Look, Otto, love, fish!'

Sarah was standing on the edge of the pier, looking down into the water, and I went and stood beside her. It was like looking down into a melted mirror with ribbons of bright green weed streaming out from the harbour wall like fairy flags and flotillas of little fish moving in and out amongst them, in and out, in and out, like breath on a winter morning. I couldn't take my eyes off them and I stood there, watching and beckoning behind my back to, 'Come and see, come and see,' but nobody came and, when I turned to see why, they were all just standing there with the same stupid, stunned look on their faces.

I looked at Tifty and she put her hand to her mouth and turned away. I looked at Max and I said, 'What?'

And Max looked at me and he said, 'Otto. Love.' And then he found something interesting to do with the camel's bridle.

'And brandy,' said Varga. 'We need more brandy. In fact, I always seem to need more brandy. Isn't it time for lunch?'

I've got to tell you, that seemed like a bloody good idea to me so I said that, yes, it was time for lunch and the camel was paying, so we loaded him up with the broken cash box on his back and set off the way the little fisher boy had gone, following the sound of distant music.

That was a mistake. We wandered about like Hansel and Gretel, but what started out as a no-more-than-ordinarily narrow lane quickly wound its way by twists and turns deep into the town walls and, just like a river winding between cliffs of stone, the further we got from the entrance, the narrower it became. Before too long there was no room for the loaded camel to pass and still no sign of any place to eat and the music seemed as far away as ever.

Max ducked down between the camel's knees and took him by the bridle, 'Come on, boy,' he said, 'back up. Back up.'

We all stood back a bit, where the alley was a little wider, to give him room to work, but the camel's patience was exhausted. He had behaved like a gentleman on the train and, by the way that he took to the water, you might have believed he came from a long line of ducks but, this time, he'd had enough. Nothing Max could say – and they were firm friends, Max and that camel – would persuade him to move. He stood there like a rock, not even bothering to belch or spit, just calmly chewing the cud, blocking the passage and looking at a spot on the wall above Max's head as if he was concentrating on doing long division in his head with no remainders.

Max took that as a personal affront. He stood in the passage with his legs out behind him and his hands flat on the camel's hairy chest and he pushed and he heaved and he said, 'Come on, boy. This is embarrassing. You're giving me a right showing-up here. Come on, boy, back up.'

My mate Max was a professional strongman, remember. He bent iron bars in half for a living. He lifted stuff. But that camel would not shift. He planted his big hairy feet on the stone floor and he refused to move. There was a lot of grunting and snorting, mainly from Max, it has to be said, and the rest of us stood around not really knowing what to do when, all of a sudden, the camel let go about a gallon of red-hot piss. Now I'm not very sure whether it was the effort of wrestling with Max that brought that on or whether it was intended as a bitter camel insult, but tactically it was a mistake. It made the flagstones slippy and the camel's back feet began to slide. By the time he noticed what was happening and started scrabbling around to get a grip, it was too late. Max started going forward and the camel started going back and the camel went back and Max went forward and they came rattling down the alley together, one in front of the other like a train, so Tifty had to grab the Professor and jump out of the way as the camel went crashing backwards through a pair of double doors and Max went falling forwards, still holding the bridle, sliding on his belly through a lake of camel urine. Well, I don't say it was the funniest thing I ever saw, but by God it was hard not to laugh.

And somehow, whatever it was that had made us walk in silence up that little lane and left us with nothing to say to one another, even while Max was wrestling with the camel like Jacob wrestling with the angel, whatever it was that had suddenly settled between us just because Sarah called me 'love', was just as suddenly swept away again, as easily as that door was swept aside by the camel's arse.

Tifty loved me, I have no doubt of that because I loved her, but she could never say it because the next night she would be loving Max.

Max loved me, that's for sure, and I loved him, but we never said it because we were men and mates and that's not what mates do.

The Professor really didn't care whether I lived or died, but he loved Sarah. It was for Sarah's sake alone that he had come along, after all, because he was her father and he planned to die at her side. He loved her ferociously, but he had heard her use that word to another man. Do you think fathers feel that betrayal less keenly than husbands?

No, all of us needed a little time to make sense of what had been said, which, after all, was much, much more serious than what had been done, and Max, my mate Max, made things normal again. The bursting of that door, the hinge-bouncing clatter of it, sorted us out the way a bang of the fist on top of the wireless will do it. Max retuned us. Max got us back on the station again. Same old programme as before, playing the same old music, just coming through a bit clearer than it was.

Not that everybody was delighted by our arrival. In the moment that the camel burst backwards through the door, a flood of angry little men with the look of Gypsy brigands came pouring through the gap like bees from a hive.

There was a lot of shouting which made no sense to me, but it sounded like, 'What the hell are you doing in the cellar with my daughter?' in Hungarish and, when Max got to his feet and pulled the camel back through the doorway, several angry hairy men came with it, yelling and screaming.

There was no reasoning with them. I had no way of explaining that our camel had slipped in its own piss and broken their door by accident, and we couldn't even walk away since they were blocking the alley in one direction and it was too tight for the camel the other way.

The Professor said, 'I'm very sorry, my boy, but I can't

make out precisely what they are saying. There's something Turkish about it, although it's not Turkish, and I'm nearly sure they said they are going to kill you. Or maybe us.'

Just then, the smallest of the hairy men reached over his shoulder into his shirt collar and, when his hand came back, it was holding an open razor which he laid over the camel's family jewels. He grinned with both of his yellow teeth but, luckily for him, Max was at the other end of the camel and he couldn't see what was going on or at least half of those teeth would have ended up on the floor. But Max was yelling and shouting and the hairy men were shouting back and the girls were getting jumpy and the camel was looking agitated and it seemed to me there was always the danger of an unexpected bodily function, which would not have been good, and Varga, the little coward, had wormed his way behind me and got his back against the wall and, in short, it looked as if something was about to kick off until, all of a sudden, a pair of milk-white hands appeared, barely showing over the heads of the crowd and clapping together – clappity-clap – like a teacher demanding quiet in the classroom.

The hairy men fell silent like good little boys and they stood aside to make way for a tiny woman, covered from head to foot in gold-embroidered Arab robes with her face hidden under a veil. She hissed at them in that strange language that the Professor could not understand and then she went, 'Ffshhhhht! Ffshhhhht!' and clapped her hands again and they all retreated, backing away through the broken door, smiling as they folded their razors away and – here's the thing – bowing as they went.

The veiled woman said, 'I have told them that you will pay for the damage in coins of gold and that you require food for a party of six. It is even now in preparation.'

'And for the camel,' Max said.

'And brandy,' Varga said.

'These too will be provided. All things will be provided for those who can pay. All things.' Then she held out her hand and she said, 'These men know me as the Eye of the Dawn and obey me. You may address me as Mrs Margaretha MacLeod. Welcome.'

I took her hand and kissed her gently on the fingertips. 'Thank you for coming to our rescue,' I said. 'I am the Graf von Mucklenburg, Keeper of the Camels of His Imperial Majesty, the Emperor Franz Josef,' which was quite a grand claim but not quite as grand as being 'the Eye of the Dawn'.

Anyway, it failed to impress her. 'The Graf von Mucklenberg?' she said. And she gave a little titter. 'No, you're not, you silly boy. You are Otto Witte, acrobat of Hamburg, newly arrived from Budapest by way of Fiume. Come in and eat. We've been expecting you.'

You might imagine how much of a surprise that was to me. I like to think that nowadays I would take a shock like that on the chin, since I am a good deal older and I have got used to the idea that – while I am pretty smart – there are other people who are much smarter than I am. We learn these things as we go along and some of them take a while. First comes the terrible knowledge that we can live without our mothers. Then we begin to understand that we will die one day and then, very gradually, we realise that we can be outsmarted. Beyond that, a very few of us achieve the great insight that there are other people in the world besides ourselves. These people are called 'saints' and they are usually made to pay. Since the bombs have been quiet for a bit and there is just the slimmest of chances that I might live through the night after all, I will leave you to judge how far down the path of enlightenment our great leader has trod. Enough said.

So, there I was, my jaw dropping to the floor, following on behind Mrs MacLeod like a stunned ox and asking myself over and over how she knew so much about me and never thinking who it was that knew so much or why a Scotchwoman was talking Scotch to a band of Gypsy brigands in a hidden courtyard of Dubrovnik.

The others were just as amazed and just as worried – all except for Varga who was laughing like a drain. 'See? I knew it all along. Didn't I say it? I knew you were no gentleman. I knew it.'

But my mate Max gripped him warmly by the cravat and said, 'Listen! It doesn't matter whether he's a grand duke or a gutter sweeper, he still took you on and he beat you fair and square. Now get in there and eat.'

We all trooped in through the broken green doors and we found ourselves in a narrow courtyard, crowded with people. At one side there was a platform – not what you would call a stage – covered in Gypsy brigands, each of them armed with a musical instrument – drums and shawms and violins and clarinets and tiny fairy bells and accordions – but there were so many of them in the orchestra that they spilled off on to the floor, where they sat round in untidy heaps, tuning up or sharpening long, thin daggers.

At the other side of the courtyard there was a house, three or four storeys high with all its windows hidden behind pierced sandalwood shutters, but the ground floor was open, with square wooden pillars holding the front of the house up and a kind of a veranda covered in fancy rugs and pillows.

Waiters in baggy trousers were running up and down the front steps and disappearing into the building or running out again with great round trays loaded with food for the dozens of customers crammed around the tables that filled the place.

All these people must have been sitting there in obedient silence while we stumbled about outside, waiting, listening, holding their breaths, but now the whole place was yelling and screaming, shouting orders for food, demanding coffee, sucking blue smoke from hubble-bubble pipes and blowing it up to the open sky, rattling dice down on backgammon boards and kvetching about the score. I was impressed. That silence showed a certain amount of military discipline and, more than that, it meant they knew we were there all along, just as Mrs MacLeod said.

She signalled to one of her Gypsy brigands, who led the camel away to the stables – but not before Max took its saddlebags off and laid them across his own shoulders. My mate Max wasn't going to leave the cash box any place he couldn't see it. We followed on behind Mrs MacLeod, threading our way between the tables towards the veranda, where a long man with a henna-red beard and a jaw like a wolf was lying amongst the carpets and the cushions, smiling at us as we came.

He stood up to meet us, bending a little to Mrs MacLeod as she passed and offering his hand while she sank, cross-legged, into a bank of richly patterned cloth. By God, he was a tall man. I might have been standing on the bottom step, but he was big and he was wiry. When he shook my hand, the arm that fell from his cloak was hard and stringy, like one of those fancy Italian hams you used to see hanging in the delicatessens in the old days, and he had a grip like a pair of nutcrackers.

'Witte,' he said, 'lovely to meet you at last.'

And then, because I was still too busy gaping to say anything, he greeted the girls, bending to kiss their hands so his fiery beard brushed their fingers. 'Miss Von Mesmer. Countess Gourdas, I am enchanted. Ladies, if there is anything you wish for your comfort, you need only say.'

I was past being surprised that he knew all our names.

'Professor, welcome. May I help you to a seat? Let's put you here and get you some coffee. Herr Fregattenkapitän Varga, good afternoon. Schlepsig. Glad to meet you.'

He got us all arranged, sitting on the floor on cushions around a low table, a thing like a huge brass gong set on little turned legs with a fancy enamel coffee pot and a stack of tiny cups, like porcelain eyebaths waiting to be filled. The long red wolf scattered the cups around the table and began to pour.

Nobody drank.

'Please take a little. It will refresh you. It's quite safe. You are quite safe. Food is being prepared for you. We can offer you anything you require.' Then he leaned back on a huge cushion, resting on one elbow with his legs folded up underneath him like a spider waiting to pounce, and lifted one of the tiny cups to his mouth. When he put it back on the table, it was empty.

Still nobody drank. Is there anything more terrifying than the reassurance that you are not about to be killed? But I snatched my cup from the table and swallowed it down. It was like a mouthful of fire and I could feel the skin peeling off the roof of my mouth, but I was damned if he was going to show me up.

'Oh, bravo!' said Mrs MacLeod from behind her veil.

'You see? Nothing to fear,' said the long man.

The others began to sip their coffee, but he and I simply sat there, on opposite sides of the table, looking at each other, and it was no easy task looking at him, believe me.

His eyes . . . I don't know what it was about them. His eyes were like a desert or a mountain top. Not empty eyes, not dead, but he had looked at terrible things that had left them scoured and rubbed clean. They say the eyes are the windows of the soul. Well, the soul that looked out of those eyes was blown along on a cold, dry wind, screaming at the world as it went. Martyr, monk or maniac, I was never very sure what he was, but whatever he was, it showed in his terrible eyes.

I dropped my gaze, but he waited until I looked back again before he spoke.

'So, I understand you are the rightful King of Albania.'

'Is there any brandy?' Varga said. 'Do you have any brandy?'

Mrs MacLeod raised a slim, pale arm, all a-clatter with bangles, clicked her fingers and muttered something at the brigand who raced to attend her. It gave me a moment to think.

I said, 'You seem to know an awful lot about my business, but I don't even know your name.'

'Names are a confusion and I pick up so many. I wander

about. I stop for a night in this village or that and in the morning I find myself with somebody else's coat and a new name. So far as I know, you have only two, and look at the mess that's landed you in already.'

'Tell me one of them.'

'At home, amongst my own people, they call me Sandy Arbuthnot.'

I felt the Professor suddenly stiffen beside me but he said nothing.

'An Englishman then?'

'Not quite, Mr Witte. A Scotsman. Some would say that's a thousand times better or a hundred times worse. I make no such claim.'

'Scotch. Like Mrs MacLeod.'

'Oh no. Mrs MacLeod is Dutch. Only her name is Scottish. Our connection is purely professional . . . most of the time.'

She gave another of her little titters.

'And may I ask how you earn your bread?'

'Well, not by jumping through hoops in a circus ring, Mr Witte – although there's nothing wrong with that. No, I go to and fro in the earth, and walk up and down in it, you might say and I keep my ears open as I go. It's how I came to hear about you.'

Varga's brandy had arrived. He pulled the cork with his teeth and set about emptying the bottle, filling cup after tiny cup in quick succession. Tifty finished her coffee and held her hand out with an expression of boredom, but her cup rattled against the bottle as he poured.

'What have you heard?'

'That you're the next King of Albania, of course. Not that I knew it straight away. Sometimes a strange little bit of information comes along and it means nothing, then another piece of the picture falls into place, and another and then all becomes clear. First there was all that strange telegraph traffic announcing that the little Turkish prince was on his way. But why from Budapest? Of course, none of that would have meant anything but for the code. I must admit I've scratched my head over that, Mr Witte. Very good stuff. I can't make head nor tail of it. Then some anxious signalling from your navy chums, Mr Varga. That lovely yacht of yours has gone missing and the story of your unfortunate duel has got out, I'm afraid. Your colleagues fear you may have taken her out and sunk her out of shame. In fact, I rather think they expect it.'

'Fat chance,' said Varga, and he poured himself another brandy.

Mrs MacLeod laughed one of those frozen little laughs again, like hailstones tinkling over broken ribs.

'Very wise,' said the long man. 'Anyway, then we heard about a robbery at a circus in Budapest. A great deal of money stolen and a missing camel – perhaps the same camel that was seen at Fiume. Everything began to make sense. Budapest. Coded telegrams. A camel travelling south with the Graf von Mucklenberg and his party. And then your description circulated, Mr Witte. You bear an astonishing resemblance to that Turk, you know. All the pieces fit.

Clearly, you are the next King of Albania, which is disappointing as I was rather hoping to do that job myself.'

'Please don't let me stop you.'

'I'm afraid it's quite impossible. Your code has ruined it for everybody. The Turk himself may have some trouble getting crowned because of that.'

I looked around the courtyard. 'Surely, with this army of yours, you could be on the throne by tomorrow afternoon.'

Mrs MacLeod laughed out loud and the long man said, 'Oh, Mr Witte, an army is no good. Armies require supplies and orders and communications. Armies can be repulsed. Armies can be engaged with and battled. But a few resourceful friends could slip into Albania like the rain. And we are not an army. We never go together but we are never apart. A few here, a few there, we know one another intimately but we have never met, each one of them is a brother to me and none of them has ever heard of me, wherever they sleep – in a shepherd's hut in the mountains, in the mansion of the Bey – I am with them, always and everywhere, they obey me instantly and I issue no commands. We are not an army, Mr Witte. We are—'

'I know who you are,' said the Professor. 'For God's sake, Otto, give him Albania. Give him the camel, give him the money, give him anything he wants and let's get out of here.'

Mrs MacLeod said, 'If we wanted those things, don't you think your throat would be cut by now?'

'You could have a go,' said Max.

Mrs MacLeod turned to the long man. 'Oh, I like him. Look at the muscles on that one.'

'I know,' said Varga. 'Gorgeous.'

And then she clapped her hands and said, 'Your food is ready.'

I wasn't interested in food. I was trying to remember what I'd done with Varga's pistol, and then I noticed Tifty's gloved hand fluttering over the catch of her bag. I patted her gently. 'Let's have something to eat,' I said, and she took her hand away.

Waiters arrived, with their round-cornered waistcoats and trousers like flapping sails. Don't ask me for notes on what they delivered. I don't remember that meal like I remember the lunch at Varga's place. I was too scared. I had a frightened countess on one side, groping for a gun, a blind professor on the other side, trembling like a violin string – afraid even to hear a name spoken aloud – and I was sitting down to dine with a couple of maniacs, surrounded by their gang of assassins. I think I was entitled to be a little bit scared.

'So you don't want Albania, Mr . . .'

'Arbuthnot,' the Professor said.

'Mr Arbuthnot.'

'Oh, I couldn't care less about wearing the crown of Albania for myself, Mr Witte, but it is of intense interest to the British Government who does. They feel I should not. I imagine they don't want the second son of an earl getting ideas above his station and putting himself on a par with the dear old King Emperor. Downright snobbish of them, if you ask me, so I think it might be rather jolly to have the old fellow shaking hands with a former circus acrobat instead, but I need to know this: whose side are you on – apart from your own?'

I remembered all that damned silly nonsense I'd said to Sarah on the night passage, stuff about how I would govern always and exclusively in the interests of the people of Albania, 'Mostly my own,' I said.

The long man said, 'You sound like you'll make a fine king. But here's the thing.'

'Can't you hurry this up?' said Varga.

'Yes, can't you hurry this up?' said Mrs MacLeod.

He turned those eyes on her for a long moment. 'Do you think you might like to dance, Mrs MacLeod? I'm busy chatting to the king.'

'Ooh, yes. Why don't I dance? What a good idea.'

Mrs MacLeod stood up from her bed of carpets and cushions and walked to the edge of the veranda on kitten feet. It was as if a rocket had gone off. All the eating and drinking stopped, all the shouting and arguing, the backgammon and the gambling, everything stopped. Men stood up from their chairs. They moved their tables to the walls to make an arena for her. The place was silent. But there was something, a thrumming, like the noise a guitar makes the moment after it stops playing, a noise you could feel even though you couldn't hear it.

Mrs MacLeod stood in the midst of them, like a candle ready to be lit, swathed from head to foot in Arab silks, waiting for the music.

I said, 'She told me they obey her. She did not lie.'

'No,' he said. 'This is why.'

The music started, long, mournful chords, the sound of birds flying south for the winter. Mrs MacLeod stood without moving.

The music played on, saxophones and melodeons, tiny fairy bells and the twanging of a Jew's harp, the music of blossom falling.

Mrs MacLeod raised her arms over her head and, suddenly, she was naked. Absolutely naked. Every scrap of silk that had covered her from the crown of her head to her ankles was suddenly lying in a pool about her feet – everything except for that little strip of cloth that hung across her nose and mouth and it only made her more naked than if she had been naked. The horns wailed. Drums beat. And she danced. She danced for every man in that place. She danced *with* every man in that place and she offered herself to each of them and none of them dared to touch her, but that noise, that plucked guitar noise, got louder and stronger. It was the sound of men watching her, the breath in their lungs, the sound of them wanting her.

'It's a remarkable thing, is it not?' said Mr Arbuthnot.

'Remarkable,' I said.

'I've seen better,' said Tifty.

'They follow her because she is a witch,' he said. 'She charms them. Every man there is ready to have the flesh cut from his bones for her sake because he entertains the wild hope that she may love him. One day. For a day.' He turned his back on the dance. 'As we were saying . . . you must understand, Mr Witte, Albania is part of the Great Game. She has a coast, and anything that touches the sea touches Britain. The Turk has lost her and the Turk desires her. Germany desires what the Turk desires, and Russia desires the opposite. The Balkans are a running fuse, aimed right at the heart of Europe, Mr Witte, and they are about to explode. I don't mind that. Explosions interest me. But I need to know in which direction you will be pointed when you go off.'

'I haven't decided.'

'I'd urge you to choose. It's my turn to dance.'

Tifty let her breath out in a long whistle and the Professor smashed the head of his cane down on to the table. 'Don't let him dance, Otto! Don't let him dance. Don't!'

But the long man just laughed and, anyway, how could I prevent it?

The woman was approaching. Mr Arbuthnot stood up, took off his fine, blue cloak and wrapped it around Mrs MacLeod, who sat down in his place.

'Did you like that?' she asked.

Sarah glared at me.

'Oh, never mind her. You can tell me later.'

'What's happening?' said the Professor. 'Tell me what's happening.'

'Nothing, Daddy. Mr Arbuthnot is going to dance, that's all.'

'Sarah, don't look at him. Look at me. Don't look at him. Ignore it.'

Let me tell you now that I don't believe in magic. I know

there is magic in the world, rainbows and babies and snowflakes and dandelions, the love of a man and a woman, sunrises and all that, but the rabbit out of a hat stuff, sawing girls in half and table tapping, no, I don't believe in any of that. So don't ask me to explain what I saw. All I can tell you is what happened, and if you don't believe it, that's all right because I don't believe it either.

Arbuthnot went out and stood in the middle of the courtyard, feet together, arms spread, and he raised his long wolf jaw to the sky and he began to blow. His lips were formed in a tight O and he blew, like a silent whistle at the bright noon sky. All around the courtyard the men lining the walls did the same, they turned their faces up to the sky and they blew. There were dozens of men there, more than a hundred, all of them blowing thin blue trails of tobacco smoke at the sky, cigarettes and hookah pipes all puffing upwards and – this is the part I don't believe – the sky darkened. The smoke rose and, as it rose, it thickened and grey clouds crept in over the rooftops and hid the sun.

There was a fiddle playing, the same two wheezy see-saw notes over and over, in and out, like an old man in winter, in and out, in and out, in time with Arbuthnot's breathing. Soon the whole place was breathing with him. I was breathing with him and the fiddles scraped and the clouds boiled over the sun.

Two men carrying lamps came and stood with Arbuthnot. He looked down at them and smiled a welcome and then he began to turn, slowly at first, then faster and faster, and the men with lamps went round about him, faster yet, and their lamps swung out like comets as they danced, trailing smoke like incense. The fiddle music got faster and faster but fainter and fainter until it died away and, in its place, there was a single throbbing, rumbling note, like the music of a mill wheel turning, like a mechanical thing, ringing out from the throats of all those men. I have heard music like that since then – but only once – far away in the east when one day I came through the woods and found a waterfall plunging between velvet-green pine trees into a cavern which I could not see. I don't know, maybe that's what the music of heaven sounds like. From all around the room more men came out of the shadows to join the dance, leaping through the circle of fire, over and under amongst the swinging lamps, and the music went on and on and the smoke drifted like fog and the lamps swirled until they weren't there any more and I was lying on my back in a field of cut corn looking up at the stars, and the sky went on forever and I could see everything. I could see the whole earth laid out in front of me until it curved away to the dark ocean; I could see the swirls in the skin at the tips of my fingers, the weave in the cloth of my shirt, the jewel eye of the tiny fly that was crawling there and it was exactly the same as the stars.

I don't know how long it lasted, but the music changed again. The singing faded and turned into a clash of knives and shrieks and howls and pot-lid clangs. The men in the circle were looking out at us with gargoyle faces, beckoning us to join the dance. Tifty was beside me, whimpering, rocking back and forwards like a trapped thing. She put her hand inside her bag and gripped Varga's pistol and I laid my hand on her arm — not to prevent her but for the love of her — just for the touch of another human being and to still my own fear. Sarah covered her face and sobbed and tears were running down from the Professor's dead eyes and Mrs MacLeod shrugged off her blue cloak and laughed and laughed and the music didn't stop. It would not stop.

And then the courtyard was empty and we were sitting on the veranda, Mrs MacLeod was wrapped in cloth again and the sky was clear and I was asking the long man, 'Who are you?'

'I think the Professor knows,' he said.

'I know. God help us, I know who you are.' He gripped his cane very tightly and he said, 'They call themselves the Companions of the Rosy Hours.'

'Just a name. Just one of many,' said Arbuthnot. 'But I see one of your companions is gone. You are only five. The Fregattenkapitän seems to have slipped his moorings.'

My heart sank. 'He's gone and stolen his boat back.'

'Quite impossible. My brothers have been looking after it since the moment you arrived and our young friend ran ahead to show you the way here. Varga cannot take the boat and he cannot leave the city. If you want him returned to you, that will be done.'

'Everything is provided for those who can pay,' said Mrs MacLeod. 'Would you like his throat cut instead?'

'I don't care if he lives or dies, but I need somebody to sail me to Albania.'

'Oh, I can do that,' said Arbuthnot. 'But, Mr Witte, please believe me, there is a gale coming. It's going to blow through the whole of Europe and I don't know what will be left after it has passed. You may sail through it with me but, I promise you, you will not sail through it without me.'

'Then it seems I have no choice,' I said, and I shook his hand.

The Professor held his head in his hands. 'Better sell your soul to the devil. These people are maniacs. They are demons.'

'Oh, it's far, far worse than that,' said Arbuthnot. 'Some of them are poets.'

You know, writing this story down has given me a wonderful opportunity to look back and consider how little I knew in those days. The fact is, I knew damn all about damn all and I bet you're just as bad. If this little pile of paper survives, if it's not incinerated in the blast or exploded into a million bits and scattered from here to Cologne, if it's not varnished with brains and completely unreadable, then you might learn something. But you probably won't.

Everybody thinks they know it all, and even those wise enough to know different have to find out for themselves.

Napoleon thought it might be a good idea to invade Russia until he found out it wasn't. You and I might think that is a useful example. Certainly, any time I have been tempted to invade Russia, I have held the image of Napoleon before my eyes until the fever passed off. Our great leader, on the other hand, decided to try the experiment for himself and, as it turns out, Russia is just as big, just as cold and just as unfriendly as it used to be, and Moscow has been moved a good deal to the right since Napoleon got there, which explains why we didn't.

Now, I know what you're thinking. You're thinking I've got a brass neck to complain about other people invading Russia when I was on my way to grab Albania, and I take your point. But, in my defence, I have to say that a few friends and a camel on a stolen boat isn't much of an invasion force. I know it's only a matter of degree, but circumstances count for a lot. I'm no lawyer, but it seems to me there's a big difference between finding a few coins lying in the street and bursting into a man's house, whacking him on the head and stealing his wallet. You are free to disagree if you like, but back then Albania was just lying in the street, waiting to be picked up.

But the point I wanted to make was that wisdom and experience come with age, at just the sort of time when you are too feeble to do anything with them, when you couldn't invade Albania even if you wanted to and, anyway, you can't because you don't like to be too far away from a toilet.

And I say 'tend to come with age', because it didn't take me long to work out that Arbuthnot was wise beyond his years. He was certainly younger than me and much, much younger than the Professor, but he had worked out that stuff about poets being worse than devils and I have found that to be generally true. Not that I have known many poets. They turn up only rarely in music halls and circus tents, but I know what he meant: that it's all right to dream of a better world, so long as you don't actually get off your backside and do something about it.

You might dream of a world where all property is shared

and kings are abolished, as poets do. Or you might dream of a world of order and neatness, you might think that things would run so much more smoothly if only people could be good and decent and clean and hard-working and reasonable and respectable. That's all fine. But if you do something about it, there's always going to be somebody who's difficult and awkward and uncooperative, somebody who wants to paint a different kind of picture or write a different book, somebody who wants to earn more than is polite or grow a slightly bigger nose than you might like, and pretty soon that person is going to have to get a smack.

Arbuthnot knew this. Arbuthnot had been to the top of the mountain and, while he was up there, he had a good look round at the world and decided that most of it was pretty bad and not worth keeping. But, instead of dreaming a new dream for those bits, he decided to concentrate on the bits he liked and dream the old dream about those as hard as he could – though it cost him his life. I liked him a lot.

The Professor did not. I don't say he was afraid of him, although, to tell the truth, I think I was, but he was wary. If the Professor had eyes, he would have kept one of them on Arbuthnot, the same as he would if we had gone sailing with a basketful of cobras.

I don't know how it happened, but the Companions of the Rosy Hours disappeared like water through a sieve and we were left to sail out of Dubrovnik, on Varga's boat but without Varga. Just me, Arbuthnot, Max and his camel,

Mrs MacLeod, Tifty, Sarah and Professor Alberto von Mesmer.

He banged my shins with his cane and sat down beside me. 'Good evening, Mr Arbuthnot,' he said.

'It's Otto.'

'I know, but I wanted to know if he was near.'

'He's up at the front.'

'You mean, he's in the prow.'

'He's in the prow.'

'And the woman?'

'Mrs MacLeod? She's with him.'

'Good. I must say Sarah's making a surprisingly good job of steering.'

'Max is steering,' I said. 'Sarah's with Mrs MacLeod.'

'Get her back, Otto. Bring her here right now.'

'It's all right. I'm watching and, anyway, Tifty's with them. She seems to be having a dancing lesson with Mrs MacLeod.'

You bet I was watching. Clothes off or clothes on, Mrs MacLeod was worth looking at, and when Tifty was trying to outdo her in a private show, well, that was something to see even if the camel stood between them with a look of haughty disdain.

'With Mrs MacLeod? That doesn't reassure me, Otto.'

'Honestly, she'll be fine.'

'My boy, you have no idea who you're dealing with. Arbuthnot is a madman. He walked alone through the deserts of Yemen – something no white man has ever done – and the savages there left him alone because they said he was touched by God.'

'Maybe he is.'

'He quotes Satan! All that "walking up and down on the earth" stuff – that's straight from the mouth of the Beast.'

'He can sail!' I said. 'He can get us to Albania.'

'And what about Varga? What happened to Varga? He could sail but he simply vanished. That's a little odd, don't you think? A little convenient?'

'I don't care about Varga. For God's sake, Professor, we stole his yacht and brought him here at gunpoint. You can't be surprised that he ran off.'

There was a burst of laughter from the prow.

'What was that? What's going on now? What are they doing? Where's Sarah?'

'She's fine. I can see her. She's having a good time.'

And she was. She was having fun, just a little way away on the other side of the boat, and for all she thought of me she might as well have been on the moon, but my heart flew to her – sweet, ordinary, pretty Sarah standing there between those two glamorous women, like a snowdrop between two hothouse orchids. She looked around and smiled as if to say, 'Look at me! See how clever I am!' but, although she danced as they danced, she was like a little girl tripping about in her mother's high heels.

Arbuthnot waved to me from the other side of the ship. 'Mr Witte, a word please. A moment of your time.'

He sprang up, easy as an acrobat, just as I would have done, crossed the deck and lay down beside me. He was never one to stand when he could sit, Arbuthnot, and he didn't believe in sitting if he could lie down.

'What are you up to with my daughter?' said the Professor.

'Nothing improper, I assure you. In fact, that's exactly why I wanted this little chat, Witte. I'm afraid we have to throw the Graf von Mucklenberg over the side.'

The Professor gripped his cane like a cudgel and I suppose I must have looked a bit put out because Arbuthnot said, 'Not you, Witte, you understand, but the Graf has outlived his usefulness. He was a handy chap to have around in Budapest and Fiume, but by the time we arrive in Dirac he will have served his purpose. It's time to hang him up in the wardrobe and put on Halim Eddine instead.'

'None of this explains why you are teaching my daughter obscene dances.'

'Professor, each must play his part. Witte will play the king and, I assume, you will be his wise vizier. Every king needs a body servant, faithful unto death, and Schlepsig seems ideally suited for the task so that leaves the ladies. I thought the king would need some dancing girls, and the thing about dancing girls is they have to dance.'

'What's wrong with secretaries?' said the Professor. 'They could be secretaries.'

'Really, Professor! Lady secretaries? That's very modern of you. I don't think the Albanians would find that at all believable and, anyway, lady secretaries would immediately be separated from the king. On the other hand, His Majesty will have ready access to his dancing girls at all times.'

I saw a problem at once. 'Can I marry a dancing girl?'

'Once you are king, Witte, you can marry the damned

camel, if you like.' Which was his kind way of saying that, since we would probably all be dead in a week, my marriage plans hardly mattered.

'In that case,' I said, 'it sounds like a fine idea.'

'Good. Now let's have a look in that dressing-up box of yours.'

So we spent the rest of the afternoon dressing up, swapping clothes, cutting braid off a naval jacket left hanging in Varga's closet, stitching it back on to something else, trimming, cutting, letting out and taking in. The girls sat round the saloon table sewing and sewing and Arbuthnot sat drilling me in how to say my prayers like a proper Turkish prince, how to stand, the best ways of ignoring people, everything that a real king has to know.

Most important of all, we took the red felt cloth that once hung on a rope advertising Spindelleger's Spectacular Equestrian Circus and Menagerie and, more recently, nestled Spindelleger's cash box, picked the letters off and turned it into three passable fezzes..

'You'll do,' said Arbuthnot. 'You might as well arrive naked as arrive without a fez.'

I think we made a pretty convincing show, and I was particularly pleased with the trousers the girls made for me – very military-looking, tight on the shins and loose on the thighs – the sort of thing they wear in the cavalry. Tifty had been through her jewellery box for me and we broke a few cheap bits up and glued them together again to make a big gaudy star to pin on my breast pocket.

'Every inch the king,' said Arbuthnot. He sounded a

damned sight too proprietorial for my liking, as if he thought himself in charge of my adventure, but there wasn't an awful lot I could do about that. I couldn't get into port alone, and Arbuthnot was the only power on earth that could keep Mrs MacLeod on the leash.

'And what will you be wearing?' I said.

'Me?' he said. 'Me? Oh, don't worry about me. Nobody will see me – unless I want them to. I will wear the air. I'll be dressed in the sky and the houses and the trees.'

'He's good at that,' said Mrs MacLeod.

'I'm good at a lot of things.'

'Oh, he is. He's good at a lot of things.'

The sun went down. By morning we were in Albania.

I suppose you've seen through that, haven't you? I suppose you're sitting there, reading this and wondering how it is that I can spend page after page getting a ticket for the sleeper train or picking apart every detail of a camel's natural functions like a veterinary encyclopaedia and then, all of a sudden, we all wake up in Albania. Well, I've had a bit of a rethink about that. There's no point telling this story unless I tell the truth. You're never going to believe me unless I tell you the unbelievable parts and you're never going to believe what a hero I was unless I tell you the unheroic bits too so, the fact is, between 'the sun went down' and 'by morning we were in Albania' there was Mrs MacLeod. There. Now you know.

Any farmer will tell you that if you want to get a really good look at your cows, the thing to do is ignore them. No, if you want to see a cow, there's no point chasing it. The damned thing will lumber off to the other side of the county out of spite. But go in the field, pay them no heed, lie down and suck on a straw and, before you know it, every cow from miles around will come up and lick your ears. And if you're in the mood to make new friends, the thing to do is to set up an easel. You might sit in a tavern all night and never have anybody speak to you, but take out a paintbox and start dabbling and that draws people like flies. They can't seem to stay away. A man painting a picture is a kind of public entertainment second only to a hanging, and everybody else feels free to join in, either so they can ooh and ahh over how well he's doing or snigger behind their hands because he's making such a mess of it, although I don't think it's fair to make fun of anybody who is trying his best to do something difficult.

Well, in just the same way as cows can't stay away from a man lying down and gawkers can't stay away from a man with an easel, there's a certain kind of woman who wouldn't give a certain kind of man the time of day unless she saw him happily settled with another woman. On his own, a man like that would never stand a chance with a woman like that. She'd be too grand for him, too beautiful. But let her once catch a whiff of another woman on him, let her sniff a little bit of happiness hanging in the air, and she'll be on him like a terrier on a rat. It's a matter of pride for a woman like that. She doesn't want that man for herself. She just wants to prove that she could have him if she wanted.

That's what happened to me.

I moved my bunk when Varga disappeared. With Arbuthnot and Mrs MacLeod on board we had to shake things up a bit. As a lady, you might think that she would be entitled to the nice cabin, but she was not the only lady on board. Why should she have the captain's cabin ahead of Tifty or Sarah? And I was damned if Arbuthnot was going to get it. Hell's teeth, he had enough fancy ideas about who was in charge of the expedition without putting his feet up in that snug little hole, so I claimed it, as of right. Not that Varga lived like a prince or anything. His cabin was not much bigger than the closet where he hung his extra uniform, but he did have a door, which was something. I don't know why, but somehow the boat seemed smaller than the train and, what with her father being so close by, it didn't feel right for me and Sarah to be anything more than friendly, door or no door. But that didn't hold Mrs MacLeod back any. Somehow or other in the middle of the night, when it was as black as the inside of Professor von Mesmer's spectacles, she managed to find her way into my room.

God knows how she did it. The little brass catch on the door never even clicked, and I didn't wake up until she was standing by my bed. And that was all she did. She just stood. I don't know how long. She knew that, if you wait long enough, the electric current of another person in the room will wake anybody. If she had come to rifle my wallet, she would have been quick about it for just that reason. But Mrs MacLeod wanted me to wake, so she stood still.

There was a smear of starlight at the window and the shape of her head broke it in the corner and I knew – although I don't know how I knew – that she wasn't Sarah.

And that was my chance. If I had spoken then, if I had yelled, if I had ordered her out, if I had even whispered it, she would have gone and her power over me would have been broken, but I said nothing and that made me guilty. Other people have done as much out of terror, because they hope that, by saying nothing, something will pass over them, some dreadful thing will happen to someone else and they will be spared, but I can't make that excuse. I had seen her naked and I had heard that terrible laughter but, still, I was not afraid. I was greedy. She brushed me with her fingers and I let her. She curled them around me and gripped me and pulled something out of the heart of me and I let her. It was the first time in my life that such a thing had happened and I had no joy in it. But then, I had never been in love before.

So now I can say it. By morning we were in Albania.

I lay in my bunk that night and, when I looked out of the porthole in the morning, there was nothing to see but a harbour wall. We were in dock.

It came as a shock. There was a dreadful feeling of things not done and the sure knowledge that I was about to be badly caught out, the way it used to feel on a Monday morning when you've forgotten your homework and the school bell is ringing.

I can still feel the flat sting of those boards on the soles of my feet as I ran up on deck. There was no sign of Arbuthnot, but the whole damned boat was strung from end to end with little flags and, hanging from the stern, a big red blanket with a double-headed eagle on it, looking very much like the country cousin of dear old Franz Josef's eagle might look after a heavy night on the town followed by an unfortunate interview with a steamroller.

Entertaining as that was, I was more interested in finding Arbuthnot. There was no sign of him on the harbour wall and no sign of him on board ship but, once I'd established that the cash box was still safely under Max's feet, I was a good deal less concerned.

And, as well as leaving us the cash box, he left us Mrs MacLeod too. She clapped her hands lightly and ran about on tiptoe. 'Overture and beginners, everybody! Eyes and teeth, eyes and teeth! Five minutes to curtain up!'

But she stopped rushing when she saw me coming down the passage in my nightshirt. 'Good morning, Otto.' She gripped my collar, finger and thumb, a pinch to stop me in my tracks. 'I hope you slept well. You must be at your best today, Majesty. Now hurry along and get dressed.'

It just took a moment and then she let me go and went back to yelling at everybody else as they fumbled with buttons and hopped about on one leg hauling on their socks and boots. 'Five minutes! Five minutes!'

Just a moment, but Sarah spotted it and she gave me a long look.

Like a fool, I looked back at her. 'What?'

'I don't know, Otto. What?'

I went into my cabin and pinned on my jewelled star, pretending that it made me a king, pretending that I was true to my word – and I had been. 'No more Tifty' – that's what I said. But any man who ever had a mother worth the name of 'mother' knows the difference between right and wrong, and I was wrong.

That was neither here nor there. I straightened my fez in the mirror and I went ashore.

I don't know what it was I was expecting but, I have to say, it was more than what I got. The harbour wall was adequate, I suppose, and Max got the camel straight off the yacht and right on to the quay with no trouble at all, but the boats in the dock were nothing special and the town didn't look like much. There was a bit of a hill at the back of it with a sort of a castle on top, but the rest of the place could have done with a good shave and a brush of the hair.

'Looks rough,' I said.

'It's hardly surprising,' said the Professor. 'The Serbs knocked it about a bit in the war. Don't you ever read the papers, my boy?'

'Yes,' said Sarah. 'Don't you ever read the papers?'

'My dear, remember you are addressing a king,' said Mrs MacLeod.

And Sarah said. 'Yes. That's what I used to think too.'

She was within her rights, I suppose.

The place was dead. I don't think I counted three smoking chimneys in the whole faraway town and there was nothing to see in the harbour but gulls.

There was a broken fish box lying on the quayside with the dried husk of a starfish glued to the planks and bleached in the sun. I kicked at it with the toe of my boot and a bit of old crab shell fell out, the bony plate from underneath, all ridged like a tin roof and two huge claws clasped together, a thing torn apart, holding hands with itself, saying farewell to itself, consoling itself in its death agony, locked into the shape of a crown. It was an unhappy omen.

Sarah had a handful of little pebbles. She was chucking them into the water one at a time. 'So much for, "Eyes and teeth, everybody." So much for "Overtures and beginners."'

Tifty agreed. 'So much for "Five minutes everybody." You'd think there would be somebody to meet us. A town like this – well, a strange boat arriving should be front-page news.'

Max said, 'No brass band, so far as I can see. Do you want me to go into town and have a scout about?'

'Brass bands will be provided,' said Mrs MacLeod. 'All things will be provided for those who can pay.' And, with that, she set light to the biggest, fattest sky rocket I have ever seen, before or since. Don't ask me where she got it from. She might have kept it in her handbag, she might have had it down her drawers for all I know. All I can tell you is that there, on the end of the pier, she had a big, fat rocket standing on a metal frame and she took out a match and sent it fizzing up into the empty sky.

It was daytime so, as fireworks go, it was a disappointment. It climbed and it climbed and it seemed to be heading right for the castle on the hill and then it sort of lost interest and painted itself into an ugly brown inkblot beside a small, bored cloud. It didn't look like much but, by God, it made a noise like the Last Trump and I don't know about the others, but I damn near wet my pants and the camel reacted in the usual way.

Mrs MacLeod was hopping about from foot to foot, clapping her little hands with delight. 'Your presence is announced, Majesty. Brass bands will be provided shortly.'

I looked back to the ugly little town, and all the way up the hill I caught the glint of opening windows. It seemed we were noticed.

Now, if we were at the pictures, this is where a card would have come up on the screen saying, 'In another part of the forest' or 'Meanwhile, in the castle of the Count' because a lot of stuff is about to happen in this story which, by rights, I couldn't possibly know anything about until a lot later. Also, I should point out here that, when the Albanoks were speaking, I couldn't understand a blind word they had to say and the Professor had to fill in the blanks later on but, for your sake, I will translate as we go along.

So, in another part of the forest, an elderly man with a grey beard and a grey suit and a high-collared shirt tied with a black tie heard his windows rattle in an unexpected blast, got up quietly from his desk and went to see what was happening. But before he'd even got to the window to find out, the door of his office burst open and a ratty little man with slicked-back hair and a moustache like cheese-wire and a nose like a carrot stuck in the middle of his face came running into the room.

'Take cover, Prime Minister. We must flee. The bloody Serbs have returned to finish the job.'

'Calm yourself, Zogolli. Presently we will flee, squealing like women, but first let us look out of the window.'

The old man did not say, 'Shut up, you pathetic coward!' because he was kind and wise and because he had suffered terror before and he knew the mark it can make on a man's soul. It does, always. For the most part the marks scab over and turn to scars. Some find that the marks never heal, the wounds stay open and ready to bleed at the slightest shock. Zogolli was one of those. The old man knew that and he was generous. Only those who have known fear can be brave. Courage is not courage if there is no fear to conquer. To praise a man for courage without fear, that would be like praising the Professor for staring at the sun without flinching. But courage is a kind of muscle, like love, and the more it is used, the stronger it gets. If it is not used, then it shrivels away.

Prime Minister Ismail Kemali walked to his window on small feet and looked down into the harbour. He stood, holding his arm out behind himself. 'Bring me my glass, Zogolli. There on the bookcase.'

The little man scurried like a rat round the desk, grabbed the brass telescope that stood waiting, just where Kemali said it would be, and hurried across the room to give it to him.

'There is a boat in the harbour, Zogolli. Quite a fine little yacht, bedecked with flags like a bride for her wedding and, unless I am much mistaken, she flies the eagle of Skanderbeg – our brave little eagle.' He snapped the telescope shut again. 'But no sign of Serbs, my friend. Be of good cheer. Now, why don't you go down to the harbour and find out what they want?'

He said this because it was a simple task, with no danger attached, but one which would still require Zogolli to master a little nervousness. It would be exercise for his courage muscles, like the weights and medicine balls the doctors give to wounded men, but Zogolli was already thinking how he could avoid it.

'I'll go at once, Excellency,' he said, and slipped out the door.

'Oh, Zogolli?'

The door opened again.

'Have you made any progress with those coded telegrams yet?'

'Nothing, Excellency. It is impenetrable rubbish, all of it.'

'Very good. Report back immediately.'

We didn't have long to wait on the quayside before we saw a boy on a bicycle come bouncing over the cobbles from town, rattling and squeaking all the way. He stopped halfway round the dock to adjust his hat and, when he got close, we could see it wasn't much of a bicycle. The front mudguard was held on with string and the back one had gone completely which, to my way of thinking, was completely the wrong choice since it's the back wheel that throws up the most spray, but the boy on the bicycle didn't look like the sharpest tool in the box.

Somebody had given him some kind of military cap to make him 'official', but apart from that he was dressed in ordinary street clothes. He left his bicycle propped up against the harbour wall, took the clips off his trouser cuffs, put them in his pocket, walked up to me and saluted.

When he spoke to me I did my damnedest to ignore him. I looked down at the shiny toe of my boot. I flicked an imaginary spot off it with my riding crop. I looked up at the sky until long after he'd delivered his message and then, without saying anything, I turned my back on him and pointed vaguely in the direction of the Professor.

The boy was either very dutiful or very used to being treated with contempt, because he trotted off without a word of complaint and started again.

He stood at attention and said, 'Good morning. As the representative of His Excellency Ismail Kemali, Prime Minister of the interim government of the free and independent state of Albania and of the entire interim government of the free and independent state of Albania, I have been despatched to offer greetings . . .'

That was when his bicycle fell over with a clatter. He turned to look at it for a second but continued standing proudly at attention and flicked his eyes back to the front, 'greetings and to enquire, respectfully, what is your business in the free and independent state of Albania?' Then he took a step backwards, flung a salute that set his military cap rocking on his head and yelled, 'Greetings!' which seemed to be pretty much the sum of his message.

The Professor said, 'What is your name, boy?'

'Sir, Fatmir, sir.' And then he started off again, 'As the representative of His Excellency Ismail Kemali . . .' until he finished with another shout of 'Greetings!'

'Very well, Fatmir Effendi, return to your masters with greetings and inform them that the heaven-born one, the great and powerful prince Halim Eddine, and I, Abdullah, his most unworthy and miserable servant, his vizier, the slave of slaves, are come at last. Tell them that the heaven-born one, the great and powerful prince Halim Eddine, has heard the anguished cries of the proud people of Albania, that he has wept for them, that his heart is sore for their sake, that he heeds their plea and that he has come to give them his wisdom and his strength and to take up the burden of the throne and crown, not for his glory but for theirs.' Then the Professor reached into his pocket, held out his hand and said, 'And take this for your trouble.'

The boy reached out but, before their hands met the Professor opened his fist and dropped three gold coins, ringing, on to the cobbles.

Fatmir hunkered down, grabbed the money with more salutes and promises – 'Yes, sir! I'll tell them, sir. Yes, sir' – and cycled off, unsteadily, back to town. I watched him wobbling his way along the dock with one hand on the handlebars as he gazed in disbelief at his new-found wealth in the other.

'Shrewd move, Professor.'

'We speculate to accumulate, my boy. Now the word of your great wealth will spread through the town and the government — such as it is — will think us so rich that it will never occur to them that we have come to rob them.'

Do you think I should have gone to the shelter? That's a damned stupid question, isn't it? Obviously you think I should have gone to the shelter. Of course you would. You're picking your way through what's left of my lungs and liver, all strung from the chandeliers in amongst a few broken bits of caravan so, obviously, you think I should have gone to the shelter. The truth is, I'm scared of the shelter. I'm scared here so it hardly makes a difference, but I'm absolutely terrified of the shelter. Last year, do you remember, in that really big raid we had – the first really big raid? – there was a direct hit on a shelter. God knows how many people died down there. Three hundred? Might have been four hundred. God knows. I always hated the shelters, but I couldn't go back after that. Not after that. I hated them. They were never clean. Those attendants used to come round and squirt DDT out of contraptions like bicycle pumps to keep down the lice, but that just made me think of lice and, if you even think of lice, you can't help but scratch and wonder if you've got them. I bet you're scratching right now, just reading this. I always hated going down those steps anyway. It was like walking down into your own grave, burying yourself alive. I was always scared down there – just as scared as I am here, but here I can babble to you. Here I can make a noise to whistle the fear away. Down there it was a constant battle not to say anything in case it turned into a scream. I hated it. But sometimes something would happen. Somebody would tell a joke or say a nice thing or offer a cigarette. Something kind. That was like a candle, and whoever did it, man or woman, would be set apart a little. People would point them out and share in their kindness simply by giving them credit for it. Still, I hated it. And those bloody watering cans full of disinfectant. If the place was clean, they wouldn't have to go to so much trouble killing germs, now would they? All that disinfectant swilling round just brings to mind public lavatories, and who wants to sleep in a public lavatory? It doesn't matter what they do – they always stink of damp wool, armpits and piss, those places. It's an old-man smell. I recognise it. I am an old man. I don't want to have to smell other old men. And I don't want to die like that, like those poor buggers in that shelter. Can you imagine what it must have been like, what they must have suffered? I said we deserved it, the bombs, for following that strutting lunatic into hell, but they didn't deserve that. I try not to think about them, with their kids, and other people's kids, people they didn't know and cared nothing for, jammed in there, with those iron doors clanged shut behind them and then that bomb falling and they wouldn't all have died in the blast, surely. They couldn't have. Some would have, but some must have survived for a bit with people screaming all around them in the dark and stuff falling on them and things on fire rushing over them and the smoke coming creeping in to smother them and no escape anywhere, stuck inside there with the doors locked. People turn into animals at times like that. They claw and scratch and fight to try to save themselves. They don't give a damn about anything or anybody else. Nobody's to blame. You can't blame them for it. You can't. But I don't want that. I couldn't bear it. That's why, when that bomb fell this afternoon, I came here, to my own place, with my own stuff. I should have started this story sooner. In the summer, when the days were longer, I could have sat outside on my step and written it. Now it's winter. It's nearly the end of the year. It's nearly the end. I have been very foolish.

To go on. Give me a moment.

I suppose the boy Fatmir must have taken a bit longer to get back up the hill on his bicycle than he took coming down, but before the sun was much higher in the sky he was back at the castle carrying his three gold coins and his news and, not many minutes after that, he was standing in the empty office of Ahmet Zogolli while his coins were slapped down on the desk next door.

'Excellency, he's come! This Halim Eddine – the Turkish prince. He is here, scattering gold coin like a dog scatters fleas.'

Kemali took the coins from the table one by one and slid his spectacles down his nose, the better to examine them. He said nothing at all until he had studied each one closely and then he said, 'This is interesting. Gold coin. All genuine, there is no doubt about that and – did you notice? – all of them Austrian. Now, why is our new-found Turkish prince handing out Austrian gold? Has Turkey run out of gold? Do the Ottomans mint no gold these days? Is the treasury of the Topkapi empty? And why did he give this gold to you? That seems remarkably ill-mannered. A prince meets the official envoy of government and hands out a tip as if to a servant? That is strange. And you had this from his own hand, you say?'

Zogolli stood for a moment chewing on the pencil line of his moustache as Kemali rolled a gold piece slowly along the edge of his desk.

Eventually Zogolli said, 'Excellency, due to pressure of work and the important business of those telegrams which you specifically asked me to decode, I chose to delegate investigations at the harbour to a trusted lieutenant.'

'Did I not also specifically ask you to go to the harbour?'

'Excellency . . . pressure of work.'

'Who went?'

'The boy, Fatmir.'

'Dear God. What an impression to make. Is he outside? Bring him in.'

Zogolli hurried to obey and Fatmir stood in front of the Prime Minister's desk, holding his official hat in his hands.

'Boy, you met some people at the harbour today.'

'Yes, Excellency.'

'And one of them gave you this money.' Kemali held the gold out in the palm of his hand.

'Yes, Excellency.'

'Take them.' He waited while the boy picked up the coins, one at a time. 'And give them to your mother. Now listen. I have returned this money to you and nobody – I promise you – will take it from you again.'

'Except my mother.'

'Except your mother. I gave you the coins so that you would tell me the truth and only the truth. There's no point making up stories because you think I'm going to give you some money if you tell me what I want to hear. The money is all yours. Now explain to me exactly what happened when you went to the harbour. Leave nothing out. Tell me everything you saw and everything you heard.'

So the boy Fatmir told his story, about the six strangers with their camel, about his message faithfully delivered and all that was said in reply.

And Kemali said, 'What was done was well done. I wish I had more men like you. Go home now and make your mother happy.'

When the boy was gone, walking home this time because the bicycle belonged to the government and was not to be used for profitless private journeys, the Prime Minister turned to Zogolli and said, 'Call out the guard, summon the band and have my hat brushed. It is time we went to meet this Halim Eddine to welcome him into his kingdom.'

We waited. We got back on the boat. We got off the boat again. We looked in the water, trying to see some fish. Some of us went on the boat again. Sarah ran out of pebbles to throw in the harbour. We stared at the little flies dancing quadrilles together over the abandoned fish crates. We looked out to sea in search of something interesting. I remember there was a long white cloud in the shape of a dragon, with a long snout and a long neck, wings and everything, and I stood there, watching it and, just about the time that it turned into an elephant lying on its back, we heard the music.

The kindest critic would have to say that it was far from the greatest music in the world – in fact, I reckon Spindelleger's Circus could've put together a better band – but there was something familiar about the strange combination of clarinets and accordions. God knows what tune they were supposed to be playing but, they thumped it out *con gusto*, with plenty of cymbals and a good deal of bass drum as if to prove that it was meant to be a military band, playing a tune for marching. And yet it made me think of hayfields and starlight and I couldn't remember why.

'Brass bands will be provided,' said Mrs MacLeod, with triumph.

'For those who can pay,' said Sarah. Her mood had not been sweetened by the wait.

Max suggested we should line up and I agreed, so we put the girls at the back, the camel, Max and the grand vizier in the second row and me standing out a little in front, looking bored witless.

'How's my fez?' I said. Everybody thought it was fine.

The delegation of loyal Albanoks took their time coming along the quayside, with the band oompahing away in front, a straggle of official-looking men in morning coats and top hats behind and an honour guard of bashi-bazouks squashed in between. They looked pretty much what I had expected from the state of the town, with an odd collection of rifles on their shoulders, swords trailing along and striking sparks off the cobbles and an assortment of uniforms that could have come straight out of our own dressing-up bag. Still, I counted at least sixty – not including the band – and any one of them was better armed than all of us put together.

But I wasn't too concerned about them. Soldiers are soldiers, they obey orders; I was more concerned about the men giving the orders – the men in the top hats.

Kemali was easy to spot. He was there, in the middle, a mild-looking man who had had the courage to turn his back on the Turkish Empire and somehow keep his mad little country free of the Serbs. I liked him at once. All around him his colleagues were shambling and tripping, pretending that they knew how to march in line – something even the soldiers were none too sure about – but not him. He walked along as if he was taking a stroll in the park, with never a thought for the band or the soldiers or the trails of kids and townspeople who had come out to see the show.

God in heaven, it was slow progress and then, when they finally arrived, the band had to step aside and queue up along the harbour wall, still oompahing away, so the politicians could push their way to the front and the soldiers could form up in rows for inspection. And then we stood and looked at one another for a bit, Kemali and his little band of patriots and me and my mates, waiting for a break in the music so the speechifying could begin. I tried to look kingly while Zogolli chewed his little moustache ragged and Kemali looked at me like an indulgent uncle, rolling his eyes towards the band as if to say, 'Children! What can you do?'

At last, with a final fart of the euphonium, a drum roll and a clash of cymbals the music curled itself into a ball and died of exhaustion.

Kemali waited for a moment, until he was sure there would be no surprises from the horn section, then he stepped forward, a thin smile showing through his velvet beard, and he took off his shining top hat with a wide sweep of the arm but, before he could open his mouth to speak, Zogolli pushed himself forward.

'I have the honour to introduce His Excellency Ismail

Kemali, Prime Minister of the free and independent state of Albania.'

Of course I didn't understand a word of it, but I was employing my patented 'Angry Hungarian Father' method of translation so I harrumphed in a profound and kingly way which was intended to signify, 'That's nice.'

Then Kemali himself took another pace to the front, continuing that long, slow sweep of his arm to edge Zogolli out of the way with a look that said, 'We'll talk about this later,' leaned forward in a gentle bow and he said, 'Honoured sir, on behalf of the government of the free and independent state of Albania, my colleagues and I welcome you to our nation. I invite you now to inspect the honour guard.'

He put his hat back on and I shook his hand, mumbled kindly at him through my magnificent moustaches and walked stiffly beside him, nodding from side to side as I went.

What a crew they were. I walked up and down three long rows and I don't think I found two hats the same amongst the whole bunch. Trousers too short, trousers too long, jackets with buttons missing, boots – they mostly had boots except for the boys – that hadn't seen a polish for months. I didn't know whether to laugh or cry, but these poor buggers had held out against the Serbs and I felt suddenly very proud of them.

And then, at the end of the last row there was a long, tall man with a wolfish jaw in a sergeant's uniform, standing at 'present arms' like a bloke who knew how to stand at 'present arms'. I was surprised to see him. I did my best not to show it but I gave him a good going over anyway, tugged on his buttons a bit, brushed a lot of imaginary smuts off his uniform, straightened his belt up before I walked off to rejoin my mates, brushing my gloved hands together with a lot more harrumphing.

I leaned over for a confidential chat with the Grand Vizier Abdullah, just so I could bring him up to speed on a couple of things. 'So what do we do now?'

'Well, we can't stand on the pier all day anyway. I think it's time we took the party indoors.' He turned his face towards the crowd – I'd seen him do it in the circus and he seemed to have an instinct for that sort of thing. 'Prince Halim Eddine the heaven-born one is gratified by the welcome of the people and ready to begin discussions on high matters of state regarding the future of the throne of Albania to which he has been called in this time of the nation's most need. All those who have business with the Heaven-born one may approach and they will have audience. Through me.'

Naturally I had no idea about any of this stuff but I could tell that, whatever he was saying, it wasn't making much of an impression. The politicians stood there with their hats on. The band failed to strike up. The ragged townspeople said nothing. The urchins picked their noses and a gull made an uncomfortably loud cry.

I leaned in close to the Professor again and harrumphed a bit more. 'Tell them that the proud people of Albania have endured too much and, within the month, as soon as I have carried out the necessary re-equipping of our gallant forces, we march on Belgrade to bloody the noses of the Serbs and restore the national honour.'

Then the cheering started. One voice at first, just one, from right at the end of the very back row of the honour guard, then a hat went up, then another and the cheering spread and the urchins took their fingers out of their noses and their mothers danced about and their fathers clapped and the music began.

Poor Kemali had to shout to make himself heard. He was yelling at the top of his voice but I cupped my hand to my ear and made a great show of not catching him until the Professor was forced to shout too – confidentially – in my ear.

'He says we should go up to the castle and have a chat.'

Max tapped the camel on the back of the leg and got it on its knees. 'Mount up,' he said, 'Your Majesty.'

'And throw money,' said the Professor, 'but not much money.'

So that's what we did. We went up to the castle with the band playing and the soldiers waving their caps on their rifles and the girls dancing and the people cheering and me scattering coins as we went – but only a few and only every fifth time that I dipped my pockets – and waving at the crowd as if I had a toffee wrapper stuck to my fingers.

Just before we reached the castle gates Sarah came dancing up close and tapped on the toe of my boot. 'I think we might get away with this,' she said.

'I think we might. I think we just might.'

'Otto, what happened with Mrs MacLeod?'

'Nothing happened.'

'Otto!'

'She's trying to make trouble, that's all.'

I don't think she believed me. She was right not to.

'Otto, you do know I love you, don't you?'

'Yes, Sarah. Yes.' And then the camel gave a lurch through the castle gate and knocked my fez off on the arch as we went so I was spared saying more. As I came into the courtyard Mrs MacLeod was dancing with a tall sergeant and singing as she danced, 'All things will be provided for those who can pay. All things will be provided for those who can pay,' over and over. It gave me the shivers.

Did you see what I did there? The oldest trick in the book. Chapter 1, paragraph 1 in the politician's manual: 'If you want the people to love you, start a war.'

And I didn't even have to read the instructions. I was entirely self-taught, a natural. I didn't have to stop to think about it; I just took to it like a duck to water. It was instinctive. In a bit of a hole? No problem, let's just kill a few people – or a lot of people. The more the merrier.

I looked at those poor bastards I had come to rob and I could tell that they didn't love me. But that didn't matter because all I had to do was give them somebody to hate – then they would love me! And they did. It worked like a charm. It always does. I never stopped to consider who might die, who might suffer, who might lose arms and legs and eyes, how many widows there might be, how many orphans. I never gave it a thought. I just invited them to a war and, damn them all to hell, every last one of them, man, woman and child, RSVP'd saying, 'Thanks a lot, we'd love to come.' And you know where that ends, don't you?

It ends up with an old man pissing his pants in a tin caravan, waiting to get blown to bits.

What the hell is wrong with us? What is it that's cracked or twisted or bent inside our heads? We all queued up to join the party when the Kaiser asked, and even four years of that shit wasn't enough to cure us. Twenty years later, just enough time to grow another crop of sons, and we're at it again, killing each other. We can't get enough of killing each other

Those poor bloody Albanoks had taken a pounding off the Serbs – God alone knows how many of them died, and there was hardly a house in that town without its share of bullet holes – but they just couldn't wait to get started again. You would have thought that if some madman turned up in town with a plan for another nice war they would have queued up to lynch him but, no, the military band struck up and everybody started marching. Every time. Every bloody time.

Still, I can't complain. It worked for me. When I came through the arch on my camel with half the town following, the other half had already run ahead to start the celebrations. There were cooking fires set up all over the courtyard with pots boiling over them. Street vendors brought their barrows up from the marketplace to cash in on the fun. Children were running round every place, and all around the courtyard people were singing and dancing around little groups of musicians – small, hairy men with the look of Gypsy cut-throats, who gazed adoringly at Mrs MacLeod.

No, war or no war, my conscience was clear. I had no more concern for the Albanoks than I did for that girl in the beer cellar. Everybody was having fun. Everybody was a volunteer. Everybody was sitting round swapping stories about how well they knew me and what I'd said to them and all the money that I had thrown around – not that they caught any themselves, but that bloke over there, he had a friend who got five, no, seven, no *fifteen* gold pieces! It was exactly as Sarah said it would be, clever, beautiful Sarah, who knew and understood that it doesn't matter how life is, it's how it appears to be that counts. It doesn't matter what's right in front of our noses, it's what we see that counts, and it doesn't matter what the truth is because the only thing that's worth a damn is what we choose to believe.

You should've seen the welcome when I arrived, how they clapped and cheered. I've seen the same thing in the boxing booth. Some farm boy, fresh from the fields, well fed, well rested, on his day off, meets up with a rum-soaked, punch-drunk, middle-aged slugger with a nose too broken to breathe through, ribs aching, crying out for another drink, on his tenth fight of the night, and he lands a lucky punch and the rummy goes down and the crowds cheer in that same hungry, look-at-me way. They all want a piece of the kid. They all want to be his pal. They all rush up to shake his hand and clap him on the back. Except they didn't touch me. You can't slap a king on the back. You can't shake hands with a king – not unless he asks you. That would be disrespectful. So they picked on Max instead, as the next best thing.

They were all over him as I went up the castle steps, girls rushing up to be kissed, men rushing up to give him a drink. Me they just looked at. It can be lonely, being a king.

'Be good,' I said.

'I'm always good.'

'And look after the camel.'

'I always look after the camel.'

'And don't get drunk.'

'I always get drunk.'

'And look after Sarah – and Tifty!' But I don't think he heard me.

I went bounding up the steps and stood on the top landing outside the castle door, waving like a windmill as the people cheered and shouted. I looked down and saw the Professor at the foot of the staircase, turning his head from side to side, searching the crowd with his blind eyes while people surged and jostled all around him like waves around a drowning man. I would have gone to get him but I reckoned there was still time for one more wave and a cheer or two and, when I looked back, Kemali was coming up the steps with the Professor on his arm and Zogolli as his rearguard.

The doors of the castle opened, servants bowed us through and, with a final cheer, we went inside.

Kemali showed us to his private office, ordered coffee, cakes and extra chairs and, since it appeared he was ready for a nice chat, I shook my whiskers at him, gave him one of my special 'harrumphs' and turned round to look out the window, legs apart, fists knotted behind my back. Down below, down at the bottom of the hill, I could see the harbour and our little boat – Varga's boat – all brown and shining like a polished nut, waiting for us, and the sea, twinkling as if somebody had taken a bucket of stars and spilled them out, all the way to the horizon, the way my mother used to swill water across the stone floor in the cheese house. Looking down from up there I suddenly felt how far we had come – not just from Budapest, but from a circus caravan to the steps of a throne. We had climbed very high and it was an awful long way back down, so the only thing to do was to keep climbing.

There was a knock at the door and two men entered carrying plates of cake and trays of rattling, chinking coffee cups. I sat down and, when everybody was served and the waiters had gone, Kemali turned to me with a tolerant smile and said, 'Now, what do you want?'

Well, naturally, not knowing what he had said, there was only one thing to say to that. I shook my head slowly, as if in despair at his amazing denseness, said 'Fssht!' at him through my moustache and took a big gulp of coffee.

'I think,' said the Professor, 'what the Heaven-born one means is that his intentions must be obvious.'

'Not to me.'

'Oh, but they are to me,' said Zogolli, slicking down his oily hair.

Kemali gave him another one of those 'I've been meaning to have a word with you' looks.

I ate a cake. It kept my mouth busy, and when it was

197

well stuffed with coffee-soaked cake I said, 'Let's all invade Serbia,' in a booming voice.

'Forgive me, Excellency, I didn't understand a word of that,' said Kemali. He looked at Zogolli. 'Did you understand a word of that?'

Zogolli shrugged.

'And there you have the problem in a nutshell,' said the Professor. 'The Heaven-born one speaks very poor Turkish.'

'But he's a Turk.'

'Barely a word, I'm afraid.'

'But he is the son of the Sultan himself.'

'Therefore no ordinary Turk, and therefore he speaks no ordinary Turkish. The Heaven-born one spent his youth enclosed in the Harem and there he learned a beautiful and stately dialect, formed in seclusion centuries ago and preserved, perfectly, behind the walls of the Harem, as if in amber.'

Kemali sat with his mouth open until he decided to fill it with a bit of cake. He chewed thoughtfully for a bit and then he said, 'You're telling me he speaks no Turkish except for some secret dialect dreamed up for women hundreds of years ago.'

'Exactly,' said the Professor.

'I can't believe it. I've never heard anything so ridiculous. Have you ever heard of such a thing, Zogolli?'

'Oh yes, sir. Everybody knows all about that. It's really quite famous.'

Kemali turned back to the Professor. 'And you too can speak this strange language?'

'Of course.'

'May I ask how you came to learn it?'

'Because I also grew up in the Harem. As well as acting as his all-unworthy vizier, I am the uncle of the Heaven-born one and brother – indeed the favourite brother – of the great Mehmet, Sultan and Caliph himself.'

'The favourite brother of the Sultan,' said Kemali. 'Forgive me – that is a remarkable claim.'

'But surely it is obvious. When, in accordance with the will of God, dear Mehmet came to the throne, all our other brothers were garrotted but, in his great love and charity, he merely blinded me. May I live a thousand years to sing of his generosity.'

'Oh, a thousand years is barely enough,' Kemali said. 'So, to cut a long story short, you want us to accept a king who cannot communicate, a recluse who has spent his life locked up with his mummy and his aunties.'

'What a ridiculous idea! His Excellency Halim Eddine, the Heaven-born . . .'

'Actually, I should probably mention, the free and independent state of Albania is very modern in its outlook. This "Heaven-born" business? It's a bit old-fashioned for our tastes. We're looking for a more down-to-earth kind of king, one whose farts don't smell of roses. Forgive my interruption – what was it you were saying?'

To his great credit, the Professor never even cracked a smile over that and, while I helped myself to some more cake, he went on, 'His Excellency Halim Eddine is by no means a recluse. Yes, he passed his early years in the seclusion of the Harem, but the days of his youth he spent in study abroad, mastering the arts of war at the German Imperial Military Academy. He is the model of a modern monarch and he speaks excellent German.'

Kemali jumped up. 'He speaks German? *Wunderbar!* And then he turned to me and said, 'Welcome to Albania.'

I had no idea what to say, but then the Professor said, 'I have just been explaining the unusual circumstances of Your Highness's upbringing in the Harem of the royal palace, how it is that you speak no Turkish, despite being the son of the Sultan, my brother, who mercifully blinded me instead of having me strangled, and that you speak excellent German, thanks to spending years at the Imperial Military Academy,' and stuck his face in his coffee cup.

'Thank you very much,' I said. 'Thank you very much.' I said it again to give myself a moment. Then I put my cup down on Kemali's desk, stood up, flicked the cake crumbs off the front of my uniform and shook him by the hand, saying, 'Thank you very much,' again, just to make sure.

There was a lot of vigorous hand-shaking for a bit and then Kemali said, 'Now, what do you want?'

'Just one more slice of cake might be nice,' I said.

'Oh, if only kings could be satisfied with a slice of cake – don't you agree, Zogolli?'

Zogolli simpered.

'My dear sir, if a slice of cake was the height of your ambition then you really would be the ideal monarch.'

'Well,' I said, 'I am a man of simple wants. Modest accommodations—'

'There is a palazzo. A small shell hole in the roof. Nothing that couldn't be fixed.'

'In that case, I—'

'A country estate not too many miles from here – farms, woodlands, a lake.'

'All of this is more than ample.'

'Naturally, anticipating the needs of any future sovereign, the interim government has established a personal treasury based on a percentage of all harbour dues and customs duties.'

'Naturally and I feel sure—'

'It has already grown to some four millions of leks.'

'Really? So much? Is that a lot?'

My grand vizier, Professor von Mesmer, nodded into his coffee cup. 'Four million anything is a lot.'

'I see you have provided admirably for my arrival. And is there a harem? I brought a few dancing girls with me but, perhaps . . .'

'No,' said Kemali, 'there is no harem.'

'Pity. Pity. Never mind, we can sort something out later. Anyway, it all sounds excellent and I think the thing to do is to get my bags moved in and then we can get on with the whole business of a coronation and running the country. And so on.'

Kemali smiled at me with that soft, uncle-ish smile of his and said, 'Yes, but what do you want?'

I shook my whiskers at him again. 'Hasn't this been explained to you? Surely you've been told? Tell him, Mr Grand Vizier.'

The Professor took a big breath and he repeated his speech from the pier, all that stuff about hearing the anguished cries of the proud people of Albania and taking up the awful burden of the throne.

'Yes, yes,' said Kemali. 'I understood all that. The thing is, I've racked my brains and Zogolli here, well, Zogolli has been through all the files – haven't you, my boy?' He gave a little chuckle. 'Anyway, the thing is – and you'll laugh when you hear this – but nobody can seem to recall sending for a king.'

Max was surprisingly disappointed about the harem. We were about halfway down a bottle of brandy in my private quarters and he was still going on about it. 'No harem? No flaming harem? I mean you, an Oriental potentate, and no harem — how are you supposed to hold your head up?'

'Franz Josef seems to manage without one.'

'He's an old man.'

'And the Kaiser.'

'Well, if you ask me, and not to appear disloyal or anything, I don't think the Kaiser's all that bothered about that sort of thing, but I am.'

'Christ,' I said, 'you've got Tifty here. She's enough for any man.'

'Oh, you know what Tifty's like. She's like liquorice. The more you get, the more you want, and I think it's a diabolical liberty not supplying a king with his reasonable requirements. It's like asking somebody to bring their own beer to a wedding.'

But I'm getting ahead of myself. We were at the bit where

Kemali told me, in the kindest way possible, that nobody had invited me to become king after all.

I suppose that's what they call 'a cliff-hanger' at the pictures. Somebody pulls a gun, the audience gasps and then the credits roll with a few little flashes of what's to come in next week's thrilling episode. It's exciting – but only because you don't know what's coming next. Will he live? Will he die? Well, you know I lived. That's why I'm waiting to die in my little tin caravan now. So there's no point in a cliff-hanger. There's no point in wondering, 'How is the brave, handsome, daring and courageous Otto going to get out of this one? Is the adventure over? Can he still become King of the Albanoks and escape with his life?' when you know very well that I did both of those things, since it says in my papers that I am seventy-three years old and the former king of Albania. It's there in black and white. It's an official document. It must be true. Do you think your government would lie to you? Think carefully before you answer, and write nothing down. I am going to make what passes for a cup of tea.

That was a waste of time. This stuff is tea in the same sense that little girls sit you down between a doll and a stuffed poodle, hand you a cup and tell you that it's tea. This tea is tea, complete in every respect except for one of its vital ingredients, the other of which is hot water. Still, it's a comfort. Going through the ritual. Boiling a kettle. Pouring it into a pot. Pouring it out again into a cup. That's what makes it tea in just the way that a bit of paper is money or a circus acrobat is a king – because we all agree that it is and for no other reason. I suppose there must be some memory of tea left in that pot, something that can be soaked up from the brown stains on the inside, tea in homoeopathic doses, a souvenir of tea I drank a thousand years ago without stopping to consider the wonderfulness of something like that, brought from the other side of the world just to be drunk in a time before the world conspired to blow itself up.

I want to go to bed. No, there's no point going to bed. Lying in bed I'd be just as cold and just as scared as I am now and I'd rather sit here and talk to you than lie there talking to myself. What I want is to be asleep, deeply, deeply asleep, but not so deep that I can't notice how warm and comfortable I am. I want to sleep the way I did when I was a little boy, when sleep would suddenly overtake me as I sat beside the fire, fall on me like a great unshakeable weight and, after a bit, my father would pick me up and carry me off to bed, my face against his neck, and I would know I was going, carried off through the air in strong arms that would never let me go, to a bed where the sheets were cold but only until my little furnace body made them warm again. Now my bed is always cold. I have no heat left in me. I must be getting ready for a long, cold sleep.

But, before that, I have to tell my story.

When Kemali told us that he couldn't remember sending for a king, well, that was the first time I felt really scared. I remembered all the things that the Professor had told us – about how the only Turk the Albanoks liked better than a dead Turk was a live one they could torture to death, and how he fully expected to be sitting on a sharpened spike by the end of the week, and I didn't like it.

But working in the circus teaches you to think quick, and when you're doing that, when the knives are flying through the air, when the horse kicks, when the barrels are falling or the tightrope turns out to not to be where your foot thought it was going to be, then time changes. For the people in the audience, it's just a tick of the clock but, up on the rope, it's all the afternoon. If you get it right, you've got all afternoon to get it right, hours and hours to do the thing that you know how to do before you've even thought about doing it. If you get it wrong then you've got all afternoon to fall down and down and down to the sawdust, trying to remember how to fall, and cursing yourself all the way for where you went wrong. It's a miracle to me that anybody ever bothered with making a clock or that clocks can be taught to measure time the same for everybody when it goes by differently for all of us. When I was a little boy there was a whole year between Christmases. These days, each year lasts a month, but last week I was a boy of twenty.

So there was Kemali looking at me, and me looking at Kemali, and time passing at one speed or another while Zogolli stood puffing on a cheroot and blowing smoke rings at the ceiling.

I had already worked out that Kemali was no station-master. I couldn't push him aside with the threat of a stern word from the Emperor, but I reckoned he would expect a little bit of righteous indignation and whisker bristling.

He didn't get it. Instead I stood up sharply and said, 'I see I have been the victim of some kind of practical joke which, you must understand, is as much of an insult to the throne of Turkey, my father and my family as it is to me. I cannot say what the consequences of this may be, but I will exert myself to the utmost to prevent war falling upon the people of Albania as a result of this outrage,' and I clicked my heels together and bowed like a clockwork soldier. 'Uncle Vizier, we depart.'

I think they might have been willing to leave it at that but, while I was standing at the door, waiting for some-body to open it for me, I said, 'You realise, of course, this has no effect on your coded instructions *whatsoever*!'

I stood looking at the door. It did not open. I said, 'The door! Please.'

'Actually,' said Kemali, 'we were wondering what the coded section of your telegrams said.'

I never even bothered to turn around but stayed ramrod-straight with my back to him. 'Don't say you've lost the code books.'

'Something like that. The confusion of the war. You may imagine how it is, Excellency.'

'Out of politeness I should pretend that I find myself amazed by your incompetence but, alas, my patience is wearing thin. Now, will you open the door or must I do even that for myself? My command is waiting.'

'Your Excellency's command?'

I turned round with a snarl. 'Kemali, the coded section of those telegrams was intended to inform you of the exact time of my arrival and to notify you that all Turkish forces still stationed in Albania have been placed under me. They were to form the core of the army of the free and independent Kingdom of Albania. Now they remain a sword of the great Ottoman Empire, lodged in the heart of this sorry little country.'

The old man sat down with a thump and I thought Zogolli was going to swallow his cheroot. Kemali said, 'Do you intend to occupy Albania again?'

'A king can hardly "occupy" his own country. On the other hand, I am not a king. I am a pasha, and occupation is what pashas do rather well. Kings are answerable to no one. As pasha, I await my instructions from Constantinople. As I said, I will do my utmost to spare the country.'

'This is intolerable. Albania is a free and independent nation.'

I sat down on the edge of his desk. 'My friend, any room you are in, there is freedom and independence. Outside that room . . . nothing. But don't worry. You have made all the necessary arrangements for a king and, when you do, at last, decide to send for one, who knows, he may even be acceptable to the Turkish forces stationed here. He's sure to make a far better king than a humble soldier like me ever could. Perhaps Zogolli here –' I reached up, took his dangling cheroot from his open mouth and puffed on it – 'perhaps Zogolli would be a good king. What do you think, Zogolli? Would you like that?'

Zogolli said nothing. He just stood there, looking at me down his long, carrot nose, but when I blew smoke in his face and shouted 'Boo!' at him, he almost jumped to the ceiling with terror.

'Yes,' I said, 'I feel sure Zogolli would make an excellent king. Now I have things to be doing.' I took the Professor by the elbow and all but dragged him out the door and into the corridor. 'Just keep walking,' I whispered. 'We're getting out of here. Max is in the courtyard with the camel. Get on it and get moving.'

'But Sarah! Where is Sarah?'

'Don't you worry about Sarah. I'm going to get her. We're not going any place without Sarah.'

I was trying to hurry down the passage but the old man was like an anchor holding me back and his cane was going tappity-tap on the stone flags, and behind us the sound of chairs being pushed back and men yelling at each other in Albanok and the calm, mellow voice of Kemali and doors slamming and feet hurrying, and up ahead the shape of the castle door with light showing all around it where the winds blew through in winter, and, louder and louder as we walked towards it, the sound of an angry hive – 'Ooom-bret, ooombret' over – and over and I knew we were dead, I could hear it in their voices, and when we opened that door there would be nothing but bullets and pitchforks and the last thing I ever saw would be my mate Max with a rope round his neck and Sarah and Tifty tossed around by a pack of savages like broken dolls.

'Right, Professor,' I said, 'here we go!' and I gave the castle door a kick and walked out, ready to die like the king I never was.

It was like opening the door of an oven. The bright light of the courtyard and then the chanting, 'Ooom-bret, ooom-bret' like a punch in the face. I've heard it since. I've heard it again, that same rhythmic, rocking chant. I've seen it in the newsreels. I've seen the crowds surging around an open-topped car. I've seen the night sky lit up with thousands of burning torches and I've heard that empty, hungry howl again. It is an ugly thing. 'Ooom-bret, ooom-bret . . .' But then they saw us and it changed and, for just a second there was silence and then wild, crazy cheering and mad, screaming delight.

The Professor was pulling on my sleeve. '*Mbret* means "the king". They are calling for their king. They want you for the king, Otto!'

I pushed my fingers through my hair, tugged my tunic down, shot my cuffs, tried to look a little more kingly and a little less like somebody who was getting ready to run for his life and I waved at the crowd with my famous, toffee-paper wave. And then Kemali and Zogolli and the rest of them came out of the door and joined us at the top of the castle steps.

'Do you hear them?' I said. 'Do you?'

Kemali said nothing.

'Maybe you should tell them that you didn't ask me to be king. Maybe you should tell them you are waiting for a better offer – or you could give them Zogolli instead and see how they like that.'

'I think we both know that the king of the Albanians is already standing here and he is not my good friend Zogolli.'

Kemali offered me his hand again. 'Welcome to your kingdom, Your Majesty.'

When we shook hands the crowd went insane. Delighted gunshots started going off all over the courtyard and the crowd scattered as a gigantic Rolls-Royce came skidding through the castle gates with bandits hanging all over it, filling the running boards and clinging to the roof and a troop of wild horsemen clattering alongside, guns popping like carnival fireworks.

I saw my mate Max fighting his way up the stairs to stand beside me as the bullets were going off, ready to put himself in the way of trouble, when a man with a bigger brain and a smaller heart – which is ninety-nine men out of a hundred – would have done their best to go the other way. But he was still smiling.

'This is it, Otto. We gave it our best shot. Nobody's fault. Just the roll of the dice.' He took my hand and said, 'It's been a treat. See you soon.'

'But they like us! They like us! They don't want to kill us. They want me for their king.'

Max wasn't paying any attention and I doubt if he could hear me anyway, what with the gunfire and the shouting and the men on their horses chasing our camel round and round on the cobbles. He turned to face the stairs, where half a dozen ugly thugs who smelled like a goat shed and made the Companions of the Rosy Hours look like prima ballerinas were coming up to greet us.

He grabbed the first one by the throat and pushed him over the balustrade, down into the courtyard below, where the roof of the Rolls-Royce broke his fall. The second he lifted bodily and swung over his head while knives and pistols and good gold coin came raining down from the bloke's pockets and he wriggled and he screamed and cursed. I don't know what Max planned to do with him, whether he planned to throw the bloke down on his mates or whether he planned to stand there like a colossus, holding an armed man over his head while his body was riddled with bullets, but – as you already know very well – no bullets came. Instead, the ugly, goat-smelling men stopped in their tracks, put their guns away and broke out into applause with a stream of Albanok that sounded like a bucket of gravel sieved through barbed wire.

'I have no idea what they just said,' said the Professor.

'Warlords from the north,' said Kemali. 'Five clans of them. It's a difficult dialect, but they seem to like your friend. They admire his strength and they wish to put their swords at the service of the King of Albania. Also the hetman of each clan offers a daughter to Your Majesty. The girls are in the automobile – which is a little bent. It appears Your Majesty will have a harem after all.'

'Well, that's good news,' said Max.

'Yes,' I said. 'So you can put that bloke down now.'

So that was how me and Max came to be in the royal apartments discussing my government's policy on the supply of harems.

After my public acclaim and once Kemali came to realise that he really didn't have much say in the matter, it was all pretty straightforward. The warlords kicked their girls out of the Rolls so one of them could lie on the back seat and use his feet to push the dents out of the roof, and then I got on board for a stately progress through town to the palazzo that had been set aside for me. Naturally there was no room for Max and the others. I had to sit there, all alone in the back seat with nobody for company except a driver who smelt like ripe cheese and big hairy men with bad teeth hanging on the running boards to keep the crowds back. Using my patented 'Angry Hungarian Daddy' method, I was able to translate their pleas for more royal cash to be flung out the windows, but I just smiled and waved and told them cordially to get stuffed in a language they could not understand.

It took a couple of runs before the rest of the royal party

was able to join me in my palace, so I had the place to myself for a bit and I went off to hunt for secret passages. I didn't find any. It was all pretty much as I'd expected: a pleasant, comfortable palazzo up a drive with a grand, central lobby and fancy curving staircases and a hole in the roof where the early-evening sun peeped through, courtesy of the beastly Serbs. It could be fixed and I've slept in worse places. This is one.

I walked along the upper landing and counted sixteen rooms on two wings with statues and paintings and pianos and fancy fireplaces and beds big enough to hold a dance in. Downstairs there was a ballroom with a chandelier as big as the moon, all wrapped in dust sheets and dangling from the roof like a hanged ghost, and a dining room with a table the size of an ocean liner and chairs lined up all around it and, beyond that, the kitchens with copper pans swinging from hooks and chattering at me as I passed and an iron range that filled the whole back wall. It was stone cold, of course, and I was tempted to get it lit, but really that's not the sort of thing a king's supposed to do. In fact, I doubt if a real king would have the first idea how to start a fire. That's what you have servants for. So I didn't bother in case it gave me away. Not being helpless is a sure sign of not being a king.

When I heard a car horn and the sound of tyres on gravel I went back to the lobby so I could stand on the stair looking stately and, sure enough, a few seconds later the door swung open and the smell of goats and wet dog and cheese came flooding in ahead of a lot of hairy Albanoks wrapped in greasy sheepskins.

Max was bobbing about in the middle of them like a cork in the ocean, complaining bitterly that he had been forcibly parted from his camel, and Kemali was there, a huge handkerchief clapped across his nose against the stench while, in the light of the headlamps, I could see soldiers helping to unload the girls from the back of a cart.

Kemali took his handkerchief away from his nose just long enough to wave it at me. 'Excellency, Excellency, we must begin the arrangements for your coronation. There is much to discuss.'

'Must it be now?'

'Time is pressing, Excellency.'

'But I have so many other concerns.'

'What could be more important than your coronation?'

'Many things, Kemali. For example, I seem to have mislaid my grand vizier.'

'He's outside. I saw him earlier.'

'My camel has vanished.'

'At the castle, Excellency.'

'Don't we have stables here at the palace? I need to make arrangements for the accommodation of my staff: my uncle, my manservant and, of course, my women.'

'Your entire household has been transported.'

'Then I hope my household has been expanded to include a cook, because I'm starving and my dinner is far more pressing than my coronation but, of all the pressing concerns which beset the King of Albania, the first and the most pressing is that the royal apartments are full of large hairy men.'

'Excellency, they insisted on coming. But naturally there is a cook. Several cooks. The warlords and their followers expect to be fed. There are duties of hospitality.'

'Kemali, if I was forced to endure that intolerable smell, I promise you I could not keep down a bite. Make them go away. Promise them all the raki they can drink, enough to drown themselves in, enough to wash away that vile stench, and put it on my account, but for God's sake tell them it's up at the castle.'

'Yes, Excellency. If it means we can, at last, discuss matters of state.'

He did. He was nothing if not helpful, old Kemali. He climbed up the stairs behind me and banged his cane on the banister until the yelling and screaming died down and then he made his announcement.

I could tell from the cheering that they were pleased, but still they didn't go home. A couple of them rushed past me, picked poor Kemali up by the lapels and carried him back down the stairs with his cane waving in one hand and his top hat waving in the other as he yelled, 'They are delighted, Excellency. They offer thanks. They bless your name – and they demand that I accompany them as a hostage. I will tell the guards to remain with you.'

And so he left, carried out the same door he came in at five minutes before and back to the same castle in the same Rolls-Royce but, even then, not all the Albanoks went with him. My seven new fathers-in-law lingered about in the lobby saying goodbye to their daughters, 'Get good sons. Do as your mother said and you will end up as the favourite wife. I have to go and do some serious drinking now and, after that, we've got a war to fight,' and then they crowded out the door with a lot of handshaking and some breath-takingly foul embraces.

With the Albanok warlords gone I was all alone with my new brides – apart from my mate Max and a bloke with a knife stuck in his belt who was wandering round opening doors accompanied by two boys carrying a lot of chickens and stuff.

'He must be the cook,' said Max.

'For God's sake, help him find the kitchen,' I said. 'It's through there,' and I waved vaguely in the right direction.

So, after that, I really was alone with my harem and, once I'd got over the smell, I had to admit they were as choice a string of fillies as you could have asked for. They lined themselves up on the polished marble floor and they knew how to fall in a lot better than that guard of honour I'd met in the morning. A couple of them were just school-girls and they were obviously going to have to be excused from the parade for a few years at least, but the others were more than acceptable and in a range of colours and sizes suitable for any occasion.

I walked down the line to introduce myself, 'Hello, I'm Otto. I'm the king.' I put out my hand, but the first in the queue had no idea what to do with it. She looked at me and she looked at my hand and then she looked at her own feet, so I reached out and put her hand in mine. You would've thought I'd wired her up to a battery. She jumped about a foot in the air and all the other girls shrieked – and then burst out into giggles. Well, they caught on pretty quick and the second one took my hand with no prompting and the little sisters joined in and the giggling got worse and, when I gave my whiskers a bit of a curl they damn near swooned away. The last in the line had a real twinkle in her eye – I'd seen that look before and it needed no translation. By God, she was a healthy-looking, well-fed girl with a balcony you could've used for reviewing the troops and an arse on her, well, you might have cut steaks off it. She didn't wait to be asked but stuck her hand out and, when I shook it, she laughed, way down deep in her throat.

'Listen, liebling,' I said, 'if you think holding hands is racy, I can tell you, you're in for a treat with Otto.' And then, because she was gorgeous and because she was saucy but, mostly, because I could, I got a grip of her backside and I gave it a good squeeze. 'Just you wait and see what I've got planned for you.'

'So what have you got planned for her, Otto? Why don't you tell us all about it?' And there was Sarah, standing in the doorway with her dad, Mrs MacLeod and Tifty and, behind them, the sergeant of the guard, a long, tall man, grinning a wolfish grin.

So, like I said, that was how me and Max came to be in the royal apartments discussing my government's policy on the supply of harems.

He arrived at my room with a plateful of chicken in one hand and two bottles of brandy threaded through the fingers of the other so he had to do back-heeled kicks against the door instead of knocking.

You might think that two bottles sounds excessive, but we were like kids in a sweet shop and, anyway, I damn well needed it.

Sarah was not pleased when she caught me sweet-talking that fat girl. Not pleased at all. If she had gone off like a rocket I think I could have stood it better but she didn't do that. That wasn't Sarah's way. She was hurt and she went all silent and frosty, colder than a witch's tit, all sharp and icy. Raging would have been easier to cope with but she just stood there, her eyes sparkling, waiting for me to say something while her dad glared at me with those hideous blank blue-black window panes and Mrs MacLeod smiled her clever smile and Arbuthnot stood there in his ragged Albanok uniform, trying hard not to laugh.

I had nothing at all to say. I could've said, 'What business is it of yours?' but that was the sort of thing only a king could say, and nobody knew better than Sarah that I was no king. Anyway, it was her business entirely, and mostly because I agreed that it was. Sarah and I had said things to each other and meant them. I loved her. But I wasn't used to all the things that went with that yet – as Mrs MacLeod had proved.

The silence went on. The girls of the harem stood there in line, looking sheepish and embarrassed, and then the fat one said something which Arbuthnot helpfully translated.

'She wants to know if this is your chief wife.'

'Tell her to shut up.'

'Yes,' Tifty said, 'tell her to shut up. Come on, Sarah, darling, let's go to bed. It's been a trying day.'

They were halfway up the stairs, linked in, arm in arm, Tifty blazing with indignation, Sarah frosty with rage, when the door to the dining room opened and Max came out.

'Dinner in half an hour,' he said. 'That's a pretty good cook. He got the stove going in no time with a bottle of something. Turns out you can drink it as well.'

Tifty called down to him, 'We're going to bed, darling. Bring the bags.'

'But don't you want your dinner?'

'Yes,' I said. 'Stay for dinner.'

'Is that a royal command, darling?'

When I didn't answer they continued up the stairs with, 'The bags, please, Max.'

I stopped him as he passed. 'Find some place to put these ones as well — and for God's sake don't tell me where, in case I get any big ideas.'

Max whistled at the harem girls and they followed him dutifully up the stairs, stopping at the bottom to shake hands with me, one after the other, as they went.

'I think I will go to bed too,' said the Professor.

'No dinner for you either?'

'I seem to have lost my appetite,' and off he went, tap-tap-tapping his way behind Max.

'Turn right at the top,' I said.

And that just left Arbuthnot and Mrs MacLeod. 'Won't you go in to dinner?' I said, and I waved them towards the dining room. 'Forgive me if I don't join you.'

I couldn't have stood it. I went upstairs to find a bed. It wasn't hard in that big house, and I chose the room with the balcony, big double doors with a gilt eagle over them and a really quite rude statue of a girl with no clothes on standing on one leg. When girls do that sort of thing in theatres, the cops try to shut the place down. If they do it in art galleries, Sunday-school teachers bring their grandchildren to look at them. Life is strange.

Anyway, I lay down there on the big bed and I suppose that was how I was when Max found me with his plate of fried chicken and his two bottles of brandy and his heartfelt concerns about the provision of harems.

'Arbuthnot and the woman are sitting down there

gabbling in foreign,' he said. 'I was like a spare bride at a wedding so I thought, blow that, I'll go and see Otto and we can celebrate.'

'I don't feel much like celebrating.'

'Well, you should. It's not every day that you get to be King of Albania. By God, for a while there I thought we were done for, but you pulled it off.'

I found myself wondering if there was any point in being King of the Albanoks if Sarah didn't like me, and whether it might not be better to be with her in a little caravan than without her in a palace. Of course, I didn't say any of that to Max but it must've shown in my face.

'Have a drink,' he said, 'she'll come round. She has to understand that you're a king, with kingly duties to perform.'

'There are kingly duties and then there are kingly duties. It's not like launching a ship or cutting the ribbon on a new bridge, you know.'

'Otto, I'm telling you, if you don't start cutting a few ribbons off those girls and launching a few of their boats, there's going to be trouble. It's expected. It would be rude not to.'

He was right, of course. A harem is a handsome gift and it wouldn't do to turn it down. Those warlords from the north might take that as a personal insult, and we wouldn't want gossip. It wouldn't do if the word got round that the new king didn't like girls, and it just goes to show that you should be careful what you wish for.

So we carried on in that vein for a bit, speculating on

which of them should be the first to have her boats launched or whether it might not be best just to jump in with a full-scale review of the fleet, and we were pretty much through the first bottle when there was a knock at the door and Arbuthnot arrived, with the tip of Zogolli's carrot nose poking through the door behind him.

Arbuthnot announced his arrival with a lot of exuberant saluting and foot stamping and, while Zogolli was waiting to make his entrance, my mate Max got his boots off the royal bed, grabbed the bottles and ducked into the next room.

'My dear Zogolli, what a pleasure!' I stuck out my hand and I could've sworn he flinched. He was probably still upset with me for saying 'Boo!' to him earlier. 'What can I do for you?'

'Majesty, Prime Minister Kemali presents his compliments—'

'Let me get you a refreshment. Max! Max! Have we any brandy? I beg your pardon, you were saying, Zogolli?'

'Majesty, Prime Minister Kemali presents—'

'Won't you have a seat? I don't believe in undue formality, although maybe we should see about some sort of audience chamber. I don't really know my way about the place yet. Yes, go on.'

'Majesty, Prime Minister Kemali—'

'Do you think you could arrange that?'

'Arrange what, Majesty?'

'A chamber of audience. A proper one.'

'It will be arranged, Majesty.'

'Forgive me, you were saying . . .'

'Prime Minister Kemali presents his compliments, Majesty. He is unavoidably detained at the castle.'

'As a hostage.'

'Entertaining Your Majesty's fathers-in-law. He has instructed me to present the plans for Your Majesty's coronation for your comment and approval.'

'Wonderful. I promise I'll look at them thoroughly in the morning.'

'Majesty, they require your immediate attention.'

'But when am I to be crowned?'

'We thought about three o'clock.'

'Tomorrow?'

'At three o'clock.'

'But the King of England can't possibly be here by three o'clock! What about the Kaiser? What about the Emperor Franz Josef? What about the President of the United States and the King of Italy? If the free and independent kingdom of Albania is about to take its place in the family of nations, we need them here to see it.'

'Majesty, these matters are addressed in the papers you hold in your hands. There is no time to lose. The free and independent kingdom of Albania cares nothing for the approval of other world powers. There will be time enough for your brother monarchs to welcome you to your throne, but first we must get you on it!'

And the truth is, that suited me fine. The faster the better, as far as I was concerned. I flipped through the pages in my hand. 'Will there be children?'

'Majesty?'

'I want children scattering petals as I go. Symbolic of the rebirth of the nation, looking to our strong future.'

'We will provide children.'

'Try to provide clean ones.'

'Majesty.'

'No rickets. No scabies.'

'Of course, Majesty.' He scribbled some notes in a little leather folder.

'Very important, children. I'd like to open a school as soon as possible.'

'Yes, Majesty. I'll look into that.'

'And will I go to the coronation by coach?'

'We have no coach, Majesty. We can offer you a Rolls-Royce.'

'Ah. Yes. But the roof?'

'Easily repaired, Majesty.'

'Perhaps I could go by camel.'

'Your Majesty's camel appears to have been mislaid.'

'Really? Oh, well, never mind. I'm sure it'll turn up. How are we placed for horses?'

'We have some very fine horses, Majesty.'

'Then I'll ride. The Royal fathers-in-law can be my Companions of Honour and him –' I gestured flappily at Arbuthnot, who stood slouching by the door – 'he can be the Captain of the Guard.'

'But, Majesty, that man is a mere sergeant.'

'Promote him. Make a note.'

Max appeared at my elbow with the brandy and poured

two considerable glasses and Zogolli stood up to toast me.

'I drink to you, my king, and to Albania, free and independent. A long life and a long reign and –' he clicked his heels as he had seen somebody do sometime – 'to victory!'

'To victory,' I said, with all the bloodthirsty, baby-on-a-bayonet relish that only a man who has no intentions of getting any place near the front can muster. 'So, if that's all, Zogolli, I'd better turn in. Busy day tomorrow, you know. Thank Kemali for all his work with this . . .' I waved the papers at him, 'this very valuable advice. You can assure him that I will read it thoroughly to prepare myself for tomorrow and I'm relying on you to make those arrangements we discussed – some clean and attractive children.'

'No rickets,' said Zogolli.

'Exactly. Petals, horses, fathers-in-law, guards, oh, a nice school to open as soon as possible, and that visit to the Treasury.'

Zogolli put his glass down and looked quickly at his notes. 'The Treasury, Majesty?'

'Yes, the Treasury. Didn't I mention? Make a note.'

'The Treasury, Majesty?'

'Isn't that where we keep the crown?'

'Yes, Majesty.'

'Don't you think I should try it on? Perhaps before the coronation? Just to check for the fit?'

'Of course, Majesty. Essential.'

'Good. Shall we say nine o'clock? My man will see you to the door.'

We waited quietly, Arbuthnot and me, until Max came back up the stair and then it was time for another toast.

'I don't mind telling you,' Arbuthnot said, 'I had my doubts but, credit where credit's due, I think you might just pull this off.'

I raised my glass. 'You know, I think we might.'

And then there was another knock on the door.

Remember I warned you about all the things I couldn't possibly know and all those conversations I couldn't possibly hear. Well, not long after Arbuthnot arrived in my room with Zogolli trailing along behind, a sign should have flashed up on the screen, a black sign with curlicue borders and big, white letters that said, 'Meanwhile, in another part of the palace . . .'

Then the letters disappear, the black sign fades and reveals a shadowed corridor, dungeon dark, and there, at the turn of the stair, there comes a light – a lamp carried in a woman's hand. The woman is very small. She walks quietly but with a firm tread. She wears a modest dress of plain grey wool. Her hair is tied back from her scrubbed face. She wears no jewel. It is Mrs MacLeod, the woman who commands the myrmidons of the Companions and who, for the promise of a kiss, could send any one of them, laughing, to meet death, and here she comes now, as dull as a June sermon, as modest as a butterfly.

Mrs MacLeod comes on quiet feet. She stops outside a

closed door. She hears familiar voices. She knocks. The voices are stilled. The door opens.

Mrs MacLeod says, 'Good evening, Countess Gourdas. I apologise for disturbing you so late at night. May I have a word with Miss Sarah?'

Tifty says nothing. Tifty throws a glance back into the room. Tifty nods. She turns back to Mrs MacLeod and says, 'Please come in.'

Sarah and Tifty had established their angry little nunnery in a pretty rose-coloured room at the back of the house, overlooking the darkened garden.

Standing there, with the yellow light of a dozen candles bouncing back from fancy gilded mirrors and the wind sighing in the trees beyond the window, Mrs MacLeod looked like a suitable penitent, seeking admission to their order.

She said, 'I have come to talk to you of the king.'

Sarah finished dabbing her eyes and tucking up her hair and blew her nose noisily on a tiny scrap of handkerchief. 'I suppose you mean Otto,' she said.

'Otto is the king. The people have acclaimed him. The government, such as it is, has been obliged to accept him, and the army is eager to obey him. Otto is the king because everyone agrees that he is.'

Sarah smoothed down her skirt and stood up straight. 'What is it you would like to tell me about the king?'

'Only that you are about to make a terrible mistake.'

'You need not concern yourself about that, Mrs MacLeod. I am well aware of the kind of man he is. For a little while I was badly mistaken, but now I see my way clearly. I'm sure Mr Witte will make a very good king, but he is not the man for me.'

'Forgive me,' said Mrs MacLeod, 'but that's exactly why I came to warn you. The king is a good man and, again, forgive me, if you don't know that it is because you have not met enough of the other kind.' Without taking her eyes off the fireplace Mrs MacLeod said, 'If the Countess Gourdas has a different view on this matter, I will defer to her and say no more.'

There was a long moment of silence. Tifty had spent most of the evening examining my character and finding nothing good in it, but that was just to go along with Sarah for the company and because they were friends and part of the great, suffering sisterhood of wronged women, but she couldn't honestly believe that I was a bad man?

Mrs MacLeod took a deep breath and said, 'Countess Gourdas and I, well, we are part of a kind of freemasonry of unhappy women who have seen things, known things, done things and suffered things which you have not. We "meet on the level and we part on the square" and we recognise one another by the secret signs of our society. Some clubs are more exclusive than others, but ours is unique. Other clubs attract new members by advertising. Ours wishes to have no new members recruited. We advertise in order to drive new members away.'

Mrs MacLeod stared deep into the fire. After a time she

said, 'You have a father. I had one too, but not like yours. I could hardly wait to flee from him, so one day, when I saw an advertisement in the paper from a respectable officer looking for a wife, I shook the dust of my little Dutch town from my feet and I ran. I ran to the other side of the world, as far as I could go without starting to come back.

'My father had taught me what a bad man is, so I knew at once that Captain MacLeod was a worse one. He planted two babies in me and he took them from me, but before I left he gave me something else too, something vile and unclean, a little souvenir, a promise of a mad, ugly death.'

Sarah's hand flew to her mouth but Mrs MacLeod went on telling her story to the flames.

'I lived with the women of the islands. I watched them. I learned from them. I danced their dances. I walked amongst their gorgeous statues, their blossoms, those tinkling temple bells chiming in spice-scented breezes; I played with their children and I remembered my own and my heart became flint. And I changed. Little Grietje went to sleep and, when she woke up, I had taken her place. I made myself new, like some terrible black butterfly emerging in a new day. Grietje was gone. I was the Eye of the Dawn. I was Mata Hari. I danced the temple dances the women had taught me, but I danced alone – and I danced naked.

'All things were provided for those who could pay. Men loved me. How could they not? And when they loved me, I stung them with my secret sting. I took their love and their money, perfume, fine jewels, everything they could offer me. I took their hearts and crushed them, but my revenge was not enough. Always I thirst for more. Their stupid careers, their politics, their wars, governments, kingdoms and empires, I will tear them all down and still it will not repay my babies.'

Sarah was standing, grey-faced, at the window. 'And Otto? You came to tell me that you have destroyed him too, that you stung him with your secret sting?'

'My dear, no. I assure you, he is quite safe, believe me. I care nothing for King Otto. This has nothing to do with King Otto. A man like that will go on through life without doing too much harm to himself or anybody else, with or without a woman like you. My concern is only for you. I want to warn you. I hold myself up to you as a terrible example. I made myself into a dagger to attack the world of men but, my dear, that dagger cuts on both sides. With every thrust, I slice through my own soul.'

Sarah said, 'What do you want me to do?'

'Do what you already want to do. Otto is a good man. They are scarce. Bind yourself to him as if with iron chains.'

Tifty said, 'She's right, darling. She's right. You should grab him. It's not every girl who gets a king.'

And then Sarah started snivelling again and the tears she had tried to hide came back. 'How can I when he's taken a harem? He's down there just now, planning which one to have first, like an old granny with a box of chocolates.'

Mrs MacLeod took her gently by the hand. 'Oh, don't you worry about that, my dear. I think we can sort something out.'

I've been for another pee. I don't like doing that in an air raid. What if I was doing that and a bomb suddenly dropped on me? Imagine if that's how you found me. That's not a very dignified way for a king to die. What a stupid thing to worry about – as if it matters, as if there's any dignified way to die. Anyway, I expect I'll be spread over half of Hamburg by the time you get here and I very much doubt that my underpants will survive enemy action. All the same, I don't like going in an air raid, but there's no help for it. You wait until you're old and you'll find out. Everything changes. When I was a young man it seemed like I had a brain the size of a walnut and a bladder as big as a coal scuttle. Now I'm so old and wise it's as if my brain has filled out in my head like a schoolboy in last year's trousers, but I can't go half an hour without pissing. So I went – air raid or no air raid. And my hot-water bottle is cold again. I don't think I can be bothered putting the kettle on, and anyway, if I had to watch it spitting and dribbling again, that would probably just set me off too.

Not that I use it for anything else these days. Poor old thing sits there like a baby sparrow fallen out of its nest, and if the girls of the harem went to work as a team, I don't think they could make him fly again.

Speaking of the girls of the harem, me and Max and Arbuthnot had just settled down to enjoy a little nightcap when there was a knock at the door of the royal apartments.

Arbuthnot put his hand on his sword with a kind of 'Are you expecting somebody?' look, and Max, who never really paid enough attention to bullets, got his shoulder against the door and said, 'Who seeks audience with the king?'

We heard laughter on the other side of the door – the kind of filthy laughter that only Tifty could produce.

'Don't be silly, darling. It's me. And I've brought some friends.'

Max flung back the door and there was Tifty with all the girls – Mrs MacLeod, my Sarah and the entire harem, every member of it red-faced and blubbing. They started out quietly enough, like good little houris, but as soon as they saw me they set up a wailing and a howling like cats going through a mangle.

Tifty and Mrs MacLeod went clucking and fussing around them, trying to quiet them down a bit, but Sarah paid them no heed at all. She just came right up to me, put her arms round my neck and gave me a big kiss and a tug on the whiskers.

And then I said the wisest thing of my entire reign. I

said, 'Sorry, Sarah,' which made her very happy but seemed to turn the cat-mangle by another couple of cranks.

'For God's sake, Tifty, can't you make them shut up? What the hell is wrong with them?'

'Darling, can't you tell? They are in love!'

That was only to be expected. My whiskers were looking particularly magnificent that day and my boots particularly shiny, and in normal circumstances I would have been only too happy to dry their tears and give them each a right good cheering-up, but circumstances had changed, not least because Sarah was standing right at my elbow.

'Arbuthnot,' I said, 'I'm relying on you to translate here. You tell them from me that the king thinks they are absolutely gorgeous, every one of them. Tell them that the king loves them all very dearly, but that I am promised to this lady here.'

'Is that wise?' he said. 'Their fathers are in town, blind drunk and armed to the teeth. Kicking their lovesick daughters out on to the street might not be the best plan.'

'Just do it.'

But before he could begin, Tifty almost burst her corsets laughing that filthy, syrupy laugh of hers again. 'You might have turned little Sarah's head, but you're not that much of a catch. Darling, they are not in love with *you*! It's not *you* they are crying for. Silly man, your harem girls are all in love with village boys back home.'

And then the cat mangling started again. 'Oh for God's sake, Arbuthnot, talk to them. Find out what's going on.'

Well, he did his best to soothe them, but they would

not be soothed although, to be fair, Albanok is not a very soothing language, and Arbuthnot's cooing sounded a lot like a lullaby sung by a mother cheese-grater to her cheese-grater child. Still the howling and the yowling went on and they seemed to me to be encouraging each other to screech a little bit louder and sob a little more hoarsely. Before long Arbuthnot – who was not a patient man – lost his patience with them and started yelling and shouting and, just for a second, I thought that might work. They looked at him like startled rabbits and, thank God, the screaming stopped. Then it started again worse than before and the girls fell on one another's necks, weeping and sobbing until Sarah and Tifty and even Mrs MacLeod gathered them up in their arms and joined in the crying, while they all gabbled at each other in a mix of unintelligible tongues.

But it's an exhausting business, uncontrollable weeping, and after a bit they were too tired to bother with it any more and they all sat down.

It seemed like a good idea to offer round the last of the brandy – purely as a restorative – and, little by little, the snivelling died down as Tifty gathered up the dribbles of brandy and emptied them out into her own glass.

I told Arbuthnot to ask them again, but nicely this time, and it took him a few attempts because they all wanted to join in and speak at the same time, but eventually he got it all out of them.

God forgive me, I've forgotten all their names, but they all had the same story to tell. This one, Lotte, wanted to marry Fritzie, but Fritzie was just a poor shepherd boy and her daddy hated him and he tried everything to break them up and scare Fritzie away and, when he wouldn't go, Daddy went just about mad crazy until this morning when he heard the new king had arrived and he hit on a plan to get rid of his girl for good.

And this one, Rosa, wanted to marry Jupp, but she was the last of six girls and there was nothing left for a dowry so she was going to be left at home on the shelf, an old maid, looking after her brother's children until her hair went grey and her teeth fell out and she had to dine on nothing but bread soaked in warm milk – at least until this morning when her daddy heard that a new king had arrived and, well, you know the rest.

Arbuthnot went round them all, each in turn, and after each telling there was more caterwauling and crying and sympathetic embracing and cries of 'Oh, you poor thing', in Albanok of course.

'In short,' said Arbuthnot, 'it seems Your Majesty is regarded as no great catch.'

'But I'm the king!' I said.

'Apparently a fifth share of a king is less to be prized than a shepherd boy with full vacant possession.'

'Oh, I understand that completely,' said Sarah.

'But there's more – Your Majesty is too old.'

'Too old!' I gave my whiskers a ferocious shake.

'Old enough to be their father, it seems – indeed older than most of their fathers.'

'They start damned young in Albania, by God!' I thought

that might raise a laugh but nobody laughed with me because they were all trying so hard not to laugh at me, so it just sounded silly and whiny.

'In short, they wonder why a man of your age is not already surrounded by strong sons and if there is something wrong with you.'

I sat down on the royal bed with a thump and everybody forgot that they were trying not to laugh. 'Something wrong with me? You tell them from me, Arbuthnot, that if I were not promised to this lady here – who is much nicer than any of them – then they'd soon find out there's damn all wrong with the King of the Albanoks. Go on! You tell 'em!'

Arbuthnot translated but the girls seemed unimpressed. They made no reply to me, but instead they turned moony gazes on Sarah, waiting for what she had to say.

'It's true. It's true,' she said, but that cut no ice with them, not until Sarah put her hands together as if in prayer and drew them apart and drew them apart and drew them apart until their little eyes popped and their little jaws dropped and they collapsed into giggles and showered Sarah with excited yammering congratulations.

'Aww, bloody hell,' said Max. 'I've seen you naked.'

'Yes, but darling, you've never seen him angry,' said Tifty.

'Bloody hell,' he said again.

'Darling, yours is just as nice, believe me.'

'Bloody hell.'

I was feeling a lot happier now, and it was quite clear

that the girls — and everybody else — were looking at me in a different light.

'But none of this solves the problem,' I said. 'They don't want to marry me, and I damned sure don't want to marry anybody who doesn't want to marry me.'

Sarah said, 'I think they might have changed their minds now.'

'Too bad. They missed the boat. But I still don't know what to do with them.'

Sarah sat down beside me on the bed. 'When I don't know what to do, I always ask my dad.'

She was so clever and so pretty that I just had to kiss her. 'Summon the grand vizier!' I said. 'What's the point of having a vizier if you don't consult him? Do you think he's still up?'

'I'll go and see.'

So she went and I sat on the bed and the girls of the harem looked at me and looked at each other and whispered behind their hands and giggled some more and I felt a bit smug and I grinned at Tifty and then I caught Max's eye and I looked at my boots and we went on that way for a bit until Sarah came back with her dad in his big blue dressing gown with his hair sticking up at all angles.

Professor von Mesmer stood leaning on his cane in the middle of the room and he said, 'What can I do for you?'

'I'm sorry to get you out of bed,' I said, 'but I need your advice,' and I explained the problem.

'I don't see the problem,' he said.

'Look, it's very simple. These girls don't want to marry me and I don't want to marry them, but if I don't marry them, their fathers will be upset and somebody might get shot.'

'You can't marry them.'

'But I have to.'

'But you can't.' He tapped his way along the line of harem girls. 'There are five of them. You are allowed no more than four wives. You can't marry all of them, so you'd best marry none of them and avoid giving offence to one angry father.'

'Then they will all be angry.'

'Probably not. Elevate them to positions of honour. Name them as Royal Sisters and send them home with enormous dowries.' He turned his black gaze to the girls and gave them a quick burst of Albanok. 'Would you be happy with enormous dowries?'

They laughed and clapped and danced and came to hug my boots.

'I think they will be happy with enormous dowries. Now, can I go back to bed?'

'Yes. Thank you, Professor. Go back to bed and get some sleep. We're having a coronation tomorrow and I will need my Grand Vizier at my side.'

That was that. Everything was sorted out. Everybody was happy. Except for Max, who shook his head and said, 'So you're going to send them all back without even so much as a trot once round the park. What a waste.'

And everybody went back to bed. Everybody except for Sarah. She didn't go back to her bed until much later.

241

There's one other thing. I told you I wasn't going to lie but I lied. I lied about forgetting all their names. The fat one, the one with the nice arse, she was called Aferdita. It means 'dawn'. Pretty name. Unusual. If we had had a girl, we were going to call her Aferdita.

I hope just about everything I've told you is something you can understand, something you've done for yourself. All right, you might never have stolen a boat and sailed away to the south, but you've probably been on a boat – at the very least you've seen a boat and you know what the sea smells like. And I hope you know what friendship is. I hope you've had your share of fun with girls – or one girl. I hope you've had a little drink from time to time. I hope you've been happy. I know you've been scared. God knows we're most of us scared most of the time these days so we have all these things in common, and it's not like I have to begin every page as if I was describing 'green' to a man born blind. But there are damned few men in the world – damned few men in the history of the world – who have ever lived this part of my story because there are damned few men who were ever crowned. I was crowned. Me, Otto Witte, acrobat of Hamburg, I was the crowned King of Albania. Who alive can tell you of his coronation day? Franz Josef, gone – and the one that came after him, whatever his name was. No more Kaiser, no more Czar. Portugal and Spain, both relieved of duties and excused boots. There's that bloke in Italy but I wouldn't bet on him seeing the war out, and poor, stammering George in England, with his stout little wife and his palace bombed full of holes, but he only got his crown because his brother didn't want it anyway. Norway, Holland, Belgium, Greece, all chased away. All in exile. All kings without a country. Like me. No, it's a small club – no more than a handful of us who can say, 'I remember the day of my coronation.'

A coronation is a big thing. It's like a wedding day, and when a bride gets married she soaks up every moment and tells herself that this is the day she will remember forever. But she doesn't, of course. Bits of it stay in her head. Odd flashes here and there, the idea that, once, she had a wedding day, but not much more than that. The memory gets put away and, not being used, it gets stale and fades away like old flowers pressed in the back of a book.

A woman who loves her son for thirty years, watches him grow, sees him become a father with babies of his own, she forgets. She forgets the way he smelled, the funny things he said and did. She forgets because there is simply too much to remember. But the baby dead in the cradle, he is never forgotten. Never. He is remembered every day, believe me.

And I suppose that's what it's like for kings. A bride can't spend her life thinking about her wedding day because she's too busy with the business of being married, and kings don't sit around thinking about the day they were crowned because they've got too much ruling to do. But that never happened to me. My coronation never faded. I have taken it out and polished it every day of my life since then. I have remembered, every day, that once I was a king.

So, as they say, to begin at the beginning. I slept like a baby and I awoke at half past six when Max arrived in my room like a troop of cavalry crossing a cobbled street and flung back the curtains. 'Up!' he said.

'I don't think you've quite grasped the role of trusted retainer and faithful manservant.' My head was thick with brandy and my tongue had more fur on it than a month-old cheese.

'Up! Breakfast. Dining room. Come on, you're getting crowned today.'

God, I remember how that felt. I was about to get crowned. If my mother had said I was going to get a prize at the village school I could not have been prouder, although it goes without saying that getting yourself crowned is a lot easier than winning a prize at the village school. At least it was for me. I flopped back into the warm pillows to enjoy the thought of it for a little longer, but Max tugged the blankets on to the floor and threw an enormous velvet dressing gown in my face.

'Up!' he said. 'Dining room, now!' And he left.

I suppose, since we had got through the best part of two bottles of brandy between us, I should have felt a lot worse than I did. The truth is, I felt pretty chipper. The blood was singing in my ears, my eyes were bright and I fairly sprang down the long staircase to breakfast, but when I got there, the cook was more than averagely stupid. He stood at my elbow, asking over and over what I wanted to eat and, although I told him, over and over, 'Eggs!' it didn't make a blind bit of difference. Eventually I had to get up from the table and walk down the corridor to the kitchen in my bare feet so I could show him: 'Eggs!'

All my friends were already there, sitting together round a scrubbed pine board with steaming pots of coffee and piles of freshly sliced bread and mounds of golden, buttery scrambled eggs.

The moment he saw me, even while I was yelling, 'Eggs!' at the cook, Arbuthnot dropped his fork in his tin plate, pushed his chair back and stood at attention. And, by the time I'd stopped yelling, 'Eggs!' at the cook and he was getting on with the business of rattling pans and kicking the stove and swearing at his boy, all the others were standing at attention too.

'What the hell are you all doing here?' I said. 'There's a perfectly good dining room next door. Come and have breakfast there.'

'I'm afraid that's not possible, old man.'

'And why are you all standing there saluting?'

'Oh, we can't salute, old man. Improperly dressed. No headdress and all that. Saluting's completely out of the question. But we can brace up a bit to demonstrate due deference.'

'Due deference?'

'We don't want Cookie catching on. He thinks you are an autocratic oriental potentate and we are your cowering minions, remember.'

'Oh,' I said. 'Yes. So you won't be joining me for breakfast then?'

'That's the Officers' Mess,' said Arbuthnot, 'and we are distinctly "other ranks", I'm afraid – except for the vizier of course. He could join you.'

'Yes, Professor, you could join me.' But whether he was still upset about catching me goosing Aferdita the night before, or whether he just couldn't be bothered, he made some damned stupid mumbled excuse and stayed right where he was.

'Right then,' I said.

'It's just for a bit,' said Sarah, 'until things settle down. You know.'

'But we won't be able to join you for dinner either, old boy. Except for the vizier of course.'

'Of course.'

I stamped off back to the dining room, as loud as anybody can stamp in bare feet, and I sat down, alone, at one end of my long, shiny table with my fancy cutlery and my fancy crockery and my fancy linen napkin as thick as a sail and I longed for Sarah and the rest of them and a tin plate and a wooden spoon. I wanted to sit in the kitchen with them, but that's the No. 1 rule of kingship: a king can't do what he wants. A king has to do what other people want. You might think there is very little point in being the king if you can't even eat your breakfast where you want with the people you want and you might be right. But then, on the other hand, you've never been a king, so you don't know how sweet it tastes.

Anyway, after a bit the cook came with my coffee and my eggs and I sat and munched my way through them, alone, with nobody to speak to and nothing to do except look at my big silver candlestick like a bull looking through a gate.

It didn't take long to eat breakfast. When you're sitting round with friends you want to linger over coffee and rolls. You want to chat. You might even want to stay sitting down so you don't have to go out in the rain and spend all day carrying coals or driving a plough, but I was on my own, with nobody to talk to, so it didn't take long for a couple of spoons of eggs to go down. I sat with my coffee and looked at the candlestick. Above the empty grate I heard a hobnailed pigeon landing on the chimney pot and start his stamping around and his coo-coo-cooing. The clock ticked in the empty room. I drank some coffee. The cup chinked in the saucer. I drank some more coffee. I looked at the heavy red curtains. I drank a bit more coffee. I counted the curtains while the pigeon danced and cooed at the top of the chimney. Six windows down the length of the room. Each window with two curtains, each curtain with a long, lavish, tasselled tie-back of brocaded velvet holding it back from the window. I did some sums. I counted up in my head. I had an idea. I finished my coffee, got up from the table and bounced my way along the length of the room, snatching up those curtain ties as I went, and on, out the door at the far end and up the stairs back to my room.

There was nothing to be afraid of. Nobody could accuse me of stealing my own haberdashery. If the King of the

Albanoks wanted to take down his curtains, that was nobody's business but his own. Still, I felt like a hunted thief until I had them safely stuffed in my saddlebag.

I went across to the fireplace and gave the bell pull a good jangle, waited a bit, jangled it again and, before long, Max came in.

'You're meant to knock,' I said. 'You're the one who's all for keeping up appearances.'

'There's nobody around to see. What do you want?'

'I want a shave and I want my boots polished. You don't have to do it, but I can't. If you won't let me eat my breakfast in the kitchen, I can't very well polish my own boots.'

'Fair enough,' he said.

'You don't have to do it. Get the kitchen boy on it.'

'Otto, mate,' he said, 'I would be proud to polish the boots of my king. And I'll bring some hot water for the shave.'

That's what he said. My mate Max Schlepsig said that. To me. He could have picked me up with one hand and flung me through the window if he'd wanted, but instead he offered to clean my boots. And he was as good as his word. In the time it took to go downstairs and turn the tap on the range, he was back with a bloody great jug of scalding water.

I made sure to thank him properly because Max was my pal and a better man than I was and we were just play-acting that servant stuff, but when I went to take the jug from him he said, 'No, Otto. Let me. I mean it.'

So I sat down in the big leather chair by the window

and Max came and tucked a towel under my chin and wrapped my face in hot, wet cloths, as gentle as any mother with her child. I heard him mixing up the lather in a bowl sloppity-sloppity-slop, and then he took the damp cloths away and painted it on my chin, around my magnificent whiskers, up my cheeks, right to the edge of my ears.

'This is going to be the best shave you've ever had,' he said. 'If you took the circus cash box back to Vienna and emptied it out on the floor of the Imperial barbers, you couldn't get a better one. When you stand up to get crowned today, the Albanoks will know they've got a king to be proud of. You're a good bloke, Otto Witte, and a good friend to me, and we both know that I'm shaving you this way because I can't kiss you and I'm doing it to show you that I love you because I can't tell you.'

Of course he didn't say any of that. Max took his razor and passed it over my chin with never a word, over my cheeks and over my throat as gentle as a lover's kisses. He said nothing at all, but that was what he meant.

The little French clock on the mantelpiece was halfway through chiming nine when we heard the tiger purr of the Rolls-Royce outside.

Zogolli and Kemali were sitting, top-hatted, in the back seat, gloved hands resting on silver-topped canes, claw-hammer tailcoats tucked carefully under their backsides in case of creasing, and there was a gigantic Albanok brigand standing on the running board, wearing a jacket which a sheep had been wearing not long before, all strung about with bandoliers and bristling with pistols. He held on to the door jamb with one huge fist, and in the other he held a trace that led to a string of fine horses, trotting along behind.

I flung open the door of the palazzo and stood in the hallway for a moment to let myself be seen in a striking and majestic pose but, most importantly, to make it look like somebody else had opened the door for me. I had worked hard on my reputation for kingly helplessness and I didn't want to dent it by extravagant gestures like polishing my own boots or opening doors for myself.

'Good morning, Prime Minister!' I said, rubbing my hands together. 'Zogolli, right on time, I see. Well done.'

I came down the steps, ready to offer my hand, but the giant brigand stepped off the running board and grabbed me first. He swallowed my hand in his, fell to his knees right there in the gravel and started blubbing like a girl and rolling his face around on the back of my hand as he jabbered at me in Albanok. I tried to haul him to his feet but he was having none of it, and he stayed there, rubbing tears and snot and kisses into the back of my hand, until Zogolli got out of the car and prised him off with the tip of his cane.

'A thousand apologies, Majesty,' he said. 'An overpouring of emotion.'

The poor bugger was still on his knees and still blubbing, but at least he'd let go of my hand. I said, 'Tell him that the king thanks him for his services in bringing these fine horses and send him to the kitchens for breakfast.'

You would've thought that I'd offered him a dukedom, and he went off, bowing and scraping and showering me with blessings all the way.

'Your Majesty has made a remarkable impression,' said Kemali, sweeping his top hat from his head with a graceful flourish.

'Good morning, Mr Prime Minister. Lovely to see you again. Did the Royal Fathers-in-Law treat you kindly?'

'I found them congenial companions, if limited and somewhat profane conversationalists, but, so long as the slivovitz lasts, they are cheerful and harmless enough. Fortunately the castle is well supplied with slivovitz. Or it was. They are sleeping it off.'

'Just so long as they don't miss the coronation.'

'Half the nation will be there, sir, the Royal Fathers-in-Law not least among them.'

'Excellent news, Kemali. Shall we go?'

By that time Max and Arbuthnot, my newly appointed Captain of the Guard, with three gold buttons stitched on his sleeve and a dusty mark where three stripes had been the night before, were waiting on the steps, each offering an arm to my grand vizier to help him into the limousine. You don't get cars like that any more, cars built like a two-storey house at the back so as to make room for the hats. I miss that.

Anyway, the Professor got in and settled down while Zogolli and Kemali folded themselves in beside him like mismatched bookends and I waited, helplessly, for somebody to supply me with a horse.

Max chose one for himself and naturally it had to be the size of a fire engine otherwise it wouldn't take the weight, and he brought one for me that was nearly as tall, a great, high, stilt-legged beast that stood there, snorting fire and dancing as it waited for me to mount. Short of jumping up into the saddle with the sort of cartwheel leap that might have given me away as more of an acrobat than a king, I don't think I could have made it into the saddle if Max hadn't bent down and offered his cupped hands for me to stand in. And then we were up, riding side by side behind the Rolls. I felt like I was sitting on a moving, bouncing steeple, but I felt like a king, riding into battle, ready to fight, Max at my left hand and Arbuthnot at my right with his sword drawn and glittering. By God, that man could ride. I looked across at him and he was holding the reins in his left hand with barely a touch, textbook stuff it was, great seat, everything in the legs, you know, and I couldn't help but smile as we trotted down the drive, through the gates and out on to the street.

'Do you know where the Treasury is?' I asked him.

'Well, I wouldn't call it a Treasury, exactly. It's more a sort of a warehouse affair, old man. It's back up at the castle.'

'So it's not exactly the last word in modern security measures, then.'

'A big door with a big lock and a couple of iron bars.'

'Hear that, Max? A couple of iron bars. You could eat those for breakfast.'

'But it is in the middle of a castle. I'm sure your crown will be safe enough.'

The Rolls slowed to a crawl along the rutted mud street, and through the little oval window in the back we could see the top hats of Kemali and Zogolli nodding at each other with every bump. The horses were walking slowly, side by side, like they used to do in the park – do you remember? – when the toffs used to take their exercise under the trees and their wives would trot along in carriages at one side of the avenue and the actresses would sit in carriages at the other side, smiling and nodding and showing off their latest sparklers and there was nothing in the sky but blackbirds and rainbows and nothing falling to earth but cherry blossom.

We had to stop and rein the horses in and make them stand while the car decided whether it was worth going through a particularly challenging pothole and Arbuthnot tilted his sword back to rest it on his shoulder while we waited.

'This is boring,' Max said.

'I've known better parades. Looks like they didn't put enough posters out to tell the people we were coming.'

'And that car stinks. All that smoke. To think you used to complain about my camel. I miss my camel.'

'He'll turn up,' I said.

'Bloody Albanoks have probably eaten him – or something worse. I've seen their women, and my camel's a damned sight more attractive than most of 'em, with a lot less of a moustache. It makes my heart sick to think what they might have done to that poor beast.'

'He'll turn up.'

'Harmless, he was. And now he's steaks or some bloody Albanok's boyfriend.'

'We'll get you another camel.'

'That's not the point. Anyway, it would be *another* camel. Not the same camel. It wouldn't be my camel. Damn fine camel that, once you got to know him.'

'It was a very fine and heroic camel,' I agreed.

'Never met a better one,' said Arbuthnot.

The Rolls gave as much of a roar as a polite car like that will ever give and tiptoed carefully through the puddle.

'This is boring,' Max said again. And he was right. We'd only been in town for a day, but already I had grown to expect cheering crowds and oompah bands wherever I went. That's how it is. That's how it gets a grip of you, like a drink or a dope fiend. It's so sweet and so strong, like the applause you get for a backflip dismount off the trapeze, but it's different because they do the same for the clowns, they do the same for the performing dogs, they do the same for everybody but there is only one king. Nobody else gets that love and want and longing, as much as you get from any woman, as much as a mother can give, but magnified ten thousand times with ten thousand screaming, joyful faces, all turned in one direction, all looking at the king like daisies turning towards the sun. You get a taste for it pretty damned quick, I can tell you, and once you've had it, there's just about nothing you won't do to get it again.

Anyway, Max was right. It was boring to sit there, walking our horses behind a limousine as if we were on our way to a funeral, so I fell out of line, banged my fist on the roof of the car and yelled, 'See you at the castle, Kemali. We're going for a ride!'

That horse of mine didn't take much encouragement. A touch of the heels and he was off like a greyhound, down in the haunches and springing along under the trees with Max and Arbuthnot thundering behind, Max clinging on for dear life, Arbuthnot swinging his sabre as easy as a gentleman with his walking cane in the park.

We reached the street corner, where the hammered earth road turned to cobbles, and the horses tensed as they felt their feet sliding under them for a moment, but they clattered on, striking sparks from their shoes as they went, and the noise of their passing echoed back at us from the buildings like rolling thunder, on and up, through the narrow, winding streets, up the hill towards the castle and the Treasury.

There was a final turn, then a long straight up the hill with my horse gasping under me, nostrils flaring, breath roaring like a furnace, his great heart pumping like a ship's engine, hoofs drumming and clattering all the way to the arch where I lost my fez only the night before and where half a dozen blokes who looked a little like soldiers had managed to drag themselves out of bed to form a guard.

We pulled up and jumped from our saddles, laughing and breathless and alive, by God, alive.

The guards snapped to attention like clockwork soldiers and you could tell they were aching with pride, chests puffed up like pigeons as I walked down the line, whacking my riding crop off my boot as I went. 'I saw the king on the day he was crowned. I was in the guard.' You could see it in their eyes – they were thinking what they would tell their grandchildren.

'Well done,' I said. 'Tell them well done.'

'Well done,' Arbuthnot said, but he said it in Albanok, of course, and you could see them swelling and adding a little something extra to their stories. 'Well done. That's what the king said to me. He stopped on his way to his coronation, got down off his horse and singled me out for doing a good job.'

And, you see, already a little bit of the love they were shining at me was reflecting back at them. Already, even then, I was becoming a legend. By God, it tastes good.

'Now then,' I said, 'have you men seen any sign of a camel?'

They hadn't.

'There was definitely a camel here in the courtyard yesterday.' Looking round the place, there was every chance that the camel might still be there, hidden under piles of rubbish and old bonfires and broken bottles. 'Perhaps we could detail a work party,' I said. 'Get this place cleaned up a bit.'

'Get this place cleaned up!' Arbuthnot said.

'Now, where is the Treasury?'

'You there, show the king to the Treasury,' although he said it in Albanok but I knew he was talking about me because he said '*mbret*'. They said something back to him, but it goes without saying that I had no idea what that was and then, right that very second, we heard the klaxon horn of Kemali's Rolls – honk, honk and a long lean on the horn, honnnnnnk, as the car came squealing through the castle gates and into the courtyard.

Zogolli wound down his window and leaned out. 'Majesty, might I, that is, might one ask, what are you doing here?'

'Isn't it obvious?' I said. 'The Treasury. The crown. I came for the fitting, to try on the crown.'

And then Kemali leaned out of the Rolls and said, 'But, Majesty, the Treasury is stuffed with cash. The Treasury is brimful of money, money which belongs to the people of the free and independent kingdom of Albania and to you, my king. We needed something rather more suitable, something with the most modern and impregnable security. The Treasury is no longer at the castle. We moved it.'

I went to look out the window. I still have a window, which is a pleasant surprise, and the snowdrifts have gone, that little blizzard of ash all blown away, and God knows what blown with it, God knows who.

There's nothing much to look at out there. Nothing but fires, a long line of dark and the shape of the trees in the distance, very sharp, as if they had been stamped out of tin plate and, behind them, the flames reaching up to orange clouds. The searchlights are still sending up their beams. I don't know why. The sky is so bright that they could just look up and see the bombers if there were any up there, but they've gone. I think they've gone. I haven't heard any booming and banging for a while. Maybe it's stopped. I think they'll be back. They come when they like now. Americans by day, English by night. Or the other way about, I forget. I've seen them leaving their trails in the sky, ignoring us, flying away to the east, saving their bombs for somebody more important or more unlucky and, God forgive me, I've been glad that it's their turn and not mine. God forgive me.

But I don't know why I'm telling you this. You've seen an air raid before, you've thought those thoughts too. 'Not me. Them. Do it to them. Not me. Not my house. Not my wife. Not my kids. Do it to them.' It's not very heroic. Not very kingly. And it's how we ended up in this mess in the first place. We shouldn't speak of it more. We won't speak of it more. Anyway, that wasn't what I wanted to tell you.

When I was looking out the window just then, watching the fires burning, I caught sight of myself reflected in the glass and I knew it was me, of course, and yet I hardly recognised myself. I'm an old man. I knew that, but it still came as a shock. That's not the face I see when I remember the farm. It's not the face I wore in the circus. It's not the face they saw at my coronation. I look at that face and I wonder, Is that me? Is it? How can I be that little boy on the farm? How can I be the man that all those girls went mad for, the man all those Albanoks cheered for, the man Sarah loved? I wonder sometimes where all those other Ottos have gone, if they are still in me and I am still in them or if they've gone and they exist only in photographs, the way that I existed in the window a moment ago. Just a brief reflection in the firelight until the flare died down and I was gone again with nothing left to show but the steam of my breath on the glass. Where did I go? Where did the time go? The King of the Albanoks, where is he? And that little boy? How did he get inside this caravan with a city burning all around him? That poor little boy.

Let's not talk of these things.

So we were at the castle, me and Max and Arbuthnot, when Kemali announced that he had moved the Treasury. I suppose I should have been pleased. After all, you can bet that old Franz Josef didn't keep his crown jewels in the kitchen cupboard, but I liked the homespun innocence of keeping the cash in a leaky old back room. Still, it seemed the Albanoks had decided to grow up a little and that's a bittersweet moment for any father looking at his children. Also, it made withdrawals more difficult in case of temporary cash-flow difficulties and other emergencies.

'Majesty, time is pressing,' said Kemali. 'We have a busy day ahead of us. If we are to examine the crown – as you requested – we must go now. This time, perhaps you would care to ride with us.'

So I got in the car with them, facing backwards, which I don't like, staring right at Alberto von Mesmer's great black glasses as he sat jammed in between Zogolli and Kemali, with the horses trotting behind.

The car made much better progress on the cobbled streets of the town and we rattled on, as merry as a marriage bell, back down the hill and towards the harbour. We turned a corner into a street of solid, respectable merchant houses, some of them with gates and gardens.

'Our finest citizens make their homes in this quarter,' said Kemali.

'My own family stays just here,' Zogolli added. 'That house there with the very fine railings.'

'Very fine,' I agreed, and the Professor sat, ramrod straight, looking at the back of the driver's head. 'And our finest citizens, what do they do?'

'Do, Majesty?'

'To pay for those lovely houses? Do they farm? Where are their estates? Where are their factories, the great combinations of capital and labour adding daily to the wealth of the Albanian people?'

Zogolli looked at Kemali and Kemali looked at Zogolli and, before we had bumped through too many more potholes, Kemali said, 'I think it would best be described as "trade", Majesty. Import and export of high-value goods.'

'So they are smugglers,' I said. 'I see. Our finest citizens.'

'That is a vicious caricature,' said Zogolli. Even Kemali seemed surprised to see him so exercised. 'Our people – your people – have done what they could to survive centuries of tyranny and warfare. Not all of us, Majesty, have the rare good fortune to be born the son of the Sultan. These –' he waved a gloved hand at the mansions passing by on either side – 'these are the best and the bravest. These are the ones who have risked the most, gambled the most, survived the longest. Give them peace and good governance and see what they will do.'

'It is what they long for,' Kemali said, 'and already they love you.'

It was true. He nodded the top of his cane towards the passing houses and each one was decked in flags and flowers and garlands of ribbons and painted banners with a lot of Albanok writing that I took to be 'Long live the King' and

263

similar kind sentiments. Somebody had even taken the trouble to paint a sheet with an image of a man on a camel – a camel with ridiculously spindly stick legs, I grant you, but the magnificent whiskers of his rider were a tribute to the talents of the artist.

'Some day soon,' said Kemali, 'I imagine these fine houses will be transformed into the diplomatic quarter, a long row of embassies, the peaceful sovereign outposts of friendly nations eager to establish relations with Your Majesty and his government.'

'That would be you,' I said.

He nodded graciously.

'And me,' said Zogolli.

'Not forgetting me,' said the Professor, 'as vizier.'

'Does it pay well, this Prime Minister business?'

'So far, I am pleased to say, I have managed to escape with my life, which is far more than ever I expected.'

'And I come of good family,' said Zogolli, as if that explained everything.

Kemali winked at me. It was quick, but I got it.

'What is the advice of my government regarding the world situation? The world is an armed camp. Will there be war? And, if there is war, which side should the free and independent Kingdom of Albania choose? Or will we have a side chosen for us?'

Kemali spoke to me quietly, as he would to an idiot child. 'Majesty, Majesty,' he soothed. 'to talk of war is preposterous. There can be no war. The whole world knows that Germany and Austria and the Ottomans are allied together, just as the whole world knows that Russia and France and the English are allied together. A war would be catastrophic. A war would involve a clash of worldwide empires. A war would bleed Europe white. It is unthinkable, it is madness and, for that reason, it cannot happen.'

Poor Kemali. Because he was not himself a madman he could not conceive of a world of madmen. Because he was not insane, he could not believe that kings and countries, governments and empires could all of them go insane at the same time. Because he was reasonable and rational and kind he could not see the terrible truth that was staring him in the face, the way that Arbuthnot, who was none of those things, had seen so clearly.

The car gave another little jolt as it turned down the hill and, within just a few streets, we found ourselves in a commercial area of narrow lanes and warehouses.

'We're here,' Kemali said.

'I anticipated something grander. More statues. A few bronze lions. Maybe a horn of plenty, spilling out coin.'

'Majesty, as I think I tried to explain, we removed the Treasury for reasons of security, not for reasons of pictur-esque beauty. Let me demonstrate.'

As we got out of the car, Max and Arbuthnot were tying the horses up to a drainpipe. My ministers brushed the creases out of their fancy frock coats and Kemali went into his pocket and came out with one of those little folding leather wallets in his hand, the kind of thing that's fitted with a rack of tiny metal spring hooks inside so you can carry your keys around without spoiling the line of your pockets.

I was expecting the Treasury of the free and independent Kingdom of Albania to come with a much bigger key, something more impressive, the kind of thing you could use to tether a Zeppelin in time of need, so you might imagine my disappointment when Kemali produced a tiny little sliver of brass, the sort of key Tifty might have used to open her toilet case.

I looked at Max and he looked at me and, when Kemali put the key in the lock and the whole door shook and trembled and bowed inward at his touch, well, neither of us could keep a straight face.

'You are quite sure that this is the right place?' I said. 'You did say you moved the Treasury for greater security.'

Kemali folded his wallet of keys shut and said, 'If your Majesty would follow me.'

He pushed at the flimsy front door and we all followed him into a small whitewashed room. The only light came from an unglazed window at the back – more of a hole in the wall than a window – protected by a couple of iron bars which my mate Max could probably have pulled out with his teeth if he decided not to smash the door down instead. It was pretty dark, but there was light enough to see that the place was empty. No money. No crown. No nothing.

Kemali went to the back wall and took down a hurricane lamp from a hook, lifted the glass, lit it with a match and held it high. At the other side of the room Zogolli had done the same and, at his feet, what had looked like a fireplace in the shadows opened into the beginnings of a staircase leading down into the earth.

'Would you follow me, please?' he said, and we all trooped after him, Zogolli leading the way and Kemali bringing up the rear with the Professor leaning on Arbuthnot's arm and Max looking about from side to side like a frightened bear, just in case some phantom should suddenly leap from the shadows.

The stairs went down and curved a little to the left so you couldn't see the top from the bottom, and the light from Kemali's lamp shone back from the damp walls. At the bottom of the stairs there was a short passage and then another flight of stairs, only this time they were cut through solid rock. Behind me there was the tap-tap-tap of Professor von Mesmer's cane and Arbuthnot speaking kindly, 'A step here, worthy vizier, and another and this is the last.' In front of me only shadows, but I began to see why the Treasury had moved.

The walls of that passage were solid granite. There was no way of guessing how thick they might be and nothing but dynamite could cut a way through them, and there, at the end of the tunnel, dark and grey as a thundercloud, was the reason we had come – a wall of steel that blocked the width of the passage, with a door set into it.

Kemali held his lamp up proudly. 'Majesty, Excellency, gentlemen, permit me to introduce Atlas.'

Sure enough, 'Atlas' was painted on the front in fancy gold letters, along with a picture of a bloke who looked a lot like my mate Max, carrying the weight of the world on his shoulders which, I'd noticed, was something that Max was prone to do.

'Is he not magnificent?' said Kemali, like a bloke presenting his first grandson, and we all agreed that, indeed, he was.

'Majesty, my friends, Atlas is built from manganese steel two inches thick – the very stuff that King George and the Kaiser use to build the gun turrets of their magnificent battleships. Perhaps if one of them could float into this little passage, the guns could be brought to bear against Atlas and, who knows, he might even crack. But that's not very likely to happen. This is a very little passage with not much water in it.

'On the other hand, even the toughest steel can be cut – otherwise how could these ships be made? – so let me explain that, behind the walls of this magnificent safe, two enormous cannonballs hang from soft metal chains. If a thief should manage to come here, undetected, dragging his gas cylinders down these stairs, if he should apply his torch to Atlas here –' he gave the steel walls a friendly slap – 'though that torch be hotter than the fires of hell, Atlas would not budge. Instead he would become unbearably hot, those soft metal chains would melt, the weights would fall and sixteen separate bolts, each thicker than my thumb, would shoot into place securing the doors against attack.'

'Magnificent,' I said, because it seemed to be the thing to say.

'Thank you, Majesty.'

'And how did we come to acquire this astonishing piece of engineering and set it here, in this impenetrable tunnel?'

'Oh,' said Kemali. 'Well, if your Majesty recalls our conversation earlier, I mentioned the lively contribution made to commerce by some of our finest citizens.'

'The smugglers, you mean?'

Zogolli gave an exasperated sigh. And Kemali said, 'One of our leading merchants tragically passed away.'

'You mean he was killed.'

'During an unfortunate misunderstanding involving the Italian navy, Majesty.'

'That is indeed tragic.'

'Consequently this valuable business asset became available.'

'And it is quite impregnable.'

'Absolutely, Majesty.'

'But you can open it, Kemali?'

'No, Majesty.'

'Well, that's not much good, is it? What's the point of a safe if you can't open it?'

Kemali gave another one of his patient sighs and explained, 'Majesty, please observe: on either side of the door there is a combination lock. I cannot open the vault, and Zogolli here, he cannot open the vault, but, together, Zogolli and I can open the vault.'

'Very good,' I said. 'Let's get on with it.'

'Impossible, Majesty. I do not know the combination of that lock and Zogolli does not know the combination of this lock. The greater part of the riches of Albania is behind these doors. The four millions of leks set aside by your waiting people as your Majesty's personal wealth are behind these doors and the crown of the free and independent Kingdom of Albania is behind these doors. That is too great a burden of temptation for one man to bear.'

'Very good,' I said again. 'Let's get on with it.'

Zogolli stepped forward, holding up his lamp. 'If I could prevail upon you to come back to the surface with me, Majesty.'

'You want me to leave?'

'Only while the Prime Minister opens his lock. Then he will leave, I will return and open my lock, and the crown will be in your hands.'

'But I am the king,' I said. 'Am I not to be trusted with my own Treasury?'

Zogolli said nothing. Kemali said nothing. I bristled my not inconsiderable whiskers at them. It turned into a staring contest until Kemali said, 'Four millions of leks, Your Majesty. Every lek is your own. If your Majesty wishes to withdraw all four millions, or only one single lek, you are free to do so, and, at a word from you, day or night, Zogolli and I will come to this place and open the doors. The rest – the crown and the Treasury – are a sacred trust.'

I didn't know what to say. The message was pretty clear. Whatever was behind that door, it was none of my damned business and, king or no king, whiskers or no whiskers, they weren't going to let me near it.

'Very well,' I said. 'I will withdraw with my gentlemen.'

And then Professor von Mesmer spoke up. 'Those stairs are so difficult. Down the stairs, up the stairs, down the stairs again. Such a trial. In the circumstances, and while respecting the worthy and honourable requirements for the security of the Treasury, might an old blind man be permitted to remain here?'

We waited in the little whitewashed room for a few moments, standing around awkwardly with nothing to say to one another until we saw the light of Kemali's lamp come bobbing up the stairs.

'I left the vizier alone in the dark,' he said. 'In my heart of hearts I know it makes no difference to him, but it pained me to do it, as it would to abandon a child down there.'

'It's only for a short while,' said Zogolli. 'I'll go to him and call you in a moment.'

Zogolli disappeared into the tunnel, and very soon the glow of his lamp vanished too. I imagined him in the first passage, walking doubled over so his top hat would not scrape the ceiling, then looking at his feet on the stone stairs, down and down, then in the tunnel through the granite to where Professor von Mesmer was waiting, alone in the dark just as he was always alone in the dark. I pictured Zogolli down there, setting his lamp down on the floor of the passage, taking his silly gloves off and putting them in his pocket, lifting the lamp close to the combination dial, so many turns right, so many turns left, so many turns right, a mechanical click that only the Professor could hear.

'You may come down now,' faint and far away and echoing.

Kemali said, 'Majesty, we have only one lamp and the stairs are steep. I suggest you lead the way and I will try to stay in the middle of our little group to share what light there is.'

To tell the truth you could probably have got more of a glow off a well-slapped backside than we got off Kemali's lamp, but I put my hand against the wall and made my way down the stairs safely enough, with the others coming at my back.

Ahead of me, at the end of the second passage, I could see Zogolli's lamp standing on the floor and then two figures, their outlines painted with yellow, the way the thin edge of the moon stands out against the velvet sky.

But the doors of the vault were still closed against us and Atlas was still glowing in the lamplight, the world still balanced on his shoulders.

'Open up!' the Prime Minister said, and Zogolli spun a ship's wheel set in the steel door. If well-oiled cogs and finely engineered gears and tiny bits of machinery turned and spun and slotted into place, they did it too quietly for me to notice and, when Zogolli gave a tug on the wheel, the doors of the vault glided open with barely a murmur.

It was all I could do to stop myself from running forward into the dark and plunging my hands into all that lovely money, but instead I picked up Zogolli's lamp from the floor, lifted it high and, with as much dignity as I could muster, I walked into the vault with Max and Arbuthnot crowding behind.

Have you ever imagined what it would be like to walk into Barbarossa's cave under the mountains and find the old king sitting there, asleep in his golden throne, treasure chests piled high around the walls with pearls and diamonds falling out of them, rubies and emeralds glinting like dragon scales, stacks of gold bars just lying in heaps on the floor and great drifts of coin spilling out of busted barrels all over the place? Well, this was nothing like that. We walked from the dark of the passage into the dark of the vault and there was nothing to see. It was just another dark room and, even when Kemali arrived with his lamp, there wasn't much to see.

The walls were of granite, just like outside, the floor and roof the same, black granite and it seemed that Atlas was not so much a safe as a great steel wall, thrown up to block the mouth of the cavern.

Somebody, probably the unfortunate, patriotic busi-nessman who donated the place to the Albanok people, had built wooden horsebox contraptions against the sides of the cave – you know, the kind of thing they use to divide up a stable so each horse gets a little room of its own. Kemali raised his lamp and pointed to one of the divisions. 'This,' he said, 'is Your Majesty's portion.'

Max hurried across the vault to stand at my side and I heard the quick tap-tap-tap of the Professor's cane behind me.

'What can you see?' he said, perhaps a little too eagerly.

'Boxes,' Max said, 'a lot of boxes.'

'More like crates, I'd say, Uncle Vizier. Heavy wood crates, long and narrow, eight of them, bound round with copper wires and with a rope handle at each end.'

'Half a million leks in each box,' the Professor said, and he said it as if somebody had offered him new eyes.

'The loose change, a few thousand leks only, is kept in my office at the castle, should Your Majesty have any modest personal needs,' said Kemali. 'Now, over here is the portion belonging to the state.' He swung his lamp towards the next horsebox, but on the way the light fell on a rack of rifles, all standing at attention with ammunition boxes at their feet.

'What the hell are they for?' I said.

'Oh, just something the last tenant left behind, Majesty. Tools of the trade, I imagine. But this is why you came.'

The government horsebox was stacked with crates – far more than I had in my personal Treasury, but I suppose that was fair enough. To tell the truth there was barely room for us all to stand in there, what with all the crates of cash stacked up, higher than the lamplight could reach, but in the middle of the floor four crates had been set on end together in a square to make a sort of column and, on top of the column, there was a red leather box about the size of a coal bucket.

Kemali put his lamp down on one side of the box, Zogolli put his lamp down on the other and, for a time, inside that black cave at the bottom of the world, we stood in silence.

At last Kemali said, 'Majesty, almost five hundred years ago a great hero arose in Albania. He fought, as I have fought, as Zogolli has fought, to free this land from Turkish rule. His name was Gjergj Kastrioti Skanderbeg, the Dragon of Albania who threw off the yoke of the Ottomans – if only for a little while. He is loved and admired by all free Albanians to this day. Skanderbeg stands for all that we have achieved.'

The old man stopped speaking and then, with a mother's tenderness, he opened the red leather box.

'Behold the crown of Skanderbeg.'

The crown of Skanderbeg was not what I expected, and I think it's safe to say I had never seen anything like it before. For one thing, it wasn't a crown. A crown is made of gold. A crown is lined with red velvet and trimmed with fur and covered with jewels. Above all else, a crown is sort of crown-shaped. But this crown – my crown – wasn't a crown at all. The crown of Skanderbeg was a soldier's helmet, the sort of helmet a knight would have worn in the olden days. This thing was burnished blue steel, made to withstand the blows of Turkish scimitars. Around the base there was a band of burnished leather with enormous brass bolts, like you'd use to fix a ship's boiler. Stuck through it all the way round and about halfway up there was another leather band, edged top and bottom with gold and studded, north, south, east and west, with big golden roses, each the size of a pocket watch.

Now, it would be unkind to say that the crown of Skanderbeg was the ugliest thing I have ever seen, but if we had offered it as a prize in the shooting gallery I don't think there would have been many takers. The strangest bit about the whole thing was the golden goat's head sitting on top, large as life, horns and all, ears pricked up and staring out at me with nasty goaty eyes. I picked the helmet up and I held it in my two hands and I stared back.

'Your Majesty is moved,' said Zogolli.

'I don't know what to say.'

'I understand. It is no small thing to hold in your hands the helmet of our country's hero.'

'I don't know what to say,' I said again. 'I just can't think of what to say. But it's absolutely lovely – it really is – and in surprisingly good condition after five hundred years and all those battles.'

Zogolli cleared his throat. 'Actually, Majesty, it is only a few weeks old. We had it made specially.'

Kemali gave him one of his special looks. 'Perhaps it would be fair to say that this is not so much the crown of Skanderbeg as "symbolic" of the crown of Skanderbeg and all that it represents to the free and independent Kingdom of Albania. The real one is in Vienna.'

'This one is real!' Zogolli squeaked.

'It certainly seems real to me,' I said, and I gave it a knock with my knuckles. 'Yes. That's real enough. I think, maybe, once I've put it on and I really am king, we should have a word with old Franz Josef, man to man, and ask him if he wouldn't mind sending the other one back, postage paid.'

'Majesty,' said Kemali, 'you must understand that when

you put on this crown in the presence of your people today you will become the new Skanderbeg, the defender of a free people. Like me, you are a Turk and a Mussulman. We represent everything that Skanderbeg – a Christian prince – struggled to oppose but, like Skanderbeg, we are Albanians, Zogolli and I by birth, you by choice. Today you will be invested with the belt and sword of a Mussulman prince and crowned as a Christian king, uniting all your people under the crown of Skanderbeg.'

'I regard that as a high and holy duty,' I said, and I meant it. If I was going to be the King of the Albanoks, then I was going to be the best bloody king those Albanoks could wish for. 'I will do my best, Kemali, I promise you. I pledge my life in service to this country and its people. Now, don't you think I should try it on?'

I don't imagine you have ever worn a crown, and even if you could, even if you found yourself alone in some royal treasury, I bet you wouldn't try one on, just for a laugh. There's something more than superstition that goes with a crown. It's more than metal and jewels. It stands for something and it can only ever belong to one person at a time. That's why we make paper crowns at Christmas – or we used to – because it's funny, it's ridiculous, it's a mad idea that just anybody can go about as a crowned king.

And that ugly metal thing I was holding in my hands, it wasn't even a real crown. It was just a soldier's helmet, but all of us in that dark cave agreed that it was a crown and that made it a crown. It was *the* crown.

I lifted it up. I hesitated. I turned to Kemali. 'Shouldn't you do this?' I said.

'Someone will assist you later, Majesty. For now, if it is too tight, we will remove a little of the padding. If it is too loose, we add a handkerchief. Go ahead.'

I dipped my head. I fitted the crown to it. I stood up at my full height, shoulders back, whiskers bristling. Nobody said a word.

Later, after we had packed the crown away in its leather box, after we had climbed the stairs back to the blinding half-light of the little whitewashed room and just as we were about to get back into the Rolls, Kemali took me by the hand and whispered, 'I worry about poor Zogolli – his little outburst about the crown, you know. Sometimes the poor boy can't seem to tell the difference between what is real and what is imaginary.'

'Very few of us can, Prime Minister. The important part is to tell the difference between what is real and what is true. If he can do that, then he'll do for me.'

My back hurts. And my ribs. Maybe it's from when I fell off the ceiling earlier, when I was trying to do that 'allez-oop' through the trapdoor of the Budapest cellar, remember? But I don't think so. I think it's from the bomb this afternoon. That gave me an awful shake-up. I felt all my bits jangle inside me and that's not nice. I have pains in my heart. I can feel it beating in my chest. That's not nice either. For a long time now I've been falling apart. When I was a young man, which was the day before yesterday, I never noticed my body. It just worked the way a watch works, all the little bits knitted together and sliding past each other and doing their job, tick-tock.

Nowadays I can feel my heart beating and I can't help but wonder when tick-tock is going to reach tick-stop. I can feel the air going down into my lungs. I can feel the food sliding down my gullet and landing in my stomach – when I can get food. I have to be careful what I eat – although I can't afford to be fussy – but some of the stuff they give us well, you know, if it doesn't bung me up it shoots right through me and, whatever it does, I can measure it every inch of the way. My knees click, my hips click, my ankles and my shoulders and my wrists click and every bone in my back is a separate, aching bead on loose elastic. It's like old age has got me up on a butcher's block and taken me to bits, joint by joint. It's as if my body is starting to break up while I'm still using it, like a ship falling to pieces just short of port.

But maybe that's nature's way. Maybe it's easier for us to move out of a house that's already falling down – not that it matters to me since the Royal Air Force is quite likely to serve a notice of eviction before morning so I'd better get on with this story.

When we arrived back at the palazzo in the Rolls, with Zogolli holding the crown of Skanderbeg on his knee like his granny's big red handbag, the place was in an uproar.

More staff had arrived – before he left, promising to send back the car, Kemali said he'd sent them – and they were running in and out of the house, carrying sides of beef and cases of champagne and crates of crockery and working away to titivate the ballroom ready for a night of celebration while the girls, Sarah and Tifty and Mrs MacLeod and the rest, were running about in between them, carrying smoothing irons and crimping irons and curling tongs and lots of other dangerous stuff that could set light to the curtains.

Sarah hurried past me on the stairs, 'I'll make you a sandwich for later, Otto, love. You'll need something to keep you going!'

'You can't go about making me sandwiches. We have staff for that kind of thing.'

Max said. 'You can make as many sandwiches as you like for me.'

'And what about your aged father?' the Professor said, but she was already running off, trailing a long dress over her arm.

I watched her go. Sarah was always nice to watch and I spent a lot of time doing that, one way or another. Watching her go away was as heartbreaking as watching the swallows go at the end of summer. Watching her coming back was like finding crocuses broken out along the path. Watching her standing still was like drinking hot chocolate on a winter's evening – hot chocolate with a dash of something in it. By God, she was lovely.

The vizier put his arm through mine and leaned in close. 'Do you think I might have a private word, son? There's something I want to say to you.'

'Me too,' said Max.

'Why don't we go to your room? You can show me the way.' And he looked at me with those black goggles and squeezed my arm.

Don't you hate that, when somebody says, 'We must talk,' and then says nothing at all? There's this thing that simply must be said but it can't be said there and then, only someplace else and a bit later on. And the way he called me 'son' was odd. And the way he held my elbow. It wasn't like an old blind man looking for help. It was as if he had gripped me so I couldn't run away, as if he was pushing me along, through the crowds of housemaids running about with their arms full of plates or waddling under great nodding vases of flowers, past the sweaty red-faced soldiers with their too-tight collars buttoned up, rehearsing where to stand, and the men teetering on stepladders, unsheeting the chandeliers.

We made our way back to the royal apartments, the ones with the questionable statues and the steamrollered eagle over the door, me arm in arm with the Professor, Max and Arbuthnot a little behind. But when we reached the door and, naturally, I stood there like the village idiot, waiting for Max to demonstrate once again how it worked, the strangest thing happened.

Sure enough, Max flung back the door and stepped into the room, holding it wide so the Professor and I could pass through, but when Arbuthnot stepped up, Max threw out an arm and said, 'Not you!'

All credit to Arbuthnot – his hand flew to his sword and he looked ready to use it, with that jaw of his set and his wolf's teeth showing, but Max never moved. He just stood there like a tree, one arm out, daring Arbuthnot to chop it off, if he thought he could.

I said, 'It's all right, captain. These are my friends. They don't mean me any harm.'

Arbuthnot let his sword slide back into its scabbard. 'I'll be waiting right here, Majesty. You need only call,' and the door slammed in his face.

I think the Professor took that as a signal to begin. He folded his arms and took a deep breath but I wanted to keep him off balance for a bit so, before he could start, I cut him short.

'You don't mean me any harm, do you, Max?'

'Now, you know better than that, Otto.'

The Professor coughed. 'Maybe I could explain.'

'I'm talking to Max!' I said. 'So, we're still pals, Max?'

'Still pals, Otto. You know that.'

'There you are then, Professor. That's me and Max still pals. All sorted out. Now, what can I do for you?'

I suppose that, just by being a little bit short and a little bit disrespectful, I hoped to show the old bugger that he couldn't boss me around, and I think it was pretty clear that Max wasn't going to be doing any bossing around on his behalf. 'Yes, Professor. Go ahead.'

'Otto, I was wondering how long . . . that is, Max and I were wondering how long you plan on keeping up with this pretence?'

'What pretence?'

'How long do you intend to continue with the charade that you are the King of Albania?'

'But, Professor, I am the King of Albania. Haven't you noticed? You are standing in my palace. My servants are scurrying about every place, doing my bidding. I have a castle and a government and an army. Only a few minutes ago I was wearing my crown and it fitted like a glove, and a few moments from now I will wear it again to the acclaim of the entire nation. Are you suggesting I'm not the king? Are you suggesting all those people are misguided?'

What a fool I was. Not half an hour before I had shaken

hands with Kemali, spouting all that high-minded nonsense about being able to tell the difference between what was real and what was true, and there I stood, half an hour later, ranting at a blind old man. He knew I wasn't the king. From behind his black glasses he could see the truth that I refused to see.

He leaned on his cane and sighed. 'Otto, did you mean that stuff you told Kemali, all that stuff about doing your best?'

'I always do my best, you know that.'

'And pledging your life in service to the Albanian people, did you mean that too?'

'Of course I meant it.'

'Your whole life?'

'My whole life.'

'My boy, sometimes a lifetime can be painfully brief. You may have pledged the Albanian people only the rest of the week. Otto, we can't get away with this. The Great Powers won't allow it. Somebody is going to want their country back.'

'It's my country!' I said, in the sort of voice you hear in the playground, the sort of voice that yells, 'It's my ball!'

'Otto, please, if not for my sake, then consider Sarah. Let's fill our pockets, grab what we can and run for the back door.'

It was the wisest advice I ever had, but I would not be told. A man has to listen to his friends but, damn it, kings don't. Kings have a higher calling. Kings answer to a higher power. They call it duty or destiny or the national interest or sometimes they just call it 'God', but whatever they call it, it puts them beyond advice and it excuses them from picking up the bill.

'What do you think, Max? You're in this too,' I said.

'Whatever suits you suits me, mate. That's how it's always been. On the other hand, fun's fun, but keep your arse off the pillow. That's what I always say, and I have found it a useful maxim for life.' Actually, he did say that a lot, along with, 'There will be tears before bedtime,' and, 'It's all fun until somebody gets an eye out,' and 'Don't come running to me when you break both your legs.' Max was a surprisingly cautious bloke considering that he spent his working life swallowing swords and lifting small ponies over his head.

Anyway, I flopped down into the big sofa in front of the fire. 'Lads,' I said, 'you're looking at this all wrong. You're looking at this like you were part of a gang of carnies on the run with a stolen camel. I'm seeing this from the point of view of a king. We can do some good here. Schools. A hospital. Port improvements. Drains. This is a chance to make the world a better place, introduce a bit of law and order.'

The Professor snorted. 'Otto, do you really think an impostor and a camel thief is the man to bring law and order to anybody? Dear God, man, you've even lost the camel. How you plan to keep control of an entire nation when you've got no idea where your camel might be is beyond me!'

'It had nothing to do with Otto,' Max said. 'It was me. I lost the camel.'

'Nobody's blaming you, mate. But look, this is exactly what I'm talking about. I can't be wasting my time all day worrying about what happened to the damned camel.'

'It was a bloody good camel.'

'And I know you loved it dearly, Max, but still, I have to think about other things. Arbuthnot is outside that door with the British Empire at his back and, worse than that, those madmen from the Companions. They could be anywhere. I have no idea who they are or where they are. I have no idea if the whole town is choked with them or if he simply invented them. I don't know. The Turks are to the south, and they might not know much but they know they didn't send me. The Serbs are to the north, spoiling for a fight, and the Royal Fathers-in-Law must be pacified.'

'All the more reason to cut and run,' said the Professor. 'You've been to the Treasury. Four millions of leks, Otto. It's enough.'

'No. I'm staying. I'm riding a tiger here and the one thing I can't do is get off. But if you want to go, I won't stop you. Whatever money is in Kemali's desk is yours. We'll shake hands on it and I'll send you on your way with no hard feelings and more to follow once things settle down a bit.'

I looked hard at Max. 'Go or stay?'

'Stay, Otto.'

'That's it sorted then.'

There was never much to see on the Professor's face. If the eyes are the windows of the soul, he had nothing but drain covers, those hideous black glasses that seemed to soak all expression away into them. Still, he looked relieved. He heaved a sigh and his shoulders relaxed.

'Thank you, Otto. You are very understanding towards an old man. I'll get Sarah and we'll be on our way.'

'Sarah stays,' I said.

'You can't be serious.'

'She stays. You can go if you want to, but Sarah doesn't want to leave.'

'You mean you don't want her to go. You mean you've decided for her. You've decided to hold her here. To spite me.' His spectacles glittered and his knuckles were white on the handle of his cane, but I was calm.

I said, 'Do you want to put this to the test, old man? I'll accept her answer if you will. Arbuthnot!'

The door opened.

Sarah was wrapped in a dressing gown I did not recognise and which was clearly not her own. It went round her twice, the sleeves were doubled over in gigantic cuffs and it fell in an awkward, tripping pool of cloth at her feet. She looked like a girl caught in the middle of getting ready to go out, after she had finished pinning her hair up but before she had finished doing her face, and she did not look pleased.

She stood in the middle of the room with a pretty little frown hiding between her eyebrows and, by God, I loved her. I knew I loved her. I knew she was why all those others had been before – so I could tell the difference; so that, when I found Sarah, I would recognise her and know. I knew she was the one I wanted to spend my life with. I knew she was the only one and, if I could not have her, there would be no other. I knew that if she chose to leave my heart would break and I might die of it, but I knew that I would stay and be the king.

I said, 'Sarah, throw some stuff in a bag and get ready to leave within the hour.'

That little frown deepened and then it vanished and her eyebrows turned down and she looked like she was trying hard not to look surprised. 'Leave? Are we leaving?'

'I'm not. I'm staying. You're leaving.'

I thought she was going to cry and I hated myself for it. It was like a slap. Her mouth made a little flat 'O' and her eyes flicked towards her father, just for a second, as if she was trying to make that link again, the way they did in the circus ring when he knew exactly what she was holding in her hands, when they saw through one another's eyes and spoke with one another's voices, but it had gone. He stood, leaning forward on his cane, looking at nothing as if he had no idea that she was even in the room.

'What about all that stuff you said on the boat?'

'What stuff?'

'Stuff about bread on tables and children in schools.'

'I plan to go ahead with those.'

'And the other stuff? The stuff about being the queen. The stuff about light duties. You didn't mean any of that?'

I couldn't keep it up after that. I grabbed her by the hand and I held her and I kissed her face. I kissed her face and her eyes and her hair and her mouth and her sweet little nose. 'Of course I meant it. But don't you want to go? Your father thought you wanted to go.'

'Well, I don't,' she said. 'I want to stay here and be the queen. You don't want to go, do you, Daddy?'

The Professor smiled a smile that glittered like a broken icicle. 'Of course not, *liebling*. Whither thou goest I will go, and where thou lodgest I will lodge. Where you die I will die and there I will be buried. May the Lord deal with me, be it ever so severely, if anything but death separate you and me.' He reached out and, when she offered her hand, he kissed her fingertips. 'Albania is our home now. Otto has work to do and so do you. I misunderstood.'

Sarah said, 'Good,' and she rubbed her eyes with the deep folded cuffs of her dressing gown. 'God in Heaven, Otto, it's lucky for you I hadn't started on my make-up. And if you've messed up this hair, there's going to be hell to pay.' She gave a big sniff. 'Ooh, I can't waste time on this nonsense. I don't know about you, but I have to get ready for a coronation!' And then she turned and hurried out of the room, as fast as she could shuffle with all that cloth around her feet, and I think she was trying to hide a tear or two as she ran.

The Professor said, 'Is she gone?'

Arbuthnot closed the door. 'She's gone.'

'Good. Get the money ready. I will leave right after the coronation.'

I am an old man now, much older than he was then. I've seen stuff, a lot of stuff, and I've done stuff too, and almost all of it – especially the stuff I've done – has made me think a bit less harshly about other people and the stuff they do. I can understand why a man would steal. It might be desperation; it might be greed; it might be the heat of the moment. I don't know, but I can understand it. I stole a camel and a strongbox once. And I can understand why a man would go with women. It might be desperation; it might be greed; it might be the heat of the moment. Women are pretty nice and, as you know, I've been with a few. But I've never been able to understand what the Professor did. I couldn't understand it then and I don't understand it now. If ever I had had a daughter, my little Aferdita, then nothing would have parted her from me. I would have cared for her and protected her no matter what. No fear could have driven me away from her; no amount of money could have tempted me to give her up. I would have loved her with a fierce love, and I know this because I have loved her fiercely all these years although she was never born. How much more would I have loved her if I had once held her in my arms, if I had kissed her, if I had smelled her?

But the Professor chose to flee from Sarah and I can't understand why. On the train, when we had our heart to heart, he was ready to face death with Sarah rather than let her face it alone, but when push came to shove maybe his courage failed him. Maybe he was afraid of what might happen to her, not of what might happen to him. Maybe that was what he couldn't face. Or maybe the thought of a little bit of cash was worth more to him than she was. 'Get the money ready.' That's what he said. Such a tiny little bit of money.

I could hardly bear to look at him. None of us could. He was suddenly embarrassing, as if we had noticed for the first time that he was a cripple.

You don't need eyes to know when you are being watched, and he must have felt us turning our gaze away from him. 'I must prepare,' he said. 'I will wait in my room until it's time to leave for the ceremony.'

Arbuthnot opened the door as he approached and the Professor paused on the threshold, swinging his cane to tap it against the doorposts, and went out into the corridor.

When he was gone, Arbuthnot said, 'Is it too early for a brandy?'

'It's never too early for a brandy,' Max said, and he took the last, half-empty bottle out of the cabinet by my bed.

I didn't say anything. I just drank.

We didn't hang about over the brandy. There are two kinds of drink: the kind you want and the kind you need.

This was the second kind, and you don't hang about with those. I had a bad taste in my mouth and I wanted the brandy to take it away. Anyway, we all had things to do, boots to polish, brass to burnish, horses to brush, epaulettes to buff and magnificent whiskers to curl – all except me, of course.

I had nothing to do but to read, over and over, the two sheets of paper which Kemali had written out for me to guide me through the ceremonial of the coronation. There is no prompter's box at a coronation, no matter how incompetent the actors, but the more I tried to learn my lines, the less they stuck in my head. Orders of precedence, who stood where, who moved, who kept still, where they moved to, who said what, when the music played, where to go in the processions . . . none of it made any sense and it wasn't fair. Those flaming Albanoks had been practising for months, learning their dance steps off by heart, but it was all new to me and, quite frankly, I couldn't keep up so I decided not to bother.

The little china clock on the mantelpiece was striking the half-hour when Arbuthnot knocked at my door and came in.

'They found you a new fez,' he said. 'We can't have you riding through town bareheaded like a beggar.'

I must say it was much nicer than the one Sarah had knocked up for me on board the yacht, with a fancy sparkler stuck on the front which must have been several times more valuable than the one I was wearing on my chest.

I put it on, slowly, two-handed, just the way I'd put on

294

the crown of Skanderbeg, squaring it up across my brow, and I must admit I was thinking of the time I would take it off again, the time I would stand to wear my crown.

I drew myself up to my full height and I gave my jacket a bit of a tug. 'How do I look?'

'Very smart, old boy. I think we're ready for the off.'

I walked out the door, pulling my gloves on so they were tight and smooth, just as they should be, and Arbuthnot came on a pace or two behind, spurs a-jingle, tall and rangy, with the look of a man who knew his business. That uniform of his had seen better days, but stretched over his broad shoulders, with his epaulettes gleaming, by God, he looked the part.

'You'll be fine,' he said, as if he could tell from my back that I might waver a little, as if he could sense that I was making a little extra effort to be brave and firm and upright, like a man on his way to have his head taken off instead of having a crown put on.

The whole house was silent, not a Sunday-afternoon silent, not even a middle-of-the-night silent, but a stopped-clock silent, the kind of silence you get in the circus when the kid on the high wire starts to fall, the silence that comes in the moment after everyone breathes in and before the moment that they start to scream. It was a moment like that, and when we got to the top of the stairs, Arbuthnot and me – no, when *I* got to the top of the stairs – the moment burst.

The hall of my palazzo was jammed with people: soldiers more or less in uniform, bashi-bazouks and fathers-in-law

295

with their troops of moustachioed brigands crowded round the door. Every step of the grand staircase had a lancer standing on it as an honour guard, every one of them with a brass helmet, polished thin and gleaming like the sun, and horsehair plumes hanging down his neck and black shiny boots up over his knees, and every one of them holding a pig-sticker that scraped my ceiling or threatened my lovely chandelier. There were packs of kids jammed between the lancers' feet, with more of them at the bottom of the stairs – little girls in dresses holding baskets of flowers and, in amongst them, the palazzo staff, maids in mob caps looking pink and prim and starched and well worth a try and the cook and his boy and God alone knows all who else, people I'd never seen before, butlers and under-butlers and grooms and boots and footmen, I can't begin to guess who or how many, and there, at the foot of the stairs was my Sarah, so small, so lovely, in a hat that would knock your eye out and a long lilac dress that fitted her the way the petals fit a rose before it opens. God knows where she found it – maybe on some foraging expedition through the wardrobes of the palazzo – but she looked magnificent, and Tifty was there and Mrs MacLeod and even the girls of the harem, all done up to the nines. I saw Sarah and only Sarah. She raised her eyes to the top of the stairs and looked up at me from under the brim of that fabulous hat and I saw her and she saw me, not a man playing at dressing up but me, Otto, a man who was striving to be all that a king should be, for her sake and then, like I said, the moment burst. The whole place went crazy with cheering and shouting, mad clapping and a lot of shouted '*Mbrets*', which I took to be kind sentiments regarding my longevity. They wanted this to work. They wished me well. They believed in me and they wanted it to be true just as much as I did.

I came down the stairs between my rows of lancers as they struggled not to watch me pass and stand, eyes front, looking grim-faced, and there was Sarah, clapping madder than all the rest, with Tifty beside her, arm in arm with Max, and both of them clapping and Tifty jiggling deliciously as she clapped, and Mrs MacLeod and the harem girls and the Professor too, because he meant it, however much he begrudged it, or because he lacked the courage to defy a mob, even a mob as genteel as this one.

It fell on me like a sudden shower of rain. I was standing, drenched in a torrent, a cataract of applause, but it was more than that. It was pride. It was hope. It was love.

At the bottom of the stairs I took Sarah by the hand and kissed her, just once, just a little bit, but it was enough to set the cheering off again – even from the fathers-in-law, who clapped me on the back and yelled garlicky congratulations at me and clearly didn't care how many girls I kissed so long as I got round to their girls eventually.

We went out together, hand in hand, into the sunshine of a day as bright and warm as memory can create, with woolly clouds unravelling across the sky while sunbeams shot them full of holes, with the trees full of singing birds and the garden full of blooming flowers, but we had to part again so that Sarah and the others could join the parade.

We knew a bit about parades, my friends and me. We'd been in a few in our time, although this one had not so many camels and elephants and a damned sight more horses than what we were used to.

Zogolli was there, dancing around like a headless chicken, shouting orders through his long carrot nose. He was as much use as a glass hammer but, somehow or other, he got it done.

The Albanoks had managed to find a couple of landaus from someplace or other, possibly on loan from some of the best and finest families of smugglers that the country had to offer. Sarah, Tifty, Mrs MacLeod and the Professor filled one of those, with the harem girls squeezed into the other, and God help the poor soul jammed in next to Aferdita.

Then my lancers came clattering down the stairs in their big unbending boots, dipping their spears as they passed through the doorway, and they began to form up.

The ladies' coaches each had a guard of two shining cavalrymen, with two more to ride beside the Rolls where a lot of official-looking blokes in very glum top hats were saving a place for Zogolli. Half the rest went to the front of the queue, down at the end of the drive, and they fell in behind the marching band at the head of the procession, just ahead of a flag party of soldiers parading the national banner and a seething mass of brigands and bashi-bazouks which the fathers-in-law were struggling to herd. The other half of the detachment went to the rear and formed up behind me. I expected Max and Arbuthnot to ride beside me, as they had in the morning, but after Max gave me a hand up to the saddle, they went back a little ahead of the cavalry guard but behind me.

'It's not me they want to look at,' Max said. 'And, anyway, it'll give the assassins a clear shot.'

The chauffeur got out to crank the Rolls and it started

first time. Zogolli stood on the palazzo steps waving his top hat like a lunatic until he was satisfied his signal had been seen, then running to take his place in the car. From the end of the drive we heard the noise of a drum – boof-boof-boof – an explosion of cymbals, the drum again boof-boof and then music, or something very like music, in slow march time. We couldn't march, of course, not until the band had started, not until the lancers had moved off, reining in their chargers to stop them treading on the heels of the bandsmen, not until the soldiers of the flag party had started, facing to the front, eyes darting to the side of the road, looking out for sweethearts looking out for them and brig-ands and bashi-bazouks shambling along like a troop of monkeys, scratching themselves and baring their teeth at the crowds and breaking ranks and running about, though the Royal Fathers-in-Law on their shaggy ponies damned near broke their horse whips trying to keep them in line. No, the last of us could not move until the first of us was well under way, so I sat there on my great tall steeple-legged horse, striving to look grim and kingly, checking and rechecking that I had remembered to bring that special saddlebag while Sarah looked up at me from her landau, smiling from under her hat and blowing me little kisses and waving me secret waves with twiddles of her elegantly gloved fingers and trying to make me laugh until, at last, we were off.

But progress was slow. By God, progress was slow. I couldn't see why until I reached the end of the drive and joined the long, snaking parade out on the street and then, from up on my horse, I could see the man at the front of the queue, the bandmaster leading his band, but he was nothing like the one in Fiume, the man that Max had punched out for poking his camel.

This bloke was like no other bandmaster I ever saw. He wore a tall white hat and a long coat, trailing the ground as he walked, all covered in fancy frogging and open at the front so it flapped about as he went. He carried a big stick, like the rest of his tribe, but instead of marching like any sensible bandmaster would march, instead of a nice show-offish goosestep, he stood with his legs apart and rocked. One foot came up, the other stayed down and he swivelled on that heel and spun halfway to the right. Then he did the same thing with the other foot, and spun halfway to the left, walking along like a pair of open scissors so that, like a ship tacking in a headwind, he made progress by going off to one side and then off to the other, when any sensible person would just have gone straight ahead.

Still, nobody else seemed to mind, in fact the Albanoks lining the roadside would probably have been put out if he had chosen not to march like a lunatic, and I suppose it all added to the general gaiety of the occasion. It certainly slowed our stately progress, which was another bonus for the waiting Albanoks, since it gave them more time to gaze in awe and wonderment at me as I brought joy and sunshine into their otherwise dreary lives.

After all that had happened and everything we had been through, it was hard to remember we had been in the country for only a few hours, but that was long enough to bring the people into town in droves.

When we clattered through the streets together that morning the town seemed almost as dead as it was when we first arrived but, quite clearly, the wise old Albanoks had simply been lying late with their pretty wives, recovering from all the fun of the night before and getting ready for another day of fun to come. But now the shutters had been flung back and the windows opened. Now the streets were filled with bright, shiny, well-scrubbed Albanoks, old men who rejoiced to see their day of deliverance had come at last, apple-cheeked children screaming for joy and waving little paper flags they had coloured for themselves, proud fathers who knew they were standing in the dawn of a bright new day for their country. They cheered, they threw flowers, they sang songs I could not understand – the songs they had sung in whispers during the years of their bondage, songs which sustained them, songs they sang now as free men, songs of love, and I loved them back for the sake of those songs and I knew it would be nothing less than a joy to rule these people.

On and on we went, I don't know where, but by winding routes through the city so that everybody in the town could get a good look at us. Slowly, slowly we went, with the bandmaster waddling at the front of the procession and that strange, reedy, whining music trailing in ribbons around us all the way.

The procession took so long that any sensible person would have had their fill of us by the time we finally passed but, no, the Albanoks stood and cheered until the last of the lancers had gone by and then ran ahead to see us go by again, which was nice, but then I was so damned handsome and Sarah was so damned pretty it would have been nothing less than a criminal waste to stop looking at us. Also I suppose there were more than a few men in the crowd who had noticed Tifty and imagined themselves throwing sugar lumps down that magnificent cleavage. God knows I had. They cheered and they waved and I smiled with no more than a regal enthusiasm and waved back with my patented toffee-paper wave when, really, I wanted to get down off my horse and shake every one of them by the hand, kiss every girl in the crowd and say, 'Look at this! Can you believe it? I'm the king! I'm the King of the bloody Albanoks!'

It was a wonderful time. And then I noticed, at the side of the street, a tiny figure watching us, standing by the roadside to watch us pass, then running ahead to the front of the procession to watch again. There was nothing unusual about that. Lots of people were doing it, especially the children, and the strange watcher was hardly bigger than a child, but there was something about him, a bitter shadow that hung about him as he went. He did not cheer as the children cheered. He never waved a flag on a stick, never applauded. They jostled to get to the front of the pavement while he hung about at the back, peering out from behind the trees, darting his head away if I tried to catch his eye. But strangest of all, while the children were dressed in their Sunday best, sent out by their mothers to enjoy the sunshine, he was completely hidden under a long grey salt-stained sea-cloak and, just once, from under the hood, I was sure I caught a flash of magnificent tiger-red whiskers.

I pissed myself. There you are. I said you'd never believe the heroic parts unless I told you the cowardly parts too, and it doesn't get much more cowardly and pathetic than that.

It was the bombing that did it. It's started again. One of them landed right outside. That's a damned lie too. It wasn't right outside, it was the other side of the park, but I heard it coming, the damned thing screaming and howling all the way down. You never hear the one that gets you. Everybody knows that. It's something to do with the physics, the angle of flight or the speed of sound or something, I don't know, but everybody knows you don't hear the last one. Not that that was any comfort to me. I heard that whistling and I knew it was headed for me, straight down my throat, and I sat there, gripping on to the table, listening to it coming for half an hour, down and down and down until it burst, way over the other side of the park, and I pissed myself. It's very shaming, but there we are. Remember those trees I told you about before – the ones that were standing out in silhouette against the fires? They've gone now. The bomb took them and they are burning too, fizzing and popping in the dark. Nothing left but broken stumps with lumps of burning wood exploding out across the grass. I find it strangely reassuring. A stray bomb like that, it must mean I'm not the only one who's terrified. One of those pilots up there decided to get out quick, hit and run, never mind looking for the docks down there in the fires. He came just as close as he had to and no closer than honour demanded. Close enough would do. Dropped his bombs and turned round as fast as he could, that's what he did, and I don't blame him. One less tree to assist the war effort of the Reich and a planeful of young men who live another night – what's wrong with that?

Anyway, I am blessed that I have another pair of trousers. I've got no tea but I have got another pair of trousers. The others are in the sink now and I do not intend to do anything with them. I can't be bothered. I suppose they call this 'resignation'. A man who expected to be alive in the morning would wash his underwear, but I'm not resigned. I'm not. As old as I am, as feeble as I am, I'm not ready to die yet. I've proved that. A man who sees Death as a welcome friend does not piss his pants when the knock comes at the door.

We should talk of happier days, when I was rather more heroic and when Death was far enough away for me to face him with a smile on my lips and an iron bladder, secure in the knowledge that he had not yet put my name in his address book.

We were on our way to my coronation, remember, and the throng grew thicker as we went because those who had waited to see us close to the palazzo ran forward to join those who had waited a little further ahead. It would have been a wonderful day to be a burglar since the whole of the townspeople had left their houses empty and come to see me, but I suppose it was safe enough since almost all of Albania's crop of brigands was busy in my procession.

Still, Zogolli's careful organisation had certainly paid off. When we arrived at the great square in front of the church and the bandmaster, with his strange rocking gait, waddled right into the centre, his musicians found there was barely room to breathe. The crowd closed around them the moment they arrived, the way into the square was blocked and our little procession came to a halt. But Zogolli had put the lancers in second place and behind them the soldiers and the bashi-bazouks. Up ahead I could see the horses plunging through the crowd, opening a way, forcing them back, and the soldiers came behind, clearing a path, holding the line until, before too long, the crowd was pushed back to the edges of the square.

They took it well, like good citizens keen to help, but the noise was indescribable and the military band might as well have stood there miming for all they added to it.

Then the Rolls arrived in the square and pulled up beside the broad steps of the church. The chauffeur got out to hold open the door and the yelling got a little louder. This was something to see.

Something was happening.

Somebody was getting out.

'It's him! It's the king! I'm telling you, it's the king! The king!'

'No, not him.'

'Not him either.'

'This one, it must be this one. The king!'

'No, not him. I don't know who that is. He must be something in the government but I bet he's important because, look, he's waiting for the king.'

He was. They all were, Zogolli and his friends in their glum top hats, lined up on the steps to await my arrival; the lancers and the bashi-bazouks around the square, the flag party standing at attention, the fathers-in-law handing their ponies to waiting boys and taking their places on the steps, all of them standing there amidst a cacophony of bells, they were all waiting for the king, but still I did not come.

The first of the landaus reached the square, the horses nervous and jittery as the cheering grew wilder and more frantic. Each new arrival made the excitement of the crowd more intense – and it was now, definitely, a crowd. There were no men and women left in the square, no children, no families, there was just a crowd, one single, breathing, heaving beast with a single pulse, a single, hammering heartbeat and one throat to howl through. There was howling when the harem girls got down from their coach. There was howling when Aferdita, the last to leave, turned and waved at them, and they went absolutely crazy when Sarah's carriage arrived.

Imagine what it must have been like for those people,

living then, in that place, waking up from years of war and misery and finding yourself in the same town square as those three gorgeous creatures.

'Who are they?'

'Countesses.'

'From Austria.'

'Grand duchesses.'

'Princesses.'

'From Russia.'

'Actresses.'

'The mistresses of the king.'

'From Paris.'

They got down from their carriage, each one more lovely than the last, hidden from the crowd until they too mounted the steps. Mrs MacLeod in a stunning gown of black and white and a hat with half an aviary perched on it. Tifty in red velvet that lapped at her curves like flames round a heretic. She paused and bent to hook up the hem of her dress before climbing the stairs and the crowd howled – just as she knew they would.

And there was Sarah, who mounted the steps arm in arm with her blind father. Can you imagine how they roared? Uniforms, pageantry, music, flags, beauty, glamour, charm and sex and then, on top of all that, a touching, girlish devotion for a poor old cripple. We knew how to give them a show to remember and, by God, they got their money's worth.

From Bonn to Budapest, Spindelleger's Spectacular Equestrian Circus and Menagerie had never produced a show like this, and then, because we always saved the best for last, because we always gave them the very biggest of big finishes, it was my turn.

There was no surprise. They knew I was coming. They could see me coming. They were baying for me, '*Mbret! Mbret!* The king! The king!' Pointing and shouting, waving madly, tossing their hats up into the blue, blue sky and screaming, but if I could not surprise them, I could at least give them what they wanted and more – far more.

They expected me to walk my horse up to the steps, dismount and there to shake hands with Kemali, who had appeared from I know not where and who stood, small and grey and imperturbable, waiting to welcome me. I did that. Of course I did that, but before I did that I put my heels to my horse's flanks and I rode. By God, that was a fiery beast. It was as if, all through that long, tedious walk around the city, with the flags flying and the drums beating, he had simply been waiting for a sign from me and then, when it came, he set back his ears, flared his nostrils, rolled his eyes and took off as if all the devils of hell were on his tail.

Of course there were no devils behind us, but Max and Arbuthnot were there, and behind them half a squadron of lancers, all a-glitter. How could they abandon me? When I rode they rode, and I galloped round the town square like a comet trailing a great fiery tail of horsemen, hardly slowing for the corners as the mothers in front screamed in terror and snatched up their children and the fathers behind yelled for the joy of it. Once around the square, one hand raised in salute to my people, hailing them, reaching out to them as they were reaching out to me, to touch as a father touches his children, back to where Kemali stood on the steps, slowly shaking his head as he would over a wild, reckless son who made him very, very proud, back to where Sarah was standing, hands clapped across her mouth with excitement, eyes sparkling with delight, back to where the soldiers of the flag party were standing at attention, facing the front, eyes swivelling to catch a glimpse of their king.

I pulled back on the reins. My horse slowed, just by a fraction. I leaned out of my saddle. I leaned out and forward and to the right, my arm extended, my hand open, and there was the colour sergeant of the flag party, a great silver-headed bear of a man, a man sworn to defend that flag against each and any and all, though it be with his life. He turned. He saw me riding right at him. We looked into one another's eyes. He knew at once what I meant to do and he knew that flag would be safe with me. He held it up. He held it up to me in two hands and I snatched it from him as I rode past. I swear to God my stirrup must have brushed the tip of his nose but he never flinched. He stood there like a rock, proudly at attention as I cantered round the square for a second time, my arm held out straight and level, the flag streaming out behind me as I rode, passing over the people like a blessing.

I had done enough. Leave them wanting more, that's what we always say.

The colour sergeant was waiting where I left him. I leaned down, handed him back his flag and clapped him on the shoulder by way of thanks and then, finally, I dismounted.

Kemali came down the steps to greet me, doffing his hat as he approached. He shook me by the hand and said, 'Very good, Your Majesty, very good. Will there be any further theatrics, or can we get on with the coronation now?'

Naturally I was as eager as the next man to be crowned, but I wasn't quite ready to stop showing off.

'Indulge me just a little further, Prime Minister,' I said. I took down my saddlebags and, with Kemali at my side, I walked out into the square and found a boy, a handsome little dark-haired chap he was, about ten years old, and I gave him my bag. I remember how he watched me coming towards him, wonderment growing in his face and, when at last the Magnificence was directly before him, he reached for his mother's hand but still found the courage to meet my eye.

'Hello, son,' I said.

'Hello, son,' said Kemali.

'I need somebody to carry this bag for me. Do you think you can help?'

Kemali said the boy was sure he could help.

'But what does your mother think?' I turned my kingly gaze on her. 'Madam, would you be willing to allow your son to come and help his king?'

Madam was more than willing. Madam was beside herself

with tearful delight. Madam called down all the blessings of heaven on my head, wailed into a handkerchief flung across her face, scrubbed that same handkerchief over the boy's chin and shooed him away with a lot of sniffles and 'Be good's and 'Do as you're told's, which I did not need Kemali to translate.

We walked back across the square, Kemali and me, the boy marching poker-straight beside us as the people screamed with delight.

Kemali said, 'It seems to me you have one more surprise in store, Majesty.'

'Oh, at least one, my friend. In fact, I hope to surprise you regularly from now on.'

'Try not to be too surprising, Majesty. Stability is a good thing in governments. Respect for tradition. My advice is to avoid novelty, eschew anything that smacks of innovation, despise the daring.'

'But, Kemali, if you had followed your own advice, my proud little kingdom would still be under the heel of the monstrous Turk. I am all for tradition – in fact, I think we should make it traditional for all the kings that come after me to parade the flag around the square. What do you think? On the other hand, "daring" is my middle name. For example, I was considering whether I might not insist on having my entire government dress in pink. I have some very interesting ideas for uniforms. Very novel. Very innovative.'

The old fox refused to take the bait. 'Majesty,' he said, 'it is a narrow tightrope to walk, but there is a clear difference between the daring and the downright eccentric.'

We reached the top of the stairs and the doorway of the church.

'Turn and wave to your people,' said Kemali. 'The next time they see you, you will be crowned.'

I turned. I waved. Max and Arbuthnot stood aside so as not to block the view. The people cheered. It was almost embarrassingly easy to make them do it, as if we were dancers, following practised steps, as if we were performers going through a routine. I waved, they yelled. We went into the church.

'Come this way,' said Kemali. 'Those waiting on the stairs will make their own arrangements.'

I obeyed as meekly as a king can and he led me into a dirty little room with a table and some chairs and a lot of discarded boxes.

'Why are we here?' I said.

'To prepare. To make ready. Mostly to wait while everyone else finds a place to sit. Have you ever been in a church before, Majesty?'

'Yes. Once or twice. A few times. When I was in Germany.' Which was true. There was the time I got christened and a few times afterwards, weddings and funerals, stuff like that.

'No doubt Your Majesty's quick mind is asking the vital question: why is this ceremony taking place in a Christian church?'

'I was about to raise that very matter.'

'There are very few churches left. The Christians were all but destroyed and driven out of Albania. They survived

315

wars and invasions, the fall of the Byzantine Empire, persecutions of one kind and another, but the firman of your ancestor, demanding compulsory military service of all their young men, proved to be a convincing argument for conversion to the faith of the Prophet. History has not been kind to the Albanians but, to those Albanians, most unkind of all.

'Yet it is the most fervent wish of your government, Majesty, that there should be no Christians in Albania tomorrow and no Mussulmans either. Only Albanians. Christians too are your subjects. They too are Albanians. And Skanderbeg is theirs. The crown itself is theirs. The very act of crowning is a Christian one, and rather than take it from them, we have chosen to give it back to them – with a few little additions. Yes, they are infidels, but endure this little humiliation, Majesty, for the sake of all the greater humiliations they have suffered. Bear this and help to make one nation.'

There was a kind of grandeur in what that fine old man was saying. He wanted Albania to be the best country it could be, just the way that I wanted to be the best of kings. Imagine living in a country where nobody cared what religion you were, where patriotism and brotherhood were enough, where you had no need to prove how much you could hate your neighbours in order to prove how much you loved your country. It was a good and high ambition.

'More than happy to help,' I said. 'Do you think we could get started?'

My voice seemed suddenly very loud because, just at that

instant, the clamour of the bells ceased as if their music had been pouring out of a tap that somebody simply turned off, leaving in its place that same empty, expectant echo I heard when the Companions stopped singing.

Kemali raised a finger as if to emphasise the quiet. There was nothing to hear now but the sighing roar of the crowd, like the sound you hear as you walk towards a faraway beach, before you reach the crest of the dunes. 'I think that means we are ready to begin,' he said.

There was a knock at the door. Arbuthnot opened it and revealed a bearded priest dressed in fabulous golden robes, a boy acolyte at his side. The man rushed into the room and knelt to kiss my hand, tears in his eyes. I almost had to drag him to his feet again as he raved and babbled at me.

Kemali said, 'He wishes me to convey the joy he feels that he is in the presence of the King, the Heaven-Blessed, the Protector of Nations, Defender of the Poor and of the Oppressed. There is a good deal more, and he has obviously rehearsed for some time.'

I took the priest by the shoulders and I looked him full in the face. 'Tell him,' I said, 'that the king is a man, like him and, like him, the servant of God and the slave of death.'

He seemed to like that and he dried his tears and smoothed down his enormous black beard with thick fingers.

'Now can we go?' I said.

'We can go,' said Kemali.

The gilded priest, with many pleas for forgiveness and humble apologies for the audacity of his intrusion and much deep bowing, formed us up into a line and led the way back into the church.

Do you remember what I told you about the bomb in the afternoon and the way I felt it growl and rumble in my chest, how it gripped my heart and shook my lungs against my ribs? My coronation was like that. I felt it in my bones as much as I saw it through my eyes.

I'm not a coward – you know I'm not – but I don't mind telling you the blood was pounding in my ears as we stood there with the doors of the church closed against us.

And the chanting started: deep, treacle-coloured singing like the slow, rolling, grinding music of a turning mill. Imagine standing under the trees of a forest when a storm is coming, when every bough is shaking and trembling, when every tree is whispering a different note and every whisper joins to become a shout that you can hear for miles, when every leaf is singing a different colour, when every sound is a motion, when you can hear every movement and see the music of it passing overhead, the way that Adam and Eve saw God passing through the garden. That's what we heard from the other side of the door – the sound of bearded priests booming like bassoons.

Then the doors swung open and the sound of the singing washed over us in waves.

The golden priest stepped forward, leading us into a darkly shadowed interior, but as I entered they began to light candles as if the arrival of the king had brought a new dawn. A tiny pinprick of yellow light appeared at the far end of the church; it dipped in the shadows and then there were two, then four, then more and more, passing from hand to hand, each lighting a candle for his neighbour until light filled the church like a rising tide. The place was packed with Albanoks jammed in like sardines, elegant ladies in fabulous hats, husbands who proudly bankrupted themselves to pay the haberdashery bills, the finest families in the city, the politicians, the clan chiefs, the officers, the brigands and the bashi-bazouks, each of them holding a leaping candle, each of them turning to let its light fall on me. The glow filled the church, reaching up to the icons of sad-eyed saints painted on every column, on every tiny bit of wall up and up until they disappeared into the shadows under the roof.

The chanting rolled on and, from the very heart of the crowd, two huge chandeliers began to rise on chains towards the roof, like a slow explosion of light, like great, bronze balloons creeping upwards, little by little, until every glorious, glowing, painted, gilded inch of those columns was on show and there, in the roof, was the face of Christ, looking down at me like a dreadful reproach. I couldn't look him in the eye, and luckily I was too busy getting crowned to wrestle with my conscience just then.

The priest's boy took Max and Arbuthnot and Kemali off to one side, but the boy with the saddlebags refused to leave me. He had his instructions – to stand by my side – and he would obey them like a dog, but I patted him on the shoulder and sent him away with the others so I stood alone, surrounded by priests and acolytes.

My bodyguard of priests closed ranks and shuffled me forward, down to the front of the church, where my throne was standing in front of a wall of icons and, most surprising of all, where Kemali was waiting with a clutch of bearded Mussulmans. I have no idea who those people were. It might have been the Grand Mufti; it could have been Ali Baba and his Forty Thieves – I didn't know then and I don't know now – but I was delivered into their tender care for one of those 'little additions' Kemali had explained about.

The priests fell back, the fathers-in-law surrounded me, one grasping each hand, one supporting each elbow, one pushing me along from behind, and they frogmarched me to a wooden stand heaped with fancy carpets where I was made to pose, like a prize boar on market day.

There were some magical passes of the hands and some no-doubt-very-sacred mumblings which Kemali hastily translated, but I couldn't hear a word of it for the Red Indian whoops of the harem girls, a howling and a shrieking such as I have never heard since – well, not until that bomb came down across the park.

The fathers-in-law silenced their daughters with scowls and threatened backhanders, then they took me by the wrists and raised my arms high.

'Keep your hands raised to heaven,' said Kemali and, like a good and obedient king, I did.

The Mussulman clerics approached and wrapped me round the waist with a scarlet sash and a sword belt of white leather, which they buckled into place.

'Keep your hands high,' said Kemali, so I did, and then another set of Mussulmans arrived, this time bearing a sword with a gorgeously jewelled handle in a scabbard which, if it was not gold, was very highly polished brass.

They jabbered at me in their outlandish tongue and Kemali said, 'By this sword you are invested as the Great King of the Albanian people, from the sea to the mountains, their master and their lord, their keeper and protector, upholder of justice, chosen of God, we acknowledge your reign. For goodness sake put your arms down.'

The fathers-in-law signalled, 'Now you can scream,' and, as Aferdita and the girls set up their howling again, I discovered why I was made to stand on that fancy step. One after another the menfolk began to fall on their faces, taking turns to come and touch my shiny boots – the clan chiefs, the captains of the brigands, the officers of bashi-bazouks, they all bowed to acknowledge me as lord. It was quite a chest-puffing moment, but it went on for a bit and then it just got to be embarrassing. I have that much to say in my own defence. There are some – and I don't think we need to mention any names here – who could never tire of people slobbering on their boots. There are certain political figures who would be quite content to have the whole world form an orderly queue and file past for a bit of vigorous boot-licking, with occasional breaks for meals, cigarettes and the usual necessaries. There are some who would take that sort of thing as their right, but I am not one of them and, if truth be told, I found the whole thing a bit awkward and uncomfortable, but it was beyond my power to stop it. I could hardly let one hetman grovel and then forbid the next. Come one, come all. No, I just had to stand there until they had their fill until, at last, even my ministers, even Zogolli and, last of all, good, kind, wise, loyal Kemali took their turn to bow the knee. That was too much to bear. I got down off my step and helped the old man to his feet.

'Most kind,' he said, 'most kind, Majesty. But we are not done with you yet.'

Kemali backed away, bowing respectfully, revealing at his back a wall of grim-faced, golden-robed priests. I stood up straight to face them, as a man would face his firing squad, and then, after a moment of silence, the chanting began again, rolling like waves, boiling like clouds, rising and falling, singing songs about God alone knows what.

Four of them broke out from the crowd, including the man with the biggest beard I ever saw, a thundercloud of a beard that exploded from his chin down to his chest and up to where his bristling eyebrows were crowded down by the weight of his golden hat. They never stopped booming and singing, not even for a moment, as they processed around me. And as they went they wrapped me about in a fine blue shawl which hung around my shoulders. The man with the gigantic beard produced a thing like a big nappy pin and fixed the two sides of the shawl shut over my breast and he began to mumble music at me again.

Kemali said, 'Say "I do"'

'*Une nuk*,' I said.

And then there was more chanting and more mumbling before the gilded priests grabbed hold of my shawl – one to each corner – and took me off on a grand circuit of the church. I was guided along as if with my head sticking out from the top of a tent, two priests on either hand, Archbishop Big Beard strolling along in front, swinging a censer on a chain, trailing clouds of perfumed smoke as we went and with a regiment of clergymen coming along in convoy and singing as they came.

Wherever we passed there was a furious storm of crossings. Men and women – and by God there were some damned pretty women – bowing their heads as we went by and marking lips and breasts with the sign of the cross; honest, upright, respectable Mussulmans who had never given a thought to such heresy before, joining in with their neighbours because it was the thing to do, because their neighbours were doing it and it was suddenly the fashion.

And we know how that goes, don't we, you and I? We know where that sort of thing ends up. We know what happens when dearly held beliefs are put aside because everybody else is doing it. We know what happens when it's suddenly all right to steal because everybody else is stealing, when it's all right to throw stones through windows because everybody else is, when it's all right to be a bully, when it's all right to say nothing because nobody else is saying anything. You know where that ends up? You know where that ends up. It ends up with an old man blown to bits in a shitty little tin caravan.

Forgive me. I got carried away, but it's passed off now. I went for a walk, or at any rate I stood up from the table and stamped up and down the length of this caravan for a bit. I might have gone further, I suppose, if I had dared to go outside, but I lacked the courage. I am too afraid to open my door in case the bombs get me, so I stay here, inside my caravan, where I am safe from bombs. It's nonsense. It's madness. It's as stupid as blaming those good people in that church all those years ago for the bombs that are falling on me now. I went to make a cup of tea but I forgot I haven't any tea. Forgive me. I have come to mistrust crowds, that's all. It's all right now. As I recall, I was telling you how the priests dragged me round the church in my tent of a shawl.

Round the church we went, everybody turning in their places as we passed, the way that daisies turn to the sun, only I was the daisy and a thousand tiny candle-suns were turning towards me.

The priests led me back to my throne and began a new bout of chanting. To tell the truth, it was boring. I had no idea what to do or even what I was supposed to be thinking while all this singing was going on. I tried to think high-minded thoughts. I strove to prepare the inner man for the awesome duty I was about to undertake. More than anything else, I struggled to keep a straight face. My eyes found Sarah standing near the front of the crowd, her weight on one foot, the other leg a little to one side so she stood like a capital R with that curve sweeping down to her heel. Do you remember what we used to say about 'a prettily turned ankle'? In the old days that was just about all there was to see and, although I'd seen all the rest, seeing that gorgeous, swan-neck curve was as good as seeing her naked again. And there was Tifty, standing near her, glowing in that daring dress. Mrs MacLeod, I knew, would be close by, too short to spot in the crush, but I could see Max, looking solemn, and Arbuthnot looking the same as he always did. He never changed, that man.

I turned my kingly gaze on each of them in turn, as if my private thoughts could reach them, but my eyes lingered on Sarah and stayed there. That dress. That hat. Those eyes. The candlelight falling on her face. The tiny, locked world of the railway-carriage sleeping car. The taste of her. The smell of her. The warmth of her. I was so deep in love with that girl and I wanted it to show in my face. I wanted her to look in my eyes and see herself reflected there and know that I loved her. She did. I hope that she did. I know she did because I saw it in her eyes when she looked back at me and, more than that, I saw it in Tifty's eyes, saying, 'Goodbye.'

The priest-song halted for a moment.

'Say, "*Une nuk*,"' said Kemali.

So I did, and in exchange the priests gave me a sceptre to hold and then we had another procession all the way round the church and back to the throne for some more singing.

'Say, "*Une nuk*,"' said Kemali, when they reached another break in proceedings, and then they gave me a golden orb to hold. Off we went round the church again, only this time we stopped in front of the great wall of icons, pictures of Christ and his mother, pictures of this saint and that saint, endless rows of them, with their long beards and their sheep's eyes. Each of them had to be asked for a special blessing. Each of them had to be saluted by name.

'Bow when they bow,' said Kemali, so I stood there in my little tent shawl, with my orb and my sceptre and, when the priests bowed, I bowed and we all got on very well. There was another age of bowing and picture kissing before we went back to the throne for another sing, but this time when they all fell silent and Kemali said, 'Say . . .' I beat him to it and said, '*Une nuk*.' I never had any problems with learning my cues.

The priests surrounding me let go of my little shawl, took a few steps back and returned with an enormous red cape that any self-respecting cardinal would have dismissed as a bit ostentatious. There was so much gold embroidery stitched into it that I reckon the damned thing could probably have stood up by itself. It was absolutely rigid, like a suit of armour. God knows how many poor little nuns must have bled their fingers white in stitching it, and when they put it round my shoulder and buckled it up across my throat it felt like somebody had emptied a sack of coal into my pockets.

Luckily I still had my pageboy priests with me and they gathered round and helped me bear the load as we set off for another tour of the church, but this time, thank God, when we got back to the throne, they let me sit down.

The singing stopped. I was sitting bolt upright in my seat with my orb in one hand, secretly resting on my knee, and my sceptre crossed over my chest and sort of leaning, just a little bit, on my shoulder, because the damned thing was starting to get heavy, and the whole place was absolutely dead silent. The whole place was holding its breath. There was a window open. I remember the cry of a blackbird that sounded out like a fire alarm and I remember the sweat, a tiny trickle of sweat, running down between my shoulder blades and the heat and the weight of that cape and I realised that it was my turn to say something and I took a big breath, ready to shout, '*Une nuk*,' in my kingliest voice, but Kemali held a finger up to his lips, so I sat there, very still instead, saying nothing at all.

Silence. Absolute silence. Then four priests came in a squadron, each one carrying a pole and, stretched between the poles, corner to corner, a sheet of cloth, like a portable roof with a tasselled fringe. They stood around me so the sheet was above my head, and then Archbishop Big Beard reached into his sleeve and produced a cut-crystal perfume bottle. He stood close to me. The priests lowered their poles. They came closer to the throne. They let the cloth sag. It fell in folds around us, hiding us in a tiny private world, a big top where we were the only performers. But that's not right. It's not respectful enough. It wasn't a big top, it was a little sanctuary, a holy place in the middle of that holy place, where holy things were done, things so holy that they could not be looked on – not by anyone.

That fat old man, with his bristling beard, was standing so close to me I could smell his breakfast and, when he pulled the stopper off his perfume bottle, I swear to you it rattled in his trembling fingers as if he was handling nitro-glycerine. He tipped a tiny flood of oil into his hand and dabbed it on my head with many murmurings. I felt it, cool and wet, in my hair, running down on to my scalp, trickling over my head, and I knew enough to know what it meant. It was more than a crown. It was the blessing and authority of God.

The priest wiped his hands across my ears and over my eyes and, last of all, with more garlic-sausage whispered prayers, he touched my mouth and then the moment was over. He straightened himself under our private little tent, and the pole carriers took that as their sign to lift the canopy high again.

I wonder if the anointing left me changed. I wonder if I was different to look at. Certainly I felt different and they looked at me differently – even Sarah, who put her ankle away and stood up straight and looked at me solemnly and then turned her face away and looked at the floor. Fool that I was, I liked that. The singing started again.

330

The canopy was back in place over my head. The priest handed his bottle to an acolyte, backed away from the throne and vanished through a door in the middle of the wall of icons. I couldn't see where he had gone, but I knew why he had gone and, when he came back carrying the crown, the music burst like a thundercloud.

Don't forget, those hundreds of people inside that church had never seen the crown before. Kemali and Zogolli had seen it. They imagined it, or rebuilt it or something, and I'd tried the damn thing on for God's sake, but the people had been waiting for it to arrive the way that children wait for Christmas and far, far more than they had been waiting for me. When I arrived in the church they were all suitably respectful and properly excited, but nobody gasped, nobody stood there with their hands clamped over their mouths the way they did when they saw the crown. Nobody burst into tears for me.

The priests sang. The people sang back. The priests sang. The people sang back and slowly, slowly, the priest with the big beard drew closer to the throne, bearing the crown before him, carrying it with his hands folded inside his sleeves like a thing red-hot from a furnace.

He reached out to me. The priests holding the canopy stretched out their free hands towards him until, when he stood over me, all four of them were touching him, as if to say that they were crowning me too. The crown was close. Closer. Closer. The crown was poised over my head. I could feel the electric crackle of it. I wanted to sit staring to the front, dignified and imperious, and I tried, but I'm only flesh and blood and I know that my eyes flickered upwards once or twice, just to see what was going on, and then there was nothing at all to see. My vision was filled by a theatre curtain of golden robes and then the priest stepped away and I knew it had happened and I could feel the crown on my head and I knew that I was the king and all the other priests stepped away and the people could see me – me and the crown together – and they went crazy with their God Save the Kinging.

Well, we had to have another parade after that, all the way round the church again and back to the throne so I could sit to receive the homage of my people, one after another, kneeling to kiss my hand, and when that was done at last, Kemali said, 'Now, Majesty, we must leave. It is time for the people to see their crowned king.'

'A moment, Kemali, I have business to conduct.'

'Another of your little surprises, Majesty?'

'I promise this is the last. I need you to translate.'

I stood up on the steps of the throne, but I had to put down the orb and sceptre and that damned cloak was so bloody heavy, so I shucked that off and laid the whole lot on the seat, and then, when I looked a bit more ordinary, except for my fancy new sword belt and my fancy new hat, I beckoned the boy with the saddlebags towards me.

I said, 'Citizens of the free and independent kingdom of Albania,' and Kemali translated.

'As your king, We pledge to you in full and equal measure the love and loyalty you have pledged to Us this day.' I might easily have said 'today', but 'this day' sounded much,

much grander and it produced the applause I had hoped for.

'First, We are happy to announce that the vile and craven Serbs have crumbled before the mere threat of war. Earlier this morning they informed our government that they have capitulated and will accede to all reasonable demands. Such is the terrifying might of the free and independent kingdom of Albania. Your strong sons will not be required of you. The national honour is restored. There will be no war.'

God knows they were happy enough when I told them we were going to crack heads together but, when I told them we'd already won and there would be no fighting after all, well, they just went crazy with delight. Kemali merely raised an eyebrow.

'Secondly, from this day, We make a solemn and binding covenant with you, Our people. We promise that your tongue, the language of the Albanian people, shall be Our language and the language of Our court and government.'

Wild applause.

'And, as a sign of Our especial favour, we wish to make certain gifts and grants. Whereas the heads of some of the nation's most ancient and noble families have done Us the great honour of presenting their daughters to Us, these ladies are to be assured of the lasting love and regard of the Crown, honoured henceforth as Sisters of the King and sent home . . .' the Royal Fathers-in-Law scowled and reached for where their pistols should have been, had they not been removed at the door, 'sent home heavy with Our favour and each endowed with twenty thousand leks from Our private Treasury that they may secure good marriages.'

The fathers-in-law put down their imaginary pistols, grinned their broken-toothed grins and clapped like crazy.

When the applause had died down again I went on: 'No king can rule without the good counsel of trusted friends. Therefore, We have chosen this day to found and institute a new order of knighthood open to the closest advisers to the throne, to those who stand as close as brothers to the king and only a little below him in honour, to those who are sworn to serve Us personally and with loyalty.

'The members of this new Order of Skanderbeg –' by God they loved that and clapped until their hands were bruised – 'will be charged with the sacred duty of speaking the truth to the king; they will be assured of access to Our Person at all times and granted the right to dine at Our table.' No more sitting alone in a swanky dining room for me.

The applause went on and on until I had to hold my hands up for a bit of quiet. When I said, 'The first Knight of Skanderbeg,' those Albanoks had no idea what I was taking about, but they understood me well enough when I called the name of 'Ismail Kemali.'

The grand old man, God bless him, was slow to answer my beckoning, but the cheers and the shouting went on and at last Zogolli and the fattest father-in-law dragged him forward.

I reached into my saddlebag and brought out a scarlet curtain tie. 'Will you swear your loyalty to me, as King of

Albania, while you live? Do you promise to give true counsel when most needed, upon your honour as a Knight of Skanderbeg?'

Good Kemali said, 'I do.'

'Say "*Une nuk*,"' I said.

'*Une nuk*.'

I laid the curtain tie across his shoulder, only now of course it wasn't a curtain tie, it was the insignia of the Order of Skanderbeg, and every man in that huge crowd wanted a curtain tie across his shoulder as Kemali had one across his.

Sadly I had only twelve curtain ties in my saddlebag: one for Kemali, five for the jilted fathers-in-law, one for Zogolli, who wept hot salt tears and repeated every word of his oath before giving me his 'une nuk'. His eyes filled with tears and his big carrot nose filled with snot while he snivelled his loyalty as if I had done something for him, as if I had paid him some special service when, if only he had noticed, Kemali had loved him like a father for years. But Kemali was not God's anointed. Kemali had no crown, and it's the crown that makes the difference.

Eventually, in spite of his lovesick slobbering, I managed to shake him from my hands and the boy stepped forward, holding up his bag so I could choose another curtain tie. Only twelve curtain ties, and seven of them gone already.

I called out 'Sir Max Schlepsig, Knight of Skanderbeg,' and my mate Max came forward, looking like an embarrassed bear.

'Me, Otto? A knight? You sure?'

335

'Can't think of anybody better. You might not be a nobleman, Max, but you've always been a noble man.'

'That's kind of you to say, but I'm more used to swallowing swords than carrying one round on my hip.'

I leaned in close and whispered, 'Shut up, Max. The world's on its head. If I can be king, then you can damned sure be a knight. Now, do you promise to be loyal and always to tell me the truth?'

'Always have,' he said, which was true. Asking Max to be loyal and true was like asking the ocean to be wet and salty.

I threw the cloth across his shoulders. 'You're in,' I said. Then I called for 'The Captain of the Royal Guard,' and Arbuthnot, looking as delighted as a man like Arbuthnot could ever look, fell to his knees and kissed my fingertips.

'What a hoot,' he said. 'I wonder what they'll make of this back home. I'd rather have this than the Garter.' I remember that's exactly what he said, although to this very day and hour I have no idea what he meant by it.

Next I called for 'The Countess Tifty Gourdas, Dame of the Order of Skanderbeg,' which sent a ripple round the church. I don't know if the Albanoks were prepared for the idea of ladies close to the throne, but when they saw her walk to the steps they probably changed their minds, and when they saw her curtsy they were utterly convinced, because by God that woman could curtsy, and if I let my hand linger just a little longer than needful when I laid the sash of the order across that magnificent bosom, it was only by way of a fond farewell, that was all.

336

And then Sarah. My Sarah. It had to be Sarah. The tenth curtain tie was hers. I announced, 'The Most Serene Lady, Sarah von Mesmer, Dame of the Order of Skanderbeg,' and, I swear to God, that whole church sighed when they saw her mount the steps of the throne. Remember that crowd? Remember them all pressed in together, with Sarah at the front? She came up out from them, like Venus coming up out of the waves, and they sighed like the waves as she passed.

All except one. All except her father.

While everybody was watching Sarah, I was watching him hold on to her as she tried to come to me, clinging to her until she was too far to touch, clawing at the empty air where her scent hung, even as she turned and promised him, 'I'll be back, Daddy,' pounding his cane into the pavement in fury, glaring at me with his black, dead eyes.

There she was, standing in front of me, so small and perfect, like a flower that suddenly appears where nobody ever planted flowers before.

'Hello, Otto,' she said.

'Hello, Sarah. You look nice.'

'So do you.'

'Would you like to be a Lady of Skanderbeg?'

'I think that sounds lovely, Otto. Thank you very much.'

'And do you promise to love me?'

'Always and forever.'

'And do you promise to roll about in that big bed with me for hours at a time and always on a Saturday morning?'

'Do all the Knights of Skanderbeg have to promise that, Otto?'

'Only you, my love.'

'Only me?'

'Always only you.'

'In that case, I promise.'

'And do you promise to tell me the truth?'

'Most of the time.'

'Fair enough. You're in.'

Thank God that Kemali had stopped translating long before it was time to lay the sash across her shoulder, but when the boy held up his bag and I reached in to take one out, I saw at once that there was just one left. It was another of those dreadful 'forgotten-to-do-your-homework' moments and the urge to scrabble about in the bottom of the bag was almost overpowering. Kemali, Zogolli, Max, Arbuthnot, Tifty and the five fathers-in-law. Sarah was not the tenth knight, she was the eleventh and I had only one curtain tie left, and there was Mrs MacLeod, with that gorgeous frozen aviary on her head, smoothing her dress down, smiling her wicked smile, sinuous as a vine, fluid as flame, ready to step forward to receive the honours that were her due.

'The last place in the Order of Skanderbeg . . .'

The pretty little toe of Mrs MacLeod's pretty little shoe peeped out from behind the hem of her dress.

'. . . will be filled by my most worthy vizier.'

The smile on Mrs MacLeod's face folded its wings and died, like a pheasant in flight. Her little toe disappeared again and she turned to Professor Alberto, urging him forward with chilly whispers.

He would not budge. She pushed, angrily, at his elbow. He did not move.

Sarah went down to him and took his hand, but he said something to her and she let him walk alone, with a few shallow sweeps of the cane, to the foot of the steps.

The place was hushed – as quiet as it had been at the moment of my crowning – and somehow the people seemed to realise that this new Knight of Skanderbeg was a little more important than the others.

'Do you promise to be loyal?'

He turned those terrible, shining spectacles on me again, those black sheets of glass, like the opposite of searchlights. 'I solemnly promise and swear my loyalty to you, my king.'

'And do you promise to tell the truth and always to offer sound counsel to your sovereign?'

'I do.'

I laid a curtain tie across his shoulder. 'Hail, Knight of Skanderbeg.'

That was when the explosions started.

You probably don't give a damn about explosions. Not any more. The whole town is on fire. There are explosions everywhere. The world is ablaze. Explosions are ordinary. Look out the window. Except if you are reading this, I probably don't have a window. Or a roof. Or walls. Explosions are a cliché. The bombs are falling over there in the dark and, when they land, it's nothing. It's a burst pillow and a shower of feathers. A lot of noise. A flash and a bang. Explosions are nothing.

But those explosions were not nothing. Not for the people at my coronation. They were like us. They had heard explosions before, remember. They knew what war was. But they thought it was over. More than that, they thought they had won. Hadn't I told them we'd won without so much as a shot fired? Not that we were about to win, not like that shit we hear on the wireless every day about how a new army of little boys and grandfathers is going to sweep the Bolshevik hordes back on to the steppes or some unstoppable super-weapon is to be unleashed on the unsuspecting Allies and knock them from the skies of the Fatherland.

None of that. No ifs, no buts, no maybes, I told them we'd won, and yet the sky was full of booms and bangs, just like our sky is full of American aeroplanes.

I told them we had won and there would be no more war, no more bombs and bullets to break their windows and rattle their chimney pots, and half an hour later it all started again.

There was just a moment after the first blast when the people inside that church stood and wondered what was happening. I looked up from laying a curtain tie across the Professor's shoulder; I looked up and I looked into the crowd and I saw the fear on their faces.

Imagine a man who has a tooth pulled. Imagine the agony of that, the pincers gripping the rotten tooth, the jaw wrenched this way and that, the fiery hot, screaming pain of it, the crunching, grinding noise, like a train wreck inside your head as it comes out by the root, torn out of living bone. But the agony reaches a crescendo, the tooth comes out like a cork from a bottle and the pain is past, an unpleasant memory, that's all. And then the dentist says, 'Now for the other one.'

That's the look I saw on their faces and, if they had any doubts that the toothache had come back, the second bomb settled the matter. From the same open window that let in the blackbird song, we heard it falling from the sky and screaming as it fell.

They knew what it meant and they were ready to run. All they needed was somebody to tell them what to do, somebody who could say it was all right to break out of the formal dignity of the coronation and run away, weeping and screaming, or somebody who could tell them to do the other thing, to stand steady, to leave in good order, return to their homes, put their wives and children safely in the cellar, arm themselves and return to defend the nation. All they needed was a leader, a proper leader and, because I was their king, the poor bastards looked to me to tell them what to do. I stood there like a stunned ox as they looked at me, as the priests and the acolytes looked at me, as Kemali and Zogolli looked at me, as every single one of my loyal subjects looked at me, as Max and Sarah and all the Knights of Skanderbeg looked at me, down to the last, who turned his black eyes on me in glittering triumph and I said nothing. Absolutely nothing. I stood there with that crown on my head like an upturned bucket while my whiskers sagged and drooped and I said nothing. I said nothing because there was nothing to say. I said nothing because I knew I had been found out. I was exposed as a fake, like a conjurer when his rabbit sticks its ears out of a secret pocket and all the little boys in the theatre point and shout. So I said nothing and, when the third bomb fell and they all began to move and heave, like fish in a net, when panic was hanging over them with all the weight of a summer thundercloud about to break, when they were ready to start trampling over other people's children and their own grand-mothers in a rush for the doors, the voice they heard was not mine.

That third bomb fell, and in the silence that came after – as if that wasn't nightmare enough – I heard that mad sing-song voice again: 'One, two three! That sounds like my cue!'

All around the walls men were emerging from the crowd and throwing back their cloaks or dumping heavy coats to reveal naval uniforms – and rifles.

One of the golden priests caught a rifle butt across the shoulder as they herded him into the middle of the church. There were angry gasps and a scream or two and a couple of courageous Albanoks went to help him and things were looking as if they might get pretty ugly when the crowd parted and that little shit Varga came walking towards me, carroty whiskers blazing, a salt-stained sea-cloak flung back off his shoulders and a pistol in his hand.

'Varga,' I said, 'great to see you. We hoped you were dead.'

'Shut up, you fraud.' He walked slowly up the church, pausing at every step to strike threatening poses and jam his pistol up somebody's nose until at last he reached the steps of the throne and it was my turn. 'Shift, camel boy. Stand there.'

I went down the steps, Varga went up and he began to address the crowd. 'People of Albania, I imagine that for the most part you are too ignorant and stupid to understand a word that I am saying. However, I am relying on the fact that, even in this backward and barbarous country, one or two of you must have been to school. You can pass the word to your stupider countrymen.'

Nothing happened so Varga waved his pistol around a bit. 'Well, go on then!'

Here and there in the crowd, men began whispering to their wives, who began whispering to their neighbours. Word spread. They were not happy. Varga seemed satisfied.

'Stupid Albanians,' he said, 'it is my unpleasant – but delicious – duty to inform you that this man –' he pointed down at me – 'is not a king.'

He waited a moment for the news to spread. 'I met him a few days ago when he presented himself to me as the Graf von Mucklenberg, Keeper of the Camels to the Emperor of Austria. Feel free to translate, darlings.'

I felt my ears redden as the whispers burned around the church.

'And a few days later, after an act of gross piracy when he stole my lovely, lovely yacht, he presented himself to you as the Turkish prince Halim Eddine.' Varga spoke slowly so the translation, in all its awfulness, could sink in.

'In fact, he is neither of these people. In fact He is Otto Witte, a circus performer of some small note, wanted by the police in connection with the theft of a cash box and a camel.'

The whispers turned into gasps. I knew that Kemali was standing behind me somewhere, but I couldn't look at him. I kept my face to the front. Those hundreds of sad eyes were easier to endure.

'Consequently,' said Varga, 'we won't be needing this any more,' and he reached out from his place at the top of the steps, gripped the golden horns of the golden goat on top of the crown of Skanderbeg and lifted it from my head.

The whole church drew in its breath with a hiss and it seemed that Varga had gone too far, but he pointed his pistol here and there in the crowd, just to show who was boss, and he said, 'Calm yourselves, my dears, calm yourselves. You have a crown – of sorts – now all you need is a king and, oh fortunate people, a king has been provided for you, a real king, a proper king, a man of noble blood, a man who has never stolen even a single camel in his entire life. Most importantly of all, he has been chosen for you by the Emperors of Germany and Austria-Hungary, thereby ensuring you of the continuing love and friendship of the most powerful sovereigns in Europe. Here, catch!' And he tossed the crown towards the priest who crowned me, who caught it with tears in his eyes.

There were furious mutterings in the crowd but Varga dismissed them with another wave of his pistol, 'Oh, shut up, you noisy, nasty, ungrateful, stupid stinky Albanians. This is for your own good. Look what happens when you're left to run your own country – you end up with a circus troupe in charge! But be of good cheer, because you'll soon have a lovely new king and a nice new government. Just as soon as we've shot the old ones.'

He signalled to the sailors standing round the walls, 'Round them up. And the rest of you – GO AWAY!'

The doors were flung open and men with rifles started herding the people out. They didn't need much encouragement but, when they were all gone and their candles with them and the place had fallen back into shadow again, Mrs MacLeod was left. The click of her heels, the tap of her parasol, that black and white dress, like a nun and nothing whatever like a nun. She raised her chin and waited.

'You,' said Varga. 'I remember you. The last time I saw you, you had forgotten where you put your knickers.'

'Oh, I'm always doing that,' she said.

'I like your hat.'

'Isn't it charming?'

Varga cocked his pistol and took aim. 'I could shoot you for it.'

'But you might make a hole in it.'

'I'm a very good shot.'

'But it's a very big hat. Hard to miss. Don't you find it draws the eye?'

'It does, yes.'

'Hard to look away from it, don't you think? It's the sort of hat you just want to keep on looking at.'

'Yes.'

'I'll tell you what – why don't I give you this lovely hat as a present, from me to you?'

'That would be kind. Thank you.' With his thumb, Varga uncocked his pistol and put it back in its holster, and Mrs MacLeod drew out a long jewelled pin and removed her hat.

She held it in front of herself as she walked, slowly, slowly, between the columns, through the shadows of the church towards Varga. 'It is a lovely hat, isn't it?'

'Lovely.'

'It really draws the eye.'

'It does. It draws the eye.'

'People find they can't stop looking at it. Don't you want to look at it?'

'I do, yes. I want to look at it.'

Mrs MacLeod came on like a cobra. 'You want to look at it so you *should* look at it. You should always do anything you want to do. You must do everything you want to do and you want to look at this lovely hat so you must look at it. Really, you must. You do want to look at it, don't you?'

'Yes, I do.'

'Then you must. You must look at the hat.'

'Yes. I must look at the hat.'

'Yes, look at the hat.' She was at the throne, standing beside me at the foot of the steps, holding the hat out to him, its jumbled, frozen aviary trembling a little in her grasp, and Varga came down the steps to take it from her.

He held it in two hands, looking deep into it as if it was a window to another world, and we looked at him looking at it and we wondered.

After a time Mrs MacLeod said, 'Imre. Imre? Imre, darling?'

Varga looked up.

'Weren't you going to have these people arrested?'

He looked round like a man waking up and seemed surprised to notice the sailors with their rifles and the rest of us, standing round waiting to be shot. 'Yes,' he said.

'And put in prison.'

'Yes. Arrested and put in prison.'

'And shot.'

'Yes. We'll shoot them tomorrow.'

'But not me, Imre. I'm not with them. They didn't ask me to join their silly Skanderbeg club.'

Varga was fully awake now – or as close to awake as the little ginger lunatic ever got. 'Not you obviously . . .'

'Mrs MacLeod.'

'Obviously, not you, Mrs MacLeod.'

'You see, I'd very much like to meet this new king of yours. I feel sure he and I would get on very well indeed. And there's something I'd like to give him.'

Varga smiled a knowing smile that barely flickered out from under his enormous moustaches. 'I'm no judge but, from what I recall, I feel certain he would like to meet you.'

Mrs MacLeod made a pretty nod to acknowledge the compliment. 'But you haven't told me his name,' she said.

'The new king?' said Varga. 'His name is Wilhelm.'

She gave me a look. 'Does he have a second name?'

'Wilhelm von Wied.'

'Really?' She put a tiny gloved hand in front of her mouth and laughed like silver bells. 'It's too rich. Wilhelm von Wied and Otto Witte. It's almost as if somebody sent a telegram and ordered the wrong king – isn't it, Captain Arbuthnot? Oh, do you think I might have my hat back?'

'Of course.' And he gave it to her as if nothing could have mattered less.

'So we're agreed then? You're not going to arrest me? And those five silly Albanian girls and their smelly old fathers – you won't be needing them, will you? And

Countess Gourdas – you know, I'm sure the new king will want to meet her too, so let's keep her, and you can shoot the others – but not until the morning.'

'No, not until the morning,' Varga said. 'And not Maxxie. Not poor dear Maxxie. He's too nice to shoot.'

But my mate Max said he would really much prefer to be shot quite a lot than to live an extra day as Varga's special friend. Well, that wasn't what he said but it was pretty much what he meant.

'Shame,' said Varga. 'Have it your own way.'

And then Zogolli broke ranks. He'd been standing there, chewing on his gloves and trying not to cry, but when he saw that Tifty had been saved, and Max had wasted his chance to get away, the little coward cracked.

He flung himself at Varga's feet and soaked his shiny boots with tears. 'Not me. Don't shoot me. I know about government. The new king will need a government. I can help. Not me!'

It was horrible to watch. And it did no good. Varga took out his pistol and slapped the boy away with a crack across the head.

Poor Kemali. I could see his heart was breaking. The old man rushed forward with groans and cries and went to help. My Sarah would have gone too but I held her by the hand and shook my head. Bad enough for Zogolli to suffer that humiliation without a woman showing him how a man should behave.

So there was Kemali, getting blood all over his fancy gloves and muttering soothing noises, and there was Zogolli, spitting bits of broken tooth out on the floor, and Varga, the little madman, couldn't even be bothered to look at them.

He put his pistol away and said, 'His Majesty King Wilhelm has no need of cowards in his government. You will be shot along with the rest of these traitors.'

Zogolli couldn't take it. The courage that Kemali had tried to teach him failed utterly, like a bit of elastic stretched too far. He just snapped. He jabbered and he yelled, he raged and he wept and he howled. The poor bastard went to bits. Like those people in the bomb shelter. He wanted to live, that's all. It's not such a bad thing. I can't find it in my heart to blame him for it. My mate Max could lift beer barrels straight up over his head, and you wouldn't make fun of a bloke who couldn't do that. Zogolli didn't have the strength, that's all.

There was nothing to be done. We just had to stand there and let him get on with his snivelling while we tried hard not to do the same, but, credit where credit's due, he didn't piss his pants and that's more than I can say. It went on for a long time. It's hard not to notice somebody for that long, but we all pretended and then, at last, he stopped his howling with all the ease of a child and he stood up and he wiped his face and pushed his fingers through his hair and spat a little more blood and he said, 'You can't shoot me.'

Varga cocked an eyebrow at him.

'I know where the vault is. The national vault of Albania. I know where it is and I know the combination. You'll never find it without me, and you'll certainly never get it open.'

Kemali looked at him in horror and he said something in Albanok which needed absolutely no translation, and then he did an astonishing thing. I expected a punch – a slap at the very least – but that never came. Instead he took hold of the curtain tie fixed across Zogolli's shoulder and he tugged it until the button popped and he threw it on the ground.

The old man said, 'There used to be twelve of us and our king, but you betrayed him and left us. The Christians will recognise that story. They know your name. I choose to die with my king.'

'Excellent choice,' said Varga. 'We'll see about that tomorrow.' He grabbed Zogolli by the lapels. 'I like you. You can stay. You ladies, come with me. Send the peasant girls away with their horrible, stinky daddies.'

Armed men moved in and tried to drive the fathers-in-law off, but they refused to leave me. 'Tell them to go,' I said. 'Get out while they can,' and, after a bit, after Kemali translated, they shook my hand and left. It took three of them to carry Aferdita and she screamed fit to bust a gut.

The sailors formed up, ready to march us out, and I was scared and I was sad and I was ashamed. I'd let so many people down. I'd made promises to the Professor. I wouldn't listen when he warned me and he was right and I was wrong and now he was about to die and so was Sarah – just as he always said. I was scared and I was sad and I was ashamed but, by God, I was proud too. I was proud that she had chosen to dare this thing with me. I was proud of her standing there beside me.

'Can I take your arm, Otto?' she said, and I didn't say anything because I was afraid that I might cry, so we all fell in together, Sarah and me and Max and the Professor, with Arbuthnot strolling along beside them as if he had been on his way to a glass of champagne and a plate of oysters.

'Good luck, Tifty,' said Max.

'Good luck, darlings.'

'Yes,' said Mrs MacLeod, 'good luck.' And she brushed the front of my tunic with the tips of her gloved fingers, 'just to smarten you up a bit. You should look nice for your firing squad.' I could have punched her.

They marched us out.

'You'll never get away with this,' said Kemali. 'You can't just snatch a country like an apple off a market stall, not with this handful of thugs. You've terrified Zogolli into joining you and I am ready to die, but that square is filled with loyal Albanian troops. They will cut you down.'

'Really?' said Varga. 'How do you think I got here so quickly? Where do you think these sailors came from? Where do you think the bombs came from? Look!'

He flung back the doors and the light flooded in and there, above the square, looming over the rooftops like the angel of death, was a balloon, a giant silver balloon, a Zeppelin with an enormous double-headed eagle painted across the nose like a screaming butterfly pinned in a case and, beneath it, a gondola bristling with guns.

'Faster than the wind,' said Varga, 'and as high as the clouds – so high up that none of your pissy little popguns can reach her – but not so high that she can't look down on every shack in this godforsaken dung heap of a country and bomb it flat. Behold your proud army.'

He threw his arms wide and we saw the square, empty except for a mother weeping into her handkerchief. The boy beside me dropped his saddlebags and ran to her.

I don't think I ever told you about my mother's Uncle Fritz. He lived on a farm a few miles east of Tübingen, and as I recall he was in charge of the dairy or something like that. Anyway, Great-Uncle Fritzie went off to market and he had a good day and he stopped off for a little bit of wurst and a little bit of beer and then the snow came down and it snowed and it snowed and it snowed. Poor old Fritzie couldn't get the cart through the blizzard and eventually, after two days and nights, he had to leave it behind, put the horse in a stable and tramp home alone, walking along on the tops of the hedges, so deep was the snow.

Well, after hours of walking he reached the farm and he found his way to his cottage, where the door was completely covered by drifts, but he shovelled them away with his big farmer's hands until he could see the keyhole and he opened the door and fell inside with half a ton of snow, which he flung out again so he could shut the door. Then, because Uncle Fritzie was no fool, he broke up some sticks, put them in the grate of the range and got them going and, after that, he went out to feed the cows.

As you might imagine, that took a bit of time, and all the while those sticks were burning away in the grate, and they burned so long that they set light to a little pile of logs there in the grate with them and soon Uncle Fritzie's kitchen was good and warm again.

Out in the shed, Fritzie was thinking how nice it would be to get back indoors where everything would be so pleasant and cosy and bright, and he was looking forward to turning the tap on his range and drawing off some nice hot water and making himself a pot of coffee and drinking it while he warmed his feet against the bars of the fire.

But what Fritzie didn't know was that all the pipes had frozen while he was away and the copper water tank on his little kitchen range was stoppered up with a big blob of ice and the fire was blazing away merrily and the water tank was getting hotter and hotter and the air inside was expanding and expanding and the seams were getting tighter and tighter and every rivet was straining like the laces on your granny's corsets.

So Fritzie got finished with the cows and he made sure they were all set for another night on their own and he shut the door and he climbed back on top of the snowdrift and he started to tramp back to his little cottage. And, when he was about halfway there, he noticed that his bootlace had come undone and he thought, Well, to hell with that, I'm not going to bother doing that up because I'm going to be taking these boots off in a minute anyway. But when the snow came in and chilled his toes he thought, Damnation, I'm going to have to tie this lace after all.

Of course all that took no more than a moment, since Fritzie had the benefit of more or less a lifetime's experience in tying bootlaces in a range of colours and sizes, but it meant that, when the rivets on the water tank finally gave way and his kitchen was filled with little bits of exploding copper and clouds of scalding steam, Fritzie was still outside the door and, when he finally came in to survey the scene of horror – a mere bagatelle compared to what is about to happen to my little caravan any second now, mind you – what did Fritzie find but the copper spigot of the water tank, blown across the room and sticking in the back of his favourite chair, right where his heart would have been?

The details of this story have been engraved on my memory from boyhood, as Great-Uncle Fritz was sufficiently impressed by his narrow escape from death to sit down and write a full account of it to every member of his family, including us. We got a lot of enjoyment out of that letter and we made my mother – who had a beautiful speaking voice – read it out over and over.

Us kids were all sitting round the table, listening again to the story of how Great-Uncle Fritzie cheated death, when the letter came telling us that two weeks after his boiler blew up he got kicked in the head by a cow and died.

I only tell you this to illustrate a point, the point being that what's for you will not go past you. Call it fate, call it destiny, call it luck, call it what you like, the point is that you just can't beat it.

You've heard so many stories like Uncle Fritzie's that you've already forgotten it. Would you sit round the kitchen table with all your brothers and sisters telling that story over and over again? Of course you wouldn't. It's ordinary. It's a bore. I'm sitting here now, in the middle of this air raid where the perfect, unchangeable geometry of a hundred falling bombs has spared me, and in a little while another bomb will come and it will blow me to bits. There's no accounting for it but you've seen it a thousand times all across this city. It's the luck of the draw and nobody gives it a thought. This one lives, that one dies. That's life. You either laugh or you cry. It's just luck. Good luck, bad luck – one is not more remarkable than the other, so I don't want to hear any disbelieving complaints about the rest of my story. I told you when I was a coward, so I expect you to believe me when I tell you how brave I was. Uncle Fritzie dodged a flying spigot and died of a kick in the head, and I lived through a firing squad so I could keep a date with an English bomb.

And this is how it happened.

I don't suppose you have ever been marched to your execution arm in arm with the woman you love. It is a depressing situation.

We all knew we were going to die, but that is the terrible burden we all carry from childhood. Everybody dies, and we are all part of everybody so we all die. Just not yet. And 'not yet' is a great comfort. 'Not yet' is a large and comfortable place to hide. 'Not yet' is a country that stretches a long, long way off, even when the little passport booth

357

which marks the border with the Republic of Right Now is just around the next bend.

So we all knew we were going to die, just not yet. Not until the next morning and that was a long, long way off. Still, we must have made an unhappy little procession, strolling along through the streets with armed men on every side – and how those streets had changed. It was as if a plague had struck the town. The crowds had vanished back into their houses. The doors were barred, the windows were shuttered, the streets were silent and once, as we were going down through a narrow lane, Sarah caught the heel of her shoe in a loop of thin rope, a broken string of bunting that somebody had torn down in too much of a hurry to hide properly. I stooped to untangle her, holding her little foot, that slim ankle I had gazed at in church, the same slim ankle I kissed in the railway carriage, and I was certain I had kissed it because there was no tiny part of her I had not kissed and I wanted to kiss every little bit of her again and fight for her and save her but I knew that would have taken us across the river from the Kingdom of Not Yet to the Republic of Right Now. I didn't want to go there so, instead, I wiped my eyes and I stood up and I offered Sarah my arm again.

'Thank you, Otto,' she said. My God, she was so brave, my girl.

We walked on in silence because there was nothing to say and whatever there was that we wanted to say we didn't want to say in front of other people. That's what Not Yet means. It gives you hope. We hoped. We hoped that there

358

would be another time when we would be alone to say those things. One more time. My friend, I am here to tell you that there are never enough such times. Don't wait for the next one. If there is a chance to say, 'I love you,' say it because, believe me, the border post of Right Now is much, much closer than you think.

Very soon we reached the gates of the castle, where there were no guards waiting to be overwhelmed by my wonderfulness, no crowds cheering me through the arch, nobody running around trying to catch the gold coins I scattered as I passed, no camel to help me knock my hat off, just an empty courtyard, ringing with the tramp of boots.

Varga was gleeful. 'Which way to the dungeons?'

'Dungeons?' said Zogolli. 'Why do you want the dungeons?'

'Where did you think we would be keeping them? What did you think this would mean? You picked your side, Ziggo, but there's always room in the dungeons for one more if you care to change your mind.'

Kemali managed an enormous gob on the flagstones. 'There's no room for the likes of him in any dungeon of mine. I refuse to be imprisoned with that traitor.'

'So that settles it. Now, which way to the dungeons, Ziggo, old boy?'

Zogolli led the way across the courtyard to a heavy door, but when he got there Varga was trailing behind. 'I'm sorry, I was just looking at your nice wall. Isn't it simply the perfect spot for a firing squad, children? Unless you've seen one you'd like better.'

'All the walls are the same to us,' Kemali said. 'Every stone in them is a stone of Albania.' By God I wish I'd said that, but the old man had a way with words that I couldn't match.

Varga pulled a face and went to look in the door of the dungeon. 'You must be joking. You have got to be joking.' He reached out and pinched Zogolli by the end of his carroty nose. 'I want some place to store traitors, but your dungeon seems to be full up already, Ziggo. What's it full up with, Ziggo? Tell your Uncle Imre!'

He hauled Zogolli towards him and jammed his head through the door.

'Champagne,' we heard faintly.

'Yes, Ziggo, champagne. Your dungeon is full of champagne.'

'We got it for the coronation. For the celebrations.'

'Oh, you got it for the celebrations. Well, it's a simply lovely dungeon you've got down there, Ziggo, but don't you think it might be a little bit cramped with all that lovely champagne in it? Not exactly ideal conditions for storing traitors on the night before their execution.'

'I don't mind,' I said.

'We could move the champagne,' said Zogolli.

'Oh, we could move the champagne . . .' Varga sneered back.

'You mustn't trouble on my account,' the Professor said.

Max agreed. 'I make my living swallowing swords. I reckon I could manage to swallow a few bottles of champagne tonight.'

'Or you could swallow a bullet right away,' said Varga. He turned to Zogolli with a sigh. 'These things have to be done properly. I promised these people they would be shot at dawn and, damn it all, man, shot at dawn they will be. It's tradition. And when they are shot, they will not be roaring drunk on champagne.' He seemed bored with squeezing Zogolli's nose and he let go with a final twist. 'Now then, what's up there?'

The castle of Durres is blessed with two towers, long, graceful swans' necks that rise up on either side of the gate, one a little higher than the other. I suppose in years gone by they might have been useful for hurling things off, should uninvited guests come calling. They must have seemed very high and hurling things off them must have seemed very clever, but that was before anybody thought of an aeroplane.

'What's up there?' said Varga, and off he went towards the taller of the two towers with merry cries of, 'Come along, children, come along,' while his thugs marched us up the stairs behind him. It was one of those winding stone staircases where almost every step is an odd height, some a little too low, some unexpectedly high – not because the builders did not understand the stonemasons' art but because they knew it so well. They knew that the garrison of the castle would climb up and down there every day and before too long they would learn the steps of those stairs like the words of a familiar song, but an invader would stumble over their jangling music, just as we did, Varga leading the way, Zogolli behind him and a straggle of soldiers in front and behind, clattering their boots on the stairs, banging their rifles off the narrow walls, with us in the middle, Sarah in her long skirt, the Professor with his cane. But we struggled on, with Zogolli calling out at every floor, as polite and enthusiastic as those lift attendants they used to have at Warenhaus Hermann Tietzl, 'Ground floor: guardroom, wood stores, coalsheds. First floor: tools and brushes, offices.'

'And up here?'

'Empty.'

'Not quite high enough. What's up here?'

'Nothing. Nothing, so far as I know.'

Varga kicked at a big oak door bound with iron bands. 'Open this.'

Somebody opened it and we all went inside. It was as empty as an eggshell, with a stone floor and stone arches that rose up three or four times the height of a man and crossed over to form the roof. The walls were completely blank, just plain white plaster, except where the stones of the arches had been left bare, and there was only one window, high up – so high up we couldn't even see it, but it was there, at the end of a narrow tunnel, cut through the thickness of the wall and down into the room, where a little light came out just below the domed ceiling.

'What's upstairs?'

'Nothing,' said Zogolli. 'The stairs go up to the roof.'

Varga nodded to the sailor by the door. 'Go upstairs and check,' and we all waited meekly until the man came back and reported, 'Flat stone roof, sir. Walls to waist height all the way round. Excellent views. Ideal guard post.'

'Wonderful!' Varga turned to us. 'Gentlemen, Fräulein, this is where you will spend your last night on earth. I hope you will be very comfortable. I expect you won't.'

He herded his sailors down the stairs with just a couple waiting behind to keep us covered as he backed out of the door and closed it with a heavy slam. 'Goodnight, children. Sleep well. Put three men on the roof. Damn it, open up again.'

The door opened and Varga came back, a man behind him swivelling his rifle round the room. 'I forgot. One last surprise for you, Witte. Turn round.'

I was slow to obey.

'Turn round or I'll have you shot right now.'

I did as he said and I felt steel cuffs bite into my wrists.

'Goodnight, for the last time,' Varga said. 'I'm looking forward to shooting you tomorrow, Witte.'

'Try not to miss this time,' I said. The door slammed and three bolts hammered home.

We were locked away in a stone prison cell halfway to the moon. Those handcuffs were completely unnecessary but Varga did it anyway, just because he could and because he enjoyed a little bit of pointless cruelty. These days they would probably make him Reichsminister for Kindergartens and he'd feel right at home pulling little girls' pigtails and giving their baby brothers Chinese burns.

I wasn't that bothered – for God's sake, he was going to shoot me for sure and doing it in handcuffs wasn't going to make that any worse – but Sarah was upset. When she put her hand on my shoulder she had that hurt look, the same look she had the morning after Mrs MacLeod came to my cabin, but then it was for her and this time it was for me and her eyes were damp.

'All right, Otto?'

'No problem,' I said, and I lay on my back and drew up my legs. I'm not saying it was easy, but I managed to squeeze the loop of my arms over my arse and down my legs and over my boots and, when I sprang to my feet, the cuffs were no longer behind my back. 'Ta-daaah!' It was a simple trick for a fit man with an acrobat's training, and of course my wrists were still chained together, but I was a bit more comfortable and it cheered Sarah up.

'Oh, well done,' said Arbuthnot, and he gave me a tiny ripple of applause, but he was already on his way to try the door. 'Not even a bally keyhole this side, but by the sound of it there's some pretty hefty ironmongery out there.'

He turned round and back-heeled the door. It never even shook. He tried it again.

'Shut up in there. Try and get some rest. It'll make the time pass quicker.'

I felt Sarah's hand in mine, saying with a touch what we all of us thought: We don't want the time to pass. We need every second. Time is short. We are going to die.

Are you thinking that now, friend? You should be.

Arbuthnot kicked the door again.

'I thought we told you to shut up.'

'More than one of them,' Arbuthnot said. 'What did she give you?'

'Who?' I looked at Sarah. 'She hasn't given me anything.'

'Not Sarah, Grietje.'

'Who's Grietje?'

'Mrs MacLeod. What did Mrs MacLeod give you?'

'She didn't give me a damned thing.'

'I saw her. At the church. Just as we were marched off. She touched you and said you had to look nice for your firing squad.'

'And I'm telling you she gave me nothing.'

Arbuthnot looked at me with a patient look and began

passing his hands over my tunic with a pickpocket's grace. 'Why don't you people notice anything? You look but you don't see; you hear but you don't listen.'

I pushed him away with my chained hands. 'Sod that. Never mind wasting time telling me how useless I am, what about this new king? Otto Witte . . . Wilhelm von Weide. Why am I here?'

'Did you think it was your idea?'

'I thought it was my idea,' Sarah said.

'It's a coincidence,' Arbuthnot said.

'Shit.'

'Coincidence. That's all. These things happen. What are the chances –' he ran his hands over my breast pocket, lifted the flap, dipped inside – 'that the Central Powers would choose a king with the same name as yours – or nearly the same name as yours? What are the chances that you should bear such a resemblance to a rival claimant?'

'For God's sake, the man I resemble doesn't even exist. I don't resemble anybody but myself.'

'Coincidence, that's all.' He went on patting me down. 'What do you want to believe? That innumerable clerks from the Secret Intelligence Service of His Majesty's Committee of Imperial Defence sat in London, scouring cuttings from hundreds of small-town newspapers from across Germany, from all over Austria and Moravia and Bohemia and Hungary, looking for a likely candidate, and that they picked you? You, an unheard of acrobat in an unknown circus troupe, wandering round the backwaters of the Habsburg Empire? And you think that, somehow, those hundreds of labouring clerks used the combined resources of the greatest empire the world has ever known to send you wandering across Europe, that they mobilised the Companions of the Rosy Hours to speed your passage, all in the hopes that, armed with no more than native cunning, you might install yourself as king and all while you never suspected a thing, all while you thought it was your own idea? Is that what you choose to believe?' Arbuthnot had almost run out of places to rub. He folded two fingers of each hand and slid them under the epaulettes of my tunic. 'Aha!' and then, like a stage magician or an uncle at a Christmas party, he produced . . . 'Grietje's hatpin. She took it out. She didn't put it in again and she gave it to you. That was very good. I never spotted it and I was watching hard.'

'But she abandoned us,' I said.

'Oh, wake up, old man. She turned what was left of Varga's brain to mush, she got the most powerful clan chiefs in the country away to safety and she extracted Countess Gourdas who, I feel sure, is even now helping to create a diversion.'

'Then why, for Christ's sake, didn't she save Sarah too?'

Arbuthnot jabbed the point of Mrs MacLeod's hatpin into the lock of my handcuffs. 'I don't think you would have been too happy at the prospect of Miss von Mesmer causing a diversion of that type, now would you, Otto?' The left handcuff clicked open. 'This one will be a little quicker. It's just a matter of . . . there.'

The cuffs rattled on the stone floor and, naturally, since my hands were free again, I used them to hold Sarah.

'I'd have done it, Otto,' she said. 'I'd do it for you.'

Arbuthnot waited quietly for a bit. Embarrassed, like Max and the Professor, the way we had been when Zogolli broke down snivelling in the church. That was something we should not have seen. We were intruders there and they felt themselves intruders in the private place which Sarah and I had built for ourselves in the space of our arms.

'Otto,' Arbuthnot called us back into the cell. 'Otto, believe me, Mrs MacLeod is out there fighting. The Companions will flock to her, but at dawn tomorrow she will abandon the fight and think of nothing but saving her own soft, pearly skin. If you don't want to watch Sarah walk to the wall in the morning, we have got to get out of this room. Now think, man.'

Faintly, from far away, we heard a sound like the beating of swans' wings approaching.

Be funny. Tell me a joke. Come on, make me laugh. Now! You can't do it, can you? So imagine if your life depended on it. Imagine if somebody told you they were going to shoot the woman you loved unless you told a joke – now, right now! Or in five minutes or five hours or five days. The mind dries up in the face of something like that, shrivels like moth wings in a candle flame, so imagine how I felt. Find a way out, Otto, that's all you've got to do. You're locked in a room at the top of Rapunzel's tower, armed with nothing more than a borrowed hatpin, the door is locked with giant iron bolts, there are armed men outside and, if you somehow manage to escape, they will shoot you and everybody you know and love but, on the other hand, if you don't escape, they will shoot you and everybody you know and love. Answer on only one side of the paper. Time starts NOW!

And I couldn't think of the answer. I couldn't think of the answer. I couldn't think of the answer. There was nothing in my head but that thumping, whistling beat over and over like an executioner taking endless practice swings of the axe.

'What the hell is that bloody noise?' but before anybody could answer me, we heard Varga running up the stairs, gasping out orders as he came: 'Get out of my way. Move. Move. What is that stupid bastard doing? Make him stand off. He has to stand off. And they can't tether to this tower.' He went running on up towards the roof, yelling as he went, 'Not this tower! Not this tower! This is a *verdammte* prison. The other tower!'

And then I knew what to do. Not down, but up. Out of Rapunzel's tower, into the Zeppelin and away on the clouds. All I had to do was get out of the room and get Sarah out of the room and her father and Kemali and Max and Arbuthnot, get them all out of the room and have them wait on the roof while I boarded a Zeppelin full of armed men, overpowered them and stole their airship. Then all I would have to do was haul my friends aboard and fly away to freedom. I'm sorry, I had no better idea.

'Max,' I said, 'get me up to that window.'

That was a piece of cake for Max. He cupped his hands into a stirrup and bounced me up the wall.

'Down again. I should take my jacket off.'

Max put me on the floor, took my jacket, hung it in his teeth and cupped his hands again. He would have thrown me up and down that wall all day if I'd asked him. He was like that and, with Max holding my heels, I reached the gap under the window easily.

It was a sort of a square tunnel, about twice as long as me and not much broader than my shoulders, sloping up to a window, an ordinary little window with a wooden frame and no bars. The masons hadn't bothered to finish it off too carefully. It was nice and rough and that made for an easy climb, but Max would never fit. I knew at once that Max would never fit. He'd get the rest of us up there. Max would stand there and lift me up, he'd lift Sarah and her father and Kemali and Arbuthnot, and then he'd sit down quietly and wait to be shot if I asked him, if I just explained that, 'Sorry, mate, you'll never squeeze in, but me and the others, we might have a chance.' He'd give us a hand up and say, 'It's no loss what a friend gets. Good luck!'

I wasn't halfway up the tunnel when I knew we couldn't do that. I'd rather be shot with Max a hundred times than let him be shot once alone and, anyway, Sarah wouldn't go without him. She was down there in that room, as terrified as I was, being brave for my sake, for the sake of her father, clenching her teeth together to keep from screaming, and I knew very well that scared her more than the thought of a firing squad. She was scared to scream because she knew that, if she started to scream, she wouldn't stop until they stopped her with a bullet. She was afraid of breaking like Zogolli. She was more afraid of that than of anything, and I knew because I was afraid of that too.

I reached the window. It was just a little thing, split into four panes, one of them cracked, and the wood was dried out and papery since it was so high up in the tower and so far away down an awkward tunnel that nobody had ever thought to give it a lick of paint or a rub of oil. It was old and done for all right, but I'm damned if I could get it open. Lying there in that stone shaft, facing up to the sky, I could see nothing but clouds passing by and I could touch the frame of the window, I could get my hands on it, but if I tried to push it open, I just ended up pushing myself back down the tunnel. I tried to hold on with the toes of my boots. I tried to brace myself against the walls with my elbows, but nothing worked. The harder I pushed, the further backwards I fell, and the old window stayed stuck.

'What can you see, Otto?'

'Not much. I'm coming back down. Stand clear.'

I let go of the sides and slid down the tunnel. Falling out was even easier than climbing in. I even managed to keep my legs straight and my feet together when I landed. 'There's a window,' I said.

'So we can get out?' said the Professor.

'We need to talk about that.' I gave the knees of my trousers a good brush. 'There's one window in one side of the tower but I can't see out of it. Well, I can see out, but I can't see down so I don't know what's outside. I think I could get the window open, but we need to think about that carefully. There are four sides to the tower. Three of them look down into the castle courtyard and only one of them faces out to the town, so we need to consider—'

'Forgive me, but there is nothing to consider,' said Arbuthnot.

'We have no choice,' said Kemali.

The Professor shook his head. 'If you attract their attention by breaking the window, they will shoot us.'

'But they're going to shoot us anyway,' said Sarah. They were finishing one another's sentences again.

I looked at Max.

'Whatever you think best, mate.' That was all he said. My mate Max.

I knew what I was going to do. There was no choice. They were right, even if Max had to stay. Even if I had to stay with him. 'Max,' I said, 'I need to go in again, backwards this time.'

He stood there like a rock with his arms held out while I did a handstand on his upturned palms. By God he was strong, but so was I in my way. I stayed there, straight as a candle, as Max raised his arms up to shoulder height and then higher still until he was standing with his arms raised high over his head and me, upside down above him, as if he was reaching up to a mirror or I was reaching down to one. I found the lip of the passage with the toe of my boot. I tipped and tilted. I folded my body into the tunnel and I began to crawl backwards. Max gave a relieved grunt as my weight came off his palms. He wouldn't have done that five years before.

I crawled. I scraped my palms. I wished I'd brought my gloves. I scraped my knees. I crawled. I crawled backwards and uphill until my boots bumped the window and then I kept on crawling, with my feet resting against the glass so my legs bent – as far as they could in that narrow place – and everything was tensed up and then I started to push. The glass cracked like a breaking bone. I kept on pressing. The glass broke – plink. Inside the tunnel the air was suddenly fresher. I felt for the break in the glass with the tip of my toe and tapped at it, over and over, a dozen tiny kicks, until it fell out. I poked my toe into the gap and carefully worked it round the edge. More tiny kicks. I knew I was going to have to kick that window right out of the frame and I wanted all the glass gone. What could have been sillier than to stick myself in the leg and bleed to death, upside down in that little shaft, with all my friends corked up inside? So I took my time. Four panes, each one carefully kicked out and cleared away and each one scattering a hundred sparkling, tinkling bits of glass out into the sky and down to the ground and yet nobody came. There was no shout of alarm, no sound of angry Austrian sailors running up the stairs to come and shoot me in my tunnel, and that made me feel good. They hadn't seen. They hadn't noticed.

All the glass was gone. I braced myself. I kicked backwards – hard, again and again. The wood splintered and I kept kicking until there was nothing left to kick.

It was time to leave. I began to crawl backwards again. My foot caught on what was left of the window. I dragged my toe over it. And the other one. Both my boots were sticking out into the air and the weight was pressing on my knees as I crept up the rough stone tunnel. Backwards a little further. My knees came out. I kept on wriggling and pushing, working against the stone walls with my hands, flapping like a landed fish. A loose nail from the broken window frame caught in my trousers and I felt them rip but I kept on, bouncing my thighs out into empty space until at last I had my backside sticking out the window with the broken window frame and the edge of the stone wall digging into me. It wasn't comfortable, but at least it meant I could bend my legs.

I lay there, half in and half out of the window, rough stone and bits of broken wood sticking into my guts, my arse hanging out into fresh air, kicking at the wall, trying to find a toehold, gradually sliding backwards into nothing, with those jagged bits of timber clawing at me as I went. And there was nothing there. There was absolutely nothing to stand on but I kept on squirming my way backwards out of the window, more out of desperation than hope, because if I couldn't find a way to get Sarah out of there, then I might as well throw myself off the tower and pray that I hit Varga on the way down.

My shoulders were through the gap. There was nothing keeping me from falling into the air but my elbows and the flats of my hands and by now I was sliding, properly sliding, out the window. I caught hold of the bottom of the window frame with my fingertips and I wished like blazes that I'd worn my fancy gloves, but there was still nothing to stand on. So I did the only thing I could do.

I let go and I fell for about a hundred years or the time that it took to drop a hand's breadth, where I clung to the window ledge and dangled, reaching out with my toes – and they found something solid. There was something there.

I pulled myself up again a little, put my feet flat against the wall and hung there, like a monkey, looking down between my legs to get the lie of the land, and there it was – one of those little, pointless bits of masonry they put into old buildings and, if anybody ever knew why, he's long dead. It was only a tiny ribbon of stonework and it stuck out from the wall by about half the width of a shoe, those parts where it hadn't already dropped off on to the heads of unsuspecting Albanoks, but half the width of a shoe is about three times the width of a slack rope. For a man like me that was as good as the king's highway. I put my feet down on the ledge and tested my weight on it. It held, so I turned round. Hands together on the window ledge, I let go with my left, held my weight on my right and swung round so my toes, which were pointing in, were pointing out and my back, which had been facing thin air, was against the wall.

I hung there quite comfortably, with my heels on the ledge, supporting myself against the castle wall. It was nothing for a bloke like me. In fact, if anybody had bothered to organise the Albanian All-comers Standing-on-a-Ledge Championships, I reckon I could probably have reached the finals. That sort of thing is bread and butter for a circus acrobat. Anyway, I surveyed the situation.

Luckily I was on the one side of the tower that faced outside the castle. To my left I could see the other tower and, streaming out from it, high above and far away down-wind, like a kite on a string, the glinting silver shape of the tethered Zeppelin.

The whole town was spread out in front of me: the mansions of the very finest families, the trees along the avenues, the palace that had been mine for a night, all the broken jumbled rooftops, all the little winding streets tumbling down the hill to the harbour and Varga's yacht and the blue sea and the gulls, flying free, all the way to the edge of the world. And I could see how to get there. The wall beneath me was cracked and broken with odd stones missing here and others standing proud there. I could reach them. I could plan a route all the way down to the trees that crowded round the bottom of the tower, then branch to branch down to the bushes at the bottom and I could wait there until dark and I could get away. I could get away. But the others couldn't. Maybe Arbuthnot could, but not Max or the Professor or Kemali and not Sarah. She couldn't escape. I turned round and I climbed back up the wall. I climbed so high that I could stand on the broken window ledge and breathe, big breaths that filled my lungs while the salt wind blew in from the sea and shook my magnificent whiskers and the clouds raced past and the sun shone and the blood sang in my veins and the birds sang.

'Goodbye,' I said, and I swung my legs up and I dropped into the tunnel, down and back into the cell.

They were all gathered round the bottom of the shaft,

waiting, hopefully and Max was there to catch me by the boots and lower me down to the floor.

And then they saw my face. 'There's no way out,' I said. 'I'm sorry. I tried my best, but there is no way out. I'm sorry. We'll think of something else.'

We didn't think of anything else. The Professor tapped round the walls with his cane, measuring the place, but he didn't find any secret passages, and Arbuthnot kicked the door a couple of times but the guards always answered and, even if they hadn't, it wouldn't have mattered since we were stuck on the wrong side of a thick lump of wood. It didn't take long to run out of ideas and, after that, well, there was really only one thing to think about and we tried hard not to think about that.

All the light in the room came from the shaft that led to the window. Eventually, because there was nothing else to do, we sat down on the floor and watched that odd yellow rectangle moving across the opposite wall. It crept along like the moving finger that terrified that bloke in the Bible, changing shape as it went, growing in brightness as the shadows darkened and deepened in the rest of the room until, at the end, there was just a single point of light down in the corner and we all sat there, as if we were gathered round a deathbed, and watched it go out. Hope went with it. In the sudden dark of the cell we could hear the border guards of Right Now calling out and telling us to have our papers ready for inspection and we knew that, when that spot of light appeared again on the wall, it would be the end.

After a bit Kemali said, 'From the moment we raised the flag of Skanderbeg, I knew in my heart it could end in only one way. It doesn't matter. Albania will be free. I know that. Maybe tomorrow I will do one more thing to help make her free. And I think we could have chosen a far worse king for my country; indeed, I am certain that a far worse king has been chosen for her now. I regret nothing.'

Arbuthnot sighed. 'God save us from enthusiastic amateurs. Does anyone mind if I smoke?' and before anybody could answer, he struck a match and lit a cigarette. 'Anyone else? I think I have enough to go round. And one for the morning.'

'I was saving my cigar,' Kemali said. 'But I think I may smoke it a little with you. For the company. I have matches.'

'I'd take a smoke if you had one to spare,' said Max.

'If I may,' said the Professor.

I saw their faces in the flare of the match, the deep, velvet black of a cellar darkness behind them like an Old Master painting and the line of Sarah's nose and the curve of her cheek where she lay with her head in the crook of my arm and a narrow band of light that marked the edge of her beautiful body and I thought about the bullets tearing into her and the match went out.

She kissed me then in the dark, very gently and sweetly,

and we went away together to a corner and held each other. That was all. On the other side of the room we saw those three little red lamps of burning tobacco and they might have been stars or the lights of ships so far away were they, so black was it, and we kissed and we kissed like kids. That was all.

'You went outside,' Sarah whispered.

'No, I didn't. There's no way out.'

'Yes, there is. You went in feet first when Max lifted you in and you came out feet first when he lifted you out. There isn't room to turn around in the tunnel so you must have been outside.'

I didn't say anything.

'Stop trying to think up a lie. I'm clever enough to spot which way your toes were pointing so I'm clever enough to spot a lie.'

'I got outside, but there's no way down.'

'No way down for you or no way down for an old cripple and a girl like me?'

'My darling, there is no way down.'

'Otto, you could have gone. You should have gone.'

'You know I couldn't. You know that, don't you? And you know why.'

Then she kissed me some more. 'Yes, Otto, I know. Because there is no way down. Not for me.'

'And not for me either.'

'But what about the others?'

'Max would never fit in the tunnel. Kemali would never make it. Arbuthnot might have one chance in a hundred but not in the dark. I'll tell him in the morning if I must, but there's no need. Something will turn up before then. Tifty will come to get us, just you wait and see.'

Poor kid. She wept and trembled against me then, very quietly, trying not to make a fuss, hiding her face in my shirt in the merciful darkness while my silent tears rolled down and soaked my magnificent whiskers.

Time passed. It does. Whether we want it to stay so a moment of joy can last forever or hurry away so that pain can be past, whether we want to delay the moment of parting or make Christmas come a day early, nothing changes it. Time passed. It passed for us at the same ticking pace that it passed for that little bastard Varga down in the dungeon drinking his way through my coronation champagne. Time passed and the room grew chill. The wind picked up and began to howl down the shaft from the window, whistling and moaning as it came and as cold as the moon.

'The Bura,' said the Professor.

He was standing behind me as I looked up the shaft watching the clouds race by, all torn and scrappy and silvered with moonlight, and I knew he was doing that thing again, where his head would click like one of those old-fashioned clockwork dolls and a stream of words would fall out.

'The Bura is a violent katabatic wind – from the Greek for "downhill" – observed in the evening, which blows down the eastern side of the Adriatic. It is produced by cold air from inland mountains rushing towards the relatively warmer coastal areas, usually in the winter months, although it can arise unexpectedly, depending on weather conditions, threatening shipping and causing structural damage to buildings.'

And, just then, just when the Professor's clockwork ran down, a black line like a pencil score appeared across the clouds, just for a moment, appeared and disappeared again with a sound like a whip crack.

'Poor Zogolli,' Kemali said. 'They will be sure to shoot him too, once they find out that he knows only half the combination to the vault. Still, he may be warmer than this when they do it.'

'And we will be still colder before too long,' said the Professor, and then it happened again, that dark line across the sky and the whistling sound of a whiplash, as if the clouds were ripping open.

'Find those handcuffs,' I said. 'They're on the floor someplace. Use your matches if you have to. Use them all up – you won't need them tomorrow. We're getting out of here!'

'There's no need.' The Professor made a sweep of the floor with the tip of his cane. 'I think these are what you want,' and there they were rattling on the stone floor, glinting like the pennies on a dead man's eyes. 'But you said there was no way out.'

'There *was* no way out, but now there is. Sarah will explain. But it doesn't matter any more. I'm getting out and I'm coming back. Max, get me into that hole. Sarah – I'm coming back! I'm coming back!'

I went down the tunnel like a ferret down a rabbit hole, climbing and crawling as fast as I could go, with the handcuffs dangling from my teeth and scraping off the stones as I went.

The wind was something ferocious – and colder than a witch's tits – but up I went, spidering my way along the tunnel, toes and elbows, knees and fingers, until I reached the broken window frame.

But I didn't stop there. I waited, just inside the lip of the tunnel, inside the blackness, looking out at the angry clouds, and sure enough the whip crack came again – loud as a gunshot this time and so close that I felt the wind of it in my face.

I flinched before it, but the next moment I squirmed forward so half my body was sticking out of the window, my arms held in front of me, my back arched, looking up to the furious sky, and then I could see it. High above me I could see the Zeppelin, pitching and yawing at the end of her tether like a salmon on a line as the Bura shrieked in my ears. It must have been hellish up there. They had let out their ropes so the machine rose clear of the castle towers, but they did not dare cast off into the teeth of that storm and now the Zeppelin was bouncing around up there, down by the nose as the rope tightened and slackened and swung. The next time that rope went past my window I was going to be ready for it, and it was coming, cutting through the air like a sabre, hissing like a cobra. I could hear it, bouncing and scraping off the castle wall down there in the dark, and then it stopped, suddenly, with a violin-string twang, and I knew the cable had snagged on that little bit of stonework where I stood earlier in the day, and I knew it wasn't going to stick.

I'm telling you this like it took forever. I'm telling you this like I stopped to think about it, like I measured up all the lines and the distances and the angles, but that's not what it's like for a man like me. Men like me, we're used to ropes, we're used to jumping and throwing and catching, we're used to dangling out over a gap, we're used to having our lives hanging by a thread, we're used to walking in the hours between heartbeats and falling and reaching out and catching on and flying and flying and flying.

I leaned forward to catch the rope. I leaned forward and I leaned a little more and a little further and then the rope came free and it hit me in the chest with all the force of a bloody train. I came out of that window like a worm wriggling on a hook, soaring upwards as the line went tight and, every moment, hanging on like grim death. I'm not being funny, but a lesser man could never have done it. Max was strong enough but he was too big. He couldn't have got through the tunnel and, anyway, he wasn't fast enough, he wasn't agile enough. I was quick and I was strong and, more than anything else, I thought of it. Not that it was my idea, but I'd seen it done in a show in Vienna once, although that was over a cage of tigers but no higher than the dress circle. The point is, I remembered.

Hanging there on the cable, biting down on the chain of those handcuffs, I wished to God I hadn't. The pain was monstrous. The wind had gone out of me, my chest was burning with the sting of the rope's blow and a couple of ribs must have gone. I knew when the rope stopped moving it was going to hurt like a bastard, and it did. Have you ever played with your mother's beads? Ever taken one end of the string in each hand and pulled it tight? Then you know that when you do that, all the beads bounce on the string, and that's what happened to me. I bounced on the string like a bead. It was hell – like getting beaten with red-hot pokers – but I clung on like a limpet. Nothing gives a man strength like terror does. I was hanging on a bit of tarry rope four storeys up, dangling over a castle ditch in a howling gale with a giant airship rolling about in the sky above me and, at the other end of the rope, the way out for me and my friends. I could see it down there, the top of the other tower where they had anchored the Zeppelin with a lamp to mark it, flaring in the gale. I was up and I had to get down.

The air came into my lungs again. Dear God, it was like breathing burning cinders. You can't imagine the pain. The rope was too thick to hold. I looped an elbow over and hung there though it felt like my arm was on fire, and I pulled myself up. Can you imagine that? Could you do that? Is there another man alive who could have done that, anybody in the world apart from Otto Witte with the strength and the skill and the courage to face such pain? And then, when I had raised my chin to the rope, and the handcuffs between my teeth were in reach, I grabbed hold of one end. It was easy to grab the other end with my free hand and I knew then I was going to make it. I was hanging there, one hand on either side of the rope with a loop of chain linking them, gripping two steel bracelets. I could have hung there all night if I'd wanted to, but I didn't want to. The wind was trying to blow the Zeppelin away again, but it couldn't get away so instead of flying along, it flew up and the rope went as tight as cheesewire and I started to slide, faster and faster, coming down that rope like a screaming comet and a damned sight faster than that bloke in Vienna, but he had a couple of mates waiting to catch him in the wings, and I had nothing to stop me but a stone wall.

And then, in the light of the oil lamp at the top of the tower, I saw two of Varga's sailors standing guard. They were hunched over against the freezing wind, rifles on their shoulders, hands tucked into their armpits, hugging themselves for warmth, but they looked up when they heard the sound of the handcuff chain coming screaming down the rope. One of them tried to swing his rifle round but, before he could, my right boot landed hard on his chin and he went spinning backwards, over the turret and down into the dark. I caught his mate smack in the middle of the chest with my left foot and he went down like a sack of coal off the back of a cart and I fell off the rope and landed right on top of him. But he wasn't dead. And he wasn't even unconscious. It's not like the picture shows, you know. You can't just knock somebody out by punching them on the nose. It takes quite a beating to make somebody go to sleep, and the sailor wasn't looking too well but he wasn't dead and he was going to get better so I murdered him. That's all there is to say about it. There is no other word. He was lying there, helpless, wondering what the hell had happened to him, and I dragged him to his feet like a Saturday-night drunk and I propped him up against the wall, sat him down on it and I pushed him right over. Poor bastard never made a sound. I pray for him, you know. Sometimes. When I remember. And for myself. But he would have done it to me. He might have been all set to join the firing squad, for all I know.

I have given him a lot more thought since then than I gave him the night that I killed him. Then there was no time to be disgusted with myself. I had to find a way down the tower and a way back up the other tower and a way out of the castle for myself and a party of five. I needed a diversion and I found one. By God I found one.

The signal lamp was still burning at my feet. I picked it up and unscrewed the tin reservoir. I reached up the rope as far as I could stretch, I poured lamp oil down it and I lit it from the burning wick.

Tar doesn't light, you know. You could hold a match to

a tar barrel all day and it wouldn't catch, but put tar in a fire and you'll never put it out again. The lamp oil lit. The lamp oil lit the tarry rope. Fire streaked up the airship tether, it gripped the rope, it wound itself round and flared out like feathers and the wind screamed and the flames soared and they raced up into the dark in a great curving wing of flame.

Those poor bastards up there must have seen it coming. I imagined them watching. I've imagined it a lot since: somebody spotting the flames, somebody wondering what the hell it could possibly mean, trying to make sense of it in the darkness as the gondola bucked around like a three-master rounding the Horn, looking down and then realising that the fire was heading straight towards them, the split second when he wondered what to do, the wasted moments while he alerted an officer and some little Flug Leutnant wasting more time looking out the window in disbelief and blowing down the communication tube, yelling at them to let go the tether, let go of everything Right NOW! But it was too late. The fire touched the nose of the airship.

Just for a second it seemed as if there was nothing wrong and then that tiny point of flame thickened and bloomed. From a dot it became a circle, and then it opened like a great orange chrysanthemum. The whole ship glowed red in the sky and then, as the outer covers burned away, I could see her ribs standing out against the fire like the wreck of a great cathedral ablaze in the sky.

Then she was falling, a burning snowflake, gently wafting

to the ground, down at the nose then down at the tail, rocking as she fell, faster and faster, coming down like Satan out of heaven, the clouds above her blazing and boiling as she fell.

Beside me the burning rope finally parted and whipped away into the night with a tormented scream and, someplace over there behind the trees, all that was left of the Zeppelin, all that was left of her crew, crumpled to the ground.

There was panic in the castle. Bells were ringing. Lights were coming on. Men were shouting. Boots were tramping down the stairs. Orders. Swearing. I peered over the edge of the tower and watched them forming up at the gate armed with shovels and blankets and little Varga yelling and screaming, staggering about with a bottle of my champagne in each fist. He took a swig – 'Come on then. Let's get on with it' – and he flung the bottle in the ditch.

How I wish I could see your face now, friend. What are you thinking? Are you thinking, The old fart's making this stuff up as he goes along?

I'm not. Remember what I told you about Uncle Fritzie? Sliding down the hawser of a Zeppelin is no more remarkable than not being killed by an exploding boiler, I can tell you.

Or are you thinking, My God, what a man! I wish I had known him. What a hero!

I'm not a hero. I dropped two boys off a tower. I burned a dozen more to death. I broke their mothers' hearts. I left their children to starve. Do you think that makes me a hero? I think that makes me a killer.

Of course, if they had been American boys or English boys I'd probably get a medal for something like that, and I wouldn't settle for anything less than a Knight's Cross with Diamonds. But they weren't English boys and I didn't kill them because I was a hero, I killed them because I was terrified and I didn't want to die. It's my only excuse, but you know what? Those poor bastards in the bomb shelter would have done exactly the same. When the place was on fire and full of smoke and they were clawing their way to the door, if somebody had said, 'Come along. This way. No need to rush. Take your time. The only thing standing between you and the exit is these sailors. All you have to do is slaughter a dozen nice German boys and then you can leave and take your wife and kids with you.' If somebody had said that, how long do you think the queue would have been?

Do you really think I could make something like that up? Something so shaming and cruel and cowardly? Why would I tell you such a thing unless it was the truth? Tifty dancing naked in a sawdust ring, the landlord's girl in the tavern cellar, Sarah in a railway carriage, wonderful beautiful things – those would be worth making up, but not this. I only tell you this because it is true, and the proof, friend, is that I am here in my little tin caravan tonight, waiting to die and, maybe, if I write a bit faster, I can get this story told before that happens.

So there I was, looking down from the tower of the castle with the wreck of a giant airship blazing away amongst the woods, watching as Varga and his men went tramping off down the hill.

I must have stayed there for a good ten minutes, watching and listening. Damn it, I think I even held my breath in case they spotted me peering out from between the battlements until I was sure they had gone.

There was a door and I opened it and went down the stairs, stopping at every turn, doing that stupid breath-holding thing, listening, waiting. I never heard a thing. The place was abandoned and, after four turns of the stair, I found myself in the courtyard.

I looked around. The cobbles were splashed with moonlight. On the other side of the courtyard a door stood open, swinging and banging in the howl of the Bura. Little burnt scraps of twisted ash were swirling in the sky and falling down slowly and piling themselves in the corners and the air was filled with a smell of burnt hair and the guards were gone. But I still didn't believe it. I ran to the opposite tower as fast as I could, not door to door but sticking to the shadows at the bottom of the walls like a mouse running round the skirting boards, trying not to be seen.

The door to the tower stair was open in front of me, and that dark passageway gaping like the grave beyond it. There was no light and, strangely, that reassured me. If Varga's guards were still waiting outside the door, they wouldn't be sitting in the dark. Still, I took my time, finding each uneven tread with my toes, putting my feet down carefully so there would be no scrape of dirt and leather. That boy I killed, the one I knocked witless before I flung him off the tower – he had dropped his rifle. I was kicking myself for leaving it behind. I had a vision of turning the stair and finding them sprawled outside the cell door smoking and chatting, catching them by surprise, shooting them. BANG! BANG! BANG! But I came round the last corner and found nobody there. I was lucky. I was spared more murders on my conscience and, to tell the truth, I had no idea how to fire the bloody thing anyway. I bet I couldn't have found the safety catch, and that business with the bolt never made any sense to me.

I went up to the door and knocked. There was no answer. I knocked again and Max said, 'Piss off. Some of us are trying to sleep.' My mate Max.

I searched round the door frame with my fingers, found a bolt and pulled it, found another one and pulled that too. And the last one. But I was careful to stand out of the way when I opened the door, just in case Max was waiting there with a ready fist.

'Told you I was coming back,' I said. 'Give us some light, Arbuthnot.'

A match flared. Sarah rushed to me and covered me with kisses and that, friend, was worth more than any damned Knight's Cross with Diamonds.

'We're going. Quiet and quick. Don't talk. Hurry. Let's go.'

Down the stairs we went, stumbling along together, match light flaring off the walls as we passed, shadows soaring up to the roof, the Professor's cane rattling, Kemali wheezing, the click of Sarah's heels.

I pulled them up short at the door. 'We're leaving here. We turn right, out through the gates and into the town. There are no soldiers left. Varga's gone with all his men. We're heading for the harbour. Back on the boat. Out the way we came in. We'll be gone before they even notice.'

We hurried across the courtyard, ash crunching softly under our feet as we ran, across the courtyard and sharp right into the castle gate. We were standing there, right in the middle of the road, when we heard the engine's roar and saw the blazing electric lights sweeping across the buildings at the end of the street, a scream of gears, the lights straight in our eyes and then Tifty leaning out from the Rolls.

'We saw your signal,' she said. 'Can we offer you a lift?'

Now, you know I loved Sarah, but my God, I never in my life saw anything half so pretty as Tifty hanging out of that Rolls. I remember it all: the car trembling like a kitten, the petrol smells whipped about on the wind, the yellow light of the headlamps bouncing around from the whitewashed walls of the narrow passage into the courtyard and shining off Tifty's copper-coloured hair.

'Get into the castle,' I told her. 'Turn this thing around and let's get out of here.'

The car surged off the way a racehorse does, down at the back to gather its power then racing forward, the beams of those giant headlamps sweeping around the castle courtyard almost like the living opposites of the Professor's terrible glasses, shining light where he shone shadows, but everywhere they turned, they showed the same swirling, fluttering black ash dancing in the air.

The car stopped and we jumped aboard like she was the last lifeboat leaving the wreck of the *Deutschland*, Sarah and her father inside with Kemali and Mrs MacLeod, Max and

Arbuthnot on the running boards at one side and me on the other, alongside Tifty.

'Hello, darling,' she said. 'Hello, Max, love.'

But it was only then, when she spoke from inside the car, that I noticed Tifty wasn't driving, and there beside her, sitting in the shadows of the cab, was Zogolli, gripping hard on the wheel and staring straight ahead so he wouldn't have to meet anybody's eye.

I yelled a warning and I drew back my fist, but Tifty put up a hand to protect him. 'No, Otto! It's all right. He's come back to us again – haven't you, Ziggo, darling?' and she put her hand on his neck and drew his head down so that stupid carroty nose nestled between her magnificent pillowy breasts while she petted his ears. 'Ziggo was just a little overtired, that's all. But he's had a good cry and he feels much better now and he's most anxious to show how sorry he is and to put things right. Isn't that so, Ziggo, darling?'

Down in the Valley of the Shadow of Fun, Zoggoli nodded faintly. He didn't seem too anxious to get out of there and start driving.

'Tifty, he's already switched sides once, he can do it again. You can't trust him.'

'Of course I can, darling,' and she reached down into her handbag, there in the dark shadows on the seat beside her, and when her little hand came up again it was holding Varga's revolver. She let me see it, she laid it back where it was and, without taking her hand off it for a second, she told Zogolli, 'Come along now, darling. Time to go.'

Zogolli sat up with the look of a man waking from a wonderful talcum-scented dream and went to drop the hand-brake but, just before he could, Mrs MacLeod slid back the partition behind his head and pressed the tip of her hatpin – none too gently – against the back of his neck.

'Drive as far as the top of the hill,' she said, 'and take the car out of gear. You can roll from there to the harbour. It's downhill all the way.'

In the seat beside her Kemali lit the stub of cigar he had been saving for his execution and he said, 'Thank whatever God you still believe in that it is not I holding the hatpin.'

Zogolli did as he was told, which was one of the things I liked best about him, and we rolled silently over the cobbles, down through the narrow, twisting streets with the rubber of the tyres kissing the cobbles, just the way the camel's feet had brushed over the night streets of Buda half a lifetime before and, as we rolled, Tifty told me about the adventures she had been having since I saw her last.

'Darling, I hope they were kind to you in prison. Mrs MacLeod and I had a lovely time in the palazzo. We waited there for a little, absolutely alone – except for the staff of course, and they don't really count as company – while Varga took you off to jail. Then after a bit he sent some rough sailors down to us with champagne – simply crates of the stuff.'

'I like champagne,' said Sarah.

'Of course you do, darling. Who doesn't like champagne? I saved some for you. It's in the boot. We should drink it on the way home. Champagne is the perfect antidote to mal de mer. Anyway, Varga's sailors told us that the champagne was intended for a party where Mrs MacLeod and I were to charm a considerable number of officers and toast your execution in the finest Krug.'

'That's nice,' I said.

'Darling, I would have done it with a tear in my eye. Then we saw the Zeppelin burning and we knew that the lovely officers would not be joining us, but we took it as a sign that you were in good health.'

Zogolli's head jerked forward uncomfortably as Mrs MacLeod gave him another little stab.

'Put your lights out. We're almost here.'

We had reached the bottom of the hill, where the road came twisting from between the houses and flattened out. Zogolli put the car in gear, but it was a Rolls so it made no more noise than Sarah snoring.

'Drive to the end of the quay,' Mrs MacLeod said, and there was Varga's yacht, neatly rigged and ready to put to sea, with a moustachioed brigand waiting at the gangplank. 'As you see, my Companions have prepared for our arrival.'

Zogolli stopped the car.

'Out!' and Mrs MacLeod gave another little prod with her hatpin. Zogolli didn't complain. He got out of the car and stood by the end of the gangplank, offering an arm to Tifty and Sarah in turn, then to Mrs MacLeod and the Professor and then even to Kemali, who ignored him with a bitter stare. Zogolli made no complaint about that either and stood looking his old master in the eye as he passed, which must have taken more courage than I gave him credit for.

But I was not prepared to turn my back on him. 'After you,' I said. 'I insist.'

'I remain here,' he said.

Halfway down the gangplank, Kemali turned round. 'What does that mean?

'It means I will stay here. In Albania.'

Kemali turned back up the gangplank – 'Let me through, let me through. Forgive me. You must allow me to pass' – squeezing his way past the Professor and rushing back on to the quayside to grip Zogolli by the shoulders. 'You can't stay here! Is this some trick? Do you think that you can persuade me to give you the other half of the combination? I will not do it! I won't! You know that, don't you? I was ready to go to the wall rather than help them. I will not help them and I will not help you to help them. My boy, they will kill you when they know how you have deceived them.'

'Oh, Kemali Efendim, if you are safe out of the country, there is nothing they can do to me to make me tell them. One half of the key is useless. Anyway, when you are gone, I will not wait here to be killed. I will take the car and drive as fast as I can to the hills. The Royal Fathers-in-Law fight on. Perhaps they will shoot me. Perhaps they will give me a gun and let me fight on with them. Perhaps they will remember that, like them, I was once a Knight of Skanderbeg.'

After that they yammered and jabbered at each other in

Albanok for a bit and then there were tears and more jabbering and embraces and finally a sharing of cigars before Kemali said, 'My boy has returned to me. We go together to the mountains to fight for a free Albania. Thank you, my friends. Now hurry. To the ship. The tide is dropping. Away with you, and Godspeed.'

He stopped to shake hands with all of us, and I was last in the line. 'Goodbye, Your Majesty,' he said. 'I have never served, nor could I ever serve, a finer king. I do not think we will meet again in life but, perhaps later, we may share a cigar together – if such things are permitted there.'

I can admit it now, I had a tear in my eye as I sat on a pile of champagne crates, watching the Rolls bounce down the quayside and disappear into the streets of the town.

And there was nothing left to say. Like the moment when they lower the coffin into the ground. Like the moment after, 'I don't love you any more.' The bottle was empty. The fire was out. It was time to go and we were leaving as we came, unnoticed, unremarked, but lighter by a camel and a cash box full of good Austrian gold kronen.

The Professor was lingering on the quayside, one foot on the gangplank and one foot on the harbour wall. I took him gently by the elbow. 'Come along, Professor. We should go now.'

But he turned those fearful spectacles on me again and he said, 'I know the combination of the vault.'

I have often wondered, in the long years since then, what might have happened if he had said that more quietly, so the others had not heard, or if he had waited to say it, waited until he and I were alone or until we were a mile out to sea with the coffee boiling in its pot and a warm bunk calling.

But that isn't what happened. Everybody else was there and they looked up when he said it, as if he had rung a bell or sounded a klaxon.

'You're lying,' I said.

'Why should I lie? What would be the point when I could be so easily found out? Even Zogolli understood that eventually.'

'Zogolli knew only half the combination.'

'Zogolli knew half and Kemali knew half. Only one man has been in the chamber when both locks were opened. I am that man.'

'But you are blind.'

'I still know.'

'We don't even know where the vault is.'

He turned his black glasses towards the town and raised his nose like a hound scenting its prey. 'From the entrance of the harbour it is three streets to the left and two streets uphill.'

'Jesus,' I said. It seemed the only thing to say. I took him by the elbow again. 'Come on, Professor. They'll be on our tails in a moment.'

He didn't budge. Instead he swivelled his head away from the town and looked towards the bottom of the gangplank. 'Nobody else seems to be in that much of a hurry,' he said.

He was right. I looked at them and I could see it on their faces. A day ago I might have shouted them down. A day ago I might have told them to shut up and ordered them to cast off. A day ago I was the king.

Arbuthnot said, 'My instructions are simple and broad: to make things hot for the other side. I should think despoiling the Treasury counts.'

Mrs MacLeod agreed. 'My Companions are loyal but I see no reason why that loyalty should not be rewarded with the gold of our enemies.'

Max looked at his feet. 'I had a lot of silly ideas about a pub in the country. I was going to call it the King Otto.'

'And I promised myself some new hats,' said Tifty.

Only Sarah said nothing at all, and I suppose that was as much support as anybody could have asked for. I stood there, looking at her, trying to come up with some kind of sensible reason why we should simply run for our lives but, damn it, I couldn't think of one. Like the gambler who sees his horse come in one time out of a hundred, we forgot that we had spent the day in a prison cell and we remembered that we had spent the night in a palace and, the longer that I thought about it, the harder it was to say no. Max wanted his little pub in the country, Tifty wanted a new hat – that was all – and all I wanted was Sarah, but we were running away with no more than the clothes on our back in the hope of finding a job in a circus again, maybe, some day. No more palaces for Sarah. No more limousines. Just long years breaking her back, sweeping up horse-apples and sleeping in a narrow bunk. And what about the kids? Why should my kids go without when the man who stole my country got fat on my money – money that could make them into ladies and gentlemen? And there was Sarah in that lovely dress, the last lovely dress she would ever own unless we got some money.

The Professor gripped my arm. 'I won't leave here poorer than I came,' he said. 'I won't. Decide for yourself. I'm going,' and he set off along the quayside, sweeping his cane in front of him as he went.

Sarah was frantic. 'Otto, go after him, please! Hurry!'

'Max, come on. Arbuthnot, load up the champagne.'

'The tide is falling fast,' said Mrs MacLeod. 'We leave in one hour – or sooner if we are found out.'

The Professor was walking as fast as a man with no eyes can walk. I had to go quickly to catch him up and, by the time we reached the harbour gates, Max came running and behind us, far away, Sarah was shouting, 'Hurry, Otto.'

Night and day were all the same to the Professor, and he made his way through the dark streets as easily as if it had been noon. He found the corner of the street with his cane and crossed over, into the shadows of a looming warehouse, and then he was off again, his cane tapping on the walls and ringing out in the silent town like a hammer on an anvil.

'For God's sake, Professor, stop that bloody thumping. Here, give me your arm.'

I took one side and Max took the other but, though we had eyes to see, we were no faster. The Professor was ready to hurry on come what may. He could not see, and that gave him a child's belief that he could not be seen, but Max and me, we hung to the shadows and made haste slowly, waiting and listening, looking about at every turn, expecting every minute that Varga and his thugs would notice we had gone and start the hunt.

'Is this the street corner?' the Professor said.

'Yes.'

'Then there are two more corners before we turn.'

We hurried on, across another side street, watching and listening at every step until we found the third street.

'Uphill here, for two streets,' the Professor said, and – damnation – he was right. There was that little window with its stupid iron bar and the sagging front door held shut by that piddling penny-bazaar lock. Max gave it a push and it opened with the sort of disappointed crunch a customer's nose makes in the boxing booth when he discovers he's not quite so tough after all.

Without another word the Professor plunged into the darkened room, swinging his cane about madly and heading straight for the stairs in the corner of the room. Max and me, we had to strike a match and get the lamp lit and stumble about on that slippery stone staircase and duck through the tunnel and, by the time we did all that, we found the Professor waiting in the deep darkness, like a lost soul seeking admittance at the gates of hell.

'Speed is of the essence, gentlemen. Time and tide and the terrible Mrs MacLeod wait for no man.' He herded us with his cane. 'Mr Schlepsig to the left, Mr Witte to the right. Now, Max, set the dial to zero.'

'I can't see. It's too dark.'

'Really? I hadn't noticed. Otto, hold up the lamp. Now can you see? Set the tumbler to zero. Done that?'

'I think so.'

'Now turn it to forty-one left.'

Slowly and gently, Max turned the knob.

'Now nineteen right. Then go left, back to zero, then—'

'Wait a minute, I can't keep up.'

'You have to get this right, Mr Schlepsig. If you are out by even one dot on the dial, the lock will not open.'

'I put my hand on his shoulder. 'You're doing fine, mate.'

'My fingers are too big for this stuff, Otto. You do it. I'll stick to punching people instead.'

I handed him the lamp and took his place in front of Atlas. 'Zero,' I called out.

'Good,' said the Professor. 'Now nineteen right and twenty-seven left and right to zero again.'

Once upon a time I was sitting in a garden when I looked up and found that a butterfly had chosen just that very moment to land on a rose at the other side of the path, and I wondered if it was the tiny noise of its feet that made me notice it. When I turned the dial to zero again, Atlas made just the exact same noise.

'You can't possibly know this,' I told the Professor.

'And yet, I do.'

'It's impossible.'

'We shall see in a moment. Turn the other dial, Otto.'

Max held up the lamp and we began again.

'Set the dial to zero. Now forty-one left. Right nineteen. Left back to zero. Right nineteen. Left twenty-seven. Right zero.'

'That's exactly the same,' I said.

'And that's how I know I am right. Zogolli and Kemali both knew only half the code. We saw that today. Kemali was ready to die to keep his secret, but Zogolli was afraid his ignorance would be exposed. Yet, when they were with me here, they each did exactly the same thing. Each man turned his dial by exactly the same number of clicks. It follows, therefore, that each must have chosen a pattern of numbers which could be referred to and recalled but which was not personal to them. Something with six figures. Something like the latitude and longitude of Durres, which, as any schoolboy knows, is forty-one degrees, nineteen minutes and zero seconds north, nineteen degrees, twenty-seven minutes and zero seconds west. Open the door, Otto.'

Max held the lamp high. I tugged on the great polished ship's wheel handle and, by God, he was right. The door swung open with a little gasp of wind, as quiet and gentle as a duchess's fart.

The Professor jabbed at the air with his cane. 'Gentlemen, the money is this way, I believe.'

So there we were, in the vault, surrounded by all that money and the personal armoury of one of Albania's leading entrepreneurs, perhaps more successful than I had been but certainly deader, and all we had to do was work out how much we could carry away.

The money was lying there in those long wooden cases and they were heavy enough but, by God, they were awkward to handle, and anybody could see they were designed for two men to carry. One set of arms simply wasn't long enough to reach both ends of the box. We experimented a little and it might have been possible, just about, for a man to take a handle in each fist and drag two boxes away, but we had the stairs to consider and, once we were out in the street, the noise would have been spectacular. Time was pressing. We had to get back to the boat.

The Professor said, 'I fear two boxes is the most we can manage. If we form a chain, the man in the middle can hold the handles of two boxes and the men at either end can share the load.'

'I suppose I'd better go in the middle,' Max said.

And then we heard it, that nasty, whiny, sing-song voice again. 'Ooh, Maxxie, you're always showing off your muscles. Come out and show your Uncle Imre – you too, Witte.'

Max dropped the crate of cash he was holding, went out into the passage and I followed.

'That's close enough,' said Varga. He was completely alone, but he had found a replacement for the pistol we took off him in Fiume.

'What now?' I said. 'Another duel?'

'Oh, don't be so bloody stupid. You've had several chances to kill me already, and anyway, you are still under sentence of death for treason. One wall is as good as another, and a wall in a cellar is better than most. Keep your hands up.'

'How the hell did you find us?' I said.

'Too easy. As soon as the Zeppelin blew up, I knew you were to blame, and the only possible way out of the country is on my lovely yacht, so I left my men to carry on putting out fires and shovelling up the cinders of our honoured dead and I told them to join me at the harbour later. I got there just in time to see you leaving.

'Why would you leave? What could possibly tempt you to abandon your escape attempt halfway, and why burden yourself with a blind man? There could be only one answer. Now, tell your cripple friend to come out of there and be shot nicely, or I'll lock him in and come back for the money in a month or two.'

The Professor did as he was told only, when he appeared in the door of the vault, he had thrown away his cane and, instead, he had a rifle firmly at his shoulder.

Varga laughed. You couldn't blame him, but when he laughed the Professor turned directly towards him. Varga stopped laughing. He ducked down and moved to the other side of the passage and, silently, he raised his pistol. The Professor shot him through the chest.

The noise of it was appalling. That sudden explosion. That bang. The metallic ring. The flash. The smoke. The chemical, burning smell. Everything roaring inside that tiny stone tunnel. Varga was flung back against the wall, slumped there with his legs at peculiar angles, sitting on one foot, the other leg stuck out in front of him and the whole of his shirt front black with blood. He looked down and dabbled his fingers in the mess and then he looked right at me and said, 'I. But.' And he died.

'Time to go,' the Professor said. He slung his rifle across his chest and went back into the vault for a moment and, when he came back, he was dragging a case of money behind him.

But Max and me, we hadn't moved from the spot. We were standing there, a noise like cymbals in our ears, looking down at Varga all twisted up on the floor and rivers of blood running down the passage, making snaky runnels in the dust.

'We have to go. Get another box of money and grab a gun. Varga's friends are going to the harbour. Come on.'

I pointed at Varga. 'How?' I said.

'He was going to kill you. He was going to kill you and he was going to kill Max and he was going to kill me and, after that, I assume he was going to keep the vault for himself. We don't have time for this.'

'How?' I said again.

The Professor took off his spectacles and smashed them

against the wall. 'Don't tell me you believed all that "blind cripple" shit? Don't tell me you were taken in by the mind-reading act. Don't tell me you swallowed all that stuff about longitude and latitude. I knew the combination because I watched them, Otto. I can see!'

There were so many things I wanted to ask. How long he had lived that way, how he had borne it, how he had managed to keep up the pretence, whether Sarah knew, how he could have existed for even a moment without turning to his beautiful daughter and simply looking at her.

More than anything else I wanted to know whether shutting yourself in darkness for years at a time left a mark on the soul, but I had seen him kill a man and I think I already knew the answer to that question.

We dragged Varga's body into the vault, bumping it over the iron lip of the door which, of course, had never once tripped the Professor up, and we left him there for anybody who might care to find him. Maybe Kemali and Zogolli came back. Maybe they buried him. Maybe he's still down there, rotting away to his bones, locked inside an impenetrable mausoleum, surrounded by weapons and treasure like one of those old Egyptian Pharaohs.

It was a difficult journey back to the street. The Professor already had a rifle and he showed us how to use one. How to snap in the magazine. How to move your thumb so that the leaf-shaped safety catch would click into place and show a dot of black enamel or a dot of red.

And then we each took a rifle, me and my mate Max, and I went in front with the lamp in my right hand, reaching back to the rope handle of the first cash box with my left, and the Professor went at the back and Max came in the middle, with a hand on the box in front and a hand on the box behind.

The money wasn't all that heavy, not for me and Max anyway, but the boxes were long and difficult to handle. I had the lamp so I could see where I was going and the Professor had already proved that he could manage pretty well without it, but we had to keep stopping so he could swap hands and then, on the stairs, the crates were too long to go round the turns so there was more stopping and I had to put the lamp down and get the crates stood on end and manhandle them round the corners and then pick the lamp up and start again, and all the while our rifles were swinging about and getting in the way.

By the time we climbed the last stair into the little cellar, with its busted door hanging open to the street, I was running with sweat and the Professor was gasping and blowing like a walrus.

I took out my watch. 'We've got fifteen minutes left before Mrs MacLeod casts off.'

'If we're not there, Sarah won't go with her,' the Professor said.

'I hope to God she does. Do you really want her hanging about on the quayside when Varga's men bowl up?'

The crates bashed off the broken door as we went out into the street. I put mine down. 'Wait. I want to look.'

Max and the Professor stood in the shadows, Max because he would do anything I ever asked him to do, the Professor because he was still catching his breath, and they waited while I went to the street corner and scouted. The roads were deserted. The terrified Albanoks had locked themselves away, waiting for the next tide of war to wash over their houses, and if Varga's men were on patrol, they had not found their way to the Treasury. Not yet anyway.

I hurried back. 'The coast is clear,' I said. 'I think we should go by the back roads, stay in the lanes for a bit and then cut down to the harbour.'

The Professor picked up his money box again. 'There is no time. We have twelve minutes left. We must go by the most direct route we can and then, if we don't keep our appointment, at least the others may see us and delay a little.'

I looked at Max, and he nodded as if to say, 'I think he's right.'

'Then let's hurry,' I said.

We formed up again, Max in front this time with the two giant money boxes streaming out behind him, like the tip of an arrow, and me and the Professor trailing behind, but it wasn't working. I could keep up pretty well, even with my busted ribs. When my share of the crate got too heavy or the rope handle started to burn my hand I could swap it over, but the Professor was labouring. He struggled along, holding his rope with both hands like a man trying to lift himself up in a bucket and with about as much success. He was breathing hot and hard and walking just that little bit slower than Max and me, dragging us both back as Max struggled to drag him forward, the way mothers do with their dawdling kids.

'Why don't I take your rifle?' I said.

'I can manage. I can manage.'

'You can't manage. Let me help or none of us is going to get out of here. The longer that you waste discussing it, the worse it's going to get.'

Max stopped walking and, grudgingly, the Professor put down his end of the crate. I helped him unshoulder his rifle.

'Do you want me to take that?' Max said. 'You don't look too good.'

'I'm fine. You've got enough to carry.'

I swung the Professor's rifle across my chest, asked him if he was ready to go and we were just about to set off again when, from someplace out of the darkness behind us, we heard that unmistakable constipated, bellowing roar, that soft slippered galloping drumbeat, and the very next moment the camel came running up.

He was nearly crazy with happiness at finding Max again and he showed his delight in the usual hot, streaming fashion, but we stepped carefully round that and, while Max held him by the head and made reassuring noises of affectionate welcome, the Professor and I roped the cash boxes together and threw them over the camel's back.

'He's been looking for us,' said Max. 'Bloody good camel this one.'

'The best. A prince amongst camels. But can we save the congratulations for later? Let's get a move on.'

From a slow stagger, we were making our way at a respectable trot. The cash boxes bounced and swung at every stride, the Professor and I clung on, pretending to hold them in place but letting ourselves be carried along as we went, and the camel ran like a carriage horse, determined that he would never again be parted from the man he loved.

We reached the bottom of the hill and the shore. We turned left, three streets to the left, and the camel strode along, eating up the distance to the harbour, grunting as he went, and then, up ahead, we could see the masts of Varga's yacht, standing out like black branches against the pewter sky, sinking on the falling tide, and we ran on and we ran on and we reached the harbour. It was there, just across the street, moonlight glinting on the dimpled water and all our friends could see us and they saw the camel and they laughed and cheered and then the shooting started.

Believe me, the noise of being shot at is every bit as distressing as the noise of shooting somebody else. The fear is just as strong, the bangs are just as loud, but when you are being shot at there's all the added fun of red-hot ricochets pinging around the place, the flat thud of bullets driving themselves into the mud at your feet, the ripping, spitting sound when they hit the water. You know this stuff, friend. You've lived through the raids. An air raid is not much different from being shot at, but being shot at is a little more personal. In an air raid a young boy far away presses a switch and bombs fall on you, and he doesn't really care if they land on you or on somebody else. When somebody is shooting at you, you know he has taken the trouble to put a bullet in his gun and look hard at you through that tiny nick in his gunsight and wonder what it would be like to see your head burst like a melon.

Luckily none of Varga's sailors were much good at it or it was too dark to see us or they had no real wish to see heads bursting. The first volley missed us completely. It was enough to spook the camel and send him waltzing sideways down the quayside away from the noise, but it didn't do us any harm. I turned and saw the flash of the second volley, angry yellow orchids suddenly blooming in the gap between the houses.

Max said, 'Run, mate. Run!' And I would've done. I was ready to run, but the Professor stumbled and fell and went down on the other side of the camel and his feet tangled with my feet and we fell together in a heap.

I waved Max on. 'Go, get the camel on board. I'll bring Alberto,' but when I went to pick him up he swore bitterly at me through gritted teeth.

'I'm hit.'

'I'll carry you.'

'No. For the love of God, my watch chain is the only thing holding my guts in.'

I went to pick him up. I could have picked him up. I was strong, but when I touched him he squealed like the martinmas pig when they haul him up to have his throat cut. He writhed away from me, but his hands were clawing at my chest. There was a hellish smell.

'Give me the guns,' he said. The bullets were pinging into the quayside all around us. 'Give me the guns,' he said. 'Give me the guns.'

'Sarah will never forgive me.'

'Tell her I died. Soon it will be true.' He screamed again as he rolled on to his belly. 'Go.' I think he may have been crying with the pain of it or maybe because of the parting, but as he lay there, writhing about in the dirt, he squeezed off a shot. They saw it, the flash of it, just as we had seen theirs, and by God it got their attention. They stopped shooting at us and went to look for something to hide behind.

The Professor fired into the darkness again and I fired so they could see there were two of us.

'Well done, son,' he whispered. 'Look after her.' He fired again. 'And say Kaddish for me.'

I left him there and ran the length of the quayside. The yacht was moving. Only the very last of the stern was still under the quay and Sarah was there, hanging over the rail, pale as a phantom in that dress, her hair whipping about like a flag in the wind and screaming as I jumped.

All I remember is Sarah screaming as the sails filled like great pale wings above us. Sarah screaming until the gunfire stopped.

There is only one more thing to tell you. When dawn came we were halfway to Venice and Sarah had cried herself to sleep in my arms. I was sitting in the stern with a blanket round my shoulders against the chill of the mist, my feet resting on a wooden box with half a million leks in it as Max steered the ship.

Arbuthnot came and sat down beside us. He had a fat cigar clenched in his back teeth and he handed one to me and another to Max and lit them from a screw of crumpled paper which he flapped about and threw over the side. 'Genuine leks, you know.'

'That was lavish,' I said. 'I hope they came from your share.'

'Oh, every one of them, Your Majesty. I opened a box earlier. And I may light several more cigars before we get to Italy. Here. Help yourself.' Arbuthnot reached into his coat pocket and produced a wad of notes. 'Take a look.'

I plucked one from the top of the heap. Arbuthnot held the rest of them up to the wind and watched them fly away without a thought. I began to see why. The paper I was holding in my hand had come from a school jotter. It was thick and pulpy and it had a faint pattern of blue lines across it with writing that looked as if it had been stamped out with a cut potato.

'They are all like that. Home-made is the very kindest thing you could say about them. I should think the crates are worth more than the money they contain.'

'It's money if we all agree it is.'

'But the Italians may take a different view.' He used the wet end of his cigar to point at an empty oval of white paper in the middle of the printing with a few words underneath. 'The King of the Albanians – that's what that says. I think they were waiting to draw your picture in later.'

As I sat there holding it, the mist soaked the paper and the colours started to run. I crumpled it up and threw it over my shoulder.

But I see that morning has come and somehow I am still not dead and that isn't much of an ending for a story like this. I'm going to tear this up and start again. I'll try to think of something better when I've had a bit of a sleep.

The German Prince Wilhelm of Wied arrived to claim the throne of Albania in April 1914. He left again in September, uncrowned.

Ismail Kemali escaped Albania and spent the First World War in Paris, where he died in 1919.

Mrs Margaretha MacLeod, known to the world as Mata Hari, faced a French firing squad in Vincennes in 1917, accused of spying for Germany.

Captain Sandy Arbuthnot served with distinction in the Great War, where he was promoted to Colonel of the Tweeddale Yeomanry. With the death of his elder brother, he inherited the title of Lord Clanroyden and, following a career in the diplomatic service, he retired to the family estates outside Ettrick, in the Scottish Borders.

Ahmet Muhtar Zogolli became Prime Minister of Albania in 1922, President of Albania in 1925 and declared himself King Zog in 1928. He was crowned in a lavish ceremony where he wore a costume of rose-pink silk of his own design. Like Kemali, King Zog insisted that he had never heard of Otto Witte. His first act as king was to establish the Order of Skanderbeg.

After a lifetime of enjoyment, Otto Witte, acrobat, crowned King of Albania and self-proclaimed World's Greatest Adventurer, died from cirrhosis of the liver in a Hamburg home for the elderly at the age of eighty-seven. He told a different version of this story.

The Love and Death of Caterina

by Andrew Nicoll

Luciano Hernando Valdez is his nation's most celebrated novelist and
he's suffering from writer's block. He's tried all his usual tricks to get back
on track, but nothing works. Until he meets Caterina. Beautiful and young,
she has idolised him since she was a child. Convinced that falling in
love with her will unlock something and enable him to write,
he pursues her and soon enough, he falls headlong into her arms.
But it's only a matter of time before he murders her.

'Elegant, wise, ironic – a gripping and impressive piece of work'
Times Literary Supplement

'The pages turn quickly, the plot thickens and rises, and when the book is
finally put down, there is little to stop you looking forward to Nicoll's next one'
Scottish Review of Books

'A deft romance . . . about male pride and its pitfalls . . . very readable'
Guardian

'The best Scottish novel I read this year'
Scotsman

'With *The Love and Death of Caterina*, Andrew Nicoll triumphantly cleared
the second novel hurdle . . . there are moments reminiscent of Graham Greene'
Glasgow Herald

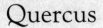

www.quercusbooks.co.uk